SMOKE
AND
MIRRORS

J.D. LAUBACH

PRINAVERSE PRESS

SMOKE AND MIRRORS

ISBN: 979-8-9912513-2-7 (Hardcover)

ISBN: 979-8-9912513-1-0 (Paperback) | ISBN: 979-8-9912513-0-3 (eBook)

Cover Art © 2024 by EA Wright
Map © 2024: Brittany Petrone from InkyandBookish

Prinaverse Press

Printed in the United States of America.

https://jenniferlaubach.wixsite.com/jdlaubach

PRONUNCIATION GUIDE

Arden: Ar-den
Atatacia: At-uh-tah-see-uh
Baptiste: Bap-tees-tuh
Benito: Buh-nee-tow
Bram: Bra-m
Calix: Cal-iks
Daphne: Daf-nee
Dia: Dee-uh
Evalie- Ev-uh-lee
Florian: Flo-ree-un
Guinevere: Gwe-nuh-vee-ruh
Hode: Hoe-duh
Lieve: Lay-vuh
Lopter: Lop-tur
Lucette: Loo-set
Madoria: Muh-Dor-ee-yuh
Malsu: Mal-soo
Oriel: Or-ee-ul
Poppy: Pop-ee
Prinav: Prin-av
Saima: S-eye-muh
Seelie: See-lee
Siva: See-vuh
Soleil: Sol-eel
Teyrnas: Tey-er-nus
Tussia: Tush-uh

Unseelie: Un–see–lee
Vera: Vee–ruh

To my husband, Jeremy, for turning my life into a fairytale without even knowing it.
I love you, and I always will.
Til the end.

CONTENTS

Trigger Warnings	XV
CHAPTER 1	1
CHAPTER 2	11
CHAPTER 3	20
CHAPTER 4	27
CHAPTER 5	35
CHAPTER 6	42
CHAPTER 7	49
CHAPTER 8	55
CHAPTER 9	66
CHAPTER 10	72
CHAPTER 11	82
CHAPTER 12	91
CHAPTER 13	98
CHAPTER 14	104
CHAPTER 15	110

CHAPTER 16	117
CHAPTER 17	120
CHAPTER 18	131
CHAPTER 19	137
CHAPTER 20	144
CHAPTER 21	152
CHAPTER 22	159
CHAPTER 23	164
CHAPTER 24	169
CHAPTER 25	179
CHAPTER 26	185
CHAPTER 27	195
CHAPTER 28	204
CHAPTER 29	213
CHAPTER 30	217
CHAPTER 31	227
CHAPTER 32	236
CHAPTER 33	247
CHAPTER 34	254
CHAPTER 35	260
CHAPTER 36	272
CHAPTER 37	280
CHAPTER 38	285
CHAPTER 39	293
CHAPTER 40	301
CHAPTER 41	310

CHAPTER 42 318

CHAPTER 43 327

CHAPTER 44 334

CHAPTER 45 343

CHAPTER 46 355

CHAPTER 47 361

CHAPTER 48 369

CHAPTER 49 372

CHAPTER 50 383

CHAPTER 51 386

CHAPTER 52 397

CHAPTER 53 404

CHAPTER 54 408

CHAPTER 55 415

CHAPTER 56 426

CHAPTER 57 431

CHAPTER 58 441

CHAPTER 59 442

CHAPTER 60 445

CHAPTER 61 450

CHAPTER 62 458

CHAPTER 63 464

CHAPTER 64 473

CHAPTER 65 477

CHAPTER 66 483

CHAPTER 67 487

CHAPTER 68   492

CHAPTER 69   495

CHAPTER 70   500

CHAPTER 71   502

CHAPTER 72   507

CHAPTER 73   512

CHAPTER 74   515

CHAPTER 75   519

Acknowledgements   527

About the Author   531

TRIGGER WARNINGS

There are things in this book that are uncomfortable, and your mental health is more important than a sale. Please read this list and decide if you still want to enter Atatacia...and if you do, buckle up...shit's about to get real.

War, blood, gore, violence.
Sexual acts.
Alcoholism and Addiction.
PTSD, Hallucinations, Delusions, Panic Attacks, Memory Loss, Violent Outbursts.
Suicidal Ideation.
Murder.
Foul Language.

Twins born in the River of Light and Dark will separate,
causing dark to devour all, until the light can shine
without restraint.
– *Proverb of Saint Ulaway, The Holy Book of Bram*

CHAPTER 1
VERA

S tanding at a merchant's table in the market, I watch my brother's
nimble fingers take items and swiftly drop them in his pocket.
Stealing things for Lieve has become an art, and everytime I witness
it I can't help but feel a little guilty, but at the same time, mesmerized.
Lieve is a thief, but that word isn't fair. He has to do it. We have to do
it – at least, for now.

Lieve's pockets are filling quickly, but out of the corner of my eye
I notice an Enforcer watching us. He's close enough now that I can
smell his musk. My hands start to sweat. I clench them to stop from
wiping them on my cape; Lieve says that's a dead give away that I'm
up to something. I try to get his attention, but he's focused on a nearby
jewelry display. His hand reaches out, and before he can touch anything,
I cough.

He scowls at me, a familiar look I've gotten used to over the years. I
widen my eyes and subtly nod my head in the direction of the Enforcer.
Lieve's eyes travel in the right direction and his face softens. *Good.* He
understands. He sighs and we leave the display and walk towards a
group of people standing in line for loaves of fresh bread.

"I could have grabbed a necklace," he whispers to me, "we could have bought an entire turkey *plus* whatever fabric you wanted."

"Not with an Enforcer watching," I hiss through gritted teeth.

A passerby's eyes narrow at my soiled skirts and tattered cloak, but I smile at her even though all I want to do is slap her privileged face. The Harvest Ball is just around the corner, so I need to practice being polite if I want to find a suitor. We came to the market today to steal enough jewelry to exchange for a ballgown.

There are a lot of people on this end of the market, and Lieve always says that's a good thing. Everytime we go to the market he reminds me that *'blending into the crowd is important.'* Like I don't know by now. We've had to resort to pickpocketing and stealing from the market to keep our shop from going under, and the bigger the crowd, the better chances we have of finding something of value to sell. We have to be careful to manipulate the pieces in some way, gold plate them, switch out the gems, melt them down to create something new…we've become skilled at it, and no one in town suspects that we sell their own items back to them; when they actually buy anything.

Lieve has talked of nothing more than finding me a man so he can rest assured that I won't starve to death this winter while he's attending Gilormo Music Academy. Of course, the reasons I'm interested in a marriage are *very* different from why Lieve is interested in my marriage. He worries about my survival, stability, and finances, and I worry about partnership, laughter, and true love.

All the best books and fairy tales have knights in shining armor, and handsome prince's that save the girl, and they fall madly in love with each other. I've told him for years that I'll only marry someone if they are charming and kind. I will only do it if I can see myself falling madly in love with them just like the goddess Dia fell in love with the mortal Oriel in the stories Lieve tells me.

It's just another difference between us. Lieve and I are supposed to be identical, but we are only alike in appearance. Nineteen years ago, we were born. I came first and Mother claimed it's because I was filled with excitement and spontaneity, the opposite of temperamental, introverted, Lieve.

A glint of gold peeks out from the pocket of a tall man with long blonde hair standing in line in front of us. He scolds me when I pretend to accidentally bump into him, and complains that I've scuffed his brand new shoes. Before I could even open my mouth, Lieve had already swiped the object from the man's pocket with practiced ease. Lieve then loops his arm in mine, apologizes profusely, and then gently pulls me from the line.

"Solid gold," he says and winks at me.

We push through the growing crowd, leaving the morning chaos to the wealthy and return to our shop. Lieve pulls out the key and jams it in the lock, swearing under his breath as he jiggles the handle until it eventually opens. Bells tied to the door knob jingle as we enter, and the usual scent of polish meets me.

I turn the worn *open* sign around and sigh as potential customers walk by the shop without even a glance in the window. Lieve is already behind the counter fiddling with everything he stole at the market, so I pull out the box of small wooden clocks he carved last week and place them on the counter for sale.

"Vera–" Lieve mutters, "look at this."

Dangling by a delicate chain is a solid gold pocket watch. Lieve pulls out a loupe from his desk drawer and holds the piece up to his eye. I take a second loupe from the drawer and when Lieve hands me the watch, my heart leaps. *I might not have to get married right away. I might be able to wait on the right man.* This watch is worth more than its weight in gold, there are rubies, emeralds, and numerous other gems encrusted on the precious metal. This watch might be the answer to all my prayers.

"It looks to be worth a small fortune, but the fastener is loose."

Lieve's blue-gray eyes light up. "Lucky we own a repair shop then."

Yeah, lucky us. We never dreamed of owning the shop, we're stuck with it. It was our father, Roe's, shop. He ran it with a friend before marrying our mother, Eloise. The friend went on to a new adventure, Father died, and Mother was stuck with it. She worked as a Lady's maid every night after closing to make ends meet while Lieve and I took on odd jobs around town. The three of us tried to keep it afloat, but then Mother caught the fever and everything went downhill.

For the rest of the afternoon I polish the items in the display window and stare at the people walking by. Men and women shopping, holding hands, laughing, kissing. I don't want to admit it, but I'm jealous. I wonder if we'll get a buyer for the watch before Lieve sets off on his own adventure, so then I can begin my own. I wonder if that watch can buy me a future far away from this old shop and all its memories.

The sun vanishes along with the shoppers from the market, carrying a piece of hope from the watch with them. Lieve works on the loose fastener as he hums the tune to my favorite song, and I smile even though it makes me a little sad. I'm going to miss him when he leaves.

"Do you think that pocket watch will make us enough money that I won't have to rush into a marriage?"

"I think it could easily afford us food for months, and pay off school loans and debts, and easily buy you a slew of nicer dresses to make it easier to find you a nicer man."

I cross my arms, "I'm serious."

Lieve places the tools in his hands on the desk and looks up at me. "I think that there aren't many people in Adamston who can afford a pocket watch as valuable as this one, and I think we haven't had enough customers buying anything of value for the last four months to consider abandoning our plan."

"*Your plan.*" I mutter.

"I'm sorry I'm leaving for school," Lieve says, "but I can't take care of you like this. You need to find a husband before I'm gone. Symphony

Conductors make hefty salaries, *eventually*, but until then I need to make sure you'll be alright."

"You've always taken care of me, Lieve. We take care of each other."

"It will be worth it, I promise."

Lieve's right. I nod in agreement and continue polishing even though I'm pouting on the inside.

As if he knows exactly what I'm thinking, Lieve huffs. "Fine."

"What?"

Lieve walks around his desk and stands next to me. "If you can find a buyer who will purchase the watch for enough money to see you through my schooling, then you can marry whenever and whoever you choose." He holds out his hand, "deal?"

"Deal!" I shriek and wrap my arms around him, inhaling the scent of pine and moss.

Lieve laughs as I bounce around the shop, shouting out all my outlandish ideas on how we can sell the pocket watch and buy ridiculous things we'll never need. Lieve promises to read to me after work and goes back to his office to tend to the ledger, so I begin scrambling to close up for the night so I can hear more of Lieve's fairy tales. While I'm counting the drawers, I hear the jingle of the door opening from behind me.

In walks a man who reeks of wealth. He flicks invisible lint from his shoulder and I swear a spark fell to the ground. He gives me a sly smile as my eyes take in every inch of his clothing. Dressed in all black, from his luxurious vest and jacket with long coat tails, to his black shoes, so shiny I can almost see my reflection, I know this is my chance. He might be the only man in Adamston wealthy enough to buy the watch. My palms sweat.

"Welcome to Oleanders, where each customer picks their own poison."

He raises an eyebrow at me and snickers. My cheeks instantly heat at Lieve's stupid slogan. I knew we should have thought of something better. The man browses the trinkets littering the shelves and my heart jumps when thunder booms at the exact same time he strikes his gold cane against the stone floor, sending sparks across the ground.

"That's a strong cane you've got," I say and point to it.

"It is, indeed."

His voice is smooth. Controlled. I can't blow this, I've got to find a way to show him that golden watch without it looking like I'm pushing it on him.

"Looking for anything special?"

"A pocket watch."

This is it. This is definitely a sign. I go to the desk to grab the watch we stole and show it to the man, but it isn't there. I open the drawer, look under the table, on the shelves. *Lieve must have it.*

I hold up a finger to the man. "Give me a moment, sir, I have just the right one for you."

Smoke billows from under the man's feet and slowly covers the floor of the shop and I freeze. *What is happening?* A faint blue glow leaks from his pocket as he pulls out a pocket watch identical to the one Lieve stole. I swallow a lump in my throat and take a step backward towards the office.

"Vera! Vera! Look at this!" Out pops Lieve from behind me, the stolen pocket watch in his hand, glowing just like its mate.

"That," the man says, "belongs to me."

Lieve, oblivious to all the smoke in the shop, scoffs, "it could, *for a price.*"

The man's expression turns wrathful and he strikes the floor again, harder. Thunder cracks as lightning flashes in the windows and I jump. The smoke thickens, turning into molten black lava, melting everything it touches. All our gems and chains, watches and trinkets, Lieve's carved clocks and music boxes, gone.

A shelf full of heavy objects tips over and Lieve pulls me out of the way just before it crashes into me. Flames erupt from the cane in the man's hand, quickly filling up our shop and destroying everything my parents worked for, everything Lieve and I have worked for. My whole life, wrecked before my eyes. Lieve grabs our cloaks as he yanks me to the back, around stacks of clocks, empty boxes, and out through the rear exit.

"Who—what—?"

"I don't know, but we need to get out of here, and fast."

Hidden in the shadows, Lieve and I dart through the empty streets. Lieve makes sure we press our bodies against the exterior of the buildings and move as quickly and quietly as possible. That task is hard. Lieve still has the stolen pocket watch and it glows bright enough to be seen even through Lieve's woolen cloak pocket. His hand clings to mine, dragging me faster and faster through dark alleyways, further and further from town.

We reach the end of a deserted alley on the edge of the village and stop to catch our breath. Out of nowhere someone grabs my wrist and wraps their other arm around my body. Cool metal slides against my throat, the blade threatening my life with its sharp edge. My jaw tenses and saliva fills my mouth. I can't swallow. I can't scream. The dagger in his hand will surely pierce my skin if I do.

"Lieve—," My voice quivers.

He turns around and growls, "Let her go."

"No." I smell musk as his not breath blows on my neck. It's the Enforcer from the market. He chuckles, "You have something I want."

"Vera!," Lieve shouts, "Duck!"

I dip my head down, barely managing to keep from getting sliced as Lieve hurls a discarded glass bottle from the ground at the Enforcer. It thumps him squarely in the forehead and he stumbles backwards. Lieve pulls me out of the alley and we run again, the Enforcer not far behind. Again, we barrel through the village, but this time we're headed towards the forest. Lieve knows every path in the woods by heart, there's no way the Enforcer will find us there.

And yet somehow, he's now in front of us. I can see the spot on his forehead already ripe with discoloration. He stands with his legs spread, ready for combat and dagger in hand. He sneers at Lieve, and then a look of satisfaction spreads across his face. I hear laughing and a shiver runs down my spine.

I know without looking. *We're surrounded.*

My palms are sweating again, but this time I don't hesitate to wipe them on my cloak, I'll need every advantage I can get. The Enforcer's brown eyes flash black for just a moment. *Did I imagine that?* I shake my head and look at Lieve, but I must not have imagined it because Lieve pales.

Suddenly, a loud clap of thunder resonates through the air. It's louder than any thunder I've ever heard. I cup my ears, protecting them from the skull-splitting intensity of it. The Enforcers look at each other in terror, covering their own ears and scattering like rats.

We run, turning our heads to watch in horror as our shop is engulfed in flames, neighbors and passersby panicking as they tend to the fire. The pocket watch flickers and another loud clap of thunder booms.

"Impossible," Lieve mutters, his face now stark white.

Lieve's eyes gloss over and he ignores me when I tug on his sleeve.

"What's impossible?" I ask him as a gust of wind whips my hair around, chilling me to the bone.

This isn't normal weather. This isn't a normal night. I must be dreaming. A nightmare. That's all this is, because if it isn't... Then it feels like Lieve's tales about the god Sol just came true. The god of storms and anger arrives with an ear splitting crack of thunder, and his arrival is never a good sign. Displeasing Sol brings destruction and chaos, smoke and fire. A curse.

Lightning flashes, snapping Lieve back into the present. Gripping my arm as tightly as he can, he drags me out of town. We sprint in the direction of the forest, thunder continuing to echo in my head. There is a catch in my ribs from all the running and I beg to rest but Lieve objects. My lungs ache and the soreness in my muscles are starting to take hold.

Only when we've arrived on the edge of town near a trail that takes you deep into the forest, does Lieve slow down. The pocket watch is barely glowing now, but it pulsates, almost like a beacon for the wealthy man with the cane.

A wolf howls and sends a shiver down my spine and I plead with Lieve to think of somewhere, anywhere else we can go. I hate wolves, and dogs, and I don't want to wander in the stark forest at night with all the dangerous night crawlers.

Lieve shakes his head at me, and with a strained voice he says, "Vera, I don't want to go into the woods any more than you do."

Lieve finds his most recent carving in the trunk of the nearest tree. Adamston Wood is hard to navigate, especially in the dark, but over the years Lieve has carved a hidden path for us in the trails to use for hunting and foraging. I admire how fast his mind works, and his ability to think on his feet. But as I'm about to beg that we go somewhere else, a painful cry pierces the air.

The hairs on the back of my neck prickle. Lieve and I lock eyes and he gestures for me to follow before darting off into the trees. I hurdle along the dirt path behind him, deep into the depths of the forest and the bare trees create an eerie scene under the midnight sky. I try not to think of Lieve's childhood stories of Sol and the Darkthings, but the screams and howls don't make it easy.

I focus on Lieve's boots and try to match my pace with his as best as I can. We run without a destination, without an end. There are no carvings on this path. *Where are we going?* I follow only knowing that we should be as far away from the screams, from the thunder, as possible.

It's hard to keep up, he's much faster than I am. I trip over roots, brambles, and stones, but he's not hindered by a skirt. The trees seem like they are whizzing by me as I pump my legs faster and faster. Our ragged breaths and the crunch of the leaves under our heavy steps fill the now silent wood, making it impossible to hide. Lieve just keeps going. He keeps running. I'm drenched in sweat even though the autumn air is cool and crisp and my calves scream in pain as I push them harder and harder, faster and faster.

After what feels like hours, we arrive at a small clearing. In the center is nothing I've ever seen before. A tree; but, not just any old tree. This tree is...*glowing*. The blue-white radiance is soft, but I can feel its power, and it's mesmerizing. The white bark leads to limbs that weep and bloom with petals of the rarest pink. It's like magic.

This doesn't seem real. *Magic isn't real.* I step closer, reaching my hand to touch it, lost in the radiance it emits. It's like nothing I've ever felt before. A warm tingling sensation travels throughout my entire body and seems to connect my fingers to the tree branches. White sparks fall to the ground with my touch and sizzle before disappearing. I can feel a pulsating energy in my hands, pulling me like a magnet. *Can this be real?*

Another cry pierces the sky and the tree's limbs shudder seemingly to the beat of my already pounding heart. Then, the tree splits with a bright blinding light, showering the ground with white hot sparks. The split opens wider and wider, creating a hole that appears through the trunk of the tree and down into the earth below it. The trunk morphs, forming into steps that lead to never ending depths. Lieve looks at me and then steps up in the crook of the trunk like he's done this a thousand times. I'm speechless as he reaches for my hand.

"Do you trust me?"

I climb up beside him and nod. He laces his fingers in mine, and together we jump.

It is an abomination for humans to share in the power of the Fae. Any offspring resulting from the sins of the Seelie will be henceforth known as Drols.
 – *Decree 978, The Unseelie Doctrine*

CHAPTER 2
LIEVE

I land on my back and jolt from the impact of the ground. I keep my eyes closed and breathe, buying myself a moment's peace. Vera is going to *bombard* me with questions.

The grass underneath my body is slightly damp and smells like rain. Insects buzz around my ears. It's summertime in Prinav. It's peaceful. *It shouldn't be peaceful.* I open my eyes and realize that Vera isn't next to me. I can't call out her name, Darkthings could be nearby and I don't want to come face to face with one. My legs are stiff as I pull myself up using the nearest tree, my body still not used to the hard landings even after all these years.

I sneak along the edges of the clearing in search of Vera. I've never jumped with anyone before, and the tree can sometimes be a trickster. I once landed completely naked, another time I was knocked out for hours, and two years ago I stabbed myself in the foot with an arrow. The landings are never consistent. It's a relief to finally bring Vera here; I've been running out of excuses for my injuries.

"Vera," I whisper loudly, "Vera!"

No answer. She has to be close. The tree wouldn't *take* her from me…*Would it?* I circle the tree, calling out to Vera, my voice getting louder and louder with every shout. Darkthings be damned, I have to find her.

Minutes go by. Then hours. I walk a little further into the forest, off the trails that surround the clearing. *She isn't here.* I thought we would land together. *Shit. Shit. Shit.*

My stomach forms a pit, and I can taste a bitterness in my mouth. The acidic liquid rises to my throat, and sweat beads across my forehead. I lean against the tree and breathe in my nose and out my mouth for several minutes, willing the bile to travel back down. The jumping tree, who Calix named Lopter after the god of mischief, is still glowing. I can feel the hum of its magic against my hands as I run my fingers against its bark, tiny white sparks sprinkling on the ground around my feet.

"Please give her back," I whisper.

Its glow flickers, then fades. I take that as a no. *What do I do?*

Calix will know what to do. The trail that leads to Barault, Prinav's capital city, is in a different section of the forest. A small, overgrown path leads from this clearing to a maze of other trails. I follow my old carvings that eventually lead to an area of the forest that the locals use for hunting and traveling. Hopefully I can find Cal roaming around with Narah, the girl he's courting; they're usually just off the main path, tangled in eachothers arms as usual.

I've explored these woods so many times that it is almost instinctual. My feet take me where I need to go. As I walk, I feel something bump my thigh from inside my cloak pocket. Pulling out the item, I see that it's that pocket watch. But it's not glowing anymore. *Who was that man and what really is this watch?* On closer inspection I notice that the fastener has broken again, and so has the dial.

When I see Vera again, I'm going to show her every inch of Prinav. She loves everything I tell her about this place, even if she believes they're just stories. Guilt eats at me for not bringing her here sooner, but I *couldn't* bring her; it's far too dangerous. The Kingdom has been at war for over a decade, and I couldn't put her in danger no matter how much she admires its legends.

My plan was to create a life for Vera and I, but I'm just as poor in Prinav as I am in Adamston. I keep having to go back to Vera and take care of her and the shop, so it halts any progress I make for us in Prinav. So, when I was rejected by the Academy, I devised a plan. I lied and said I got accepted because I thought I could use this as an opportunity to stay in Prinav for an extended period of time. I would secure our new futures while ensuring that Vera is married to someone who can take care of her. When I have enough finances to provide for Vera, I'd come back to Adamston and whisk her away to Prinav…she can bring the husband or not. The plan was foolproof, *until today.*

I pick berries to eat as I walk, and just before nightfall takes over the forest, I make it to the main footpath that leads to Barault. My feet take me from one trail, to another, and another. I've been walking for quite some time, the evening sun casts long shadows across the trails and the longer I'm without Vera, the less I want to eat. I need to find her and get out of Shadow Grove, it's far too dangerous to be here at night. The Darkthings prey on lonely wanderers, and I've never felt this lonely before.

I won't be able to make it to Barault tonight. Now that the sun is setting, I need to think about shelter. I pick up branches from the ground and carry them on my shoulder so I can use them to build a fire.

Ahead of me is a limestone cave. Calix and I used to meet here, but when he started courting Narah, the distance was just too far for him to travel often. I step inside, my eyes slowly adjusting to the dark. The cave is much cooler than the air outside, so I build a fire big enough to keep me warm all night, but not big enough to attract the creatures of the forest.

I scan the carvings I etched in the walls until my eyes fall on a small bit of parchment under a stone. Calix and I leave each letters when we haven't seen each other for a time. I scramble to the note and hastily unfold it to read Cal's words, hoping that he's found Vera and I can relax.

Lieve,

It's been far too long since we spoke last. I hope you're well, along with your sister. The Doppelgangers have taken another stronghold on the coast of Madoria and I fear King Niall is going to pull Prinav into this fight. I've been forced by Father to join the militia. I'll start training soon. If you get this letter, I urge you to return home.

Til the end,

Calix

Adamston isn't any safer anymore. The Doppelgangers are gaining strongholds everywhere, and there's no doubt that Prinav will enter this war. They helped Madoria in the past, they'll help again. A knot in my stomach tightens at the thought of Calix joining the militia. He's an intelligent, athletic, and talented sword fighter. He'll go to the front lines. I write on the back of the parchment –*Staying until I find Vera*– and tuck it back under the rock.

Exhaustion consumes me once nightfall hits, so I curl up as close to the fire as I can and cocoon myself in my shabby cloak. I fall into a restless sleep full of nightmares of Vera in danger, and Calix dying by the hand of his own Doppelganger.

~

A couple days go by and I'm running out of food and have no weapons to hunt. The trails become wider the closer I get to Barault, and food is scarce because this end of the forest is over-foraged. It's hot. My body is weak, and my muscles shake with every step. I pray for rain. I pray for something to scavenge. I pray for anything.

On day three, thunderous hooves clomp down a nearby path. My heart beats wildly and it takes me a moment to think straight. *I need to get off the trail.* I stop and hide in the overgrowth and wait. This Kingdom is magical and dangerous, and so are many who call it home. All sorts of creatures prowl the forest, and I don't want to meet any of them, especially when I'm so weak. Peering through leaves and brush, I can see a man with dark hair and tan skin riding a black horse with a purple sash around its neck. Relief floods my body when I realize the rider is none other than Calix.

I step out into his eyeline and his riding partner, Narah, lets out a shout, "Calix, look!"

"Lieve!" Calix halts his horse. "What in Ciel?"

My hands shake as I hold them up to him. "I need your help."

Calix dismounts quickly and runs to me. He grasps my arms to hold me up, my knees buckling underneath me with exhaustion. A light feeling overcomes me and I dig my fingers into Cal's arms and let the weight of my body fall into him. He guides me to the ground and all I can do is think of Vera. She's all alone, and I don't know where to start to find her. I sit on the ground as the earth spins, all while the gods take every particle of air from my lungs.

"Doppelgangers," I breathe, "they were in Adamston. So I ran to the Lopter tree with Vera. We jumped, but we didn't land together." My voice breaks. "She's gone."

Calix's face blanched. "Dops got *out of Prinav?*"

I nod. "I don't know what to do."

"Lieve–"

"That's not all," I look into his eyes. "A man came to our shop and burned it down for this." I show them the broken pocket watch and tell them what happened, what I saw.

"Sol." Narah whispers. She bites her lip, thinking. "We need Daphne."

I can see determination rising like a fire in her deep, dark eyes, and she squeezes my hand before Calix helps me mount the horse to sit behind her. I'm so weak that I lean on Narah's back, my weight sinking into her thin frame, and cling to the reins while Calix leads us to the city.

~

"When we get to Daphne's home, we must be discreet," Narah says as she pulls her light brown curls from her face. "Her family doesn't know of her gifts, so if it gets out it could ruin her status and even get her killed if people believe she's a Drol."

"I know the laws," I murmur.

Half human-half Fae. Illegal. Dangerous. Even if Daphne *was* a Drol, I would never speak of it; not if she's willing to help me.

"He'll be discreet," Calix assures Narah.

Without a doubt, Lady Daphne is wealthy. We finally arrive at her townhouse, a gated family estate. Flowering vines grow on the iron spires, and I notice they are MortaVita vines. They are dangerous, sometimes devouring those who get too close; but they also give life if used properly for medicinal purposes. Daphne must be using them somehow.

Calix ties the horse to a post near the street and we ascend the steps to the front door. The knocker is large and made of brass, and it has an engraving. *CORTWRIGHT ESTATE.* Narah reaches out and knocks.

A maid answers. She's short, covered in freckles, and has brown wavy hair tied neatly at the nape of her neck. She takes a look at Calix and I and wrinkles her button nose. Narah politely asks for Daphne to come to the door.

The maid sighs deeply and says, "M'lady is asleep." Then she closes the door in our faces without another word.

"That went well." I say.

"Oh that Marguerite," says Narah, "she's irritating."

"What do we do now?" Calix asks.

Narah bangs on the door with her fist. "Keep knocking until Daphne herself shuts us out."

Somewhere inside, I can hear a woman cursing on the other side of the door. Something crashes to the ground, glass breaking, and louder cursing erupts.

When the door finally opens, my breath catches. The woman before me is like no other I've ever seen. The glow of an oil lamp illuminates her face, and she looks ethereal. Soft red waves of hair fall across her shoulders and I yearn to touch them, even if I get burnt in the process.

"Hello." Her gaze lingers on me for a moment before focusing back on Narah, "it's late."

This is Daphne? May Bram calm my fluttering heart.

"I'm so glad you're home. We need help."

Daphne scans the foyer behind her, craning her neck, *her slender neck,* for eavesdroppers. "Come in."

In single file, we enter the foyer. I know there must be incredible artwork on the walls, expensive trinkets ready for swiping covering the tables, but I only see Daphne. This woman is a work of art herself, a masterpiece.

"Why do you need my help?"

"We need you to see someone," Narah says.

"Quiet," Daphne hisses, "my family–"

Narah reaches for Daphne's hand and whispers, "please."

Daphne sighs and then has us follow her through her family's townhouse to a closet door at the end of a hallway in the back of the house. She waves her left hand in a circular motion, and the door transforms from wood to solid brass, and the four of us step inside. The room is dark, with piles and piles of books, bottles, and parchment strewn haphazardly. A witch's apothecary.

Daphne snaps the door shut behind us, the door turning back into wood as she narrows her eyes at Narah. "I can only see the dead."

Narah's eyes dart to me and then back at Daphne. "Yes. I know."

My heart sinks. I hadn't thought Vera might be dead. None of us speak. I can't look any of them in the face but I feel their eyes on me. This woman, Daphne, might be the one who tells me I got my sister killed.

Daphne grabs a handful of vials and pours the contents together in a bowl. It creates a faint green glow in the room as tendrils of liquid smoke swirl above our heads. She ties her hair back with a black ribbon, closing her eyes and inhaling the floral aroma now filling the area around us.

"Hold my hand–" she reaches for me–, "I need a connection to her."

Daphne's hand is soft. Delicate, but not frail. I can feel her magic. The power under her skin pulsates against my palm, causing my skin to tingle and itch. She closes her eyes and the rest of us follow her lead.

I get a flash of Vera. Vera's eyes narrowing as she watches me climb the steps into the Lopter tree, and joining me for the jump. The madman from the shop right behind us, emerging ominously from the forest; and then, nothing. Black. The vision ends. And with a crack, I'm jolted back to Daphne's messy potion room.

"That's it?" I bark.

Daphne's steps are rapid as she circles the room. "I don't know where she is, but I'm certain your sister is still alive."

Relief floods my veins, as if warm water pours from the top of my head and spills down to my feet. "That's great, thank you."

"Yes–," she keeps going in circles and waves her hand–, "but there's a much greater problem."

Any relief I feel dissolves. "The madman."

"Sol," Narah states, looking for confirmation.

Daphne nods.

Sol. A god. Daphne locks eyes with me again, and I see true fear. She opens her mouth to speak several times, clearly looking for the right words to say.

"Did he jump in after us?"

"I don't know," Daphne replies. "You aren't going to like this, but we must chop down the tree."

I snap at her, "not before I find my sister."

Daphne rounds on me. "Sol may have jumped in the tree, too, and I won't risk him coming to Prinav. I know this is hard, but it has to be done." She stiffens her jaw. "If he's already burned down wherever you came from, then he might destroy Prinav on his hunt. Sol is dangerous, obsessive. I'll do it myself if I have to."

"We need to find Vera," Calix says.

"We'll need to cut the tree quickly." Daphne turns to Narah, obviously trying to get her on her side.

"We aren't cutting down that tree without finding Vera," I growl.

Daphne throws me a sharp look. "I'll do whatever it takes to keep my sisters safe."

"So will I."

We stare each other down, and then Daphne flings her hands and says, "I'll give you some time. I'll check my charts and talk to a Fae friend I have; but no matter what, that tree is getting chopped."

I storm out of the room, Calix chasing after me a few moments later with several spell books given to him from Daphne.

I snap at him, "The tree will not be cut down before I find Vera."

Calix's eyes soften, "I–"

"She's alone." Tears stream down my face. "She's alone, and I can't help her."

Never stand in a fairy ring.
— *Roe Oleander*

CHAPTER 3
VERA

Nothing is below or above me. Pitch black surrounds my body, enveloping me in darkness. I wiggle my fingers but I can't feel Lieve's hand anymore. It isn't wrapped around mine, and I panic. I stretch my arms in every direction, desperate to feel something, anything, but nothing is there. My lips grow warm with the sensation that something is covering my mouth, smothering me. I try to scream, but no sound comes out. *Crack.*

I hit the ground. *Hard.*

My chest heaves and I suck in quick breaths. I can't move. It's like being thrown into a stone wall. Opening my eyes I see trees. *Okay, I'm in a forest.* A damp, earthy smell, like pine and moss, hangs in the air and reminds me of Lieve. The smell tells me it's springtime. *Springtime? It can't be.*

Sitting up hurts. The air has been squeezed out of my lungs too tightly, and the fall so fast that I'm sure my ribs are bruised. *Where am I?* I look around and realize I'm alone. Fearful tears well in my eyes, but I know Lieve would never leave me. He must be trying to teach me something, or he's hiding.

"Lieve!" I rasp with a dry throat.

No answer.

"Lieve!" I yell louder.

Groaning, I stand up and look around, but there's no sign of my brother. I poke around, examining bushes for broken branches, or trees for Lieve's carvings, hoping I can see which way he may have gone.

"Come out, Lieve," I cry, "This isn't funny."

Where is he? When he doesn't answer I frantically pace around the clearing, wondering where he could have gotten off too. The more I look around, I wonder, where have *I* gotten off too? It's daylight. I know the woods in Adamston, well enough to know these aren't the same woods. The trees here are much older, more mature. They have a healthy amount of foliage, and the ground under my feet feels spongy and full of life. This is *not* Adamston.

The ground is trampled with the markings of creatures, and even though I'm not a great tracker, I can tell these are animals I've never met before. The more I examine my surroundings, the more I'm convinced that I'm nowhere near home. It's springtime, and in Adamston, winter was quickly approaching.

This can't be real. I steady my thoughts and try to remember things Lieve has shown me over the years, like checking for footprints. I look for indentations in the muddy earth, but I don't see the familiar tread of his boots. A miserable thought creeps into my mind. *Did he go back through the tree and leave me here?* I've been such a burden to him. *No.* He would never do that. He probably just went looking for supplies. *Did the Enforcers get him?* No…If the Enforcers caught him, they would have grabbed me too because we were holding hands.

"Lieve!" I scream.

Still no answer. I can't breathe. I grab my cloak and hold it to my mouth to muffle my cries, as burning tears flow down my cheeks. I shouldn't have screamed. I don't know what to do or where I am. I dash around the forest again, scanning every twig twice over…and then I see the stump.

A tree stump sits in the center of this small clearing, the size of the tree trunk we just jumped through. Moss grows on the bark along with wild mushrooms. It looks like this tree has been cut down for several years, but there's no question in my mind: *This is the tree we just jumped through. That was the doorway back home, and now it's gone.*

~

For the next few hours, I just sit near the stump and wait to see if Lieve comes back. He always told me that if I get lost and can't find his markings, I should stay put and he will find me. So, that's what I'm going to do.

I lean against the trunk, keeping my eyes and ears open for any sign of his return, but nightfall is rapidly approaching. *I need to start a fire.* My muscles strain to stand again, and I curse Lieve for leaving me like this. The minute he comes back for me, I'm going to tear into him.

There are a bunch of brambles just outside the clearing, but when I pick them up my fingers are wet. This isn't going to work. It must have rained recently, so nothing in these woods is going to be dry enough to start a fire. I'm not just going to tear into Lieve, I'm going to *throttle* him.

I shouldn't sleep on the wet ground, it will only get wetter and colder as night turns into morning. So, against my better judgment, I leave the stump and take the trail that looks the most traveled so I can search for somewhere dry to sleep. Hopefully I bump into someone that can help me, or I find Lieve along the way. Each step I take along the trail gives me pause. *Am I doing the right thing?* I sigh heavily. Clearly Lieve isn't coming back anytime soon, so I have to trust my gut, and my gut says to move on.

As I walk, I make V markings in the trees and tear small pieces of my petticoat and tie them around the branches along the path. If Lieve comes back to this same spot, he'll be able to find me by following the clues I leave behind. I pat the pockets of my skirts and cloak. Empty.

No food, no water, no weapons. I can last for tonight without food or water, but if I don't eat soon, Lieve will have nothing to find.

A twig snaps.

I turn quickly, ready to hug Lieve and yell at him for worrying me, but it's not Lieve that I see. There must have been a trick of the light now that the sun is setting, because I swear I just saw *Fae wings*. Translucent and refracting the sunlight, I see the wings flutter and then hide behind a large tree.

Impossible. Or is it? I'm clearly not in Adamston anymore, and at the very least I've lost my mind. In Corduroy Velmont's *Mythological Creatures and Human Interactions*, a book from Father as a birthday gift, he states that Fae might actually exist. That they live in lush forests and have thin wings. I steel myself and breathe. Everything I've read, and everything Father said, is that they are terrible tricksters. Leaves rustle behind the tree, and even though everything I know about the Fae is urging me to run away, I can't help but feel like I should at least ask if it's seen Lieve.

"Hello there," I call out.

The tip of its wing, and then the top of its head, and then eyes poke around the tree. An almost invisible glow surrounds it, like it's so full of magic that even the Fae's body can't contain it. The Fae's eyes are emerald green, and it has wispy black hair. Slender fingers curl around the tree and their wings flutter behind them like an insect.

"I don't mean to bother you–," I take a step towards it–, "but have you seen a young man who looks a lot like me?"

The Fae looks me up and down, and then steps out from behind the tree. I don't know how Fae age works, but the girl seems to be about fourteen. She wears a short dress made of moss and vines, looking as if the vegetation grows from her very core. Her skin is tinged a slight sage, and her fingernails are as black as her hair.

"I saw a man who looked like you once before," she replies, her voice as melodic as a bird song.

My heart leaps. "Oh that's wonderful, could you tell me which way he went?"

Her green eyes narrow and a cruel smile spreads across her pretty face. "I can do better than that, for I know where he resides."

"Resides?" *What is she talking about?*

"You'll have to give me something in return for this knowledge."

I swallow the lump in my throat. *What do I do?* The Fae girl's wings flutter quickly and she rises from the ground a couple inches.

"But he doesn't live–"

She folds her arms in exasperation and her wings flap faster, allowing her to float and drift away from me a few feet. "If you don't want help, *human*, you shouldn't call for us."

"Fine!" I cry before she speeds off. "What's the price?"

"A golden pocket watch." She lands softly back on her bare feet. "It has gems and rubies and things of no use to humans, but many uses for Fae."

Suddenly my heart seizes.

Her footsteps pad the ground as she walks in circles around me. "You know of this watch, I can see it in your eyes."

I take a deep breath, "I don't have it. The person I'm looking for has it, so if you want the watch, you'll have to hold up your end of this bargain first."

"You lie."

"I'm not lying, I swear–"

The Fae girl snarls at me just as a low growl rumbles the ground beneath our feet. Her eyes wide and she darts off into the thicket.

What was that?

I can't let her go, she said she saw a man who looked like me. That *has* to be Lieve. If she gets away, I may never find him. I bunch up my skirts and take off after her, my shins scathed by thorns. She's lightning fast, and to catch up, I have to dart through the woods like an animal. I have no idea where I'm going, or what that thing that growled was, but

I have to reach her. My legs burn like fire, I can't think, can't breathe, but it doesn't matter. All that matters is getting to Lieve.

The girl rushes around in every direction. I try to focus, to memorize the zigzag pattern, but it's pointless. *What is she scared of? Where is she going?* Instead of trying to remember the pattern, I look for markers. Specific trees, fox holes, stones. I have no idea if it will help, but it couldn't hurt. If I lose her, I'll need to get back on a trail somehow. Lieve always says to memorize things, places, faces, so I try.

Eventually she stops in front of a massive tree at least one hundred feet high. The low growl is faint, distant, but the girl still looks scared. I watch her as she knocks on the tree trunk and mushrooms sprout from the ground around the tree. She counts them, anxiously waiting for the perfect number and wringing her hands. One last mushroom blooms and then they all light up simultaneously. The Fae slowly begins to dissolve, and so does any hope I have of finding Lieve.

I jump out from the brush, my legs stinging with a thousand little cuts and call back to her, "Wait!"

"Bring me what I require and I will grant the knowledge you seek." And with these words, her form is nearly transparent, nearly gone.

If she has a way to find Lieve, then I can't let her go. I can't give her the watch unless I know where Lieve is. *Can't she understand that?* Even though my legs feel like lead, I dart to her. The mushrooms' lights are dimming. I'm so close, only a few more steps–

As my boots touch the edge of the mushroom ring, something whizzes under my arm and catches my cloak. I'm pulled hard to the left and find myself nailed to a tree. Instantly the mushrooms lights have darkened and the Fae has disappeared.

I tug on my cloak but it doesn't budge, so I lift it up to look at what nailed me to the tree trunk and find a hatchet. The hair raises on the back of my neck. Someone, or some*thing*, just tried to kill me. I yank and yank on the hatchet, but it's stuck. I can't move. Something stirs just out of eyesight, and there's nothing I can do.

"Are you mad?" A man shouts.

I keep pulling on the hatchet without responding, refusing to acknowledge my attacker. The man walks out from behind the brush, and I freeze. He's roughly six feet tall and wears black leather armor. Perched on one of his broad shoulders is a sword, and a quiver strapped to the other. He wears a black hood, and a black mask hiding the lower half of his face.

The man strides over and wraps his hand around the hatchet. "Well, are you?"

"No," I snap.

I continue to tug on my cloak over and over while the man just stands there watching me struggle.

"So you're just stupid then," he grunts and pulls the hatchet from the tree in one try.

And to each Kingdom a gift of protection. A sword
of Crystal and Black Diamond. A sword, a Godslayer.
To acquire each is to acquire certain immortality,
and undeniable power. The parent Gods, Bram and
Guenivere had six children, Sol, Dia, Siva, Malsu, Lopter,
and Hode. For each of the six children gods, there are
six crystal swords. The swords exist to keep the gods at
bay, and they were gifted to each Kingdom of Atatacia:
Prinav, Madoria, Teyrnas, Tussia, Seelie Court, and the
Unseelie Court. The parent gods witnessed their children
become too powerful, so they allotted each kingdom a
way to defend themselves against them.
— *Proverb of Saint Alouita, Mother of the Maiden, The Holy
Book of Bram.*

CHAPTER 4
LIEVE

C alix and I search for Vera. We scanned everywhere for any trace,
any sign of her. Nothing was ever there. Calix asks nearly every
person in the city if they've seen her, and gets only disappointment
in return. While we search, I have to keep hidden from King Niall's
officers. If I'm sent to fight in Madoria, Vera will never find me. So, I
use an abandoned shack on the edge of the city to sleep during the day
now to keep hidden. This makes looking for her more difficult, but it's
the only safe option.

A knock on the door interrupts the quiet. It's time. Calix has returned and tonight we're going deep into Shadow Grove. It's my last chance to go all the way to the Lopter tree before Daphne's deadline, and Calix doesn't know I'm going back to Adamston. He thinks we're only looking for her once more before any overlooked clues are tampered with. Daphne sent a message this morning to warn us that she's hired a team to sever the portal; that she must keep her sisters, Prinav, and all of Atatacia safe. The message said that she's sorry, but she's found nothing on Vera in her charts and spells, and that it's time to cut it for fear of Sol.

I scramble to grab my pack of food, candles, matches, a flask, and the small hatchet I found on the property. I'm going back. Vera isn't here, so now I need to try another tactic, and going back to Adamston may be the only answer to find her.

Calix doesn't wait for me to open the door, he turns the handle and lets himself in, averting his eyes. He mumbles, "I'm leaving in a week."

"I thought you had another month."

He pulls out official looking documents from his cloak pocket. "So did I."

I take the documents and scan them, reading words like *duty, training,* and *mission,* each signed and stamped with the King's seal. I flop down on the nearest chair, dust exploding in the lamplight.

"You could run," I mutter. "Join me in Adamston."

"I can't run, Lieve. My country is in shambles…" He trails off. "And Narah would never leave her family to go with me."

"You don't know that."

Calix furrows his brow. "Wait. What do you mean? You're leaving me?"

I sigh. "I've tried every spell in all those books Daphne lent us, and nothing has helped find her, and I think I know *why*. I don't think Vera made it through the tree–" I rub my temples–, "because if she were here, I would have found her by now."

"You think she's still on the other side of the portal?"

Our eyes meet. "Or still in it."

Cal blanches.

"I've been thinking about this for a few days, and you don't have to come if you don't want to–," I stand up and hand him back his documents–, "but I'm going back through the tree."

~

When Calix meets me at the edge of Shadow Grove, he's not alone. Narah came with him. I pull the strap on my pack tighter and join them at the treeline. Calix has his arm around Narah, and he kisses her cheek. Neither of them have large packs, just packs big enough to hold a few days' food and water. They aren't coming to Adamston with me.

"Didn't pack much," I say.

Narah and Calix look at each other and Calix replies, "I'm sorry, but I have to stay–"

"We'll walk with you all the way to the tree, though–" Narah interjects.

I pat Cal's shoulder and give him a sad smile. "Til the end."

The three of us head into the forest, and I take a deep breath. *I hope I'm doing the right thing.* If we run into any guards, I'll be drafted; and any hope of finding Vera will be gone. If I go back into the tree and Vera is somehow here, they'll cut it down and we'll be separated forever. Either way, one of us might be trapped in Prinav. But I can't risk her being left in Adamston alone, not if Sol is afoot.

Even just a few dozen feet into Shadow Grove, it's pitch black. Narah pulls something out of her cloak pocket, a small stone. She whispers, her lips brushing against its smooth surface, and it illuminates a soft yellow light around us. I can feel the tingle of magic in the air, the same as when I held Daphne's hand in her apothecary.

"Daphne lent it to me," Narah says.

"Smart," I reply. "We can't very well walk around with torches through the forest, attracting Darkthings wherever we go."

"She's sorry, Lieve. She tried to find her, truly she did. She wanted me to make sure you knew that. She wanted you to know she's so sorry. Sorry about Vera, about the tree–"

I give her a weak smile. "I know she is."

I lead us through the trail, Narah in the middle with the light, and Calix picking up the rear. Daphne's orb casts its light far enough ahead of me that I can easily see my carvings on each fork of the path. I stay on high alert for guards and Darkthings, I don't want to find either in the woods. Luckily, we don't come across anything dangerous, just a hare and the occasional owl.

We walk in silence until the sun rises. Calix and I want to keep going, but Narah isn't used to staying up all night. We stop to rest and eat, and she falls asleep while the sun warms up the forest to start a new day. While Narah sleeps, Calix and I practice throwing hatchets and knives. Each of Cal's throws hits the target with deadly accuracy.

"Do you know what regiment you'll be joining?" I ask him.

"Marksmen," he replies, "as part of the Hode."

"Hode, like the god?"

"Exactly. There's so many battalions in the army, but the Hode is special. My good aim got me out of the front lines and into the Hode instead. Like the god, they have three parts, like the three faces of his personality. The spies, the marksmen, and the retribution," Cal explains. "The spies go in first to get the lay of the land, just like Hode did in the battle during the Twin War, the marksmen are ready to strike, just like Hode strikes down his enemies, and the retribution are, well…they're *deranged*."

"Like Hode became," I nod. "I get it."

My aim gets better with Calix's advice as the day wears on. When I hunted back in Adamston, I used snares, rarely an arrow or a blade, and this feels new to me. New, but *good*. I fling the weapons over and over until I can hit the target repeatedly.

Once Narah wakes up, we continue. Faster than we anticipated, we reach the limestone cave. Calix and I keep practicing hitting targets for a while before we make camp. We settle in but find no signs of Vera. *I should have come here sooner.*

Vera would love what we're doing. "Adventuring," she would call it. I hope I find her, so I can tell her the truth and stop lying to her. I've carried so much guilt about keeping Prinav from her, and I hope she forgives me. Without money, Prinav is dangerous. Hell, Prinav is dangerous even if you're wealthy; but if we had money, I could afford to keep her safe here. I could afford a safe home, maybe even guards to watch over that home.

War has been brewing here for years, and now with the Doppelgangers gaining control over so many cities, I know I was right to keep her in the dark about this place, even though it was wrong. If I ever see her again, I'll never let her leave my sight. I'll spend the rest of my life apologizing to her. The only thing I want now is to know she's okay and that I didn't run out of time.

Time. I pull the pocket watch from my cloak and examine it again. Despite my best efforts to fix it, it's still broken; but if Sol has Vera, I might still be able to use it as a bargaining chip to get her back. There's a small mirror that sits in the back side of the watch behind all the faces that tell time in different Kingdoms, and I catch a glimpse of myself and snap the clasp shut. I can't stand to look at myself, so I shove it back, deep in my pocket.

~

Calix and Narah are already up by the time morning comes. I stretch, kick out the last remaining coals from the fire, and join them. *I go back to Adamston today.* The thought of going back makes me nauseous. I don't belong there. I belong here with Vera. I'm never going to be able to return after this, I'm never going to see Prinav again. I'm never going to see Calix again. He's to chop down the tree exactly ten minutes after I jump.

Calix pops from behind a tree and shrugs his shoulders. "It's your last day."

I hide a tear and nod. I don't know what to say. He walks over to me and puts a hand on my shoulder, giving it a light squeeze. "Let's get your sister."

We reach the trail leading directly to the Lopter tree much faster than usual. My heart aches with the thought of leaving this place, leaving Cal. While my mind wanders, a bird whistles up ahead.

"Did you hear that?" Calix whispers.

"The bird?"

His eyes darken. "That's not a bird."

More whistles sound through the forest and Calix grabs Narah's arm to pull her into the brush. I follow and crouch down next to them, listening for the danger Calix hears.

"We need to get out of here."

"I don't hear anything but birds, and I have to go," I say and step out of the brush. "I'll miss you, *til the end.*"

Another whistle, louder this time, rings through the forest and Calix grabs my sleeve. I jerk my arm free and race towards the Lopter tree, it's so close I can see its pink petals through the tree limbs that obstruct the view from the trail. Calix doesn't follow me. I can hear him arguing with Narah, her pleading with him to stay with her and not follow me. I get to the clearing where the tree stands and I freeze. *I made a mistake.*

I expected to see only the tree, but instead, when I get there, a group of people with translucent wings and green tinged skin stand before me. They speak to each other, the words similar to *bird calls.* These are the Fae of the Seelie Court. They seem to be voting, or trying to agree on something. An elderly Fae woman nods at a fierce looking Fae man and he unsheaths a crystal sword. The sun glints on the blade as it arcs to strike the tree.

"No!" I scream.

I race forward, but before I can step in front of the blade, I'm lifted into the air by invisible arms. The blade carves through the tree, leaking a bluish liquid and the stumps glow pulsates weakly, until it eventually fades. I'm dropped to the ground, my wrist nearly snapping, but I crawl using my elbows and collapse in front of the stump. *Vera's gone.*

I scream until my throat is raw. Pulling on my hair, rocking back and forth and sobbing. I wail. *I'm stuck. Vera's stuck.* I can't feel my body. One of the Fae snickers and white hot rage climbs up my body and flows back down my cheeks with hot tears. I dig my nails into the spongy earth and push up with all my strength. I don't know what I'm doing as I propel myself at the bastard. I'll destroy him, and if I can't, I'll die trying.

I pull the hatchet from my belt and fling it at the Fae who sliced the tree. It lands in his chest, and he doubles over, clutching the handle. I'm still as he falls to his knees. The other Fae round on me, and I brace myself for death. Then something roars to the right of me. *Shit.* A Darkthing. The massive wolf-like beast leaps into the air, its teeth bared and claws extended. The Fae cast their spells against the monster, but it's no use. Darkthing hides are nearly impenetrable.

I watch the beast rip the Fae to shreds, tearing them limb from limb, and littering the ground with their bodies. I don't attempt to move for fear it will notice me and decide I'm next. I pray there's only one of them, and I pray Calix and Narah have already started running back to Barault.

Cal's hand grips my injured wrist and pulls me out of harm's way and into the brush. We run back towards the cave, as far away from the danger as possible. By the time the screams of the Fae fade away, what just happened sinks in. The Fae must have had their own reasons to cut the tree, and we were too late. My knees buckle and I fall apart on the ground bawling until I shudder.

Tears fill my eyes and I can barely see, but I know it's Narah who sits on the ground next to me and rubs my back softly. The air filling my lungs is shallow, and the heaviness in my chest explodes with a cough. Then begins a coughing fit, and eventually dry heaving. My ribs and abdomen are tight, and my head pounds with every ragged breath.

"I'm sorry," Narah whispers over and over. "I'm sorry, I'm sorry, I'm sorry."

Prinavian Wildberries grow in the thick underbrush of Shadow Grove. Its purple hue is similar to the seeds of the Tremor Fruit. Do not confuse the two or–.
–End of Transcript Missing from files–Corde Dashar, Healer and Consort for Queen Rosalind Bone in the year of our gods.

CHAPTER 5
VERA

I yank my cloak the second I'm released. "You could have killed me."

The man tucks the hatchet into a loop on his belt. "I could have, but I didn't. I saved you."

"Says who," I snap. "That Fae said it had seen someone I'm looking for, and you–" tears well in my eyes–, "you…"

My skin feels hot. My skirts stick to my legs from sweat. The feel of my cloak tight around my neck makes me gag so I rip it off and fling it to the ground. With each intake of breath my throat burns, and my ribs, bruised from the fall earlier, tighten around my chest. *I'll never find him now.* I fall to my knees and put my palms to the earth, watching my tears land in the grass.

The man's voice softens and I hear his boots take a ginger step closer. "Who are you looking for?"

"My brother, Lieve Oleander."

In disbelief the man replies, "You're Vera."

I snap my head at him. "How do you know my name?"

There's a long pause. The man lowers his black hood, revealing brown tousled hair, and scratches the top of his head. "He's been looking for you for a *long* time."

"Wait, wait, wait," I say. "I don't understand. I haven't been away from him for more than a few days."

The man shakes his head. "I don't know how to explain this to you, but you've been missing for *years*."

Thoughts spin in circles around my head and I don't know what to think. I look around the forest for some kind of sign of Lieve, but I don't notice anything. *Is this man lying to me?* I don't know if I can trust him. What if he stopped me from going with the Fae for his own agenda? He's got to be lying. There's no way I've been missing for years, I've just arrived.

The man studies me, his eyes trailing over my hair, my clothes. I wrap my cloak around my shoulders and turn my head from him, but I still feel his eyes burning into the back of my head.

"Thirsty?"

He takes another step closer and pulls out a flask. I hesitate. My mouth is dry and my lips feel chapped. I *am* thirsty. I'm so thirsty I actually think about drinking whatever he's about to give me, even though I know I shouldn't. He shakes the flask, sloshing the remaining liquid in the container. My eyes flick from his, to the flask, and then I turn away from him again.

"No thank you."

"Don't be stubborn–"

I scoff, "I'm not being stubborn. I'm being smart. And I'm not drinking from a flask given to me by a stranger."

"I'm not going to poison you."

"Fine." I huff and take it from him.

I open the lid, but before I drink, I smell the contents. Nothing seems odd about it, but I swirl it around and sniff at it again.

"It's just water," he says.

I take a tiny sip and wait for a minute. Nothing happens. I take another sip, and nothing happens. The water tastes so good. Cold and crisp and clean. The second it touches my lips it's so refreshing I have to stop myself from guzzling it all. The man chuckles. "Told you."

"What's your name?"

He leans against a tree. "Arden."

I hand him back the flask and he clips it to his belt as I ask, "Now what?"

Arden stands up straight and gestures for me to follow him down a narrow trail. "Now we'll see if you're really who you say you are."

I follow Arden and try to figure out if he's someone I can trust. He points out various trails to me and asks me questions about myself, but I deflect. I don't want to tell him too much. He stops every few yards and shows me which berries are edible and stuffs a handful into a stained piece of cloth and tucks it in his pocket. I see him pop a few berries under his mask and eat, so I pick my own handful and eat one. It's delicious. Tart. Juicy. The flesh on the small purple berry is perfectly ripe. I shove the rest of them into my mouth and jog to catch up with him. Maybe I *can* trust him.

"We should find shelter, we aren't getting out of Shadow Grove tonight." Arden says.

I stop. "Isn't Shadow Grove in Prinav?"

Arden stops too and turns around. "It is."

"So, I'm *not* imagining things." That means all the stories are real. I look into Arden's eyes and I can't stop myself from grinning. "I really jumped into a tree and landed *in Prinav*?"

"It would seem so."

My heart leaps. *Is this really true*? Prinav. Every story, every fairy tale. Real? I laugh and jump around, startling Arden. That makes me laugh more and he acts like he's annoyed with me but I can tell he's smiling through his eyes. *I'm in Prinav.*

"This is a fairytale land." I say in awe.

"Lieve said you had a strong interest in our Kingdom."

"That's an understatement."

I then pummel Arden with questions. *Is Lieve safe? Does Prinav really have a castle? Does the King host any balls? Are the gods real? Can Lieve and I stay in Prinav?* We walk side by side and he laughs while I squeal with joy at his every reply.

Arden answers each of my questions with patience. "Yes, there's a castle."

"How big?"

"*Big.*"

He tells me that Lieve is perfectly safe, and that the King *does* host royal balls. It's generally accepted that the gods *are* real. And *yes*, Lieve and I are welcome to stay.

This. Is. Amazing.

Arden leads us to a limestone cave and we decide that's where we should make camp. I pick up sticks for a fire, luckily the ones around here aren't nearly as damp as the ones I tried to collect earlier.

"I'll get the firewood, you can just rest." Arden says.

I hand him the sticks I had tucked under my arm and sit in the mouth of the cave, watching him bring tinder inside to start the fire. He pulls more fruit and meats from a pack he has slung over his back and we eat in silence. My mind wanders at the absurd reality that I've traveled to a different realm, and as I look around the cave I see carvings.

Lieve was here.

I should test him. I should see if Arden knows that Lieve made those carvings, because I'd recognize those marks anywhere. "What are those marks?"

Arden raises an eyebrow. "You should know what those are."

I narrow my eyes. "I do. Do you?"

"They're from Lieve. He makes carvings to mark where he's been. They're a guide for him as much as they are a guide for you; and believe it or not, for me, too."

I can feel my muscles relax a bit and I take a large bite of meat and lean my back against the damp wall of the cave.

"Are you from Prinav?" I ask.

He lowers his eyes. "Yes. But not from Barault. I used to live on a farm in the countryside of Ellerton."

"And where do you live now?"

"My cabin. And sometimes, Brone Castle."

Arden tells me all about how beautiful Barault is with its ancient buildings and fountains, and how great the food is. He says that I'll love Brone Castle. He says there's a library with every book ever written about the gods, and that I can read as many of them as I want to. Arden says he'll be the lookout, and that I should get some sleep because we have a lot of walking to do tomorrow. But, I don't want to sleep. I want to learn. I want to get to Lieve.

"Trust me, it will be a long day."

Arden's right, I should try and sleep. I lay with my back against the fire and watch the flames dance across the walls of the cave. In no time at all, my eyelids grow heavy and I'm pulled into a deep, dreamless sleep.

~

The following morning I wake up alone. I look around but all I find are a few smoldering coals, the only remaining evidence Arden was even in this cave with me. *Of course he left me.* I force myself not to cry. I have to figure out what to do, how to find Lieve. Maybe I can find the Fae girl I met yesterday.

I stomp out the remaining embers of the fire and dust myself off. Before I leave the cave, I trace my fingers over Lieve's carvings and pray to the gods to find him. If Prinav is real, they might be too; and if they are, I could use all the help I can get.

I step out of the cave and look around, giving Arden one last chance to show his face before I make my way back to the fairy ring and take my chances with the Fae. I call out for him, but there's no reply. *How could I have been so stupid?* He's not coming back.

Just as I'm about to leave, Arden returns. I fling my arms in exasperation at him and he marches right up to me and grabs me. "Why are you shouting so loudly?"

"I thought you'd left me."

"That's no excuse."

"It is, so. I thought you'd *left* me."

Arden rolls his eyes. "I had to relieve myself."

"You could have told me you were coming right back."

"You were asleep."

"That's no excuse."

Arden huffs. "Fine."

All of a sudden, now *I* need to relieve myself. *Great.*

"Okay Princess," Arden says. "It's time to go."

I really, really, need to relieve myself now.

Arden's eyes narrow at me. "Do *you* need to relieve yourself?"

"Yes." I say and cross my arms.

He lowers his hood and pinches the bridge of his nose before gesturing to a clump of large bushes. When I get back, Arden says we need to get a horse from his cabin because the journey is long and he'd like to make it to Barault as soon as possible. We walk all morning, and well into the afternoon, until we arrive at a small cabin nestled near the edge of the trail.

There's not much to the cabin. I notice chipped paint on the front door, and a heavy iron lock. Potted plants line the porch and a hammock lightly swings in the warm breeze. It's made from the wood that surrounds us, and has a small garden about three meters from the front door. Rabbits nibble on the vegetables and Arden doesn't shoo them away, he steps around them and takes me to the back. Standing in the center of a large patch of grass is the most beautiful horse I've ever seen. It has a pearlescent sheen in the sun beams that dapple between the treetops. Its coat gleams with tiny rainbows that appear like an illusion on the fur. I'm shocked that it's not fenced in. Most people who own something that incredible would want to lock it up.

"Well, hello there," Arden says and walks straight over to pet its head.

"Can I pet it too?" I breathe.

"Of course."

Its fur is so thick that my hand almost disappears. I've never felt anything like it, it's softer than silk, softer than velvet, softer than satin. It's incredible.

"I've never seen a horse like this."

"They're rare." Arden nuzzles the horse's nose. "I've only ever seen two of them, this one, and its mate."

Once the supplies are gathered, we secure the saddlebags. Arden helps me mount and then hops up behind me. His strong arms hold the reins and my stomach flips. I've never been this close to a man before. I feel, *unsupervised.* Arden stays quiet, obviously experiencing a similar awkwardness. My fingers grip the saddle tightly and I hold my spine straight so I don't let myself lean back against Arden's warm body.

Sagarts, High Priests and Priestesses of the Holy Temple:
They are blessed by the gods, with powers, knowledge,
and words.
*—Talic the Meek, First Sagart of Atatacia, Excerpt from the
diary of Queen Fortuna.*

CHAPTER 6
LIEVE

The next two days are a blur of reading and failing to find answers. Calix and Narah try to get me to eat, to drink, but it's no use. I've lost Vera forever. That was my last chance at finding her, and the Fae took it away. My heart is bruised and beaten, but still pumping. However, I don't believe my heart pumps blood anymore, it pumps *wrath*. I'll come back, and I hope those Fae remember me; and if they don't, *I'll remind them.*

I can see the end of Shadow Grove up ahead, Hode soldiers guard the exit, but we can easily slip past them. I need to keep hidden if I want to stay out of this war. But Calix is leaving, and he's all I have left. All I've ever wanted is a quiet life. I wanted to play music. I wanted to feel something. I wanted to have enough food to fill our stomachs, and a house that we could call ours. That dream is gone. Vera is gone.

Prinav isn't worth anything to me anymore. Life isn't worth anything. Without someone to tell the story of your life to, there is no story to tell. We start out as living, breathing souls that walk the earth, but in the end, we're all just stories. Our lives are handed down from person to person, over campfires or in books or song. I'll tell everyone about Vera, so at least a piece of her will get to live in Prinav forever.

Calix taps my shoulder and whispers, "you can get past them, they aren't even paying attention to the left side."

"Good thinking," I say, "let's go."

Then, Calix takes Narah's hand and pulls her down the right side of the trail. This leaves me to sneak out of Shadow Grove on the left. So that's what we do. Narah and Calix go to the right to distract the guards, and be there to vouch for me if I'm noticed. I go to the left, as quiet as a mouse.

Narah and Calix wrap their arms around each other on the treeline and start giggling. Brilliant. They're making themselves look like lovers in the forest, caught up in the moment. The guards hear their laughter and one of them marches over to them.

"What's goin' on?" He shouts.

They stumble out of the woods and the moonlight illuminates them. I stifle my snicker while the guard interrogates the pair. Calix has unbuckled his belt, and Narah's hair is disheveled. It's hard not to laugh at the sight of them. Eventually the guard lets them go with a warning.

While the guards are distracted, I creep along the path away from the guardpost. My heart pounds in my chest. *Don't hear me, please don't hear me.* I keep my eyes on Calix with every step I take. He nonchalantly chats with the guard. Narah's face is flushed and she giggles as she leans her head on Calix's arm. They have nothing to hide, just a pair of love-struck teens saying their goodbyes before Calix is sent to train.

I reach the end of the path, the sound of laughter floating through the trees. If I can just run through the clearing and behind the small Abbey ahead, then I can follow the street all the way to Daphne's. Calix and Narah will meet me there, and hopefully Daphne will have an idea on what to do now.

I crouch low and peer through the brush. All looks clear. The few officers are bidding farewell to Calix and Narah, and I have just enough time to run to the Abbey if I go right now–

A guard steps right in my path at the exact moment I leave the shadows of the woods.

We lock eyes.

Before he can warn the others, I reach for his sword. Soft leather brushes across the skin of my fingers as they curl around the hilt of his blade, but he thwarts my attempt to grab it. A hard kick to the abdomen thrusts me backwards and the guard's sword is now pointed at my throat.

The guard doesn't take his dark eyes off me. His experienced hands grip the handle of the sword and tips my chin up. "Who are you?"

"Lieve, sire," I answer with a gulp. "I'm part of the Hode."

His eyes narrow. "Your accent isn't Prinavian."

Shit. He's too smart. What can I say? What could possibly make him decide not to lock me up?

Calix walks over with Narah clinging to his arm. He holds his hand out to me and I gratefully grab it as Calix turns to the guard, "You don't recognize him?"

"No," he says and watches the three of us, "I don't."

"Well, that makes sense. He's the Hode's newest spy and needs some training, so it's no wonder you wouldn't know him."

Narah is told to go home. Then the guards take Calix and I to the Knights who are in charge of the Hode. *We messed up.* A Knight pulls me into a small candle lit room when we arrive at the compound.

He sneers, "I know you aren't a spy. So who are you?"

"My name is Lieve, sir–" I swallow–, "and, I'm no one. I'm just a very good thief."

The Knight stares me down. He's tall enough that the top of his head nearly hits the ceiling. His face shows age lines, hardened by war, and his movements are precise, practiced.

"I should lock you up for even *daring* to lie to a Hode officer."

My knee shakes, rattling the uneven leg of the chair against the stone floor.

"Instead–"

I straighten in my seat.

He leans over the table, his dark eyes looking into mine, "I'll let you join the Hode. For real." He looks down his nose at me. "*If* you pass the exam."

~

I'm led, blindfolded, almost two miles from the compound. We walk outside, the smell of moss and wet earth wafting around me. A door creaks open up ahead and then I'm nudged down a spiral staircase. The musty smell signals that we're going underground. Our footsteps don't echo, so the walls must be narrow. Every ten feet or so, I feel the heat of a torch or oil lamp. *Definitely underground.*

We suddenly come to a halt. Keys jingle and the sharp click of a lock, and the groan of a door hinge before being pushed forward. A gloved hand grips my forearm and pulls me into a seat. I can tell it's made of wood by the way it creaks when I shift my weight.

That same gloved hand rips the blindfold from my face and I blink my eyes and look around. I was right. I'm sitting on a wooden chair and beside me is a wooden table. There are torches on the wall illuminating the hallway, and it's incredibly narrow and short.

Another Knight walks in and hands me a stack of parchment. He wears a uniform I've never seen before, a cream robe of sorts. Across his chest lays a red sash with tassels, and atop his head sits a crown of solid gold. There are no gems encrusted in the precious metal, but it is formed in peculiar shapes. The top spirals up to a point, and in the front are sharp wings.

The Knight who brought me here nods at the man with the crown, "Lieve, bow to the head Priest of the King's Court, his holiness, the Sagart, Baptiste Matisse"

I bow my head.

"Good to see you, Ramsey." The Sagart says as he turns to me. "This is your test–" He lays a second stack of parchment on the table–, "read the directions carefully."

Ramsey then pulls out two ancient books from under his cloak and hands them to me. "If you fail, you'll be arrested for impersonating a member of the Hode." They both stand in the doorway, Baptiste not looking back, but Ramsey nods at me "Good luck."

They lock me in.

I stand up and look around the room for a clock, but there isn't one. I pull out the pocket watch even though it's broken and place it on the table. I open one of the books, relieved it's in Prinavian, a language I can read. Then I flip open the cover of the second book and freeze. It's in Madorian. *Shit.* I rifle through the stack of parchment. I don't even recognize the language on the papers.

Shit. Shit. Shit.

There are two buckets in the corner, one with water and one empty, and a plate of stale bread. I pace around the room, running my hands along the walls and praying to any god that will listen. I return to the table and examine the book in Prinavian. The wording is odd and archaic, and I realize *it's a cipher.* It clicks. One book gives you information about the second book, and together, you can decode the parchments.

My eyes strain from reading the miniscule words in the dim light. The Priest and the Knight Ramsey didn't leave me any ink or quills, so what did they expect me to do? I read until I stumble upon a sentence, stopping me in my tracks. *The Crystal Swords can take the life of an immortal, the Crystal Swords are killers of gods.* The Fae in Shadow Grove used a crystal sword to slice through the Lopter Tree. Could that tree have been *the* Lopter? My heart beats wildly.

I continue to read and learn about Crystal Swords and True Rulers of the Thrones. I still find no answers to the ciphers. Nothing happens until I get to the last sentence on the page. I curl my fingers, just as Daphne's books advised me, and watch as the ink on the pages blot together and then disperse on the parchment. I can't believe this. *I just did magic.* I pull the cipher closer and see that I don't need the answers, because the solution is right in front of me.

"Knock on the door six times, and vow your allegiance to the crown."

It can't be that easy. I stand and walk over to the door, knock, and take a deep breath before shouting, "I vow my allegiance to the crown!"

Nothing happens. I eat the stale bread, and it's so chewy my jaw is tight and tired when I reach the end of the loaf. The water is stagnant and tastes slightly bitter. I wonder how many people read the entire parchment, how many people have come to this room and succeeded. I wonder how many people have come into this room and failed.

The flames in this small room are growing dim, morning must be coming soon. Boots thud in the hallway outside the tiny room and I start shaking. I'm either going to enter the Hode with Calix, or I'm being sent to prison. Then suddenly the door opens, with the Priest standing in the doorway.

～

The next few weeks of training are rough. On the good side, Calix and I get to be dormmates. My training consists of half days throwing daggers, sparring, and endless hours of decoding ciphers. That last bit, Calix isn't part of. He continues physical training like balance, coordination, and archery with the other marksman.

Daphne writes letters, updating me that there's been no trace of Vera. I write back letters every day, thanking her for all her help and asking her to continue keeping an eye out. Even though the tree has been cut, and I know Vera is lost forever, I can't bring myself to totally give up on her. Daphne has searched for a way to get me back to Adamston to look for her, but she's found nothing of use so far.

Lieve,

I know you get a few days of leave and I was wondering if we could have a drink. There's a tavern called Serpent's Tongue on Silver Street near my favorite apothecary. I'll be there tonight at dusk.

Daphne

The stars, they say, are the gods' eternal eyes. Each
constellation is a story written in light, a whisper
of the divine etched across the night sky, guiding
the fates of those who dare to look up. It is said
that the constellations are the gods' final gift to the
world—a celestial guide to those who seek their fates.
But beware, for the gods are fickle, and the stars are
not always kind.
—*Letter of Warning to Queen Fortuna, First Monarch of*
the Prinavian Empire, from Hesak the Prophet

CHAPTER 7
VERA

We make good time through Shadow Grove, but Arden says
we still have a while before we reach Barault. Howling
echoes in the distance. My muscles tense. I want to think it's just a
wolf, but I know better. We're in Prinav, not Adamston, and my
gut is telling me that what I'm hearing are Darkthings.

When we were younger and Lieve was upset with me, he would
scare me with their tales. Their gnashing teeth, their canine snouts,
and those razor sharp claws filled my nightmares. Now that I know
Prinav is a real place, I assume the Darkthings are too. The thought
makes my blood run cold. I used to believe he made them up to
torture me when I annoyed him, because Lieve has always hated
anything canine, ever since the day he was attacked.

When we first took ownership of the shop, Lieve had to steal food for us to get by. One day, he stole an entire cooked chicken. Our parents had both passed away at this point, so we had to fend for ourselves. As we sat under the window of the home Lieve just stole the chicken from, I was proud. I knew I shouldn't have been. Stealing was wrong; but, I was so proud of him for doing what needed to be done to keep us eating. Lieve would do whatever it took to keep us safe and fed.

The man who owned the home did not share the sentiment. He caught us under the window and called out his dog. This dog was large, with teeth sharp enough to easily rip the meat from your bones. Lieve and I ran as fast as our legs could carry us, but the dog was faster. It nipped at my skirts and pulled me down. Lieve fought the dog off me with a stick, but it attacked him in return. I felt horrible, and Lieve suffered dearly for that chicken for many days afterward.

My stomach growls.

"We're out of food, but there's a creek nearby. We should be able to catch some fish."

"I don't know how to fish," I reply.

"I'll teach you, Princess."

I smile and find it difficult not to like Arden. "You know, I'm not a dainty little woman. I ran our shop back home, and I'm a very skilled jeweler. It's just that most of the time we stayed in the city, and on the occasion where we would venture into the woodlands of Adamston, Lieve did all the work. He would be the one that did all the hunting, and wasn't comfortable with me venturing too deep into the woods with him. He said I was too loud, but now I wonder if he was just too proud to let me help."

"I think Lieve underestimates you."

Arden's right. I'm thankful that Lieve always provided, and that he always made sure I was okay, but sometimes I wonder if he couldn't see how much I'm capable of. He always took the lead in our lives, and I resented him for it. But to be fair, I always let him.

We make our way to the creek, just over a mile away. It's peaceful. The babbling of the brook has me imagining river nymphs bathing in the clear water. Arden chooses a spot to unmount, about twenty feet from the water, nestled in the safety of some massive trees on the bank.

I wish I could have come here with Lieve. I bet he loves it here, quiet and beautiful, and away from people. He loves going to the woods alone. Lieve started going off into the woods for days at a time in recent years. Thinking back on when we jumped into the tree, I remember feeling like I thought Lieve had been here many times before.

I begged to come to the woods with him, but he always said it was too dangerous, saying it was full of snares and hunters and wolves. I argued that the city was no different, but Lieve was adamant that if I was always with him, the shop wouldn't survive. Now I wonder if he's been coming to Prinav all along.

The trickling of the creek is soft and light. I watch the water flow and I'm reminded again of the fairytales Lieve would tell me as a child. The twin Gods born of a river deep in a dark wood. In those waters lived dark and light magic. They drank from the river and were given flowing magic that the parent gods infused in the water. Together they created the inhabitants of this realm, Fae, and creatures alike. Their names were Sol and Dia.

The mother and father Gods were Bram and Guinevere, the White Wave. Guinevere was the mother of water, and flowing new life, but also of tidal waves white with rage. Bram was The Father of Multitudes and the creator of all the realms and the humans. They had six children: the twins Sol and Dia, the Trickster Lopter, Hode the mad, beautiful Siva, and her twin Malsu. Each of these Gods were born in other realms and helped create the inhabitants. These Gods can be helpful or cruel, mischievous or stoic, and it all depends on their moods.

The story says that Sol was in love with Dia, and he asked their parents if they could be married. The parent Gods agreed, but Dia refused the union. She had fallen in love with a human named Oriel and they secretly married in the river of magic. Oriel became a pseudo-god, and Sol was enraged.

Sol and the Unseelie waged a war against Oriel who created the Darkthings to protect Dia. Once Sol killed Oriel, Dia was forced to be his bride. But before they wed, Dia was able to run from him and hide in a secret realm where she remains to this day.

I always related to Dia more than anyone else in Lieve's stories. Her choices were always at the mercy of others, just like me. I didn't want to run the shop, just like I didn't want to marry someone just to survive.

Arden prepares to fish from the bank of the creek. I watch him sharpen a stick into a spear and get lost watching his hands. He moves them in deliberate motion, up and down, up and down, up and down. I move closer and sit cross legged in front of him to learn. His eyes crinkle with a smile, and without question shows me how to sharpen the spear.

"Take the stick in one hand and the rock in the other," he nods as I take the objects from him.

"Like this?" I ask as I strike the spear with the rock.

"Exactly."

His gaze sweeps from my hands, then up to my lips. My cheeks grow hot and I fumble the rock with shaky hands. I strike the stick with the rock, shaving the wood over and over. I can still feel the heat of Arden's eyes on me, and after a long time of sharpening the stick with trembling fingers, I finish making the spear.

"Is it alright?"

"Let's find out." He says cheerfully.

We take off our boots and wade into the shallow water. It's freezing. Every ripple sends a wave of cold over my feet and ankles, leaving me shivering. Tiny minnows swim haphazardly around my feet and then are carried away by the light current. I take a few steps to the middle of the creek, closer to where Arden stands. Nothing big comes by me, but Arden spears two fish while I just stand here. I start to get frustrated. I'm cold. Arden spears another fish and tosses it on the bank of the creek.

Then I see it. *The whopper.*

This fish is huge. I have to catch it, I *have* to. My hands shake as I raise my spear and stab it straight into the frigid water. The fish flops and splashes, but I lift the spear out of the creek and I am elated to see it stuck on the other end. I twirl around in the water and let this moment sink in, smiling and laughing. Dancing around in the chilly current, I feel powerful.

"I caught a fish!" I cheer.

Arden shouts, "It's massive!"

Even though the water is cold enough to bite, I feel warmth. I caught a fish.

We wade back to the bank. Arden removes my catch from the spear and places it on his small pile. "I'll dry the smaller ones for us to eat on the way to Brone Castle, but we'll eat your monster now."

I'm filled with pride. *My* monster. I killed a monster. I can't wait to tell Lieve about this. Once we dry our feet and put our boots back on, Arden starts a fire and begins cleaning the fish.

"Will you show me how to do that?" I ask.

"Sure," Arden says, "sit with me."

I practically skip over to him. He goes through the steps of cleaning the fish and we tackle each of the little ones together. It doesn't take very long, but I'm famished by the time they are all ready to be either cooked or dried out.

We eat and laugh and talk until the sun goes down and I bask in the fact that I'm in Prinav while looking up at the stars twinkling in the black velvet sky. We find a spot near a larger clump of trees right off the creek and make ourselves as comfortable as we can.

"That one there–," Arden points to the stars–, "that's the constellation Lopter. It's a ram's head. Do you see it?"

I watch where his finger points. "I do."

"It always points south. Remember that, you might need it."

I nod and Arden continues to show me the constellations, each one named after the gods. He tells me basic navigation tools to use, and the stories that go with each one. Eventually I yawn, and we decide it's time to try and sleep.

Laying down for the night, my eyes dance along the backs of the pearl colored horse. The glint of the moon casts a haunting glow onto its already perfect coat, holding such mystery. My thoughts trail to the owner of the majestic beast. Arden is just as mysterious. I fall asleep to the fantasies of spending more time alone with him in Shadow Grove after we find Lieve.

Many gods have the ability to shapeshift. They are the creators of the nymphs and dryads, and often join them in their natural states. Lopter, the Trickster, has taken various forms to tease humans and Fae alike. Many have claimed to meet him as a thorny rose, a poisonous berry, and even a blooming willow.

—Excerpt from an untitled Educational Text at the Sagart Monastery of Bramhold, located in the isolated village of Glous, Tussia.

CHAPTER 8

LIEVE

C alix lets me borrow trousers, along with a linen shirt, vest, a heavy cloak, and a pocket full of coins. I've thought about Daphne a lot, but never tried to spend time with her alone. I assumed our social status would prevent us from interacting beyond using her gift to search for Vera, so I never attempted any other type of conversation.

My knee shakes under the table I chose at the back of the dimly lit tavern as I wait for Daphne to arrive. *What if I'm reading too much into this?* There's no way that she'd just want to spend time with me, I'm not suitable for her. I frustrate myself with these thoughts and empty a tankard given to me by the barmaid.

Each time the tavern door swings open my heart skips a beat, and once the sun has set I can feel my muscles stiffen with anticipation on Daphne's arrival. There's a three piece band playing music on a small raised platform and everyone in the tavern claps their hands and stomps their feet to the beat. The barmaid pours me another ale just as Daphne enters the tavern. Her fiery locks are covered by the hood of a modest cloak, but I can tell by the curve of her lip that it's her.

She pulls her hood down and several men turn their attention to her. Her eyes scan the tavern and when she spots me, she grins and walks over to my table. The scent of vanilla wafts in the air as she slides next to me, and she grabs my ale and takes a swig before she's even said hello.

"Daphne," I say with a laugh, "to what do I owe the pleasure?"

She holds her hand up for the barmaid to bring us two more ales. "I need to feel free. I need to have a conversation with someone who isn't worried about my father, or my money. I need to have a few drinks–"

The barmaid places two more tankards on the table and Daphne immediately grabs one and holds hers up, waiting on me to pick up mine. So I do. She clicks our cups together, sloshing the ale on the table and laughs before shouting cheers and guzzling her drink. Daphne and I drink and talk, and the more we drink and talk, the more I want to continue drinking and talking. She's amazing; intelligent, funny, adventurous.

The evening turns into night, and the tavern is emptying. Besides a table of men playing cards, a suspicious looking man with wiry red hair in the corner eating stew, and a pair of prostitutes having a drink before their nightly shift starts, we are the only ones still here.

"I think I might like you, Lieve Oleander."

I feel a smile tug at the corner of my lip. Daphne doesn't look at me, instead she sighs and runs her finger along the rim of her empty tankard. Her cheeks are flushed. I like her too. I like her so much it feels like my heart is going to burst straight out of my chest.

"I think I might like you too, Daphne Cortwright."

Daphne laughs, her voice a melody in my ears and I have to do something. I have to keep this moment going. I take her hand in mine and she looks at me, her emerald eyes gazing into the very depths of my soul. My head swims with her vanilla and all the ale I consumed and I don't even think, I just close my eyes and lean into her. I feel the heat of her breath and then her lips barely brushing mine, but she doesn't kiss me. She stops.

I open my eyes and Daphne is white as a sheet. She stands from our table, wraps her cloak around her shoulders and pulls the hood down tight.

"Did I do something wrong?"

She shakes her head. "Not at all, but I must get home now. It's late."

"Can I walk you?"

"I can manage." She takes a few steps and then turns around. "Would you like me to take care of our tab?"

I feel like I just got punched in the gut. Is that why she wouldn't let herself kiss me? Or did she mean she only liked me as a friend?

"That's kind of you, but I can pay for our drinks."

She nods and then with a flourish of her cloak, Daphne leaves the tavern.

My hatchet sticks in the tree more than fifty feet from me. I try to hide my smirk from my training partner, Hal, but it's hard. He was throwing accurately at forty feet, but since we retreated another ten, he's made mistakes.

Hal's hatchet clatters on the ground underneath the target. His face turns red and he looks at me with his eyebrows raised so high they almost disappear in his hairline.

"These damned blades!" he shouts.

"Are you sure it's the blade?"

"Shut it, Lieve," he sneers. "These weapons are shit."

I stifle my laugh and launch another hatchet. It lands squarely in the target, barely an inch from my first hatchet. This sends Hal over the edge, and he marches to the weapons in the tree and yanks them with such force that the handle snaps and he falls over.

"See," I say, "the weapons are fine."

A hand thumps my shoulder and I turn to see Calix.

"The weapons *are* shit–," he laughs at Hal with me–, "but I guess Lieve and I are just *that* good."

Hal throws us an obscene gesture and walks over to us. "Benito Matisse can kiss my ass," he spits on the ground. "I hit that target every time until we got these shitty blades."

~

I wrote Daphne to let her know that leave is coming again soon, and that I would like to see her again. She doesn't write back. I write another letter asking if there have been any signs of Vera. She responds with one word, *No*. The following week, Calix and I are granted a long leave, and I head straight to Shadow Grove to look for Vera myself.

After a day of searching for Vera alone, I return to my shack. Vines and weeds hide the structure from prying eyes. The door is hard to open, but I force myself in. It takes a moment for my eyes to adjust to the dark so I light a lamp and hang it on a hook. The flames softly brighten the tiny space and I realize the longer Calix and I use this tiny, one roomed hideout, the more it looks like Daphne's mad apothecary.

I pick up her notes, scribbled in a hurry on spare bits of parchment covering my desk. Her handwriting is terrible, but I can make out every word even when Cal or Narah can't. Her notes are like pieces of her and her thoughts. Every time I get one, I smile knowing Daphne still thought of me. Her notes don't say that, they aren't even notes really...they're just scribbles. Codes, ciphers, spells. It takes Calix and I days to figure them out most of the time.

I get a surge of excitement when Narah brings a note to me. Excitement that Daphne might want to talk, or to see me. I want to see her, talk to her, learn from her, but she ignores my pleas. Every note sends me spiraling.

I know she's trying to distance herself, and I don't want her to stop looking for answers to find Vera, but I almost wish she'd give up. I thought we would talk more after our date, *or whatever you call it*, but I was wrong. She just ignores me when it doesn't concern Vera. It's breaking me and I don't know why.

I flip through the pages of a book on mending watches. I try and fail over and over to fix the broken pocket watch, and all my failure does it drown me in my thoughts. I know this watch is the link to Vera. I can feel it in my bones, and everytime I fail, I feel like I'm failing Vera over and over again.

I need a drink. My hands pull at my hair as I pace in a tiny circular motion around the cramped room. While I've been on leave, I've swiped bottles left and right to drown my thoughts. I hate feeling alone and I hate only having my memories as company.

My toes hit the panel of wood that doesn't lay flat, and I land on my face. I look down at the uneven boards and remember I hid a bottle of Tussian liquor under there for the darker days. I shake my head, *don't drink it.* The bottle underneath mocks me. I just lay there, staring at the floor, imagining the bottle under the floorboards.

"No!" I scream at it.

The door rattles, and Calix walks in.

The smile on his face fades once he sees me. "Hey." He then closes the door and places his sword against the wall.

"I'm fine," I reply.

"What's going on?" His voice is casual, but I know he's trying to gauge where to steer the conversation.

"Nothing," I insist, "I'm fine."

"Narah said yes," Calix says softly. "She *actually* said yes to my proposal."

"Calix, that's wonderful. Of course she said yes." I press my hands on the ground and push myself up. "I don't want you to be afraid to tell me when you're happy."

Calix brushes the hair from his eyes. "I know, I just–," he looks at me–, "I know you aren't, and I don't want to rub things in your face."

"You aren't, and this is amazing news." I force myself to smile, "I'll always be here for you and I'm happy for you, Cal."

He grins at me. "Til the end?"

"Til the end."

Even though it *is* amazing news, and even though I'm thrilled that someone gets a bit of happiness in this world of endless doom and war, I can't say I'm not jealous. I need to drink *right now*. I miss Vera. I miss Daphne. I hate feeling like I'm being left behind.

Calix squeezes my shoulder. "Thanks for being here for me. The Kingdom is a different place than before. I'm hoping this wedding can bring some kind of normalcy back to the court." He winks at me and lightly jabs my rib with his elbow. "It doesn't hurt that my lady is beautiful either."

"She is genuinely flawless," I say, "unlike her soon to be!"

We both laugh.

I'm jealous of him. That is what life should feel like. There should be joy. There should be laughter and love and friendship. Life should be full of these small moments. Can a person have a life when they don't have happiness? I'm not sure I'll ever have happiness again.

I don't tell Calix that I've been dreaming of Daphne. Her face, her hair. Daphne will forever be just a dream, and I need to quit thinking we could ever be something. She'll never lower her station and I wouldn't want her to. I know what it's like to be poor, to suffer. She doesn't need a life like that, a life like mine.

Her dedication to helping me find Vera is unfair to her too, I know I guilted her into this mission. I need to start thinking realistically and face the probability that Vera could be lost forever, and no one can change that.

~

Months go by and The Hode is sent to do small missions. They fill every second of our day training, searching, hunting, and killing Doppelgangers. Hal was right, the blades from Benito Matisse are awful. Eventually, each of them snapped, and at the worst times. Several of the soldiers in the Hode died or almost died in hand-to-hand combat because of the faulty weapons.

Out of his own wages, the Knight Ramsey gifts the Hode new daggers. Each is onyx and sleek. The blades are so black they look like liquid, with our names engraved in gold along the hilt. Calix, Hal, and I practice with them constantly. The whole battalion is pleased with the new weapons, and we all hit our targets with more ferocity and accuracy.

My sharp aim and instincts quickly allow me to rise in rank, Calix along with me. Wine quiets my mind. I sneak exotic wines from all over the realm every night to help me sleep, and I'm still outdoing the other soldiers in my battalion. I become highly skilled in a short amount of time, even becoming instructors to new recruits alongside Calix. We're the youngest Hode trainers in over a century.

On every leave, I search for Vera. I carve markings for Vera all over the Kingdom while I ask people if they've seen her, but of course, no one has. Every face that shows me pity makes me want to swipe hard liquor. Every voice that says they cannot help me makes me want to drown in a barrel of wine.

To quiet the pain, along with drinking, I follow Daphne around. I "accidentally" bumped into her at the market, and she apologized for ignoring me all this time. She teaches me about the gifted, and the magic that lies in Prinav. Daphne is a patient teacher. She helps me learn the lore, learn to say her spells and use her type of power to do small feats, and when I make a mistake she corrects me without shaming me.

One day, alone in the cabin, I decode a piece of cipher using that same ink spell Daphne taught me. I am able to manipulate the letters on the parchment using Daphne's technique. I discover that I could move the letters in any formation I wanted them to go. Paralyzed with amazement, I watch the ink jump off the page and stand up like a person, dancing around before splashing back down into the parchment and morphing into new letters.

That isn't even the most bizarre thing. As I'm reading, words flock together like birds, spelling out something truly amazing. The Lopter tree *was* the god Lopter. The Fae used a crystal sword, a *godslayer* on the tree. I've been entering Prinav through a god for years, and now he's gone. *Dead.* Does this mean that Vera really could be gone forever? Daphne believes Vera isn't dead, but if she's alive…*then where is she?*

If I was waiting for the right time to drink the whole bottle hidden under the floorboard, this is it. I pull up the plank of wood and grab the liquor. The amber liquid inside sloshes against the side of the bottle, demanding me to drink it. The strength of the alcohol hits my face and I gag. Tussian liquor is strong.

I don't bother with a glass, I just press the bottle to my lips and let the liquor flow. The second it touches my throat, I sputter and cough. It burns all the way to my chest and I feel warmth spread over my body, getting hotter and hotter until I'm flushed and sweating. I take another burning sip, my throat searing in pain from the raw alcohol. The room begins to spin even after just a few sips, and I sit down on the floor, my fingers clutching to the bottle like it's my life.

I drink until the sun goes down. *I should tell Daphne about Lopter.* When I open the door to the cabin, insects buzz around the air. I see flaming moths flicker above the grass and my vision goes in and out of focus as I watch the lights. The color of the red flames on the end of their tails remind me of the color of Daphne's hair. *Daphne.*

I stumble through the city and end up at her door. It's late. The lamps on her doorstep are already lit. I knock, hoping that she's home, hoping she isn't. Marguerite scoffs as she opens the door, but right behind her is Daphne. She dismisses Marguerite and then stares at me with eyes full of pity. Daphne motions for me to step inside but I can't move.

"Lieve, what on earth?" Daphne asks.

My body shakes and Daphne walks onto the steps and touches my shoulder. Her soft hands send a tingle of magic through me, sending compassion through her veins to mine. Her touch forms me and breaks me, like dying and living at the same time, and I let out a choked sound. She pulls me close to her and wraps her arms around my shoulders. The scent of vanilla engulfs me and I bury my face into her neck. I wrap my arms around her waist and shudder, releasing the tears I've held back for months.

"I know," she coos, "I know."

"I miss her."

I hate the Fae. I hate them for chopping down the tree, whether it was right or not. They stole any chance I'll have to see Vera again. I cling to Daphne, sobbing on her front step while my thoughts race from desperation to anger and back again.

Daphne ushers me inside, quietly leading me down the hall. I stop at her secret apothecary, but she pulls my hand past the door. We take a set of stairs up, and she opens another door to a bedroom. It's small, but not without its luxuries. Vanilla perfume fills the air, and dozens of sweet smelling bottles lay open on the vanity. The canopy bed is made of white silk, and so are the curtains on the windows.

"I forget why I'm here," I say to her.

She waves her hand. "It's quite alright." I watch her every move as she sits on the bed and pats the mattress, "I'm sorry all of this happened."

I sit beside her. "I feel lost without Vera."

Daphne brushes my hair out of my eyes, running her thumb along my cheek. Her touch is warm and comforting. I don't know if it's because of the liquor I guzzled all evening, or of Daphne's beauty, or her kindness, but I feel I might love her.

"Do you still think we can find her?" I plead, begging her to say yes.

A single tear runs down her cheek and a sad smile forms on her face. "I don't know."

"I have to find her." I whisper.

She wipes her eyes. "I'll never stop looking. I'll always, always help you."

Recklessness consumes me and I grab the back of her head, pulling her close to me. Our lips crash into each other, our tongues tasting our shared desperation. Daphne's nails scrape my chest, and she grips my shirt to keep me close. I want more of her. I have no control over my hands as they cover every inch of Daphne's perfect body. I can feel the sweat beneath her clothing, and I want to touch her. I want to be closer. I just–I just *want* her.

Her breath catches and the sound drives me *wild*. I run my hand up her leg, hiking her night dress above her knees. She kisses me deeply, so I keep going. My hand glides up her thigh, but then she grabs my wrist, stopping me from going further.

She breaks away suddenly, clutching her chest, "I can't."

"I went too fast, I'm sorry–" I pant.

Daphne lays her head in her hands. "It's not that."

"Then what is it?"

She looks up at me, eyes brimming with tears, and I know what she's thinking. Rich Daphne, beautiful Daphne, who stopped responding to my letters. Who only speaks to me after I manufactured a meeting at the marketplace. Who attends balls and parties and feasts.

I scoff at her. "It's because I'm a nobody."

I turn from her and leave the room, closing the door behind me. She doesn't follow me down the hall, or out the front door. She doesn't follow me into the empty streets. I don't know why I expected her to, it's not like we can be together. She's part of the court, the nobility, and I'm *nothing*.

I vow that my creatures destroy you, long after I am
dead.

– *Oriel*

CHAPTER 9
VERA

The sun shines through the dense tree canopy and I have to pinch
myself to know I'm not dreaming. *I'm in Prinav.* I think about
Lieve. What would his advice be right now? *You're traipsing around
Shadow Grove with a male stranger?* A sickening thought enters my mind.
This man might be lying, and I might be a fool. Lieve might be dead.
I've only believed Lieve might be dead one other time when we were
kids, and I have the same horrible feeling.

Before I turn into a pool of tears, I head off the path and go into the
woods under the guise that I needed to relieve myself again. I panic.
I'm so dumb. How could I just go off with a strange man? I slide my body
down into a ditch so I'm hidden from view. I sit on a rock at the bottom,
and being alone creates a sense of dread. What if this is all a hoax. Lieve
would be so disappointed if he could see me. *He knows him though.* I may
have trusted Arden far too quickly, but he's been kind to me. If this is a
trick, it's an elaborate one.

I'll keep riding with him, and if we don't hit Barault soon, I'll leave.
Everything is fine. Arden knows Lieve, and he's taking me to him. I dig
my fingers into the rich soil on the side of the ditch and pull myself to
the top. Climbing up, my foot breaks through a root and I slide back

down, covering myself in dirt. My hand feels something just under the earth where I land. It doesn't feel like a rock, it feels metallic. I clear the dirt from the smooth surface underneath and find–*the pocket watch.*

Lieve was here. I use my skirt to wipe off the dirt that caked on the gemstones encrusted on the gold case. It's just as beautiful as I remember it. I can feel a magnetic kind of pull inside the watch, begging me to open it. The clasp is wedged shut by years of dirt and tarnish. *It looks like I really have been gone for years, so maybe Arden wasn't lying.* I pick at the clasp with my nails but It's no use. It's stuck.

I stuff the pocket watch and its long delicate chain deep into my undergarments. The metal is cold on my skin. This watch is worth a small fortune, and it could help me find Lieve if I sell it to the right buyer. When I do find him, it could give us a fresh start. It's a relief to have found it, knowing Lieve was really here. The weight of it, the opportunity it suggests, calms me; and I'm not going to tell Arden what I've found just yet.

Arden slowly walks near the trench with the horse. "Princess, are you alright?"

I grab a root while placing my foot on a rock jutting out of the wall of dirt and fall backwards. Arden laughs and jumps with the horse across the trench, it's pearlescent coat gleaming in the sunlight like a painting. Arden dismounts once they land and slides down the side of the trench with feline grace. I stand up and brush the dirt from my clothes while Arden tells the horse to stay still. He then walks up behind me and places his strong hands around my waist to hoist me up, the heat from his palms melting my core.

The root snaps, flinging me backward into Arden's body. "I'm sorry."

Arden rolls me off of him and sits up. I'm on my hands and knees now, our faces merely inches apart. Our eyes meet and I can see a fire blazing in his gaze. With my heart drumming in my chest, I lean in but Arden doesn't. He scoots away and stands up quickly. I follow suit and attempt to climb up the trench silently, and without his help. He climbs up and puts his hand out to me when I reach the top to stop me from making noise.

"Vera," Arden says my name slowly, "do not turn around. Only look ahead. Prepare to mount and ride as fast as you've ever ridden in your life."

"What's going on?"

"Please." Arden states blankly and helps me mount silently and joins me on the horse. But this time he sits in front so we can ride faster. "It hasn't noticed us yet, but will any minute now, so hold on tight."

I wrap my arms around him as tight as I can and dig my fingers into his cloak.

He jerks the reins. "Keep looking forward, or close your eyes."

"Why can't I look?" I whisper, my body tense as I cling to his back.

"Darkthings are here and will take everything they can from you, including your sanity with just one glance." He jerks the reins again. "Please Vera, trust me. Just look ahead."

With that, he spurs the horse, tearing through the forest at a speed I never imagined was possible. I keep my eyes focused ahead, but I may as well have them closed. The horse runs so fast they make the trees just a blur of brown and green.

A blood curdling shriek punctures the silence from behind us. *Who's screaming?* I cling to Arden tighter and press my face into his back.

There's a second shriek, and this time I make out the word "VERA!" The voice is Lieve.

"LIEVE! LIEVE!" I scream.

"It isn't him," Arden scolds. "Keep looking forward!"

"VERA! HELP!" The voice shrieks yet again.

I start beating Arden's back with my fist, pulling on his arms to halt the horse. I am in a frenzy of fear and he just keeps the horse running. "Lieve is in danger! He needs help!"

"It isn't him!"

I have to look.

It *is* Lieve. He's bloody and disfigured and a large doglike beast is dragging him through the forest. With my brother's arm clenched in its jaws, it yanks him, chasing us. I thrash and strike Arden's back over and over as Lieve screams in pain. He doesn't stop. *Why won't he stop!*

"I can see him!" I cry, and then I lose my grip.

With nothing to hold onto, I fall off the back of the horse. My body crashes into the ground, rolling off of the path. Stars burst behind my eyes. I'm flung about in a painful position on the ground, the wind knocked out of my chest. I suck in air, but the breaths are shallow and my ribs scream at me with each inhalation. Every bone and muscle feels like it's being torn from my body.

The wolf creature is still dragging Lieve's mangled limbs, but Lieve isn't screaming anymore. I have no plan, but I force myself to stand anyway. Every ounce of energy left in me pushes me to sneak closer, even though I know it's stupid. I have to help Lieve. He saved me in Adamston, and now I have to save him.

My boots snap a twig under my foot, and a bush tugs on my skirts. It's as if the forest is begging me not to move, but I don't listen. The closer I get to it, I can see more damage to Lieve's body. He looks like a broken marionette covered in blood and soil. He isn't moving.

He's dead.

My legs feel like lead and my hands shake. I can feel a liquid thickness rising from my stomach, reaching my throat. *No. No. No.* I push the nausea away and take another step towards Lieve's body. I have to get to him. I can't leave him like this. Getting closer to the path now, I can sense that something isn't right. Lieve's face looks like wax, like wax that's *melting.*

What?

The beast sniffs the air and I hold my breath and freeze. The creature drops my lifeless brother and prowls in my direction. It sniffs again and then I see its pupils dilate. *It found me.* It lunges at me, just like the rabid dog from my childhood. It leaps high in the air, teeth bared. I'm not fast enough to escape it, not strong enough to fight it, so I cover my face and brace myself for the impact. An impact that doesn't come.

Hands grab me roughly and I'm moving again, swept off my feet and back on Arden's horse. I dare to look back again and watch the beast tear Lieve's body limb from limb.

"It's not your brother." Arden says.

"It could have been!"

"You're a fool," he snaps. "This isn't a joke, Princess. Shadow Grove isn't some little story that Lieve made up to entertain you. This place is real. It's dangerous."

"I know it's real, I can see it with my own two eyes that it's real."

"Then start listening to me with your ears. You could have died *for real*."

"You're an ass."

"An ass that's already saved yours twice."

Arden keeps pushing the horse to go faster, and all I want is to get away from him. I don't want to be on this horse anymore. I just want Lieve. After we get out of range he slows down and I brace myself for another scolding. Arden doesn't turn to look at me, but he steadies himself and I hold my breath.

Arden's voice is softer this time when he says, "Believe me when I tell you, I know how real the Dakthings feel, but it isn't. It wasn't. It wasn't him."

When it's safe, we stop and get our bearings again. Lieve's mangled body flashes in my mind, and I throw up in the middle of the path when I think about it for too long. The Darkthings are worse than Lieve's stories let on. Just another way he protected me. A way he's endangered me with his protection.

I pull my cloak around me and wipe my mouth with the hem. "Lieve used to try to scare me with stories of the Darkthings, but he never said anything about *that*. Not really."

Arden nods. "I'm sure he tried."

What if it really was Lieve? Did I just lose my brother? If it was just an illusion, why do I feel like this? How do I know what to believe? Arden could be anyone, he might not even know Lieve. The stories he's told me could all be made up. A cold wave of fear washes over me at the thought. *Can I truly trust him?*

Arden reaches out to touch my shoulder but the fear creeps up my spine and makes me recoil from his touch. "I'm sorry."

I shake my head, "I don't–"

"You don't know what to believe or if you should trust me, right?"

I nod.

"My signal to you, for you to know Lieve is safe and that I'm safe is this: Lieve hates dogs."

Lieve *does* hate dogs. Lieve is one to hold grudges, and he will always hold a grudge against any doglike beast for the rest of his life. Arden knows Lieve, and I know this, because Arden knows: Lieve *hates* dogs.

Doppelgangers have taken over the stronghold in Cerelean. Troops have been dispatched. Not enough numbers. Please send help.

– Military correspondence from General Neehar of the Madorian Army to Lord Gelhert Esven, Grand Visor of King Niall Brone.

CHAPTER 10

LIEVE

I next see Daphne at Calix and Narah's wedding. They placed us next to each other to watch the vows and I could barely focus on the ceremony. Daphne doesn't say a word to me, but she glances at me through the entire thing and fidgets in her seat. Why would Calix do that to me? I told him what happened at the tavern, and I briefly mentioned going to her townhouse. After Daphne's rejection, I am so nervous to see her again that I drink during dinner and hide behind Gwen Abbey to gather my thoughts. Only, I'm not alone. Daphne has escaped the party too and is leaning against the stone wall, lost in the stars.

I watch her for a while, trying to decide if I should leave. I'm again overpowered by her beauty, her face unclouded as she studies the heavens, her hair elegantly woven into a crown. Can I risk speaking to her when I'm already too distracted by our last encounter? But fate chooses for me; for as I turn, the glass bottle in my hand shatters against the stone wall of the Abbey. I am discovered.

"Lieve." She says startled, but looking happy to see me. "I'm sorry about–"

"Stop," I whisper, though I'm not sure if I'm talking to her or myself. "I don't want to talk about it."

"Well I do," she says softly, but with all the firmness that I've come to desire in her. "I was a fool for not chasing after you."

My heart pounds. *Does she mean that?*

Daphne walks up to me and places her hand on my arm. My body stiffens. I want to turn to her and hold her, but I don't want to get hurt again. I can't allow myself back into that situation.

"That night," she whispers as she runs her delicate fingers up my arm and gives it a gentle squeeze. "It was all so fast."

"It's been weeks, Daphne, I'm over it." The lie tastes sour on my tongue. I'm not over it. I'll never be over it. My heart aches to grab her and kiss her.

"Oh," she says softly and drops her hand from my arm. "That's–," her voice cracks–, "good. Thank you for telling me."

But I can't bear to let her walk away from me. "If I let you walk away, it would be my turn to be the fool."

Daphne then jumps in my arms at once. I pick her up and push us against the stone wall of the Abbey. My hands search her every curve, searing her into my memory. In the hot summer night, her dress clings to her body, and when she wraps her legs around my waist, the fabric tears.

We explore every inch of each other, sweaty and drunk with drink and passion. Neither of us returned to the wedding party that night. We shelter within Gwen Abbey, taking the time with one another that life hasn't afforded us before. As she finally falls asleep in my arms, our bodies cast in the cool blue light of the stained glass windows, I realize I'm glad Calix got married. I'm glad he sat us next to each other. This is the best night of my life.

~⌣~

Memories of that night with Daphne are all that gets me through the coming months. The Hode is sent on several missions to eliminate Dops from cities far from Barault. They destroyed the port town of Hamat, but our efforts were able to return the town back to the inhabitants. An elderly woman housed us in her ransacked inn overlooking the sea, and I wrote Daphne letters describing what the water looked like. She told me she'd never seen waves crashing against rock, or a sunset casting an orange glow across the endless water, so I described it in detail.

From there we were stationed in the mountains near the Tussian border. Fighting the Doppelgangers in the snow was nearly impossible, and it seemed like they were used to the cold. It was as if they spent their lives freezing and could move, *kill*, easier in the rocky terrain. The weeks we had to endure the frigid temperatures were some of the hardest of my life. We lost several men, not to wounds or infection, but to relentless cold.

I wish we knew what the Dops wanted, but their motives continue to remain a mystery. Ramsey captured one on a stop heading back to Barault from the mountains and tortured him. He did unspeakable things, and got nothing in return. The Dop refused to dispel any information, and Ramsey became increasingly more brutal the longer the war continued.

An outburst from Ramsey while at a tavern near Teyrnas caused King Niall to force him to retire. Calix and I weren't at the tavern that evening, but we read in the papers, and heard the gossip from soldiers who were with him. If true, what he did warranted an end to his position. The incident caused major waves in the Hode, and Calix and I were sent documentation that we had risen in rank and to return to Barault.

~⌣~

Daphne and I had four wonderful days together before I was put in charge of my own squad. I haven't been able to leave the Hode compound for over a month and I miss her. We've been writing back and forth whenever we can, and she's hinted that her father is pressuring her to find a husband. I want to write and tell her that I would be the happiest man alive with her as a bride, but I want to ask her in person. That question deserves to be asked when the woman can see the love in your eyes, and I want to hear her voice say *yes*. We both deserve that.

I sit under a tree thinking of Daphne and fiddle with the pocket watch I continue to carry around, hoping that someday, somehow, it may help me find Vera. I've reattached the fastener, and I've secured the gems to the metal, but even that doesn't work. It doesn't glow like it did before. The cranks inside have stopped turning, and no matter what tools I have, none of them can make them spin. It's infuriating.

Sun gleams up and down the metal of an elongated blade as Calix swings it from left to right in a figure eight motion, and my attention diverts from the watch. He wears heavy armor today, and the sheer weight of it shows on Cal's sweaty face. He grimaces with every swing. Drops of sweat spray the air while he retraces his steps and continues looping the weighty sword around and around.

"Give it a try, Hal," Calix pants and hands the massive sword to him.

Hal grips the hilt with both hands and tries repeating Calix's motions, but his movements are stiff and pained. He isn't as graceful as Calix, there's no denying that, but he's trying.

"Open up your stance," Calix demonstrates, "there, that's it," then he claps when Hal does the figure eight, "bravo!"

Calix then flops on the grass next to me, his armor clanging as he hits the ground. Hal continues to practice and I lie down on my back beside Calix and stare at the clouds drifting through the tree branches. This summer has been unbearably hot and the cool grass feels good against my sweat soaked back.

A messenger appears before us and hands me a document. Hal stops swinging the sword to listen to me read it out loud. It says we're to leave immediately. I ask the messenger for a piece of parchment and give him a few coins to deliver a letter to Daphne so she knows where I'm being sent to, and that I'll write to her as soon as I can.

Calix and I gather our men and make our way through Shadow Grove and to Madoria's city of Cerelean. Lord Esven's letter states that the Dop stronghold has crumbled, but they left destruction in their wake, and Madoria's staggered forces need backup.

The air reeks of ash and blood, the smell of burning flesh hits us as Dop and human bodies are scattered along the streets. I spot Prinav military uniforms and order a couple men to check the bodies while Calix and I look around. There were none left alive.

I sigh. *What could all of this be for?* The men scatter around, peeking through broken windows while the others are checking bodies for survivors. I look at our surroundings and my blood runs cold even in the sweltering summer heat. The bodies are in the town square, and we're easy targets. We need to move. *Now.*

I scan the buildings, all made of stone. Solid. My soldiers are solid too. Each one of them has trained night and day, and most of them have eliminated Doppelgangers in battle. I feel like a conductor of a raging orchestra when we fight. Each man has their job, to *kill*, and they do it without hesitation.

Sometimes at night, I can hear a few of them cry, or have nightmares and it makes me drink again. We've lost men on my watch. The guilt almost consumed me to the point that I ran away the first time and drank until I passed out in the middle of Barault. An old man thought I was just some idiot on leave and called in the Knights to bring me back to the Hode. I'm lucky I wasn't executed for abandonment.

The feeling of being watched is strong enough to make my hair stand. I look around the streets for eyes, especially ones that flash black, but I see nothing. The buildings are close together, connected by shared walls and the streets are cobblestone, making it easier to hear anyone coming. But they'll hear us coming too.

It's eerie seeing the streets empty, and I imagine dozens of people walking around. The bakery's line going out the door, a man who owns the produce stand laughing loudly with his customers, and the butcher passing out samples. Life. There isn't any life visiting here today. Today horror visited Madoria. Today death visited.

I tap Hal on the shoulder. When his father died, his mother sent him to the Hode because she couldn't afford to keep him. He's acclimated to a soldier's life, but he's not a soldier. He's a scared kid. I brought him along today because I began to notice he was getting bullied by officers of higher rank than me. This was my only way of getting him out from under their thumb.

"We need to get out of the street," I whisper to him, "quick and quiet as we can."

He nods and his straw colored hair falls in his eyes. We start moving to the left side of the street and the rest of the group follows like a flock of birds. *Good.* I peer over the gathered soldiers to Calix, who nods.

We split our group and take two buildings next to each other. Hal kicks in the door and I'm the first to step inside. The room is pitch black. I strain my ears and wait to walk in any further until my eyes adjust to the dark. My men follow me in, our breath quickening together in the tense silence. I have a feeling this building isn't empty.

One of my men flicks a match to look around the dark space and we see dozens of black eyes staring back at us. *Doppelgangers.* For the smallest second, we all freeze. I blink, and then manage to shout orders.

"Attack!" I bellow as loud as I can.

Bows. Swords. Axes. Blood.

The match has dropped to the ground, and in the darkness of the room, arrows fly. I can feel my dagger plunge into flesh, and I pray to the gods it's not one of my men. I stab and stab until my arms cannot move anymore. All around me I hear grunts, gasps, and screams. Metal clangs against metal. Noises like animals clawing, desperate to live, echo around me. Weapons scraping against the stone walls ring. Then, almost as soon as it started, it ends. Quiet. I don't hear the sounds of pain or anger, I don't even hear breathing.

"Alright men," I say, "let's check on the others."

No one replies. My body goes numb. My chest tightens, threatening to squeeze all the air from my lungs. I walk to the wall, my hands slick with blood, and feel around for a lamp or candle. A lamp hangs on a large hook and my fingers fumble in the dark to light it as light floods the room. When I turn from the lamp, my heart stops. No one is moving. All of them lay on the ground, their limbs positioned in grotesque angles.

Bram help me. Blood touches the toe of my boot and I don't even move my foot. I just watch it gather around me, spilling in each and every crack in the stone floor. It's thick. I wonder if it will ever stop flowing. If it doesn't, I hope it drowns me. A soldier lays on the ground in front of me. He's covered in so much blood I can't read his name tag, but I know him. *Hal.*

It's Hal's blood that touches my shoes. I watch as it flows from his body while I'm frozen in place. *I am not fit to do this.* I imagine going to Shadow Grove and letting the Darkthings come for me. I should swipe as many bottles as I can carry, and drink myself into oblivion while they rip my body apart. No. Oblivion is too good for me, it's a mercy my men weren't granted.

"Gods help us," I hear someone breathe from the doorway.

I spin around, dagger drawn, and my boot slides in the mess. It makes me want to vomit. The silhouette of the man framed in the doorway raises its hands in the air.

"Lieve, it's me. It's Calix."

I drop to the ground and weep. "Cal–" I reach towards him with a shaking hand. "Cal–"

"I'm here–," He says, gripping my hand–, "Til the end, remember?"

Til the end. Calix is alive. He's alive. I'm alive. I rock back and forth on the wet floor, and with the warmth of the blood beneath me I cry, "I can't do this."

I can't look at him as he looks around at the massacre and drops to the ground with me. Calix is alive. *Calix is alive.* I cling to him tight enough to turn my knuckles white. Calix holds me and rocks me as the puddle of crimson underneath us grows larger by the minute. I wish I had died with them. I wish the puddle we're wallowing in was filled with *my* blood.

Why was I spared? Why do I get to keep breathing? Why didn't Hal, or any of the others get that chance. I don't understand what happened. I want to go home. I want Daphne. I open my eyes and see Hal's pale face and I get sick all over myself. Cal doesn't push me from him, he just rocks and holds me. *Why is blood so red?* My throat tightens. I can't breathe. I can't breathe.

Calix takes my face in his hands, "Lieve. Brother. I am here." He shakes me. "Come back to me."

I nod and we rock together and try not to look at the faces of our friends on the ground around us. Something moves outside. I look up and see that Calix isn't alone, his group of men are just outside the doorway. *Thank the gods they're alive.*

"The building next door was empty, and we heard the fighting and ran over as fast as we could–" Calix says–, "but we were too late."

An arrow whistles through the air and all of a sudden one of our men standing in the doorway drops to the ground. The rest of them scramble inside, bows and swords drawn. We need to leave, but I don't think I can move. Any minute now more Doppelgangers could show up.

"Lieve, we need to go now."

I clear my throat. "Yes. Let's –let's go."

It feels like someone else is talking, like I'm watching myself stand and go to the doorway. I focus on getting Calix out of here, but everything he says back to me seems muffled and far away. It's as if my body is a puppet, but there's no puppeteer.

We slip out the door and return to the streets. I look up and my heart sinks. Dops are covering the balconies and rooftops of all the buildings around us. I knew we were being watched. Their smiles don't reach their eyes, *their black eyes*, as they draw their bows and aim.

"Should we split up?" Calix asks.

"No." I say with authority. "Til the end, you and me."

"What should we do?"

An arrow flies right past Cal, merely inches from his face. We run. We've pledged ourselves to the end, and I follow him knowing that this could be it. We weave in between a rain of arrows around us, one after the other. Left, right, left, right, left, right. Several men drop and I want to stop to help them, but the Doppelgangers seem to have an endless supply of amo. My heart hammers in my chest as I follow Calix through the empty streets. The thud of our boots on the cobblestone sounds like hoofbeats, and I wish we had a horse right now.

Once we get out of range, the arrows stop flying and we can see the edge of the massive forest of Shadow Grove. I wonder if we could lure the Doppelgangers into the forest and let the Darkthings get them. I wonder if the Darkthings will get *us*. A part of me hopes they'll take me.

We sprint to the edge of the forest, as dangerous as the carnage we leave behind. The Darkthings own the night and everything the night touches, and it will be night time all too soon.

"We should get to the trenches near the creek," Calix whispers to me. "There might be tools left there from other soldiers."

It's a decent plan. "Alright."

There's only four of us left. Me, Calix, and two low ranking soldiers, newly recruited to our squadron. We walk in silence, diligently keeping watch for danger. Finally arriving at the piece of trench on Prinavian land, we slide down into its depths. It's nearly night now, I can see the moon peeking through the branches above us. Calix chooses a spot for us to rest for the night, even though none of us will be doing any resting.

"I'll keep the first watch," I offer as I lean my back on the side of the trench.

Calix sighs deeply and rolls his back to me. "I want Narah."

Queen Fortuna was a noble monarch. She bartered
treaties, sustained peace, and was extremely generous.

Her reign over Prinav was nearly thirty years while
married to the Prince of Tussia. At the death of Erik the
Mad, King of Tussia, Fortuna and Prince Yuri take both
thrones and Fortuna birthed Celia. Celia marries Kish and
they have a son, but child was rumored to be illegitimate.

No one knows where the child ended up after Kish
banished the babe. The babe was never found even after
Celia and Kish's deaths, and so a descendant of one of
Celia's siblings took the throne of Prinav, King Ame.
Ame's death left Prinav monarchless. Wars were waged
over the throne. Madoria Tussia, and Teyrnas fought
massive battles, and noble families all over the Kingdom
of Prinav vied for a place in the palace. Eventually, the
Brone family won.

– *Prinavian History Through the Ages, Excerpt from Chapter
26*

CHAPTER 11

VERA

I notice Arden doesn't have to lead the horse to the correct path to
Barault, it has memorized the trails itself. The trails are wider and
less muddy, and the trees grow further apart on this end of the forest,
allowing sunlight to spill onto the trail and brighten the path. The rays

create rainbows on the back of the horse and I wiggle my fingers and watch the light swim over me like magic. For all the trouble with the Darkthings, at least some parts of Prinav are the fairy tale I imagined it would be.

"Thank you for saving me from the Darkthing."

"And the Fae," he clears his throat, "remember?"

I scoff. "Like you'll ever let me forget."

"It's my duty." He sits up straighter in the saddle.

I chuckle, but then I think, what *is* Arden's role in Prinav? "What *is* your duty here?"

"I make things happen for the King."

"What do you mean?"

Arden's voice darkens, "I'm not sure you'll like that answer."

He's right. I *don't* want to know. The rest of the time in the forest is met with unbearable silence. It's so quiet I can hear the breath of the horses and the rhythm of their steps is driving me mad.

We ride until nightfall, using the constellation of Bram as our guide north. We ride until the soft gleam of civilization peeks through the trees, showering the edge of the forest in an array of color. The lights from the city act as a lighthouse, calling sailors back to shore. I'm so happy to be out of this forest. I'm one step closer to Lieve, and one step closer to getting answers.

Stepping out of the treeline, I get my first glimpse of Barault.

Holy mother of the gods.

It's magnificent. There are stone buildings with twinkling lights, and a warm golden glow emits from their windows. My eyes can't stay in one place, they dart around, barely taking in all the details. The city looks as if it's tiered. Ancient structures climb up the hills while small moss covered homes dot the mountain side. Large buildings with stained glass windows, lights flickering inside, let me peek at the legendary tales etched in the glass and cobblestone streets lead to shop windows with flower boxes and ivy climbing the walls. It's so beautiful I want to cry.

I smell lake water, and when we wrap around a group of rather large buildings, I see the lake. There are boats tied to the docks, each with flags on them. A few say *Matisse* and bear the sigil of a snake wrapped around a pomegranate, and many of the others a gray fox with its twin tails wrapped around a beautiful flower. They must be family seals of wealthy nobles.

"We'll stay at The Serpent's Tongue tonight."

"What's that?"

"It's a tavern, but there's always a few vacant rooms in the inn above it."

"Why can't we just stay at Lieve's house?"

Arden leans back and pretends to sniff me, "I would want to bathe before seeing him if it were me."

"You don't smell like a bed of roses yourself."

Arden shakes his head. "Where Lieve stays is another day's ride."

We walk by a row of shops that seem to be open later than the rest of the city. The front doors are open and oil lamps are flickering, flooding the street so you can see inside the shops. A withered old woman drapes mirrors with thick velvet fabric, and when we pass another shop, I see them draping vanities, and the third shop even drapes handkerchiefs over hand mirrors hanging in the front window.

I squint hard, straining my eyes to see more of what they're doing, but the horse presses on too fast for me to really gauge what the shopkeepers are up to. Then, when we pass by a tailor, I see that the full length mirror inside is also draped.

"Why are all the mirrors draped in linens?"

Arden replies, "it's an old superstition that gained popularity again over the last ten years or so. Your Dop can find you if you stare into your own eyes for too long. Their eyes turn as black as their soul and they'll trick you into trading places with him."

The men with the black eyes. I cling harder to Arden, remembering the madman from the shop, and the man who grabbed me in the alleyway. The shopkeepers and barbacks who are locking up for the night mill around, watching us as we pass and listening to our conversation. I can feel their eyes watching us and scrutinizing our every move. I see them peek behind their doors, desperate for gossip and scandal, or worse.

"So, the men who chased me in Adamston, those were—"

"Doppelgangers." Arden finishes my sentence.

"Doppelgangers are *real?*"

"Yes," Arden says. "Every fairytale comes from a *very* real story."

My mouth hangs open in awe.

"Doppelgangers, hundreds of them, flocked to Prinav through the mirrors years ago. It was a bloody massacre, but we got through it. A young man emerged from this very wood and slaughtered them, and the rest went back in the mirrors where they came from. That young man never left, and for his efforts, Prinav named him King."

"Do I have a Doppelganger?" I ask him. "Do you?"

"We all do." Arden says darkly.

We arrive at the Serpent's Tongue just as it begins to rain. Arden hoists his pack over his shoulder and ties the horse in the small stable connected to the building. We walk inside the tavern full of people laughing and drinking and I stand right beside Arden as he passes a handful of coins in the barbacks hand. They have a conversation too low for me to hear and then Arden jerks his head in my direction.

The barback glances at me and then back to Arden. I cross my arms, trying to get smaller as the barback then scans me up and down, raising the patch covering one of his eyes. He seems to agree to whatever they decided about me and gives Arden a curt nod toward the rear of the room.

"Let's go," Arden mutters.

Our boots squeak on the stone floor, and each table we pass stops their conversations to watch us. I don't know why they're staring at us, but the attention they're giving is uncomfortable. Arden opens a door that leads to a dark set of stairs and we climb them up, following the light spilling into the stairwell leading to the foyer of an inn.

A fire roars in the main room, and trays of fruits and meats occupy the main table. Every chair has linens and pillows, and thick fur rugs cover the wide plank floorboards. A piece of art catches my eye, it's a large painting hanging over the fireplace. The painting shows a young man in light armor, leading a battle. He rides a pearl white horse and carries a massive sword. On top of his head sits a spiked, metallic crown. I study the face of the young man, he has gray eyes and jet black hair. He looks familiar. I laugh. *He looks like Lieve.*

A plump woman with bouncy blonde curls enters the room. As soon as she sees Arden she stops. "Can I help you, Lord Madrona?"

"Two rooms."

"We've only one, I'm afraid."

Arden stiffens at her words. "Fine."

She pulls out a ledger and Arden signs us out for the room. I smile at the woman and her lip twitches before handing Arden a large brass key off the hook behind the mahogany desk placed against the wall. "Number four."

Arden nods, and I follow him up another steep staircase. There are paintings hanging on the wall, and it seems to be the different monarchs of Prinav over the centuries. I recognize Queen Fortuna from one of Lieve's stories. She has a beautiful ebony complection, and snow white hair. Legend states she was a magnificent Queen.

We keep walking up the stairs and then I see the painting of the first Brone family monarch on the Prinavian throne; Rosalind Brone. She was the first true ruler since Fortuna, but quite the opposite of her. Rosalind brutally executed every other Brone relative that could potentially take the crown from her and never wed for fear her husband would have more power than her. However, she bore eleven children with her various lovers, and the eldest was also a true ruler. That blood line trickled down for centuries, and the last monarch Lieve mentioned to me was King Niall Brone. The stories, all of them, *real.*

At the top of the stairs is a narrow hallway lined with multicolored doors. Arden walks us to our door, *navy blue,* and turns the key. It smells like coal and soot. Heavy fur rugs cover the floorboards here as well, but the fire in this room is out. Arden gets the fire going as I inspect every inch of the place. An armchair sits in the corner, adorned with doilies and throw pillows, and a matching tassled footstool. Along the wall is a bookshelf full of various literature. I run my hand along the spines, until one catches my eye: *Watch Makers.*

When Arden turns his back to me for a moment, I slip the book in my cloak before placing the cloak over the arm of the chair and look out the window. The view is magnificent. Light from the full moon shines as far as the eye can see. Larger hills fill in the landscape with homes dotted across the mountainside.

In the distance is an enormous mountain, snow capped and jagged. I can make out something else twinkling under the moon. *A Castle.* I wonder if that's Brone Castle from Lieve's stories. I bet it is, even from here I can tell it's spectacular.

"I'll grab us some food from the barkeep."

"Alright."

As soon as Arden walks out the door, I grab the book and skim the pages. I pull the pocket watch from my undergarments and study it. Eventually the latch opens, revealing a multitude of faces. Each one of them looks to be embedded with magic. There are faces with gears, some with planets and constellations, and several with the hands stuck at different times. I turn the faces over, like pages in a book, until there are none left except for a mirror in the back casing.

I stare at myself and bring it up closer to see my eye. My gray iris stares back at me, and then blinks. *I didn't blink.* I snap the watch shut and toss it on the floor, where it skids to a halt just in front of the fireplace. *Did*

I just see my Doppelganger? My breathing hitches as I think about what Arden said about staring in the mirrors for too long.

A gentle tapping startles me and I scoop the watch from the floor and stuff it under a pillow with the book before cracking open the door. Arden's brow furrows, but he doesn't say anything. He just holds up a plate of meats and cheeses and two tankards in the other. I sit in the chair and try to collect myself while Arden sits on the footstool beside me.

He eats with his back to me, just as he's done for every meal and my mind races with what ailment he's trying to hide. I don't say anything about it, only because he didn't say anything about what I'm hiding, but I admit I'm curious. I sip my ale, *what else is he hiding from me?* When our bellies are full and even the noise from the tavern quiets, we decide it's time to sleep.

Arden unties his boots, and so do I. I watch him as he places his weapons near the door and secures the lock, checking and double checking. He then stares at the bed, and then at me. I've never shared a bed with anyone but Lieve, and that was when we were children.

"You go ahead," I say. "It's the least I can do, for your service."

He raises an eyebrow at me. "My service?"

"Saving me and all."

He rolls his eyes and sighs. "Listen, Princess, I don't want to sleep with you."

"I didn't say you did, and stop calling me Princess. I told you I'm not some dainty little woman."

"Just get in the bed, I'll sleep on the floor."

"I can't ask that."

"I know, that's why I offered."

My shoulders relax, but I can't let him sleep on the floor with nothing, so I grab a pillow and two of the three coverlets from the bed and hand them to him. Arden makes a bed in front of the fire and watches me as I slide under the remaining sheet on the mattress, fully clothed.

"Goodnight, *Lord Madrona*."

He chuckles, "Goodnight, *Princess*."

I fall into a restless sleep filled with images of Lieve being torn apart by the Darkthing. His face melts, over and over, and his shrieks of agony ring loud enough to shake my bones. Fog colored eyes stare at me and blink black, and then I see myself standing with my Doppelganger over a mountain of pocket watches, covered in blood. I scream–

My arms and legs thrash, tangling myself in the bedsheets. I panic before realizing where I am and tear myself from the covers. Sweat soaks the mattress and I take a deep breath. A nightmare. *It was only a nightmare.*

Arden sits up. "Vera, what's going on?"

"Nothing. A nightmare."

He groans and pushes himself to his feet.

"What are you doing?"

"Getting in bed with you," he replies and carries his pillow and covers to the bed.

"I'm fine."

"I can't have you thrashing about all night, it will keep me up" he grumbles. "Now scoot."

I make room for him and lay on my back, staring at the ceiling while Arden climbs in the bed. The mattress sinks with his weight and the realization that I'm in a bed with a man hits me and my heart thunders in my chest.

"Do you want to talk about the dream?"

No. I don't. I don't ever want to think about that again. "No."

"Okay."

Arden lays on his back too and his fingers gently brush against mine. I don't move. I don't know if he recognizes that he's touching me, and I don't want him to stop. I need the comfort that someone is here, that I'm safe and not alone.

"I hear my parents, my sister, calling for me before they die. Nearly every night."

He feels alone too. Just like me. "What happened to them?"

"They were murdered."

I turn on my side, facing him. "Arden," I breathe, "that's—"

"It was." He squeezes his eyes shut and sighs again before turning his head to me. "So I know how bad the nightmares can get."

"I'm sorry." I say and squeeze his hand.

"Let's try and get some sleep. Goodnight, *Vera*."

"Goodnight," I murmur and turn my back to him as I pull the covers up under my chin.

I feel Arden turn from me to face the door and we fall asleep with our backs pressed against each other. And though it feels strange to sleep in a bed with a man for the first time, I'm glad the man is Arden.

It is curiouser still, that I have found traces of shells, aquatic fossils, and coral in the trenches of Shadow Grove. What could this mean for the legends of the gods? Does that suggest the River of Light and Dark once flowed through Atatacia?
—Emmit Gadory, Professor's Lecture of Archeology at Lycee Hall, Ballmire Academy, Teyrnas.

CHAPTER 12

LIEVE

I know Calix isn't asleep. I wouldn't be able to sleep if he had offered to do the first watch. The battle replays over and over in my head, blood pouring from their bodies, washing the floor crimson. The metallic stench of death still hangs over me. It's on my clothes, my blade, it's absorbed into me and I will never be without them. This day will haunt me till my dying breath. The faces of my men on the ground flash one by one, taunting me. I was supposed to keep them safe. I failed them; and now, my boots are covered in my mistakes.

The forest has a second life at night. Each hoot of an owl, each growl of the large cat or step of the stag, prick my ears. Leaves rustle in the distance and I flinch. My dagger is ready to strike, the handle soft and formed to my grip. I have to will my breathing to slow down, to focus on each noise and separate each sound. My heart beats so unevenly I can feel it in my chest. Even if there were no nocturnal animals roaming

Shadow Grove, I cannot forget about the Darkthings. My jaw clenches and I grip my dagger tighter, pinching the skin beneath my nails.

The Darkthings are otherworldly. These beasts come to you at night, or when you are too close to their dens. Darkthings use magic to trick anyone who sees it so you become easier prey.

The moon shines brightly through the treetops so I close my eyes and imagine bathing in its light. I want to take off all these bloodstained clothes and burn them. I never want to feel the sick moisture of my friends' lives on my skin again. My clothes are beginning to dry, but many spots are still damp. A breeze gently flows by and I shudder with cold and regret.

"Lieve," Calix whispers.

I turn to where Calix peers into the shadows. I focus my attention on the same spot, and see people standing in the tree line, shrouded in the dark. Calix pulls his onyx dagger out and grips the handle firmly.

"I see them." I say.

Doppelgangers.

There are three of them armed with weapons. The moon shines on the face of the closest dop and my stomach drops. It looks *exactly* like Calix. The same messy hair and tan skin stand before us, and it's disorienting to see. The Dop looks at my best friend and blows him a condescending kiss. The second Dop, a seven-foot-tall blonde giant, spits on the ground while the third, a stalky, pink-skinned woman licks her lips. We only have two choices now. Run or fight.

Calix throws his black dagger. It wizzes past me and lands in his Doppelganger's leg. The creature doesn't scream, only looks down at the blood in awe. It yanks out the dagger, dark red blood oozing from the wound, and turns back to us. It smiles, eyes flashing black, and it is the eeriest vision I've ever seen. It's as if it knows before we do, that we're going to die.

I need to get us out of here. "Men, can you run?"

They nod mutely.

"Then let's go," I hiss. "*Now*."

We run.

We run along the trench, just trying to put distance between us and them. We're too loud and exposed. There's no time to climb the wall of the trench, so our only defense is to outrun or outsmart them. I'm an idiot for letting us settle there, I should have known better. Panting and hot air blow in my ear, the Dops are right there.

The woman extends her muscular arm, fingers grasping at my shirt. I fling my elbow to the side and catch her in the ribs, but she continues her chase. I hear something thud on the ground but I ignore it and run harder, but I'm almost out of steam. This woman is *fast*. Each step gets heavier and heavier. The air is thick with humidity so each breath feels like I'm drowning in a shallow bath. Sweat mixes with the dried blood on my clothes, sticking to my skin and slowing my pace. I pump my legs faster, my thighs burning, scorching, with every labored stride.

The trench forks up ahead. I separate from Calix and the other two men, fully prepared to be the bait. At the fork, Cal turns left, so I turn right. Cal's Dop and the giant chase them, the woman follows me.

"Over here!" I shout. "Come get me!"

I continue to make noise by whistling and shouting like a lunatic. I arrive at a dead end and I can't climb up the trench fast enough, it's too high. Panicking, I spin around, the woman only a few feet from me. I swing at her. The tip of my blade cuts her bicep, but just barely.

She slaps her hand over it and then shakes off the pain. Her full lips curl into a deadly smile and she flings something sharp at me. I dodge it and stab at her again, this time hitting flesh. She doubles over and wraps both of her hands around the hilt and pulls. She can't get it out, it's stuck in her ribcage.

I barrel into her shoulder while she's fumbling around, landing her on her back. I put my boot on her chest, taking a moment to look into her eyes before I kill her. She claws at my leg, her nails scraping against the fabric of my pants. I bend down and wrap my hand around her throat, watching her lips turn violet before retching my blade from her side with brute force. Then gently slide the blade in the side of her neck, watching the blood trickle down and land in her hair.

"May Sybill imprison your very being to Ciel where no man or god can touch," I use the heel of my hand to slowly drive the dagger deeper, "and I hope you rot there."

With a soft thump, she drops her hand on the ground. A black beetle scurries away, ticking as it climbs up the side of the trench. The Dops eyes go still, the eerie blackness frozen there forever.

I need to find Cal, there might be more Doppelgangers or even Darkthings close by. I call out, knowing that if a Darkthing finds me, it will be my end. I don't care about living, I just care about getting Calix out of here. I call out over and over, praying that Cal and the others are okay, and that I don't run into anything else in Shadow Grove.

I jog to the fork of the trench and follow his path. Blood pools intermittently on the ground and my heart stops. My breathing quickens as I follow the trail of spatter. *Please don't let him be dead.*

The two men who were with Calix and I are lying face up, their throats slashed and covered in blood. Calix is unconscious at the end of the trench. He's bleeding from his ear, and there is a large gash on his calf. I climb the top of the ditch, only letting the top of my head and my eyes above the ground so I can scan for threats. I don't see anything, but I have to assume something lurks close by, biding its time.

I must get Calix back to the castle. I pull his arms and drag him, but his head bumps the ground. I pull his leg, but the gash opens more. Taking my dagger, I cut pieces of Cal's pants and tie them around the wound to attempt to stop the bleeding.

"Wake up," I mutter as I shake his shoulders. "Please, wake up."

Pressure builds in my chest, I feel like I'm going to die. I can't lose him. I shake him again, Calix's jaw goes slack and his head falls to the side. Tears pour down my face and I shake him desperately over and over. "Wake up, Cal. Wake up. Wake up."

A spark lights in my mind: *use your cloak.* I spring up, take off my cloak, and lay it on the ground. I then roll Calix onto his stomach. Over the last year, he's packed on weight from training and he's harder to move than I realized. I grunt and then roll him again, onto the cloak, lying supine.

Hair falls into my eyes so I brush my forehead and then take the end of the cloak in my hands and pull. It works. I can drag him now. My neck and shoulders strain with every pull up the incline of the trench and I lose my footing several times. Miraculously, I manage to pull Calix out. Once we're on flat ground, I tear a path through the brush. I don't care what I have to do, or who I have to kill. I'm getting Calix home.

Calix becomes heavier and heavier the longer I drag him through the woods. I get us to the creek and stop. It's rainy season and the water is deeper than normal. I don't know how I'm going to do this. I take a deep breath and drag his lifeless body to the bank of the creek and he sinks into the water. I grip him under his arms and pull. The water turns red as blood washes off us. I pull and pull, the water up to my waist and struggle even to take steps through the sticky mud. I slip a few times grappling with Cal's weight and trying to keep his head above water. He doesn't sputter, not once, as I heave him across the creek.

Once we get to the bank, I drag him up, but my heavy boots sink in the mud and I lose grip of his arms. He goes under water, the current taking him downstream, and I have to pull my feet from my shoes to go after him. Desperately, I clomp through the creek and latch onto his wrist. I find the collar of his shirt and pull his head up, blowing air into his mouth as I've seen the Healers do. Nothing.

I see a sloped bank and pull Calix out of the water. I smack his face and shake his shoulders. Nothing. Not even a fluttering of the eyes. I imagine his fingers grabbing onto me as I pull him through mud, but they don't.

I blow air again, and watch his chest rise and fall, and I cry when he takes his first breath on his own. *Thank the gods.* I retrieve my boots and then start dragging Calix away from the water, to the direction of Brone Castle. Every few moments I stop and check that he's still breathing, and I find I'm holding my breath each time I stop. My shoulders finally relax when I feel his breath against my cheek and hand. I push forward, dragging him faster. He's still here with me, but only by a thread. That thread pulls me and guides me. That thread is not only Calix's link to the living, but my only tether as well. Without it, I fear I will die myself.

Sheer desperation allows me to pull Calix to a safe spot to rest for a while. I settle us in the crook of a massive oak whose roots are larger than my torso. I hide him from outside eyes and station myself in front. *I won't let him die.*

Insects buzz around us, and a black beetle crawls across the toe of my boot. I barely have the energy to flick it off me. My eyelids burn with exhaustion and my body feels heavy. I try lifting my legs to get in a comfortable position, but I'm so tired they refuse to move. I give up trying to be comfortable and lean my head back against the bark, and in no time, I fall asleep to the hum of the forest.

At the first hint of sunlight, I haul myself from our nest of roots and moss. The summer heat has already warmed up Shadow Grove and my shirt sticks to my back. My stomach growls. *I need to eat.* Dragging Calix is draining. After I check his breathing, I wander off just a little and find a patch of wildberries.

These berries are the most delicious fruit I'd ever eaten. I chew them slowly, savoring the tart flesh. I hold the soft fruit in my mouth, letting the juice run down my chin. The berries are firm and ripe. I pick a handful of them and stuff them in my pocket before returning to the oak.

"Ugh," I hear, and my heart leaps.

It's coming from Cal.

"Oh thank Gwen!" I fall to my knees and shout to the sky, crying and laughing at the same time.

"You look awful," Calix moans, but his joke gives me hope that he'll be okay.

I give him my berries and he eats what he can.

"What happened to you?" I ask.

"The Dops attacked me and I fought for my life. I ran from them, but they were *so* fast. I couldn't stop them from killing the others." He raises his hand to touch the side of his head. "Then out of nowhere one of them hit me over the head, and when I woke up, I was here."

I rub my brow. "So, there's still at least one Dop in the forest."

"It would seem so."

"Great." I get up and look around for a long branch. I find one sturdy enough to bear Cal's weight and bring it to him. "We need to get back to Brone Castle."

Cal groans and hobbles to his feet. We fashion him a makeshift crutch and I help him walk. Then we finally arrive at the edge of the forest after what seems like hours, Mount Oriel towering in the distance. The sight makes me think of Vera, and how she would be amazed to see this view.

The mountain was named after Oriel as a reminder that life is worth nothing without love, and as a reminder to fight for those you love, even if you meet your end in the process. It serves as the backdrop to Brone Castle, and as a beacon for those who have nothing more to give but love and friendship. We smile at each other.

"We can do this." I say.

Cal's golden eyes brighten as he sets his eyes on Mount Oriel, and we step out of Shadow Grove together. I feel a renewed sense of optimism. I'm going to get him home.

And then I hear the battle cry.

To stare into the eyes of your Doppelganger, is to give them power over you. Vanity and curiosity are the gateway to destruction.

– Sermon of Saint Dominion, Sagart Priest, Member of the Holy Order

CHAPTER 13

VERA

The morning sun shines through the lace curtains on the window. I cover my face with the blanket and groan, expecting Arden to tell me to be quiet, but he doesn't. I peek at where he slept, but he's not there. In his place is a note.

Don't panic. I'll be back. The breakfast cart will be delivered soon, so eat and then take a bath. I had the innkeeper pick out a new dress and cape for you, it's waiting in the bathing room.

I smile, he left a note this time. I run my hand under my pillow and find the pocket watch and the small book are still in place.

Just then, rapping on the door mixes with the innkeepers' shout. "Breakfast!"

Bless her, I'm famished. My nose guides me to the cart. I pull it into my room and the scent of fresh bread makes my mouth water. The cart is laden with smoked meats, fresh pastries, an array of fruits, and a pot of piping hot tea. I taste some of everything. The bread is warm, the fruit tart and juicy, and the tea perfectly sweet.

I wheel the cart back out when I'm finished and a servant girl pops up the stairs to take it. Her wide smile shows a missing front tooth, and she has the innkeeper's same bouncy blonde curls. I look at the little girl, and all I see is myself. She's small, too skinny, and pale. I assumed her mother owned the inn, but on closer inspection, I can see that they don't. The girl's clothes are hand-me-downs. Her skirts are too long, and the once brilliant colors are faded, and many threads are coming undone.

"Thank you."

"You're welcome m'lady." She leans in and whispers, "the scary man with you asked me to draw you a bath. The bathing room is just over there, if you follow me."

Bathing sounds incredible. I long to wash the dirt and grime of my travels from my skin. I thank the girl and enter the bathing room, locking the door behind me. I knew my clothes were muddy, but as I undress in the light, I can see how caked they are and kick the clothes away. I'm horrified that I slept in that filth.

A large mirror stands in the corner, its solid wood and looks sturdy. A tapestry hangs over it, covering the glass. It's just as well, I don't want to look at my body anyway. I could have been pretty, but I'm too skinny, almost skeletal. Not having enough food or rest will take a hard toll on the body, and I've never had enough of either.

The water in the clawfoot tub is at the perfect temperature and I lean back, fully immersing myself, the heat soaking me to the bone. Birds chirp outside the window and I feel totally at peace. I get to see Lieve today.

On a small wooden table next to the tub are several soaps and perfumes. Rose petals, wild moss, mint, and citrus. I smell each one, letting the aroma linger in the air. I choose a mixture of rose petal and wild moss, it smells earthy and floral.

I bring my knees to my chest and notice my legs are covered in bruises. The dark purples, greens, and yellows look like watercolor paints splashed across my skin. *I look horrible.* Whoever is in the room above the bathing room stomps their feet, causing the tapestry to gently fall to the ground. *The mirror is uncovered.*

I dare a glance at myself, and I was right about my appearance. I'm as thin as I imagined. I grab my hair and raise it from my neck, turning my head from side to side to inspect my profile. My collar bones are visibly present, just another reminder that I've always been hungry. My eyes, although light and bright, have dark circles. The physical evidence of exhaustion is painfully clear. I meet my own eyes, desperate to see beauty, but I only find faults and imperfections.

I finish bathing, but I've lost track of time. The water makes you forget all your problems and just soak in pure comfort. I start to feel a little light headed as the steam from the bath and all the perfumes are making the room too warm, much too warm. *I need to get out of the water.*

I wrap myself in a towel and see the pile of clothes Arden had sent for me. The dress is a deep blue, the color of the sky at midnight, and made of velvet. Silver stars are embroidered in the bodice, and shooting stars threaded in the skirts. The constellations of Dia and Oriel. I smile and twirl, amazed at the silver fringe of the hem sparkling when I turn. I pull on the cloak next, its silver fabric also made of velvet. *This must have cost a small fortune.* I'll have to think of a way to best thank Arden for his generosity.

Now that I'm dressed, I decide to risk a look at myself wearing something that isn't stolen or second hand. This is the first thing I've ever worn that's new. Feverishly, I wipe the condensation from the mirror and stare. The dress is stunning, but it's my eyes that I notice. They flash black for just a moment and the girl in the mirror winks at me.

"Ahh!" I scream as my feet get caught in the hem of my skirt and I fall backwards into the table of soaps.

The table leg cracks and the soaps slide across the floor. *Was that real?* My heart thunders in my chest and I can't move. I pat my arms and legs, trying to convince myself that I am here, I am real. Pounding steps in the hall stop at the bathing room door.

"Vera!" Arden calls out, "what's wrong?"

Still in shock I look back at my reflection, but it's just me. Wide eyed and pale, but nothing more.

"I'm okay," I call as I unlock the door.

I find Arden with hatchets drawn, ready to pounce on my would-be attacker.

"I'm really okay."

Arden slides in the room like a cat and prowls around demanding, "What happened?"

I point to the mirror. "The tapestry fell off and when I looked at myself, my reflection winked at me."

Arden pushes past me, straight to the mirror and slips his hatchets back in his belt loop before recovering the mirror with the tapestry. "Nothing more happened?"

"Nothing more."

He narrows his eyes at me and comes close, inspecting my face, my eyes, my lips. He turns me around and lifts my arms and then drops them. He grunts, satisfied that I'm still me, and tells me to meet him downstairs in the tavern. I watch him walk down the stairs before running back to the room to grab my book and the pocket watch from under my pillow.

⁓

We walk down a long stretch of shops and apartments and it reminds me of my last day in Adamston. There are people milling about, hanging lights and garlands and several people are wearing dashing gowns, shopping and gazing at a marble statue of the King. The energy is electric. As we pass, the people stop in their tracks, some then turn and flee, others bowing to Arden. He pays them no mind, continuing to walk and pulling the horse with him. Then I notice, they only bow after he's passed. Which means, they aren't bowing to Arden at all.

They bow for me.

I nod my head back at the people bowing to me and scurry to keep up with Arden. People here are strange, why bow to me when I was only following him through the town? We mount the horse when we reach the end of the street. Arriving at a dirt path with ivy and thorns growing on iron fencing, I can see the mountain peaks, half hidden by city buildings.

Once we get past all the ivy, the path opens up. Rounding the corner, the view of the gorgeous snow capped mountain I saw last night from my window comes into view. There are several other mountain tops flanking the highest peak in the middle, each one showcasing the larger mountain's snow covered point.

The houses are spread out far from each other on this route. It makes sense, the nobles have enough money for land and stables. I'm sure these enormous manors are country homes for Prinav's finest. I find myself wondering what Lieve thinks about living in a castle. Arden said he works for the crown, and I'm hoping with their help, I'll get a job in court too.

We ride in silence long enough that I fall asleep leaning against Arden's back. He smells like...like pine and moss. He smells like Lieve. *Like Prinav.* I smile as the beat of his heart and the patter of the horses' hooves carry me off to dreams of royal balls and fancy dresses and knights in shining armor.

"Vera," Arden whispers, "wake up."

I blink and rub the sleep from my eyes as I face magnificence.

The castle is stark white, and enormous. The gate we stop at is fine gold, the moon glints on the precious metal as the guards open for us. Now nightfall, the bright moon reflects off the white stone and the castle seems to glow at the heart of an elaborate estate of marble fountains and massive gardens.

Brone Castle overlooks the estate with grandeur, its towers watching over the darkness. My chest feels like it may burst and I want Arden to snap the reins so we can get to the entrance quickly. The horses' hooves click with each step on the cobblestone. I have to bend my neck back to see the towers, my chin pointed up at the sky. My mouth hangs open in awe of the sheer size of the castle. I have always known castles to be incredible works of art, larger than a mortal mind can comprehend, but this castle is more than massive. I've seen castles in the distance who have three or four towers, and they were the largest in Adamston. Brone castle has *six*. We hop off of our horse and servants take him away, I presume to a royal stable.

Arden then turns to me and bows, "welcome home, *Princess*."

All Hail the Conductor of Death.
— *Sybill, God of Death and Ruler of Ciel, the Realm of Souls*

CHAPTER 14

LIEVE

We round the last bit of trees that hides Solemn Valley, and it gives Calix and I a birds eye view of what we face. We stop dead in our tracks. Covering the wide expanse is a massive battalion of Prinavian forces, and on the other side, Doppelgangers.

There are hundreds of them.

The battle cry sounds again. The Battle Shrieker screams once more and then the Hode's deep horn blares through the air, echoing between the rocky surroundings. I swear even the mountains tremble as the ground beneath our feet vibrates. We run in the direction of the call, but Calix can't keep up with his mangled leg.

"Go!" Cal yells.

"I can't leave you like this."

Calix winces as he takes another step, "I'm right behind you."

"Til the end." I say and run towards the noise.

Leaving Cal is terrifying, but I know I need to be there for this next battle. I have to save as many of our men as possible and make up for the lives I lost. The Dops must be stopped. They almost killed Calix, and I wouldn't be able to live with myself if I didn't try to end this. Cal deserves a Kingdom of peace, and so does all of Prinav, even if I don't deserve it myself.

Near the edge of the battle, I see *Hal.*

I gasp. His face contorts with rage and I've never seen Hal look like that…but, *it's not Hal.* Seeing his face on a stranger sends a chill down my spine. The familiar tang of bile rises to my throat as I watch him parade around the valley.

A vise wraps around my heart, squeezing and squeezing. The tightness takes my breath and I can barely move. The faces of the men who died under my watch yesterday are before me, and now I must kill them again. The earth spins under me.

Another one of the faces is my own. The man who wears my face pulls back an arrow in his bow and aims for the King, who joins the battle to rid his kingdom of these beasts once and for all. My eyes trail the arrow as it flies through the air, arcing over the throng of soldiers.

I don't feel like I'm here in this valley. I don't feel like I exist. The arrow lands in the King's eye and his majesty's head falls back with the force of the blow. He sits upright and I have a split second of hope that he will be fine, but in the same moment, he slumps forward and slides off the side of the horse as it gallops into the chaos. The crowd roars so loud I can feel it climb up my body from the ground, resonating in and around me; consuming me.

Everything turns red. Watching myself hurt the King sends a surge of rage pumping through me. The Dops will not get away with this. *I won't allow it.* With the fall of King Niall, the entirety of his majesty's army attacks with a force Prinav has never known. My men bludgeon the enemy, one by one, and two by two. I can hear the crack of bone with every strike. Axes are being driven into the flesh of the wicked, while the valley is painted crimson with revenge.

An abandoned sword lays on the ground and I pick it up. I toss it around in my hands, letting the weight of the blade fill my grip. The weight and balance is splendid. I march into the storm swinging. Screams of pain morph into music. The drums of the Hode bounce on the ground imitating the beat of my heart. I close my eyes and let the blood spill over me, washing my failures clean. I smell the metal, I taste it. Mud and blood fill my lungs and I am born anew.

My feet dance to the song of agony and my hands compose each note with every slice of my blade. My song is red. My world is red. I will not allow the music to cease until there are no more members of their devious choir. It is my mission as Death's new Conductor to show the world that I am Death itself. I am fear incarnate. *They will all sing my song today.*

Thunderous hooves stomp closer and closer. King Niall's steed is galloping straight towards me, its pearl white coat slick with blood. I grab the reins and hoist myself atop its mighty back, raising my song's baton high above my head. We stampede through the carnage, spilling blood each step of the way. Each head that houses eyes that flash black in my presence is severed from its body. They roll on the ground, mouths still open in shock, and eyes stuck as black as their souls.

I scream in rage, carving my masterpiece into my opponents. As Death's Master, my crescendo rushes through the valley at a volume only the ancient gods can hear. Each individual man is my instrument as I guide their destruction across the blood soaked earth. Together, my band of soldiers play a symphony and I conduct their every move. The screams, the roars, the drums, they are the violent melody of my heart. The power we explode is an orchestra only the citizens of Prinav could produce. My King *will* be avenged.

I continue my death song, but the bastard choir no longer sings. The last note of destruction plays as the remaining foe retreat back into the mountainside, the man with my face included. I raise my sword above my head again and scream until the valley echoes my pain. Breathing heavily, my lungs heave against my ribs when I cry out. When I look down at myself, I am covered in blood, but this time I have no shame. This time, I have not failed. I am the avenger. I am *death.*

I turn the horse around to face the other soldiers and they roar in celebration. These men are warriors. I hope they can feel the pride radiate from me. Together we eliminated nearly every Dop in this valley. I smile until I notice a small group gathered around the King. His hand is limp, and a fair amount of blood pools in his eye. The sight sends a second surge of anger through me. I am ready to ride into the mountainside and finish what the Dops started.

I dismount the King's horse and walk over to the group of healers attending to him. They work quickly, wrapping cloth around his wounds without knocking the arrow protruding from his face.

"Is he alive?" I ask.

A young man with rich brown skin and striking emerald eyes glances towards me, hesitating before he answers. "Barely."

I drop to my knees and take the King's hand in mine. He looks up at me with his uninjured eye and whispers, "Monroe, my Monroe–" before losing consciousness.

The Healer leans into me, "I can keep him alive, at least until we get to the castle."

"Whatever you need to do, do it. He's not right, he's seeing things."

Soldiers drive their blades into the remaining living Dops as the Healer looks to the others in his group and they lift the King and take him to a tent on the edge of the valley. I watch with bated breath while other soldiers help the Healers tend to the rest of the Prinavian survivors. Blue lights flicker from behind the linen of the tent, only for a moment, a moment so short I don't think anyone else saw it. That group of Healers must know magic, Fae or witches perhaps.

The Healers are inside the tent with the King for about thirty minutes and no one emerges to give the rest of us updates. Calix hobbles over to me and we hug each other tightly. Then, the Healer with the emerald eyes opens the tent and walks over to us. I'm not sure why he's addressing me specifically, there are more senior officers here, but he stops before me.

"The King is alive, but severely wounded."

Another man joins us, one I've never seen before. He wears a cloak of the deepest indigo and silver studs on the collar. He has chestnut hair, slicked back and styled with an almost wet look. His sharp jaw clenches as he sizes me up.

The man holds out his hand out to me, "I'm Lord Esven, Grand Vizor to the King."

Confused, I shake his hand, the leather of his gloves feeling soft against my rough calluses. I'm still not sure why either of them are speaking to me. "I'm glad the King is alive, but isn't there someone other than me to report to?"

Esven sighs. "Actually, no." He stands a little straighter and narrows his dark eyes at me. "I tried to talk him out of it, I tried to appoint someone else as a Regent, even myself, while His Majesty heals– but he wants *you*."

I lose a breath. "Why?"

The muscle in Esven's jaw twitches, only for a split second, and then he says, "The King trusts your judgment in battle and believes we'll have more of these battles very soon."

The fingers in his right hand clench to a fist momentarily. *Esven isn't happy about this.* I don't want this either, I can't run a country. "I don't want to be Regent," I stammer.

"It's not up to you. It was the King's last order before his mind and body went into deep rest."

"The King's steed chose you as well, it went directly to you," The Healer says. "I saw it myself."

I stand frozen, unmoving, unbelieving. "I *can't* run a Kingdom."

Esven steps forward. "You'll learn, and I'll be here to guide you until the King is back on his feet."

"Long live Sir Lieve!" Someone shouts.

I shake my head. This can't be happening.

"Long live Sir Lieve!" I hear from a second voice. Then a third. Then a fourth.

Calix looks like he hasn't taken a breath since the battle started, his eyes wide in surprise. We lock eyes and Calix mumbles to himself, a slight grin tugging the corner of his mouth, when uddenly, he drops his crutch and kneels.

I shake my head no. If he kneels, they'll all kneel.

"Sir Lieve!" Esven shouts so everyone can hear.

I stand still, not processing what is happening. The pearl horse that carried me through the battle nudges me forward. Without thinking, I kneel before Esven. He places his hand on my shoulder, and calls for a Priest to join him. A woman wearing crimson robes and a white mask with black streaks under the eyes joins us. She places her hand on my other shoulder.

"With the power of King Niall, and the voice of the gods behind him, Priestess Panteel will lead us in the ordaining of our Regent."

The Priestess hums and raises her free hand to the sky before bellowing, "this man, this soldier, is anointed by me, and by Hode, the warrior god."

Esven's jaw ticks. He nods at me to stand. Once back on my feet, I turn to look out in the valley, and when I do, it's like the ocean. Like the waves, every man kneels and bows his head as one.

"Long live Sir Lieve!" The crowd bellows. "Long live King Niall!"

Yes. Long live King Niall, for my sake *and* theirs.

The parent gods, Bram and Guenivere, constructed Crystal Thrones for their Creation. The Thones cannot be lied to, tricked, manipulated, or destroyed. Do not lie to the Throne. The Crystal Throne is Truth.

– Saint Barnabas, Grand Sagart, Leader of the Holy Order

CHAPTER 15
VERA

Two guards open the massive wooden doors to Brone Castle. My breath catches as I take in the beauty. Black and white checkered marble floors reflect the grand staircase straight in front of me. Everything shines and sparkles, even in the dim candlelight. I walk around the entrance, gawking at the statues, art work, and gold filigree adorning every corner. I can't believe Lieve has been here this whole time. I bet he's been in love with this place because I've already fallen for it and I've only seen the stairs.

"It's beautiful," I breathe.

Guards enter the foyer and talk to Arden, asking him questions and talking low to one another as their eyes flick back and forth between him and I.

"I need to take you to the throne room."

"Why?"

"Many young women have entered these very doors, claiming to be you," he answers. "And anyone who enters Brone Castle is subject to a strict set of protocols. Even me."

Who would want to pretend to be me? Arden leads me out of the entryway and down an arched corridor. His footsteps are muffled by his cloak dragging on the marble tiles, and the only thing I can think about is why I have to prove myself. I'm no one of importance.

We travel through the maze of corridors, each one ornamented in precious artwork. I scan as we walk, statues of the gods, paintings of pearl horses, and vases made of crystal line the halls. We end up at the rear of the castle, in a dark stairwell. Arden lights a torch, but I hate the uneasiness of this.

For several more minutes we continue through a damp stone tunnel with only the torch as our guide. My pulse quickens with every step and all the thoughts of trust fly out the window. I was an idiot for coming here. *Lieve isn't here.* I've given my safety to a strange man, and I'm probably going to die tonight.

A lone door, made of solid brass appears before us. Arden opens it and my jaw drops. This room houses the moon. We walk inside the small space, and everything is doused in blue white light. The light spills from the skylight, but somehow it reaches all the way down to where we are, and we are clearly deep underground. In the center of the room is a crystal throne with jagged angles like icicles and a navy velvet cushion.

I feel a tingling in the air around us. It feels just like Shadow Grove, and of the tree Lieve and I jumped in to enter Prinav. The walls are made of onyx, and silver runes are carved in the stone. I run my finger over a line of symbols and they jump off the wall, creating stories I wish I was able to read. There is a magic in this room. But what kind? Why am I here?

"Arden, you need to tell me what the protocol is now."

"Sit, please."

"Why?"

"Just do it."

I furrow my brow at him, but step over to the throne. The tingling sensation intensifies. I reach my hand out to steady myself so I can sit, and as soon as my fingers touch the crystal, my vision blurs. A buzzing, no, a humming, fills my ears as the room goes black and then flashes white like lightning. Frost climbs up my hand, stopping at my elbow and I jerk my arm away. I take a few steps back and bump into the wall.

"What the–" I say and clench my fist.

Pieces of ice break off my skin and fall to the stone floor, melting almost instantly.

"Please sit," Arden says. "You are not in danger."

I push back from him, "*no*."

Arden touches the throne, ice climbing up his hand and locks eyes with me. The ice stops at his elbow and doesn't climb any higher. "It's just how the throne works. Please just sit and say your name, you can trust me"

Even though my body is screaming at me not to, I sit. Ice immediately wraps around my arms and legs, holding me still in the seat. It's so cold it reaches my bones and I jerk to try to stand but I'm stuck. A blinding flash of light bolts in my vision and my head swims with a deep humming.

"Please state your name."

"Vera Oleander."

I feel something cold and heavy sink onto the top of my head, and the ice melts from my limbs. My head still swims as I get to my feet. I reach my hand up to feel what's on my head and my fingers brush against something metallic.

"Are you alright?" Arden asks.

"I'm fine," I reply as I remove the object from my head.

It's a crown.

Arden kneels and our eyes meet, and I see amazement in his gaze.

"What's going on?"

Arden stands up. "You're *truly* Vera, the missing Princess of Prinav."

I drop the crown on the ground and it clatters loudly against the marble floor, echoing in the small space of the throne room. "*What?*"

"I had to make sure you weren't an imposter, for the safety of the King, and for the safety of the whole Kingdom."

I begin to ask more questions but footsteps sound behind me and the brass door slowly creaks open. Sweat accumulates on my palms as I focus my eyes in the dim light to see who's entering this secret room, and find that it's a young man with jet black hair. This young man is wearing a crown of gold, the sharp peaks twisting like vines on a tree, the moon shining softly on the surface of the metal. As he fully enters the room, I start to make out more of his features. He's average height, lean, and reminds me of *Lieve*.

The man opens his mouth and a familiar voice speaks to me. "Hello Vera, I see you've discovered my throne."

It *is* Lieve.

My heart is beating so hard against my chest I can hear it in my ears. I just stand there in shock, staring like a fool.

"Lieve," I cry softly, "you have no idea what I've been through to get here." I wrap my arms around him, breathing him in.

"Vera, I've waited for the day you'd arrive for so long." He whispers.

With tears streaming down my face, I look at him and what I see shocks me to my very core. It's Lieve, *I know it is*, but he doesn't quite look like him. He's older. Subtle lines crease his forehead, and his hair has grown longer. I touch his face and feel my hands shaking. Has it really been *years?*

"Lieve–" I say in a shaky voice.

"It's alright," he coos.

"You're older." I keep touching his face, desperately trying to process any of this.

He takes a deep breath, "You've been missing for quite some time."

"And you, you've been here?"

Lieve wipes his chin and leans against the onyx wall. "I've been searching for you for nearly ten years and I honestly can't believe you're here."

If this is all true, he would be twenty-nine now, almost thirty. He has the remnants of a clean shave, and Lieve didn't need to shave before, he had a bare chin and his muscles have filled out more. I'm sure that's due to the diet he's been enjoying for the last decade. His eyes have lines around them, and he seems tired. It's Lieve, but I don't know this man. My chest aches and tears prick my eyes.

I can feel my heart breaking as I scan every inch of my now *older* brother. "Lieve, we aren't twins anymore."

"We aren't poor anymore either," he laughs. "You'll never know hunger again."

I look around the room and just start laughing, because this is laughable. There's no way it's true. I wave at his crown and at the one I dropped on the floor. "This has to be a dream."

"No," he chuckles, "I'm *King*."

I let out a burst of laughter, and hear Arden laugh too. Arden, in the shadows, leaning against the doorframe stops chuckling as Lieve gives him a cold look. The room is spinning and I don't know what to think. Lieve? *King?* The boy that stole food to keep us from starving?

"I'm serious, Vera." He picks up the crown from the floor and puts it in my hands. It's heavy. I hold my breath, unable to comprehend any more information. "And that means, you are a *Princess*."

$$\sim$$

Arden bids me goodnight, giving me a wink before Lieve walks me out of the throne room and down several halls until we stop at a large set of double doors. As we step in, I gasp. I thought the room at the inn was the nicest place I'll ever sleep, until this chamber. There are three gigantic windows, the center one is stained glass. The image inlay is a depiction of the gods Siva and Malsu. Each of them has flowing white hair and pearl skin with a collage of colors adorning their robes. The bed frame is solid gold and the linens are thick velvet covering soft silks of deep forest green.

"This room has been saved for you for many years," Lieve says to me as I walk around, touching the furnishings on each wall. I look at him in disbelief, and he smiles softly at me.

I don't understand how this is real. My fingers trace the wood of the desk in the corner, the frame of the art on the walls, the crystal knobs on the heavy doors. *Princess.* It's impossible. A large wardrobe sits on the opposite side of the room and I open it to find dozens of gowns, robes, corsets, and cloaks. I let my hands glide over the fabrics and I can feel the quality and artistry in every thread. They feel even more luxurious than the fine velvet dress I'm currently wearing.

I choose a night dress and go behind the divider to take off Arden's gift to me and I feel something metallic in my pocket. Only then do I remember I have the pocket watch. I don't tell Lieve yet. I want to fix it for him and give it to him as a present. I think he'd like knowing I found it.

My heart starts to race. Could this watch bring us back home? Do I even want to go back home? Would Lieve be my age again if we went back? I pick it up and rub my thumb over the metal then set it under a pile of linens on a stool behind the divider and return to see Lieve smiling. I want to smile too. I want to be thrilled, but this is all so strange.

"So," he draws out, "now what?"

"I'm so confused Lieve, I just–" I close my eyes and try to find the right words–, "you aren't the same."

I walk over to him and hold his hand. Even his hands have aged and reality is starting to sink in. Lieve has been here for *ten years* without me. I bet he's been distraught.

"But better than before," he smirks. "Right?"

There's the old Lieve I know. I roll my eyes at him. "That's to be determined."

"So, you aren't impressed. That's unfortunate." He walks over to one of the massive windows and I follow him. "I fitted this room just for you, the day after my coronation."

I can see sadness in his eyes and I squeeze his fingers. "I'm so sorry you were alone."

"I've had Calix. But it's not the same. I hate to tell you that I gave up looking for you several times, it just seemed like you'd never get here."

We both stare out the window in silence, letting years of worry wash away. I squeeze again and he squeezes back. "I want a tour of this massive castle and the entire story told to me starting first thing in the morning."

"Deal," he says and bows. "And a King never goes back on his word."

"Yes," I laugh, "I need every detail of how a common thief stole an entire Kingdom."

King Niall has been shot. Wound possibly fatal.
*– Correspondence from Lead Healer, Valance Debaux,
writing from the Solemn Valley, to Baptiste Matisse, Sagart
Priest of the Royal Family, Brone Castle, Barault, Prinav*

CHAPTER 16

LIEVE

I can't run a country. Brother, peasant, soldier, those things sound natural. Death incarnate sounds more natural. Regent to the King. That's not who I am.

I'm still before Esven, and if I rise, it says that I have accepted this. I haven't. I can't. I look at Esven and I can see this position won't be without consequences, and I don't want any more trouble in my life than I already have.

The Healers are running around the field, helping the injured. I can hear them shout to each other, cry when another one of our men dies, and curse Sybill for taking them to Ciel. I should be helping the injured, but all I can think about is staying still. I just want to stay still enough that I evaporate. I want to become a shadow. In some ways, I feel like I already am.

But I'm loyal to the throne. I remind myself that I am not King. King Niall reigns, and if he wants me as Regent, it is my duty to obey.

An adolescent kid runs from the back of the sea of soldiers and stands at attention before me. "I will follow you, Sir Lieve. I'm not afraid."

The boy's jaw is stiff. He has no fear, standing at attention like a real soldier. He swims in armor that doesn't fit, but his face and hands are blood spattered, and he wields a bow. "You saved us, and I pledge to you I'll never run from your fight. Ever."

"I am no King." I say softly.

"You can be if you're brave enough." He says, looking me square in the eye.

What bravery this child has to even be here, to don his father's armor and enter the fray, to be speaking your mind to the King's Regent, temporary or not. My heart swells. He reminds me of myself, taking a responsibility he isn't really ready for. He shouldn't have to be this brave, he shouldn't be here to begin with. *Wait, why on earth is this boy here?*

"Did you fight in this battle?"

He nods and doesn't break eye contact.

I place my hands on his shoulders and I feel him sink a little under the weight of my arms. "Where is your father?"

"A Dop killed him and my mother. I ran instead of fighting them and I won't *ever* run again." His voice cracks and lip quivers. "I came looking for my sister." Hot tears spring from his eyes. "She's married to Calix Bramford, is he with you?"

Calix rises to his feet and staggers through the crowd. "I'm here."

Arden turns, his shoulders sagging with relief. "Calix, I hoped that I could live with you."

Calix pulls him close and embraces him. Arden embraces Calix back with a tight grip, silently crying into his chest.

"I'm sorry about your parents." Cal takes a deep breath and then shouts, "How many more families must be torn apart!"

He's right. How many more families will the Dops destroy? Calix's own noble family isn't even safe. How many more children must wield the weapons their parents can no longer hold? The Dops and their treachery must end. And I– I must put a stop to it. I have an army at my disposal and a sword at my side. It ends with me.

Now I'm shaking, but I make my decision and stand. I will be their King, even if it means being the King of Death.

"Esven," I say. "It is with great humility that I accept this honor. I will serve our Kingdom as Regent. I pray that Siva will treat the King with a swift recovery so that he may return to the field with us."

Esven's eyes darken with something, jealousy perhaps, but he only nods in approval.

I clean the blade of my sword on my cloak and turn to Arden. "Kneel."

Wiping his eyes, Arden detaches from Calix and kneels before me. He lowers his head and I tap each of his shoulders with my blade, right side, then left.

"To all who are here, know that from today and so forth, this young man is a Knight. In his veins runs the blood of a warrior, and he is the definition of loyalty."

He lifts his head to look at me, eyes glassy, and more tears flowing down his cheeks.

"Rise, Sir Arden." The crowd erupts in applause, and Arden then returns to the group of soldiers, now officially one of their numbers. I turn to Cal, "Calix Bramford, please kneel."

Calix hisses in pain, but kneels in front of me.

I tap my blade on each of his shoulders, "This is Sir Calix Bramford, Lord Bramford of Barault proper. He is now First General, a Knight. From this day forth, he will be known as the right hand, the Witan, to the Regent of Prinav!" The crowd cheers for my friend. "Rise, Calix."

I Knight a few others, then dismiss the men to help the Healers attend to the bodies of the fallen. I help lift my men, sorting them by severity of their wounds. I hold the hands of the dying and pray to Bram that their souls be sent to Sybill with eternal peace. In my head, I swear to Hode, that they will be avenged.

Solurnalia: *Religious Yearly Celebration lasting six days. The Feast of Bram, The Four Day Festival of Light and Dark, and the Sol Ball.*

CHAPTER 17

VERA

My new room might be perfect, but I don't sleep at all. As soon as the sun rises, I slip on a robe and run down the corridor at full speed. I have no idea where the passages lead, but I want to spend every second of the day with Lieve. I spot a servant pushing a cart with silver domes covering food, so I speed up to him.

"Hello!" I plead through my heavy breaths. "Can you help me?"

The servant bows so deeply his nose almost touches his legs. "Of course, madam."

"Where are the King's chambers?" I hold my rib, a sharp pinch hindering my breath.

He stands straight up and points in the direction I was running. "That way, but he's in the dining room at the end of the hall."

"Thanks," I say and dart to the dining room.

I can't wait to wander the halls with Lieve, listening to more of his stories. I pass by other servants and they give me quick bows and curtseys. My bare feet slap the floor reminding me of when Lieve would chase me, barefoot, in some of the Noble's homes as children. He always said I couldn't hunt, and I was too loud, and that's why he never let me come into the forest with him very often. '*You need to learn to be quiet.*

How can I feed us when you scare everything away?' I would then argue with him that I didn't need him, that I wasn't loud, and that I knew how to be quiet. Hearing my feet slap the marble and stone are proof he was right. Of course he's right, and that makes me laugh.

Rounding the corner, I smack into what feels like a brick wall, tumbling backwards and landing on my bottom. I look up and see Arden standing over me. His face is covered with another mask, but I can tell he's smiling by the look in his eyes. Those same eyes graze over me, making me very aware that I'm still wearing a night dress.

My face grows hot. "Sorry," I mumble. "I was just on my way to the dining room."

"I'll walk you," he says and helps me to my feet.

I smile, and just as we're about to take a step, a man enters the hall; a *gorgeous* man. He wears formal attire that looks to be of nobility. The fabric is a vibrant deep green, and there are brass buckles on his belt. Brass pointed studs line the black leather chest strap that attaches to an asymmetrical cape of the same deep green, with a high, stiff collar.

Everything about him *reeks* of elegance. This man doesn't walk, he saunters. His jet black hair lays perfectly messy, and his tan skin only heightens the angle of his jawline. My heart starts pounding.

The man sees Arden and I and stops. "This is a surprise."

Even his voice is gorgeous.

"Calix," Arden gestures towards me, "meet *Vera.*"

Our gaze meets and Calix's golden eyes twinkle as his lips curl into a mischievous grin. "*Vera,* the *real* Vera?" He holds out his hand. "Nice to finally meet you."

My breath catches and I hold out my hand to him. "And you." My mind races and I can't stop staring at Calix's perfect lips. "We're just headed to breakfast."

Arden stiffens beside me. Maybe I shouldn't have invited Calix. Arden clearly doesn't like him. Or is it something else? Could Arden be jealous?

"I'd love to join you."

Arden mumbles to himself, but I ignore his words in favor of having a wonderful day with my brother. Two large double doors with guards flanking each side stand at the entrance. I reach out to the handle but I'm stopped by a servant. The man is tall and gray-haired, with a soft expression. He wears a coat of thick wool, and he has a pin with a twin-tailed fox emblem attached to a floral vest.

"Good morning Your Highness," he bows. "We are all delighted at your presence. His Majesty has thought of nothing more than you for quite some time. The name's Finn, if you should ever need anything, m'lady."

I smile at him, and then a roar of laughter bursts behind the large doors, startling us.

"Allow me to announce your presence," Finn says kindly.

"Oh, of course." I say as I bounce on the balls of my bare feet. I've never been announced to a room before, and I want to remember this forever.

He knocks on the door and I hear Lieve answer, *"Finn."*

Finn opens the door for us, keeping his eyes on the floor. "Entering, Princess Vera, Lord Bramford, and Lord Madrona."

Lieve is sitting in a high-backed chair at the head of the table surrounded by nobles. I can see in his face he's drunk, and it's becoming clear he's been up all night. Trays and trays of food and drink cover the wooden table along with numerous empty bottles. I'm taken aback at the sight, frozen where I stand. I don't know what to do or say. My heart sinks. This is not the morning I envisioned. Finn gives me a weak nod and closes the door.

The air in the dining room is thick, and the smell of the alcohol sits heavily in my stomach. Lieve hasn't even acknowledged my entrance, and I'm sickened by all the food haphazardly strewn over the massive table, wasted and uneaten. They continue to laugh and joke as repulsion brews within me. I clear my throat to get his attention, and finally they stop their obnoxious chatter. One of the nobles at the table looks me up and down and I see hunger in his eyes. I pull my robe tightly over my nightdress, newly aware of how exposed I am.

"You're up early," Lieve says.

I raise an eyebrow. "And you're up late."

Lieve shrugs his shoulders. "Just celebrating the return of my sister–," he holds up a large, pewter chalice–, "and my favorite mercenary."

"To Vera!" Someone shouts.

Lieve repeats, "to Vera!"

I cross my arms and glare at Lieve. This behavior is absurd. "I thought you were going to give me a tour of the grounds."

"Drink this wine–," he slides a glass all the way down the table to me and half the contents splash on the dark wood–, "Or go be a prude like Arden."

"I'm not drinking, it's barely sunrise," I say.

Lieve downs the remaining liquid from his own glass. "Your choice."

"You're acting like–"

"Like what?" He growls.

"Like a common drunkard!"

"Cheers to being a drunkard!" Lieve jeers and all his advisors laugh.

I storm out of the dining room, Lieve calling out to me like a fool, "I'm sorry!"

Finn stares yet again at the floor when I burst through the doorway. I can hear Calix and Arden talking with Lieve, scolding him by the sounds of it. Tears stain my cheeks by the time I'm back to my own chambers. *Is this attitude the norm for him now? Does Lieve drink like this often?* Frustrated, I climb underneath the thick covers of my bed. I don't like this. My hand brushes the pocket watch underneath the pillowcase and I wrap my fingers around the cool metal. *If this watch can bring the Lieve I remember back to me, I might just have to learn how to use it.*

I wake up and I'm a little disoriented. I must have fallen asleep crying. I see large stained glass windows, and hear water running and it all comes back to me.

"Who's there?" I call.

"Just myself, Your Highness," someone calls back from the bathing room.

I pull the covers close to my chin. "But you haven't said who *you* are."

Out pops a young woman with brown skin and thick brown hair braided in a crown on top of her head. She gives me a bright smile and strides over to the bed and does a tiny little curtsey. "I'm your maid, ma'am, the name's Evalie." Evalie pats my thigh. "Now my dear, let's get you washed and ready for the day."

I pull the covers over my head and grumble, "I don't want to."

"Nonsense m'lady," Evalie pats my leg again. "It's a beautiful day, and the King has requested you meet him at the main entrance."

I grumble once more and follow Evalie into the bathing room. Once I'm washed, Evalie chooses a day gown for me to wear. Reluctantly I step into the gown and stand still as Evalie tightens the corset. She then fixes my hair into a fashionable updo and pulls the drapery from the full length mirror so I can approve of her work. My breath catches. I look nothing like the person I was only yesterday.

When I look at myself in the mirror now, I don't see me, I see someone else. This young woman in the mirror looks regal. I thank Evalie for making me presentable and find myself waiting outside the main entrance of Brone Castle.

This place is its own tiny city. There are people working, laughing, and socializing everywhere. I wait on the steps of the castle entrance long enough that the sun is high above. *Where is Lieve?* The gravel scoots under my feet so that the crunching sounds drown out the conversations of the people walking by. Irritation settles in, and I'm ready to grab a servant and make them take me to Lieve so we can have a good row, but I think better of it.

I'm growing warm beneath the layers of fabric this dress has encased me in and I'm starting to sweat. The ridges of rocks from the stone wall jab my bottom and I squirm to find a comfortable position. People stare at me as I wait, and I would stare at me too. I'm sure they have a million questions. Some share wide smiles, and some sport nasty scowls. I wonder if they know who I am or why I'm here, because I'm beginning to wonder about it myself.

"Vera, there you are!" Lieve calls out to me.

"What do you mean, *'there you are?'*"

"I'm sorry," he says. "I shouldn't have kept you waiting."

"Three hours." I get in his face. "I was told to meet you. *So I did.* And I waited and waited." I clench my teeth. "Do you drink like that all the time?"

He bends down and when he answers I can still smell alcohol on his breath. "What if I do?"

"Then I would be ashamed of you."

"You're a spoiled brat, you know that?" Lieve digs the heels of his hands in his eyes and rubs them.

"Tired are we?" I say and I hope he can hear the sarcasm. "I'm not the one who's spent ten years in the lap of luxury."

Lieve lowers his hands. "It hasn't always been this way."

I cross my arms and give him a seething glare.

"Do you want a tour or not?"

I put my hands on my hips and let out an exasperated breath. *Do I want a tour?*

"Never mind," Lieve says and turns to go back inside.

"Uhhh, you win," I grumble. "Let's go."

We stroll around the estate and Lieve recounts life after the battle where King Niall was injured and he became Regent, and then, becoming King. I can see in his eyes that he's more than tired. There's something ailing him and he doesn't seem entirely healthy. He has bags under his eyes, and his lips are dry and cracked.

Shame rushes in my veins. I have always been a burden to him. I think about all the sleepless nights he endured when I was sick, or when he was hunting for us. I think of everything he did for me, that I know he's doing for Prinav. I hope he lets me help him now that I'm here.

"It really is beautiful,"I say and Lieve's face brightens.

"I could never dream that I, *we*, I mean, could ever have anything like this." Lieve runs his hand through his hair. "Even though it's been years, I still don't feel like the real leader of Prinav."

"I'm sure you're a great leader."

Lieve has always been a good leader. Everything he did for us our entire lives kept us alive. I can't think of a better person to be in charge. I want to ask why he never brought me here sooner, but so many thoughts are rattling around in my head, and...and I don't know this man anymore. Not really. I don't know what might set him off, and I don't want to argue again.

We give the pearl horses, Siva and Malsu, quick pats as we walk up and down the rows of the massive stables. I feel shy, like I don't know how to talk to him. I shake my head and try to just be present with Lieve. I'm a Princess in a literal fairy tale world. There are worse things than Lieve having a drink or two, or three.

"So, Calix told me he enjoyed meeting you." Lieve's back is to me, but his ears are red. That's his giveaway that he knows more than he's letting on.

"I enjoyed meeting him too," I say coyly, giving up as little as possible.

Lieve chuckles, "I'm betting he'll ask you to be his partner for Solurnalia."

"What does that entail?"

His eyes sparkle. "Debauchery."

I roll my eyes. "I don't know why, but that doesn't surprise me. I meant, what does it symbolize?"

"Well, the Feast of Bram is celebrated to symbolize Bram bedding Guinevere. It's mostly about indulgence. Food, lust, entertainment. It's a way to thank the gods for giving us pleasure. You remember the stories I used to tell you–"

I nod my head in reply.

"Everyone dresses scandalously, and we drink, and eat, and many of our guests begin courtship. That's what it's all about really, unmarried courtiers finding a spouse." He takes in a breath, looking giddy, and still a little drunk. "It's going to be spectacular."

"It seems like you have more fun than I want to know about," I tease.

"Probably so." He cocks an eyebrow at me, "but now only with one specific person."

"Oh really? And who would that be?"

He grins. "My wife."

"What!" I shout. The thought of Lieve getting married is wild to me.

He laughs. "I know! It's all so surreal."

"Yes, tell me about her," I say, and bounce on my feet.

"You'll meet her soon. I've prepared a small dinner for those closest to the Court to welcome you." He twiddles his thumbs. "I'm sure Calix will come to the dinner. Should I tell him you'll be his Solurnalia partner?"

There he goes again, prying, trying to get information. "I think I'd like to get to know him a little before cementing any real decision."

Lieve's straightens. "Of course, Your Highness."

I sigh and scan the estate when something catches my eye. Across the hedges I see Arden talking to a woman with long red hair, and my heart pounds at the sight of him. I squint my eyes, trying to watch him discreetly and see who he's talking to. They look serious.

The woman turns to Arden and I see her face. She's devastatingly beautiful. Her skin shines ethereally in the sun, and the light catches the angles and curves of her face perfectly. The woman almost looks like she's glowing, and I know that even if I'm the Princess, she must be the talk of Prinav. They link arms and walk past everyone, most of whom stare as well. Something about them together makes me frustrated as the two of them round the corner and out of sight. Watching this woman rub Arden's arm and lean her head against his shoulder sends a ripple of – *jealousy?*-- through me. I brush it off and re-focus.

"Has Arden ever been married?"

Lieve lets out a howl of laughter. "Arden? No. Arden is terrified of women, and he could have his share of them."

My stomach flips. I'm sure he's right. Arden is capable, strong, smart. I'm sure there are girls out there who would be interested in him, girls who like that sort of thing. They might even like the fact that he's, well, *dangerous.* Lieve must be wrong about him though. He's clearly interested in the red-head, and I've been a fool for entertaining ideas about him. Maybe I should be focusing on Lieve's friend Calix.

Lieve and I talk more, and laugh, and it feels familiar. It feels good to be with him again. This is the Lieve I know and I cling to him as we stroll, arm in arm, away from the stables and to the pond to watch the frogs jump on the lilypads. It's early spring in Prinav, but the sun is warm and the flowers are starting to bloom. It feels natural to be here with him in this place, and I'm happy we're here together, even though it isn't perfect.

I watch Lieve point at different buildings on the estate, telling me the names of the people who live in them, and the people who work here. He has created such a wonderful life, however strange it is. *Lieve is married.* That another thing I didn't get to be a part of, another thing I missed out on.

Lieve's stories are never dull, and I'm sad and a little more than jealous that I wasn't here to experience all of this with him. He still has the air of confidence, but it's not a quiet confidence anymore, it's obvious. I smile to myself. Being King has stroked his ego.

Lieve asks me more about my journey and I tell him about the Darkthings. I shudder even in the warmth of the sun, remembering what it felt like being chased in Shadow Grove. My arms get goosebumps and I rub them quickly, trying to get rid of them. "I'm thankful that Arden was in the forest with me."

"Me too." Lieve throws a stone into the pond and several large fish fight over it when it lands on the water's surface.

"I saw you get ripped to shreds right in front of my eyes."

He sighs. "I won't even begin to tell you what I see when a Darkthing is near."

After a couple more hours of talking, we're interrupted by Calix. "Pardon me," he says with a bow. "But Lieve, you're needed for Feast preparations."

"I would be thrilled to talk about drinks and courtesans with the council." Lieve laughs and turns to me. "I'll see you at your welcome dinner. My wife has given your maid some gowns for you to try."

I stand there with Calix and flick a beetle from my shoulder and watch my brother – the married King – run back to his castle. Even knowing the story of how that happened, I can't fathom all of the events that led to this outcome. Lieve has persevered through so many obstacles. I shouldn't be so hard on him for celebrating my arrival well into the morning. It was a stupid choice, but I understand that he wanted a night of happiness after all the years of anguish.

"Well," Calix sighs. "That was an eventful morning."

I scoff. "That's true."

Calix then picks a blossom from the wildflowers that grow on the edge of the pond and hands it to me. "I can tell you have a lot on your mind, so I'll leave you with this."

I take the flower in my hand and smell it, smiling at him.

"I'll call on you." He says with a wink and follows Lieve's footsteps back to the castle.

My thoughts bounce back and forth between speaking with Arden about who the woman is, and forgetting it all and seeing what can play out with Calix. Calix is handsome, charming, respectful. He's a nobleman for heaven's sake. Calix is exactly the type of man Lieve has dreamed of for me, and I can't say he's not what I've dreamed of myself. I breath in the aroma of the flower again and realize, maybe Arden was right. Maybe every fairy tale really *does* come from a very real story. And maybe Calix is my story to tell.

*It waits patiently, counting the moments until it can
nestle in the palm of the one it was destined for, its
rightful owner. The secret lies not in its gears, but in its
purpose. A compass, leading its bearer to the one who
holds its match, a reunion written in the stars.*
— *Proverb of the Maiden, Holy Book of Bram*

CHAPTER 18

LIEVE

Walking into Brone Castle as Regent is something I never imagined. Esven talks about sending out troops, and of contracts, and meetings and budgets. He's talking too fast and I can't keep up with anything he's saying. I catch that Calix is in the infirmary with Narah and Arden, and that King Niall is resting in his chambers, surrounded by Healers. I'm relieved that, at least for now, Calix and the King seem to be alright.

Esven takes me to my chambers, which are larger than the apartment Vera and I had in Adamston, and five times the size of my shack on the edge of Barault. The bed is massive and the linens are made of satin and velvet and filled with feathers. There's a bathing room, a sitting room, and even a music room. I peek my head into the music room to see a black piano in front of a large window, and various other instruments perched on stands against the walls.

"What chambers are these?" I ask.

"This was the Queen's before she passed away."

My eyes flick to the instruments in the other room. "She must have loved music."

"She did," He answers and walks to the door. "Rest up, we have a busy day tomorrow."

Esven leaves and I explore the music room, running my hands across the smooth surface of the piano. A small trace of blood smears on the ivory keys and I freeze. I need Daphne. I go to the desk in the sitting room and dig through the drawers for parchment and write to her. I beg her to join me here. I explain what happened; that I'm Regent and that Calix is injured and Narah's parents died. I tell her that Narah's little brother is here. I tell her I need her help and that I miss her.

A knock on the door sounds from the double doors along with the muffled calls of a voice I don't recognize. When I open the door I find a man standing before me. He bows and the silver threads mixed in his dark hair twinkle in the light of the oil lamp hanging on the wall.

"I wanted to introduce myself. The name's Finn, m'Lord, and I'm here to serve you humbly."

"Lovely," I say and beckon him inside the chambers as I race over to the desk for Daphne's letter. "Please deliver this message to Lady Daphne Cortwright, she and her family have a townhouse in the city. See to it that she receives this with haste."

"As you wish, m'Lord," Finn replies and takes the letter with his index finger and thumb so as not to touch the blood on my hands. He bows again and gives me a soft smile before returning to the hall.

I look down at myself. I'm covered in blood. Sighing, I make my way into the bathing room and empty my pockets. Letters from Daphne, too soiled to keep, coins, a blade the size of my thumb and the pocket watch– *wait*. No. *The pocket watch isn't here.*

Frantically, I rip my shirt and trousers off and turn everything inside out. I scour the floor and find nothing. *It's not here.* I pull on a robe laying at the foot of the bed and fling open the doors to my chambers and race down the hall. I try retracing my steps until I get to the castle entrance.

The stone outside the castle gates glisten under the light of the moon and torches, and I spend an hour searching desperately for the watch. I know it isn't here, but I continue to look anyway.

I think about Madoria, and running from the barrage of arrows, of running from Dops in the trenches, pulling Calix through Shadow Grove, the battle in the valley. I rack my brain, trying to force myself to remember where it fell, but it's no use. I have no idea where I might have lost it.

I sit against the hedges of the courtyard with my head in my hands and cry. I know it's not feasible, or even rational, but I have to get the watch back. It's the only thing that connects me to Vera. It's the only thing in this or any realm that gives me hope. Without it, Vera will truly be lost to me, lost to time, forever. My chest feels like it's being ripped apart as tears blur my vision.

～

Esven was right. The following morning I'm debriefed on some of the inner workings of the Kingdom, and I meet so many advisors and counselors my head spins. The Knights have given intel on Doppelganger sightings and I send men to various rumored locations around Prinav to dispel them. Esven seems satisfied with my delegations even though I notice his jaw tick every time a council member addresses me as Regent.

I spend nearly the entire day in meetings, and receive frequent updates that the King is stable but not yet coherent. My nerves are shot by the evening, but I'm pleased to join Calix, Narah, and Arden for dinner. I go to Calix's chambers for the meal as he's still limping from his injuries, and it's a great excuse to get away from Esven and my privy council for a few hours.

"Do you remember the pocket watch?"

"Yes, of course." Narah replies.

Calix flicks his eyes to mine. "What about it?"

"I've lost it," I say. "Just wondered if you remember seeing it anywhere. It's the only thing I have from–from Vera."

"I haven't seen it."

Narah wrings her hands. "We need to find it before Sol does."

"I know," I reply. "But I can't just leave Brone Castle to go on a mission to find it."

"You're right," Narah says. "But you *can* get a team to search for it, I'm sure they can look around. Want me to fetch Finn for you?"

Calix shakes his head. "It's too suspicious, and much too late to send out a team for this. Too many questions."

"I can't shake the feeling that it's how I'm going to find Vera," I say.

"I wish we could leave right now, but I'm injured and you're stuck here, Lieve. There's nothing we can do about this tonight. Send a team out tomorrow morning, I'm sure it can be found." Calix looks out the window. "Besides, if Sol were here, we'd know it by now."

I nod. Cal's right. I'll assemble a small team tomorrow. Sol would have burnt down the whole of Prinav if he were here, I've got time to find it. Calix moves his leg around and I can tell he's trying not to show how much pain he's in. "How are you feeling?"

"I'm okay." He winces as he finds a more comfortable position for his leg and Narah pets his hair. "The better question is, how are *you* feeling?"

I lean back in my chair and think. *How am I?* Panicked. Tired. "I'm dealing."

Narah gives me a sad smile. "We all are."

No one else says a word the rest of the meal. Narah seems like she's on the verge of tears, Arden barely touches the food on his plate, and Calix is more preoccupied with his wound than his dinner, or family, or me. Finn and a few other servants clean up after us and I bid them all goodnight before returning to my own chambers.

Daphne arrives two days later with her father and two younger sisters. I've only gotten glimpses of her in the halls because every second of my days are now riddled with endless meetings. I've used Finn to pass notes between us, and we plan to meet for an evening stroll as soon as I can get a moment to spare. My heart feels lighter during today's Dop debriefing, for tonight I'm planning to ask for Daphne's hand in marriage.

Before my next appointment, I find myself in my chambers playing the violin and letting the sad, slow, music seep into my bones. The music comforts and excites me and I get a thrill each time the bow slides against the strings. Finn rustles around in the other room and I catch him humming my tune as he works. My lip twitches with the hint of a smile and I continue to play and play and play.

A knock on the door interrupts the music, and Finn nods to me before opening the grand double doors. "Good day."

"Good day," says a middle aged man wearing an elaborate snow white wig. His eyes turn to me and he walks in without an invitation. "I take it you're Oleander?"

I narrow my eyes. "Yes."

The man reaches into the inside pocket of his jacket and pulls out a small stack of paper. I recognize my handwriting and suddenly it hits me– this is Daphne's father. With this newfound knowledge I bow deeply to him and try to smile. He doesn't return the expression.

"Correct me if I'm wrong, but are you Lord Cortwright?"

"I am. And as Daphne Cortwright's father, I'm going to request that you cease your correspondence with her."

"What if I were to marry her?"

"Out of the question."

I feel heat burn in my chest, my neck, my face. How can he say that? Daphne and I are meant for each other. He can't possibly mean that, *can he*? "And why is that, sir?"

"Because Regent doesn't mean King." He puffs his chest. "And gods willing our great King prevails, you'll return to being a common soldier."

"I would be a Knight, *sire–*"

"Knight. Not Lord. Knight's fight and die, Lords have wealth and safety. I respect your current position, *m'lord*, but this is *my* decision. Good day." And with that Lord Cortwright turns on his heel and leaves my chambers, taking my dignity with him.

General Tanin Good, Deceased. Assassin Vlori Molik,
Deceased. Private Hunter Flemming, Deceased.
Captain Muri DeLuca, Deceased. Private Jess Bricker,
Deceased. Private Kane Valoreti, Deceased. Healer,
Cassidy Lin, Deceased.
– *Hode Casualty Roll*

CHAPTER 19
VERA

Lord Calix Bramford did call on me. He sent so many flowers to my chambers that Evalie had to call in a few of her maid friends to take some of them away to their Ladies, and it still left me with more flowers than I could count. It feels strange, wonderful, but strange, to have a man show me interest. It got me thinking again of marriage, and if Lieve still wants me to marry for security, or if I'm now allowed the opportunity to marry for love.

"Are you married?" I ask Evalie.

She stops folding linens and looks at me, her brown eyes hardening for just a second or two before she replies, "I was." She then continues to fold, but I notice her hands shaking slightly.

I stand beside her and pick up a bath towel and fold in three's, like my mother used to.

"Put that down," she scolds.

"I can fold a towel, Evalie."

She huffs and pulls out more linens. "My husband died in battle a few years ago. He was–" her breath shudders–, "Muri was kind. And he wouldn't believe it in a million years that I'd end up working for the Princess."

"Where did you work before?"

"I was a seamstress, and a damn good one."

"What brought you here, then?"

Evalie takes our stack of laundry and places them where they go, in the wardrobe, the bathing room, the sitting rooms, and then drops the basket by the entrance to the chambers. "I don't want to speak ill of anyone."

"I won't judge you." I say. And I wouldn't.

"The Matisse family owned their own shop on the same street in Wixle, that's another city near Teyrnas, love–," she says and fluffs my bed pillows. "Well, my shop was doing a good deal better than theirs, and they ran me out of business. I tried getting a job at other shops, but they paid off every other tailor so they wouldn't hire me. Muri and I lost our livelihoods and we had to sell our apartment, but the money we were paid didn't last as long as we'd wanted it to. We moved closer and closer to Prinav, eventually landing in Barault looking for work. We couldn't find any, so Muri joined the Hode. He died just six months later. Eventually I asked the Matisse's to hire me themselves, but when I arrived on my first day of work in their shop–"

I walk to the other side of the bed and straighten the comforter without a word.

"--well. I got so angry about them taking my shop and my home, and I was still so heartbroken about Muri that I slapped Odette, the Lady of the shop, right square on the cheek. You see, she insulted my work and offered peasants wages for my time. I thought I'd be hung for hitting her, but a lovely young woman saw to it that I got out of trouble. She sent her maid, Marguerite, to fetch me and talked your brother into giving me work here at the castle for a fair wage. I accepted, and I've worked here ever since."

I reach across the bed and take her hand. "I'm glad Lieve was able to help you."

Evalie squeezes. "As am I."

I try to help Evalie clean, but she only allows me to do light work. I have no more tasks for the day, so I decide to find Lieve and see what he's doing.

"I think I'll try and spend time with Lieve today," I say.

"Very good! I'm sure he would be delighted. It's been such a burden on his heart without you, everyone can tell." Evalie then picks up the linen basket from the ground and curtseys to me before leaving my chambers.

I walk over to the vanity and pull the pocket watch out of the jewelry box. Maybe I'll try and get some tools and tinker with it today if Lieve's busy. I don't dare open it to look at myself. Seeing my Doppelganger in this watch, and then again in the mirror at the inn was enough to make me heed Arden's warnings.

Church bells ring loudly, and I snap my head to look out the window. I've been told there's an enormous abbey dedicated to Gwen on the estate, and I'm sure that's where the ringing came from. There must be a mass of some sort happening. Curiosity pulls me to the windowsill and I look out and watch for people walking in a similar direction. I see a handful walking through the hedges, Arden and his red-head included.

I feel oddly possessive watching them. Lieve taught me to look at body language, and I can tell that Arden and this woman are very close. Their bodies always lean towards each other, and they are handsy with one another. Actually, only the woman is handsy. She brushes hair from his face, pats his arm, leans her head on his shoulder; while Arden locks his elbow respectfully and guides her through the garden shrubbery. They're friendly, even intimate. *But are they a couple?* I can't tell, and that frustrates me to my very core.

I stuff the watch in my pocket and march out of my room. Time to forget about Arden and the woman and move on from any thoughts about him. Hell, he doesn't seem interested in how I'm fairing, he hasn't even said hello since walking me to that disastrous drunken breakfast.

Frustration fuels my self guided tour of the castle corridors, and I get lost. At the end of the hall I see Finn, so I shout for him. Finn bows deeply and smiles as I jog up to his side.

"M'lady," he says. "How can I be of service?"

"I was wanting to spend time with my brother, have you seen him?"

"I haven't, but I can help you find him if you'd like."

"Yes, thank you."

"Nonsense." A voice purrs from behind me. "I'd be happy to assist the Princess."

I turn to see Calix. He wears riding leathers and a white tunic with the sleeves rolled to the forearms. One of his sleeves loosens and Calix uses one hand and rolls it back up, his muscles flexing as he turns his wrist. My mouth nearly waters.

Finn nods and leaves Calix and I alone in the halls, and I don't know what to do with myself. "The flowers you sent were lovely."

"Not nearly as lovely as you, Vera dear."

My face flushes. Calix is charming. I feel so awkward with him, he's so handsome and confident, and I'm not used to this sort of attention. Calix gestures to walk with him, and I do. He tells me that Lieve will be in his meeting nearly the rest of the day and I try not to, but I know I'm pouting. We walk by numerous paintings on the walls and Calix tells me about them. He talks about what the paintings depict, the artists, and where they came from. Most are portraits of forgotten monarchs, the gods, or the Prinavian scenery.

Calix winces the longer we walk and I notice him rub his leg when he thinks I'm not looking. "What else do you want to know, Vera dear," he says while slowing his pace.

"Are you okay?" I ask.

"Old battle wound," he answers. "I'm fine."

I furrow my brow.

"My leg pinches from time to time. I'm used to it. Besides–," he leans in close to me and whispers, "I don't want to look weak in front of a pretty girl."

I try to hide my smile, but I know I'm failing miserably.

Then Calix turns to me, "so where have you been all these years?"

"That's the thing," I reply, "for me, it's only been a few days."

"I've never heard of that before. Lieve used to visit all the time and he aged normally."

So it's true. Lieve had come here before, without me. *Damn him.* "What do you mean, he visited all the time?"

Calix stops suddenly and mutters, "it's not my story to tell. But he visited Prinav for many years, well before you went missing."

"So, you're saying that not only are all the fairytales real, but Lieve got to *experience* this place? For *years* before our jump?"

"He had to come alone, Vera," Calix pleads. "It wasn't safe. The war lasted for so long, he couldn't chance bringing you here."

I stew in my anger, thinking up things to yell at Lieve when I see him next. I would have died to be a part of this place, and I can't believe he actually kept it from me, and was going to continue the lie. I don't care if it was dangerous, anything would have been better than what we had. *Anything* would have been better than Adamston.

We talk about Lieve, and of the war, and of Prinav in general. I get lost in the tales, saddened and angry that Lieve didn't allow me to be a part of this incredible world. Angry that he hid it from me. But the more we talk, the more I understand. Lieve just wanted to keep us stable, and he would try anything to do so; even if it meant leaving me.

Music plays from behind a door as we pass by. The song is the same song I heard in the city, and I realize now that it's the same song Lieve used to hum while he worked in the shop. I stop to listen and Calix keeps walking a few paces before he realizes I'm not next to him.

"Vera, what's the matter?"

"Nothing. I just know this tune."

Calix smiles. "Lieve got to pursue his music. He opened a grand theater in Barault, and constructed an exact, but much smaller replica, here on the castle grounds."

I press my ear to the door. "That's so wonderful for him."

"That tune–," he jerks his chin to the door–, "he wrote it for you."

Tears well in my eyes. Of course he wrote me that song. Who am I to judge Lieve? He really did everything he could for us; and although he did it the wrong way, I know his heart was in the right place.

Calix and I listen to the musicians rehearse for hours out in the hall. We sit on the ground with our backs against the wall and talk, and I find that he's easy to talk to. Friendly. Funny. It's not hard to fall for him quickly, and I find that I don't mind falling for him. I yawn and Calix offers to walk me back to my chambers, and I take him up on his offer.

When we reach the corridor to my room, I see Arden standing at my door, hand up and ready to knock. All of a sudden I feel embarrassed, like I'm caught doing something I shouldn't be doing. I don't know why I feel that way. I can do what I want, I'm unattached. It's Arden who should be embarrassed, coming to my chambers so late, and possibly with another woman waiting on his return.

He spots Calix and I together and I see him clench his fists. *What is his problem?* Calix doesn't seem to notice, or at least, he doesn't care. We come within a few feet of my door and Arden shoulders Calix and storms past us.

Calix just sighs. He then turns and smiles at me, and takes my hand in his. He winks as he presses his lips to my knuckles. "Goodnight, Vera dear."

I smirk at him. "Goodnight."

Calix walks in the opposite direction of Arden and I go inside my chambers to tell Evalie everything about my day with Calix. I look around each room of the apartments, but Evalie isn't here. I huff and slide my boots off, and then get ready to unlace my dress when I get a knock on my door.

I tie a knot and dash to the door thinking it's Evalie; or maybe even Calix wanting to prolong our goodnights, but what I find is a surly Arden.

"Yes?"

"Calix isn't right for you."

I scoff. *Is he serious?* I can feel my blood start to boil. Who is he to say who is and isn't right for me? He has no stake in the matter. I'm speechless watching Arden's fists continue to clench and unclench as I silently glare at him.

"Vera, listen," he says. "You don't know him–"

"I don't know your red-head either."

He looks taken aback. "That's besides the point."

"No, I think that's the entire point."

"You're not listening to me."

"Get some sleep, Arden. Bitterness doesn't suit you," I say, and close the door, leaving Arden alone in the hall.

Just one drop.

– Warning from the Seelie Fae

CHAPTER 20

LIEVE

A rden is a great kid. Over the next few months, I train him day and night. He's becoming a skilled swordsman, and he was already a talented archer. Training him gives me something to focus on that isn't Vera or Daphne, or Daphne's father. I've accepted my role as Regent, but responsibility weighs heavily on me.

In our sixth month of training I teach Arden how to throw hatchets. I have an assortment of sizes, all laid in a neat row. I grab one in each hand. These feel good. They could split open a skull easily if the right spot is hit. I let the weight settle in my grip, spinning them, letting them find that perfect balance.

The chill of winter arrives, and frost covers the ground. Arden hasn't worn anything but black since moving into Brone Castle, though the formal mourning period for his family has passed. I'm hoping by spring I'll see him in something other than black.

He had a birthday last week, fifteen years old. The age I was when I first discovered Prinav. Arden didn't want to celebrate, but Narah insisted that he leave his chambers for something other than weaponry lessons and tutoring. I agreed even though I understand how Arden feels. My heart is in mourning for Vera, but I can't wear the colors of grief in court. With the Doppelganger threat gone, there's men to spare to search for Vera, and the watch. A contingent roams Shadow Grove in pursuit, and Arden has asked to join the group.

Narah wasn't enthusiastic about it, but Calix and I assured her Arden would meet more people, learn more skills, and be outside in the fresh air. With his melancholy, it was hard to argue that his request should be denied. I could tell that Calix and Narah seemed icy to each other after the conversation, but it seemed like there was more to their demeanor than Arden's surliness.

Arden grabs one of the remaining hatchets that I have laid on a deer hide on the ground. The crunch of snow under his boots sounds like bones grinding against each other. I grip my hatchets tighter and then fling one into the center of the target nearly one hundred feet away and raise my eyebrows at Arden when it sticks.

Arden's jaw clenches in response to the challenge. He reminds me so much of Vera, the way he's determined to impress me, to not let me get the better of him. He moves in front of me and places his feet in the stance I taught him. Slightly bending his knees, he raises his hatchet behind his head and practices the step of the toss a few times. When he goes to throw the hatchet, it slips from his gloved hand and spins top over bottom twenty feet to the right, landing in a thorn bush.

I can see anger bubbling up as he rips the gloves from his hands and throws them on the ground. I wince as I watch him root around in the thorns, tiny pricks making delicate cuts on his hand. Arden doesn't wince at all. He wipes the dotted blood across his cloak and returns to throw the hatchet once more. This time it lands right next to mine, so close the blades touch.

"Do you know what's going on with Calix and my sister?"

I give him a puzzled look. "What do you mean?"

"They've been arguing."

I throw another hatchet and it lands on the target underneath the other weapons lodged in the wood. "Is it bad enough that I need to intervene?"

Arden shakes his head silently and looks back up the hill towards the castle. Someone calls out to us–Daphne. My heart sings. She wears a gown and cape of cardinal red, the sight a stark contrast against the white snow. I imagine each note I would play as her song. Passionate. Dramatic, yet soft. Daphne glides down the hill to us while Arden fetches the hatchets from the target.

"Sorry to interrupt Arden's training, but I need a word."

Daphne and I still wrote to one another after I met her father, but then the letters faded, and eventually stopped coming at all. Neither one of us mentioned that we stopped writing letters, nor do we mention our intimate history. Daphne thought it best that we wean ourselves from each other because the King seemed to be doing better, *thank the gods*. But that means I can't be with her, her father wouldn't allow it. A return to Knighthood ensures our future together is over. Daphne and I have been overly cautious around each other since that day, and I hate it. I don't know how to act around her, and now she's become extremely formal.

"That's fine," I reply, "what's the rush?"

I barely register her answer. My eyes focus on her soft lips and the pink resting in her cheeks and on her nose from the cold. Her eyes sparkle when the sun peeks from behind the clouds, casting her in a single ray of light and proving to me that she's the embodiment of art itself. There is nothing I've ever witnessed as stunning as her, and it breaks my heart not to tell her so.

"My sources have found something that may be of use for you."

Before I can respond, Arden joins us with an arm full of blades wrapped inside the deer hide. "So, I guess that means that I don't train today and I have extra lessons with the snobs, wanna-be Knights, and that daughter of Benito Matisse," Arden whines, sounding exactly like his fifteen years. "She's such a *bitch*."

Daphne gives him a sharp look, but he just rolls his eyes and stomps past us and up the hill.

"He's getting out of hand," Daphne says to me, like it's *my* fault he's angry.

"How should I handle him?" I ask. "He's not my son. This is a problem Narah and Calix need to attend to."

"You know they're having issues, Lieve. Narah is just as distraught about her parents' deaths, but she's not behaving this way."

"That's what she tells *you*."

She folds her arms. "Has Calix said different?"

I shake my head and then throw my hand up in Arden's direction. "It's not going to matter soon, he's joining my Hunters."

"Hunters?"

I puff my chest a little. "Hunters, to go to Shadow Grove and look for Vera."

Daphne's face hardens and I know she wants to argue. I know she thinks it's a bad idea for an angry kid to traipse around the forest looking for a lost girl. I know she thinks Vera's probably dead and I'm putting my men in danger for nothing. Whatever she's thinking though, she doesn't say it. Moments like these make me thankful I'm the Regent. It's much harder for people to scold me for my choices.

Arden shouts when he gets to the top of the hill. "And the Priest tutoring us is deranged!"

Daphne closes her eyes and sighs. "Let's go."

I follow her around the back of the castle and down the pitch-black stairs that lead to the dungeons. Daphne snaps her fingers and a small yellow ring glows on her hand, illuminating a bubble of soft light around us.

The dungeons are frigid cold, even colder than the brisk winter air above ground. I rub my hands together and blow my hot breath on my fingers before stopping at the end of a long corridor. Daphne then snaps her fingers, extinguishing the ring's light.

She whispers, a spell, or ward, and the wooden door clicks open, letting us enter into a tiny stone room. Oil lamps flicker on by themselves, casting an orange light into the dark space. There are stacks of paper in the corner, and bowls full of potions on the wobbly wooden table in the center of the room.

"Sit." She orders.

I sit on a stool and lean against the wall. Daphne pulls a vial from her pocket and gingerly places it on the wooden table. The glass is clear and shaped like a raindrop with a flat bottom. Inside is the same bluish liquid that leaked out of the Lopter tree when the Fae severed the trunk with their crystal sword.

I reach for it out of curiosity and Daphne slaps my hand away. She regards it skeptically. "A Fae friend gave me this vial. The last person who consumed it was given the gift of prophecy. But, the visions tormented them, even if they came true. He went mad very quickly." Daphne's eyes lock on mine. "They witnessed a woman who sounds to me like how you describe Vera."

My mouth goes dry. "Wha–"

"My contact said the person who drank Lopter's blood saw a young woman with raven black hair wandering through the forest alone and scared."

Lopter's blood. Lopter's blood is in the bottle, Lopter, the god who separated us. I stand up quickly, the stool tumbling over. I reach for the bottle and Daphne snatches my wrist.

"Just one drop," she warns.

I unscrew the ivory cap and swirl the blood. It fizzes just a little and smells of mud and salt water. Taking a deep breath, I hold the bottle above my head and allow one thick drop to land on my outstretched tongue. It has no taste, but it's as thick as tree sap. I swallow, the blood coating my tongue in gooey nothingness. It seems to get thicker as it travels down my throat, and I panic.

Taking in a breath is slightly difficult and I shove my hand inside my mouth to scrape off the layer of blue slime. I drop hard, my knees aching as they hit the stone beneath me, but the pain is nothing to the fear of suffocation. I reach for Daphne but she's gone. I'm in a black void.

Someone reaches back, but it's not Daphne, it's Vera. Vera's reaching for me, her fingers wiggling in desperation. I try to grab her, but my hand goes through hers.

Then smoke billows around a man dressed in black robes. *Sol.* He's battling another man with pale blue skin, white hair, and pink rams horns. That must be Lopter, for he's the same coloring as the Lopter tree. Vera floats above the ground with her eyes closed while the two fight. Sol lifts Lopter in the air with one hand, choking him. Lopter then throws a strand of sparks at Vera, cracking it like a whip and Vera disappears.

It looks like Sol is going to kill Lopter for what he did, but then everything flashes a blinding blue-white. The visions flicker rapidly. Vera running in a forest. Vera holding up the pocket watch. A man laying frozen on the ground. Vera with black eyes. Flagstones red with blood. A mirror in Gwen Abbey covered in blood and Vera screaming at her groom for help.

I blink and I'm back in the dungeons, slick with sweat. My head is on something softer than tiles– I look up into Daphne's soft eyes and realize she's pulled me into her lap. She lets out a massive sigh of relief and curls the damp hair plastered to my forehead behind my ear.

"Thanks to Siva," Daphne murmurs.

"Vera," I croak, my throat parched, as though the Lopter blood had dried it out and made it as sticky as the sap of the tree. "I saw Vera."

Daphne helps me sit up and leans me against a wall before fetching some water and helping me swallow it. Though her care warms a part of me, I have no time for it. I have seen Vera and I need to find her.

"You said the visions come true," I say.

Daphne nods, but her brow is creased with concern. "I also said the blood torments the drinker."

I can easily imagine. The water soothes my throat, but as my head stops pounding, I'm left with an intense craving. I lick my lips and find the texture of the sap remains. Euphoria fills me to the point that my core gets hot and the threads on my trousers tighten. *Shit, that's better than liquor.* Lopter's blood hazes my ability to think clearly, it only has room for more. More blood. *I need more.* I can feel an energy under my skin, flowing in my veins. I feel *good.*

"What did you see?" Daphne asks.

What did I see? I saw Vera and blood and the watch and—my cravings disrupt my thoughts, the visions become fuzzy.

"I saw Vera, Daphne. She's alive. Let's try again, let me find her."

Daphne narrows her eyes and slips the vial back into her pockets. "You were out for half an hour. We'll already be missed in the palace, we can try again later."

My fingers twitch to go after the bottle, but I am practiced in ignoring cravings. "Fine. Then you won't object to the Hunters continuing their search?" I ask, unable to temper my emotions now that I have proof of Vera's life.

"I'm sure they'll be useful to keep Darkthings and Doppelgangers at bay," Daphne says measuredly. "But I'm afraid that the forest, or Lopter himself, will not reveal Vera until she's ready to be found."

"Vera's lucky I have more faith in her than you do," I say, stalking toward the door of the secret room. "What if she dies in the forest?"

"Perhaps *I* have more faith in her ability to defend herself," Daphne points out. "And we know she didn't die. The visions will come true."

I blink, seeing those flashes again. A man in the snow. Vera's Dop. Blood. She might survive the forest, but what world is she walking into?

Our argument ends once we reach the snow above our secret chamber, and we return to the castle in silence. As frustrated as I am, I'm grateful for the clue Daphne has dangled before me. We round the corner and stop before one of the castle parlor doors and I take her hand.

"Thank you, Daphne. Please come find me after your family is gone, the search must continue."

She nods, and Esven opens the parlor doors. Behind him are two teenage girls that look strikingly like Daphne. Each with the same copper hair, plaited in a crown around their heads and the same slender figure. Standing with his back turned to the door is Daphne's father, smoking from a long silver pipe.

"Lady Daphne! And Sir Lieve, what a surprise."

I'm as surprised to see Esven as he is to see me. What business could he have with Lord Cortwright? But then I see how his eyes flicker to Daphne, how he bows and catches her hand, then brings it to his lips. Daphne smiles politely at the gesture, and consciously I must stop my fists from clenching.

"It's lovely to see Lord Cortwright again, I've been hoping to pick his brain about how to choose a bride. I'm sure such a topic might be interesting to you as well–" Behind Esven the girls giggle.

Daphne's father turns around, takes one look at me, then scoffs before taking another long drag on his pipe. I am King Regent, regardless of my desire to be so, and even that is not enough to gain his respect.

"I'm afraid I have other business to attend to." I give a nod to Daphne's sisters and they giggle again, and I ignore Cortwright.

"Without our Regent, I guess I'll have to do for entertainment then," Esven exclaims, looking smug

Daphne smiles tightly at Esven and then at her father. "I'm sure your company is adequate, Lord Esven."

Esven looks at Daphne like a fox in a hen house. The thought of him and Daphne together makes me want to throttle him. Daphne curtseys to me, Esven gives me a little bow; and then I turn from the parlor, the doors slamming shut behind me as I go. I imagine what Esven's head would look like on a pike. *What would happen if I killed the Grand Vizor?*

CHAPTER 21

VERA

The tea Evalie pours is different from any tea I've had before. Evalie says it's a family recipe as she sprinkles red dust. She adds more spices I've never heard of, causing the liquid to turn a rich brown inside the white cup. Evalie's been a patient teacher in all things Prinav, and I'm so grateful for her company. Lieve is so busy, and so is Calix, so I've become Evalie's shadow. She had to do some work at the laundry house this morning, so, until she was finished there, I've been busy tinkering with the pocket watch and waiting for her return with the tea.

I sit on the windowsill and watch the people milling around the gardens and sip my drink. It's spicy and sweet and hot and perfect. Everything about Brone Castle is perfect. I know the Darkthings and Doppelgangers are dangerous, I've seen what they can do, but on the whole Prinav seems…well…lovely. It makes me frustrated all over again that Lieve didn't tell me about coming here. I've come to terms that he believed it wasn't safe, but I can't shake my resentment about it easily.

I spy a group of young ladies giggling and talking at the edge of the hedges. Then a man brushes by them, his black cloak billowing behind. The girls stop talking and shrink against the vegetation. I can tell by the way the man walks that it's Arden.

Once Arden has passed them, they burst into laughter and giggles again, the boldest of the group even pointing at Arden and pretending to faint in one of the other girls' arms. I was right in thinking there are women who would like Arden. However, it seems that even though Arden might be physically desirable to the girls with reckless spirits, he has a reputation for being someone you don't want to cross paths with. I laugh to myself at all these girls fawning over him when none of them stand a chance when the red-head has all his attention.

"Oh my, my." Evalie chuckles.

"What?"

She smirks. "You're smitten."

"No, that's not what–"

"I know what smitten looks like." Evalie chuckles again. "And that's you."

I open my mouth to argue, but then I hear my name being called from the foyer of my apartments. Evalie brushes her skirts and straightens her back before walking into the other room, me just a few steps behind her. Lieve stands in the foyer, looking pale and tired. Dark circles haunt his light eyes, but he perks up when he sees me.

"Ah, there she is!"

"And there you are," I say.

Lieve smiles and taps his lips with his index finger. "How would you like to see a show in my grand theater tonight?"

My heart leaps. I could attend something fancy! "Oh Lieve, I would love that."

"I thought so. I cannot attend the show tonight–"

I cross my arms. What is he getting at?

"Don't pout, Vera. It's unbecoming."

"I just thought you were inviting me to come along with you. I don't want to go alone."

"You won't be. I've asked Calix to join you. It's a charity event and many of those in court are too busy to attend, or they're simply uninterested in charity. So, I need a proxy to make an appearance on behalf of the crown."

"So, I'll be going alone? With Calix?" I ask.

Lieve picks at his fingernails and then raises an eyebrow at me. "Unless you'd rather not attend."

"No, no. I'll go." I say. "Only because it's for charity."

"Oh, of course," Lieve laughs. "For charity."

Lieve tells me that he'll inform Calix that I've agreed to go to the event and then gives me a little bow before leaving my chambers. I'm so excited to go and my mind races with thoughts of Calix. Did he ask to go with me? Does this mean Calix is pursuing me? My pulse races. Evalie turns to go back into the other room and playfully jabs her elbow at me before teasing, "nope, not smitten at all."

I roll my eyes and look back out the window at the group of girls still gossiping near the gardens and my stomach gets tied in knots.

I meet Calix at the entrance to the palace theater. He wears formal attire of dark grays and whites. His jacket has silver threads and has sharp spikes around the collar and where the sleeve connects to the vest. My gown matches, dark gray skirts, silver embroidery, and spiked diamonds sewn into the neckline. I catch a glimpse of us in the window and we look positively dangerous together.

I take heed of Arden's warning again and don't stare for too long. I'm not sure if windows count as a mirrored surface, and I don't want anything spoiling this night. A doorman calls for us; pulling me from my reverie, and leads us to our seats in a private box.

My jaw drops when I finally get a view of the theater. It's enormous. The seats are all a deep red, plush velvet, and so soft your bottom sinks in the cushion. Everything glows with the soft lights of candles and lamps strategically placed around. I take in the stage, large red velvet curtains hide the scene behind, but I spot blue tiles inlaid in the deep mahogany floorboards.

In our seats are programs, and even they are exquisite. The parchment is so soft it feels like linen, and in gold lettering reads the various Acts. I can't read the language, so Calix reads the names of the songs to me, but says he doesn't want to tell me what the play is about. He says it will ruin the surprise. I bounce with anticipation in my seat and scan out over the large crowd. We seem to have the best seats in the house. The sky box, center stage.

"The theater in the city is ten times the size of this one," Calix says.

"I can't imagine." I look around the space, dazzled at the beauty.

All around, guests fill the seats in the audience and I notice that Arden has entered the theater. I also notice that the people he passes on the way to his seat shy away from him. I understand why they do it, he doesn't exactly exude a friendly demeanor, but I can't help but wonder if it hurts his feelings. The more I watch him, the more I believe he doesn't seem to care. He's barely looked at anyone around him.

He takes his seat in his own private box, but he doesn't have anyone to sit with. Then I notice the interactions Calix has with people are much different. The people bow or wave to him, and he nods or waves back in return. Several voices shout his name and he shouts back with an audible smile in his voice. I can tell he likes the attention, and many of the ladies around us love doting it out. Calix was made for the people.

Many of the people wave or point at me, too. I smile back, and most of them seem friendly towards me. However, there are several young women, and with what seems to be their parents, who scowl. They whisper with narrowed eyes and clenched teeth. They're barely hiding their disdain and jealousy behind forced smiles. I'm sure many of those young women had the hopes of gaining Calix's favor and entering the court.

The thought makes me grin. If I play my cards right, I might just get everything Lieve and I have ever worked for. There's potential for an entire Kingdom to be jealous of what I have instead of the other way around for once. Calix whispers to me, pointing out family members of the entertainers, nobles I'll meet at my welcome dinner, and a few students of Lieve's music school who were just accepted due to Lieve's scholarships for the underprivileged. I've never been so proud and amazed with Lieve.

Ushers quiet everyone down, and the red curtain on the stage opens, revealing a woman with long, dark hair, standing alone with a spotlight pointed at her. The crows gasps in unison. The woman wears a dress so translucent it looks like water, and when she moves her hips to take a step, I swear it flows. It's so quiet you could hear a pin drop, and then–Lieve's tune plays on a lone violin.

The woman wanders around on the stage and I think she's supposed to be Dia. Then dozens of candles are lit below the stage, illuminating an entire orchestra. Quietly from the back of the stage, a handsome young man with blonde hair appears. The music picks up a passionate, romantic melody, and I watch every moment of the show in utter amazement. It's Dia's story. I can't understand a single note the woman sings, but I can feel every emotion that lives in the soul with her words.

I clap with all the others when Dia defies her parent's orders to wed Sol. I cheer as Dia kisses Oriel. Tears stream down my face as I watch Oriel's demise at Sol's hand. By the end of the show, I'm completely exhilarated and drained at the same time. It was incredible, and it was all Lieve's doing.

"I am so proud of Lieve." Calix says, mirroring my thoughts.

I wipe my eyes and smile at him. "No more than I am."

We are nearly the last ones out of the theater, and I find myself looking around for Arden, but he isn't there. Calix smiles at me and I shake my head and just focus on him instead. We talk for another hour or so, strolling around the grounds in the dark. Calix makes me laugh. He's in tune with what I want, what I need. I hang on to his every word and crave his melodic voice. I'm not ready to sleep, but he walks me back to my chambers, stopping in front of the door.

"I had a wonderful time tonight, you're a magical woman." He says.

My cheeks flush. "I had a great time, too."

He runs his hand up my arm and my breathing quickens. I've never been touched like this. Calix's honey eyes sparkle and he grins at me. I trace his jawline and imagine what his stubble would feel like against my skin. Then his fingers inch around my waist, pulling me close to him. Calix leans in, and I lift my chin and close my eyes, nervous, but ready for whatever comes next.

I thread my fingers through his tousled hair and part my lips. I feel Calix's muscles tighten and my knees wobble underneath me, just as a servant walks by and snickers, breaking us apart.

Calix steps back from me, surveying me with hungry eyes as the servant makes his way around the corner of the hall. I can feel my heart beat wildly against my ribs. I'm flustered and the way the corner of Calix's lip tugs into a devilish grin makes me yearn to have his hands on me again. Two more servants walk by and the younger one, a girl around thirteen, blushes so fiercely her ears glow red.

Calix takes my hand and pulls me in close again after they pass. He whispers softly in my ear, "Vera dear, I must bid you ado or the servants are going to label me as a scoundrel."

"We wouldn't want that now, would we?"

He laughs and presses his lips against my knuckles, and then bows to me before saying goodnight. I rush inside and run straight to my bed and jump up and down on the mattress until my legs exhaust me. Without even changing, I climb under the covers.

As I'm falling asleep, my eyes flick to the jewelry box containing the pocket watch and I smile. I'm so grateful for this new beginning, and now I'm not sure if I want to fix the watch or not. I don't know what magic it holds, and I'm afraid it could take all of this away from me, just as it took my old life from me once before. I have a chance at a new life, a great life. Finally, I might get my fairy tale.

17,345 Pence Donated By Royce Valeti. 5,432 Pence Donated by Soleil Toun. 541 Pence Donated by the Matisse Family. 143 Meckles Donated by Sir Lieve Oleander from the Royal Coffers...

— Gwen Abbey Restoration Fund, Donation Log

CHAPTER 22

LIEVE

My back hurts. I've been sitting in this chair for three hours, carving runes into slats of wood for the library while my privy council argues about the most mundane problems. It's not fun, and it's not easy. I have to make decisions that will make the majority happy and I hate being Regent. I finish a rune I happened to create out of thin air during one of my lessons with Daphne, and smile to myself, pleased with the look of it.

"On a happier note," Esven says, "The Treasury has informed me that we are in a monetary surplus. Our generous benefactors of money and weaponry here in this room have strengthened our Kingdom, and with The Regent's skillful war tactics, the Doppelganger threat is steadily diminishing. But–"

"But what?" Asks one of my council members. He's a bright man of around thirty years old. His family owns stock in the spice trade with Madoria, ships for fishing and whaling, textiles from Teyrnas, and Tussian liquors. They have their foot in every open door on the continent, but they hide their enormous wealth behind charity work and good deeds.

"But, *Royce*, Prinavians are still scared. They are still upset that a foreigner sits on our throne, no matter if his choices are helping them. We need to show this court doesn't just care about protection, we care about the *people*."

Royce rolls up his sleeves revealing a tattoo winding around his bronze forearm. I can see the wheels of thought turning in his head and I'm grateful he's here. "Any ideas?"

Then a thought hits me and it burns deep in my chest. *Music.* Music always unites people, inspires them. Music makes people dreamers. My heart thunders in my chest. What if I can use this opportunity for myself? When King Niall is healed, I'll go back to the Hode... Unless...

"Music." I say.

Every head turns. Esven's jaw ticks, telling me I'm on the right track.

Royce smiles. "Elaborate."

"Well," I say. "Music is something people grasp onto. For religion, on the battlefield, in nursery rhymes. It's a universal equalizer. If we somehow brought music to everyone–"

"Genius!" Royce exclaims.

Esven scoffs. "So, how do we go about giving music to everyone in Prinav?"

"Scholarships." I answer and stand from my chair, excitement flooding my veins. "We turn the chapel in the west wing into a theater, and we bring students here to learn. We could house them, feed them, educate them. Brone Castle would be a beacon of charity and art."

"You mean *you* could."

"No," I say. "I just have a passion for the underprivileged, seeing as I *am* an underprivileged, orphaned, *foreigner*."

A man stands at the end of the table. He wears deep purple robes, the day dressings of a Sagart Priest. I recognize him as the Priest who gave me my test to get into the Hode. Matisse, I think he is. The Priest twirls his ice white hair around his finger and smirks at Esven. "You said it yourself, Esven, the citizens are upset about Lieve being on the throne. This will help."

"Won't the people be enraged at the thought of a holy temple being turned into a concert hall?" Esven growls.

Royce interjects, "not if we restore Gwen Abbey."

The Priest smiles. "That just might work."

Calix walks in at that exact moment and pulls out a chair next to mine, plopping down in it with a sullen expression. "The Abbey is beautiful but needs major improvements. If we have the funds, we should do it."

I smile at him and clap his shoulder, but he just nods at me and leans back in his chair. I sit back down and let Royce and the others discuss the details, and by the end of it, we have the plans drawn out for the two projects. I want to jump up and down with joy, but everytime I turn to Cal to express it, I can see that he's sinking deeper into anger. He and Narah must be at odds again.

Everyone leaves the room after the meeting, leaving Calix and I alone. I make my way to the window and stay quiet in the hopes that Calix will tell me what's ailing him. As I stare out, I see Narah and Daphne seated on a bench, Narah clearly crying. I glance over at Cal and he's wearing the same expression as he did when he first entered the meeting. This can't continue.

My impatience gets the better of me and I blurt out, "what's going on with you and Narah?"

"Nothing."

I sigh. So, it's going to be *that* type of conversation. "Calix–"

"What do you want to hear? That my marriage is imploding? That I'm a useless husband? Will that make you feel better about Daphne?"

I slap my hand on the table. "Enough."

Calix opens his mouth to argue, but then his lip quivers and he buries his head in his hands. "I'm sorry. It's just–she–she hates me, Lieve."

"She doesn't hate you." I say softly. "I just saw her with Daphne in the courtyard, just there in the window. And she looks distraught."

Calix sniffs and wipes his face with the back of his sleeve. "She won't even look at me. She thinks I'm having an affair."

I gasp. "What?"

"I've been coming to bed later and later. I know it looks suspicious, but I can't sleep."

"Why?"

"She's pregnant."

Everything stops. I don't know what to say.

"She's pregnant, Lieve, and she thinks I'm having an affair because of Arden."

I furrow my brow. "What did Arden say to her?"

"He said he thinks I'm cheating on her because I'm out so late, and Narah believes him. But Narah said she loves me and Arden screamed at her. He told her she was stupid for staying with a scoundrel like me and that she's defiling the Madrona name." Calix sneers. "He told her she'd be better off *dead* than to stay married to me. He's made her not what to be around me and I can't make her see the truth. She won't listen to me. She'll barely even sit in the same room."

"You're *not* having–"

"No. I'm not." Church bells ring loudly and Calix nearly jumps from his seat. "I didn't think they were going to start the renovations *today*."

"Look, I'm sorry I asked if you were being unfaithful."

He lifts his hand and walks over to the door. "It's okay." He then nods in Narah's direction and murmurs, "I just want the fighting to stop."

"It will."

He gives me a sad smile and closes the door behind him.

~

That evening I invite Arden to dinner so Calix and Narah can have a meal alone. I tell Arden that I've talked to Calix about the arguing, and I'm sure it will all pass soon enough. He just nods his head, barely listening, barely eating. I wish I knew if they'd really be okay. I wish I knew if Arden would be okay. I watch Arden, and he reminds me of Vera when she's in a bad mood. Stubborn.

The thought makes me start thinking about the future, and the ability to see the future. I start getting irritated that Daphne hasn't sought me out to try again with the Lopter blood. Without Sol's pocket watch, I have no other way to see if Vera's still alive. The blood might even be able to predict when, or if, Sol could arrive. Isn't that important enough to use it again?

Even though it's against Lord Cortwright's orders, I send Finn with a letter to Daphne's chambers after Arden leaves. I ask her for the blood, or to help me *see* Vera again. I beg her to teach me more of her word spells like I used when reading the runes all those months ago when I watched the ink jump from the pages like a flock of birds. I don't know if there's a spell that can help me, but I'll try anything. I know her magic that can help. I can feel it in my bones.

Grief is merciful to no one.
— *Roe Oleander*

CHAPTER 23

VERA

I reach for a wildberry and I bump hands with Calix. He nudges the bowl closer to me and I take a small handful and push the bowl back towards him. I lean my back on the wide oak and eat my berries as Calix tosses a few of them in the grass for the birds. They remind me of the pearl horses. Every bird flipping around the vicinity is also pearlescent, the tips of their feathers sparkling in the bright spring sun. They chirp happily and I'm happy too. I close my eyes as sun rays peek through the clouds and tree limbs and hit my face.

Calix notices the color of the birds too. "They're like Siva and Malsu, aren't they?"

"They are!" I exclaim.

"You know," Calix purrs. "Some say they can shapeshift."

I pop another berry in my mouth. "Wouldn't that be grand? To be able to turn into something entirely different? Something beautiful and free, like that?"

Calix turns to me, thinking to himself before answering. "I would imagine it would feel powerful; to know you can be and do anything."

"When I was riding with Arden in the forest, I sometimes thought the horse was smarter than an average horse."

Calix pretends to be shocked and pulls me to my feet. "Well, if those horses are the gods, we must ask them to let *us* shapeshift! Hurry, Vera dear!"

I laugh and run after Calix through the field and down the hill to the stables. Calix doesn't go inside, he darts to the back and I follow him with curiosity. He sneaks off around the corner and I jog to catch up with him. I'm nearing the turn, and then Calix snatches me and pulls me close to his chest, knocking our heads together. Calix laughs as he rubs his jaw, and I tentatively touch my forehead where we collided.

"Come here," Calix murmurs.

I step forward and Calix pulls me in again, this time without injury. I tilt my head up and get lost in the liquid gold of his eyes. His warm hand caresses the small of my back and I arch into him and lean my head back more. Calix kisses the soft skin of my neck, and then nibbles my earlobe. I can feel my heart race, but I find that I don't want to stop. I nuzzle my cheek to his, the stubble he had before now gone, and his skin soft against my own. Calix uses his fingertips to gently turn my head to face him and he gives me a slow, soft, kiss.

I blink and behind Calix stands Arden. I give a tight smile to Calix and nod that Arden is just behind him. Luckily Arden's back is turned as he brushes one of the horses and I pray that he didn't witness the kiss.

"Why, hello there." Calix pulls me by the hand towards Arden and the horse.

Arden snaps around to us and suddenly I feel guilty. My cheeks burn as Arden's eyes fall on our laced fingers while his posture stiffens and he nearly snarls at Calix. "What are you two doing here?"

"I could ask the same of you."

"I'm working to take care of things around here, unlike you." He snaps. His eyes dart to mine for a split second before glaring back at Calix.

"I admit I've been–*distracted*," Calix snaps back. "But your attitude is unnecessary. We both know I work hard to care for the Kingdom."

"Not it's women." Arden mutters under his breath.

"Excuse me?" Calix hisses.

"You didn't take care of Narah."

"Why would you bring her up like *that?*"

Arden hesitates for just a moment, and I can visibly see his body shaking with barely contained rage. "Because you've clearly forgotten her. You've moved on."

Calix's eyes darken. "I have *not* forgotten her."

"I certainly hope that's true." Arden responds coolly.

Calix opens his mouth to keep arguing, but I cut him off. "That's enough. Both of you."

Arden tosses the brush to the ground and marches towards Calix, and he drops my hand and stands his ground. I hold my breath and wait for a brawl. Arden looks as if he's going to fight him, but he doesn't. Instead, he shoulders past Calix. He doesn't stop to say anything to me either, and he doesn't look back as he heads towards the woods on the edge of the palace estate.

Calix then blows air out loudly and then brushes his hands on his trousers, turning to me. "I'm sorry about that."

The air is still thick with tension and I'm not sure how to respond. "What happened between you two?"

"I'd rather not get into it right now, if that's alright."

"Alright," I reply.

But it's not alright. I want to know what's happened. Why don't they like one another? I thought it was about me, and maybe a part of it is, but now I see there must be more history in their disdain.

Calix and I ride separate horses around the grounds, the pearlescent pair sticking close to each other. We talk of Siva and Malsu, and Calix tells me a grand story about the siblings making a golden trunk full of treasures and gifting it to Oriel.

I'm enjoying the story, but I have a hard time focusing on it. I want to ask again about the fight with Arden, but everything is so new with

Calix that I don't want to overstep. Calix has returned to his cheerful, charming, self, but I haven't returned to the curious, smitten, Vera that Calix expects. All I can think about is Arden and what he said about Narah. And for that matter, who *is* Narah? And what happened to her?

"What's troubling you? You seem off."

I bite my lip. "Who *is* Narah? "

He takes a deep breath and sighs. "My wife."

My heart sinks. *We kissed.* I kissed a *married* man. What is Lieve thinking, trying to set me up with him? I breathe in deeply from my nose as I fail to hide my disgust with him. No wonder Arden has been so surly with me.

I don't want to be rude, and somehow I manage to mutter, "you're married?"

Calix stops the horse. "She was murdered."

Our eyes meet and my resolve crumbles. "What?"

"A Doppelganger."

My eyes flick to Arden's footpath to the woods. I want to know more, but I'm not sure if it's my place to ask. This is a sensitive subject and I want to give it the respect it deserves.

I grab Calix's hand across the horses and give him a little squeeze, "I'm so sorry."

His hand is warm. I want to believe that he has feelings for me and that as bad as that is, there can still be hope. That people can get second chances, because Prinav is a land of second chances. He lets go of my hand and gives me a small smile. My heart aches for him, and for Arden. I don't know how Arden is involved, but he must have known Narah too, and cared for her deeply.

"She was lovely," Calix says. "And a lot like you."

I tilt my head at him and ask, "how so?"

Calix's eyes look misty as he considered the question. "Narah was adventurous and strong willed–"

"Stubborn?" I ask with a chuckle.

Calix laughs. "Far too stubborn for her own good." He looks at me with those intense golden eyes and whispers so softly that I barely hear him say, "And beautiful, just like you."

My face flushes. The horses trot at a gentle pace and I think about Narah and what she meant to Calix. I hate that he had to go through that loss, but I give another prayer of thanks that he and I both get another shot at life. We might even use this second chance on each other, maybe even on love. I see now why Lieve has been pushing Calix on me. He sees what I see. A second chance for us both. A shot at love. Calix is truly everything Lieve planned for me, and as crazy as it sounds, he's everything I've ever planned for myself as well.

Knowing the future doesn't mean you should change it. Changing the future doesn't always make the outcome successful, and success does not always mean happiness.

– Lark Fledgling

CHAPTER 24

LIEVE

A few weeks go by and Daphne has not given me anymore of Lopter's blood. It enrages me that she won't give it to me, that she hides it from me. I've gone down to her potion room in the dungeon, I know that's where she keeps it, but I cannot break her wards. Even using the spells she taught me, I can't get in. I've begged and pleaded for it, but she remains steadfast in keeping the blood from me. She agrees that we can try again, but states I'm currently still too eager. She's afraid I'll be obsessive over it and claims she can already see the torment the blood has started.

Daphne's father hasn't changed his mind about our courtship and due to that, we communicate less and less each day. And due to that, I've turned to drinking more and more. Even through my inebriation, we got great results from the announcement about the music academy. But after a fumble of Lord Matisse, we now have just as much backlash about "desecrating" a temple, and the people don't care that we're renovating Gwen Abbey. I wonder if things would be better if I weren't Regent. These thoughts make me want to guzzle bottle after bottle. Not only to drown my sorrows over still not finding my sister, but also to try and feel as I felt when the drops of euphoric death hit my tongue.

It's debilitating to be refused that flood of power once you've experienced it. While my Hunters are searching for Vera and the pocket watch, I also have them search for any Fae who might be distributing "illegal potions" and to bring them to me discreetly.

Sharpening my blades is therapeutic. I scrape a new hatchet across a whetstone, though its edge has not yet been dulled. It doesn't need sharpened yet, but I've already sharpened the other twenty hatchets on the ground around me and now I'm irritated. Arden is supposed to be helping me this morning, but he's late. He's been late frequently, and I wonder if Daphne might be right about him. He probably needs more care than Narah, Cal, and I can provide, but we are all he has. I pull a flask from my cloak and take a swig. The dark liquor is bitter on my tongue, but it warms my chest in the frigid cold.

"Lieve!" Someone shouts, "Lieve!" I hear panic in the voice.

It's Arden. He flies down the hill and closer to me, his eyes wide with fear. Bloody footprints trail behind him on the snowy flagstone, my chest tightening with the sight of it. Blood on flagstones. *Could the visions already be coming true?*

"What is it!" I shout, running to meet him, hatchet in hand.

His voice breaks as he cries, "Narah is dead! Someone killed my sister!"

Arden's hands are stained crimson, and the blood streaks his cheek when he raises his hand to wipe his face. I don't know what to do. I scramble to think, and then rage boils my blood.

"Show me," I growl.

Arden tries to steady his breath. He grips my forearm, still wet with his sister's blood, and guides me inside the castle. We run through the marble halls until we arrive at a large double door.

"Stay out," I hiss and crack the door open.

I peek inside to see Calix on his knees beside Narah's body. Blood flows slowly from her head, puddling under him. My legs shake. I take a step inside the room and freeze. Blood. Thick, red, blood. Just like the massacre in Madoria. I shake my head and look at Calix again. His arms and face are smeared red and he stares at Narah, motionless. *What monster would kill her?*

I drop my weapon at the door and kneel beside him. "Cal, what happened?"

"She's dead," he says blankly. "I walked in and Arden was standing by her head." His eyes travel to Narah's light brown hair, and then follow the pool of blood that leads under his knees. I flinch. Poor Arden, to have found his sister like that, all alone.

Narah's blood is growing darker, thicker. My stomach churns with the memories of the men I lost, the nearly same pool of blood I've knelt in once before. I can't think straight. I need Esven on this at once. I turn to tell Arden to fetch him, but Cal reaches for my wrist and stills me. "Do you think Arden did it?"

Something wizzes past me and lands sharply in the solid wood desk mere inches from Calix's head.

"I would *never* hurt her!" Arden roars, so loud it rings in my ears.

"Liar," Calix sneers. "I saw you over her body."

"That's enough," I spit. "Arden would never hurt Narah."

"I told you Narah was pregnant," Calix says. He then grips the handle of the hatchet and pulls it out of the wood with one good tug.

"Cal, be rational," I say and reach for the dagger at my hip.

But Calix's face has twisted in grief, in rage. This isn't the man I have fought beside for years.

"Little Arden has been sulking for months, getting the attention he craves from everyone around him, causing trouble at every chance he gets," he says coldly while shaking the hatchet in Arden's direction. "Arden couldn't take the fact that his *beloved* sister wouldn't be doting on his every move, that she'd soon have more important things to worry about than him. I told you he once wished her dead, now he's gone and done it."

"He's been troubled," I step closer and use my arm to try and lower Calix's, "but he's not a *murderer*."

"I *love* Narah!" Arden roars again, launching himself at Calix.

I grab him in mid air and the dagger in my hand slices his bottom lip open. Blood flies across the room like rain. I set Arden down and he's holding his face and screaming. With shaking hands I try to press on the cut, but Arden pushes me away and looks at me with quiet rage and glares. "Fuck. You."

"Guards!" I call out while trying to get close enough to Arden to stop the bleeding.

The room is then filled with people. Calix is still holding the hatchet Arden threw at him, a scowl etched on his face. He's still gripping the handle firmly.

"Drop your weapon, Cal." I order.

Calix's eyes darken and he stares at Arden with absolute disgust.

"*Now.*"

He lets the hatchet drop to the ground and it lands with a loud rattle on the stone floor. I snatch it before he can think of picking it up again. Calix doesn't say a word, he just stares at Arden like a bull waiting to gouge a bullfighter.

"Take Lord Bramford and Lord Madrona to separate chambers and guard them. Get a Healer for Arden, but neither are to leave their rooms. They are not to communicate with anyone. And fetch Lord Esven."

A guard grabs Calix's arm and pulls him out of sight and down the hall. Calix struggles with the guard the entire way down the corridor shouting obscenities at me and screaming that I'm being ridiculous. Meanwhile, a second guard gently puts his hand on Arden's shoulder, guiding him out of the room. I sit with my back against the wall, Narah's scared eyes boring accusatorially into mine. Another friend's blood spilled, in a castle I'm supposed to control. I cannot protect these people. *How did this happen?*

"Any other orders, Sir Lieve?"

As I stare at the blood on the ground another idea emerges. Perhaps Daphne could use her abilities to see what happened.

"Fetch Daphne Cortwright, and be discreet."

He clicks his heels together and retreats.

I look at Narah's face, once full of life and warmth, now drained of all color. Her face is contorted in an expression of surprise and fear. Did she know her attacker? *Could* it have been Arden? *No, he'd never.* Calix, too, would never raise his hand to hurt an innocent, let alone his beloved wife and unborn child. They're both lashing out in grief, but they both loved Narah. So the question remains: *who did this?*

～

Arden and Calix are both questioned extensively by Esven, and he comes to the conclusion that neither one of them killed Narah. The reassurance that neither of them committed this heinous act gives me some consolation. As soon as he's finished delivering his report to me, Daphne arrives, escorted by a guard.

"M'lady," Esven says in exaggerated concern. "I'm sorry to hear about Lady Narah. The crown and I will do everything we can to catch her attacker."

Daphne's eyes snap to me and she starts to hyperventilate. "Lieve," she pleads.

"Come with me, Daphne." I jerk my chin at Esven. "You're dismissed."

Esven's nostrils flare and he turns on his heel, stomping all the way down the hall. Daphne pays him no mind, she clings to me while I walk her over to Calix and Narah's chambers.

I stand in front of her, lifting her chin so our eyes meet. "This is going to be a terrible sight, and I know this is unfair, but I need your help."

Her lip trembles and tears flood her eyes. I put my hand on the door and crack it open, blood visible from where we stand. Daphne's breath catches and she digs her fingers into my shirt like claws. The door opens just enough that she and I can fit through and I snap it shut behind me. When Daphne sees Narah lying on the ground, blood beginning to congeal under her hair, she crumbles. Then screams of horror burst from her chest before she cups her hands over her mouth and shakes.

I sit on the ground beside Daphne and wrap my arm around her shoulders. She buries her face in my chest and I swear I feel the ground shudder with her sorrow. My fingers get lost in her hair as I try to comfort her as best I can before asking her to watch Narah's last moments. It's awful of me, selfish, cruel even…but it's the only way to try and find out what happened.

"I need a bowl," she mumbles.

I stand up and lock the doors so no one can barge in as Daphne pulls out powders and vials from her pockets and spreads them out on the floor. Carefully stepping over Narah's body to look on her vanity, I find a jewelry dish and dump the rings out. I hand Daphne the dish and she mutely mixes the liquids and powders together with shaky hands until a familiar floral aroma and faint green glow hover over the makeshift potion bowl. A tear falls from her jaw and lands on the floor.

"Ready?" I ask.

Daphne turns her eyes from Narah and scoots closer to her, taking one of her hands in her own. Daphne gently rubs her thumb across Narah's palm while I maneuver myself so I can hold Narah's other hand and still reach across to Daphne.

I've touched dead bodies, but this is different. Narah's skin is cool, and her fingers are becoming stiff. I reach out my other hand and Daphne grabs hold. Almost immediately I get a vision. Narah fighting with Arden, and then Arden leaves the room to go to training. Then Calix walks in, they bicker a little, but then he rubs her belly and they kiss each other before he walks out of the room too.

The perspective changes, and it's as if we're in Narah's eyes as she looks out the window, snow falling softly outside. A door creaks open, the sound of a boot shuffling on the wooden floor, and before Narah can see who walks in, a loud crack resonates against her head. The room looks blurry, and I'm overwhelmed with nausea. Cold metal slices through the skin of my back, *no, Narah's back*, the blade penetrating through the ribs over and over again. Narah's knees buckle, she doubles over, cradling her womb. Fear and confusion quicken my breath. Then someone pushes her body forward. Her head smacks the stone floor and everything goes dark.

I blink and I'm back here with Daphne. Daphne drops Narah's hand and backs away, crying uncontrollably. I crawl to her and pull her in my lap, petting her hair while she cries.

"I'm sorry," I whisper through my own tears. I have to close my eyes and focus on the fact that Daphne needs me, because the moment I whispered, *I'm sorry*, the memory of Narah whispering the same to me when the Fae cut down Lopter nearly tears me apart. "I'm sorry, I'm sorry, I'm sorry."

~

We hold a small ceremony for Narah and lay her to rest in the royal cemetery on a rainy afternoon. The court remains suspicious of both Arden and Calix, but I gave a decree that stated that they are not to be accused of the crime. It has been difficult navigating the suspicions of those in my court and standing by the side of my right hand man and my loyal little Knight. After hearing each of their statements, it seems impossible for either of them to be connected to Narah's death. Each of them are devastated, and I am determined to give them vengeance and closure.

Arden is sitting alone on the ground, several feet away from the burial site, picking blades of grass from the mix of rain and snow and crying silently. The large tree at this end of the cemetery is acting as a shield to the storm traveling this way. He's wearing a mask over the bottom half of his face, I assume to hide the nasty cut I gave him. I feel awful for it, and I pray he knows I didn't mean to hurt him. His eyes have dark circles under them, and he seems weak. I make a mental note to keep track of his eating habits and make sure he consumes at least one meal a day.

Near the grave, Calix stands in the rain with Daphne in front of the pile of soil covering Narah's body. The Priest holds out his hand to Calix. He limps over to him and the Priest makes a cut across his palm, letting a few drops of blood land on Narah's grave. Then the Priest wraps Cal's hand with a rag. Daphne calls Arden over, and after his blood is spilled, Daphne gently wraps his hand.

The Priest hums, Arden and Daphne humming with him. They sway together. I close my eyes and listen, the memories I have of Narah spilling into my thoughts. Her magnetic smile, aggressive loyalty, and spirit flowing through me. My chest vibrates and a deep humming emits from my throat, adding harmony to the others. When I open my eyes, Calix is staring at the ground silently and pressing on his cut to stop it from bleeding while Daphne and Arden continue swaying.

The Priest then opens his arms to address the remaining people in attendance. "For when you pass, your remains become one with the earth. But for those true to the gods, Sybill welcomes them to the fold. May the warm embrace carry our dearly departed, to feast forevermore with the mother. And may Lady Narah become the mother she should have been in this mortal realm."

Arden balls his fists, the linen wrapped around his hand blooming dark red. Daphne puts her hand on his back and I see the faintest glow move from her fingertips.

My heart stops.

I look around, thankful no one saw. I see Arden's shoulders relax and he loosens his fist. Daphne must have been calming him down. *Good.* We don't need another outburst from him today.

"Who shall take guardianship of Sir Arden until his sixteenth birthday?" The Priest asks, his eyes looking directly at Calix.

Calix moves forward to accept, but Arden cuts him off, "I take on my own guardianship. I'm just under sixteen, and I am soon to be a Hunter in the Regent's Court."

"Does this please you?," the Priest asks me.

Daphne snaps her head around; she clearly wants me to say no. But I cannot leave Arden to Calix's guardianship, not when both are still hurting.

"Sir Arden may be in charge of his own guardianship, but he must abide by customs that Lady Cortwright deems appropriate, and he must continue his lessons with his schoolmates until he is legally of age. Only then may he enter into my band of Hunters."

The Priest looks at Arden. "Are we in agreement?"

"Yes."

"Then it is so."

Daphne walks past me with Arden. "Good call," she says softly and picks up her skirts, sloshing through the mud back to the castle. She puts her arm around Arden, whispering in his ear.

Calix and I are now alone and he seems like a different person. I hate that he's grieving and it pains me that I have no idea who has done this to him. I've carried a rage inside me since that day and it's begging for release. I've still been drinking day and night and I'm nearly obsessive in my attempt to retrieve the Lopter blood from Daphne. The visions are starting to come true, so she needs to let me use it again. I feel useless. I don't know how to find Narah's killer, and I don't know how to move forward. I have nothing to give Calix but my friendship, so I embrace him and then leave him alone so he can take all the time he needs to say goodbye.

I then slosh through the mud too, trailing behind Daphne and Arden. The rain melts the snow on the ground, creating slush for my boots to sink into. Guards open the doors for me at the entrance and I kick my boots against the stone on the side of the castle doors and remove my soggy cloak. My chamber servant, Finn, draws me a bath and pours me a glass of wine before leaving me to my thoughts.

I don't understand any of this. I want to fix it, but without the blood, without Daphne's magic, I have nowhere to turn. I sink into the scorching hot water and lean my head against the curve of the tub, washing this awful day off my skin.

I don't know what to do, Georgia. I'm pregnant, and
Killian is so excited about the baby that there's no way
I can tell him it's not his. I can't tell him what happened
to me, he'd go after the bastard and try to murder him if
he knew what that man did to me that night after mass. I
think I'll have to have this baby and pretend it's Killian's,
for all our sake. I pray to Bram I can grow to love it. I
hope I can love it. It's not the baby's fault. Do you think
I'm doing the right thing?
– *Unmailed letter from Lady Sasha Toun to her sister, Lady*
Georgia Asteron. Found by Lady Soleil Toun, daughter of
Sasha, days after Sasha's death.

CHAPTER 25

VERA

I eat breakfast on the terrace, peering out over the garden to people
watch. I spy Arden, again with the stunning red-head, on the other
side of the hedges. She hands him some kind of letter, but I can't tell
the nature of it because their backs are turned to me. Arden lowers the
hood of his cloak as he reads, and then brushes his hand through his hair
before giving the paper back to her.

Evalie comes outside with a woman I haven't met yet. Her curly dark
hair is coiled around on top of her head in intricate braids and knots,
and she wears a flowy, white dress. On her neck are chains of the most
delicate gold and her fingers are adorned with gold rings, many with

diamonds embedded in the metal. They must cost a fortune and my mind wanders to our shop in Adamston.

I'm quickly pulled from my thoughts when she curtsies and says, "Your Highness. It's grand to meet you!"

"And you. Although I hope you'll forgive me, I don't know who you are."

She smiles broadly, showing dazzling white teeth. "I'm Lady Soleil Toun. I plan extravagant balls and events all over Atatacia, and my services are unique in nature. I also own many of the theaters in Prinav, as well as some–*other*– businesses. "

I'm fascinated. A woman who has her own money. Her own power. A Noble who rebels but is still part of society. Interesting. I gesture to my table. "Join me?"

"I'd love to," she replies and plops down in the seat across from me.

Evalie dips her head and rushes off to grab a cup of tea for Soleil. I gesture to the plate of pastries in the center of the table and Soleil grabs one happily. I watch her with curiosity and wonder why she's here, why she wanted to meet me, other than I've piqued her own curiosity.

"I bet you're wondering why I'm here," she says.

I laugh. "The thought crossed my mind."

"I've come to ask if your chambermaid would be willing to make a pair of dresses for me, for the feast and ball."

On that note, Evalie returns with tea for Soleil. I thank Evalie, and before she turns to leave, I stop her. "Evalie, Lady Toun has requested that you make her a pair of gowns. Would you be willing?"

Evalie's face brightens. "I would be honored."

Soleil raises her cup in a gesture of thanks. "Lovely. I'll pay handsomely." She takes a sip and licks her lips. "Is there nothing you can't do? This tea is incredible."

I smile at Soleil. "So, you know of her talents?"

Soleil lowers her head to Evalie and replies, "I was Evalie's most frequent customer–in another life."

"True." Evalie sighs. "And it's a pleasure to see you again."

"Evalie," I say. "Please sit with us."

"Oh, I couldn't." Evalie takes a step back. "It's not my place anymore."

"Please," I say.

Soleil pushes out the empty seat next to her and pats the cushion. "Sit."

Evalie sits down next to Soleil and brushes her skirts nervously. I scoot the pastries towards her and she takes one, tearing off a small piece and placing it in her mouth.

"Now," Soleil leans forward and her lips curl into a devilish little grin. "Tell me about slapping Odette Matisse, I would have paid a sack full of gold to have seen it in person."

The three of us laugh and talk for the next couple of hours. But Arden's red-head reappears in the distance, looking as if she's searching for someone. Probably for Arden. I roll my eyes and try to remain in the conversation, but I know I'm not hiding my sour face.

Soleil notices that I've become tense and stands. "Evalie, it was so good catching up with you. I do hope to do this again."

"It was a welcome surprise." Evalie says, her face beaming.

"And you," she says to me. "It was a pleasure to meet you, but I must be off. I'm meeting an old friend, Daphne, and I believe I've just seen her looking for me. I was supposed to meet her at the entrance to the hedges nearly twenty minutes ago to talk of her sister's engagement. Daphne's mother passed years ago, and as the Lady of her family, she requested my services. I don't want her to think I've stood her up."

"Daphne? Do you mean the red-head who accompanies Arden Madrona from time to time?"

"I do."

"Are they a couple?"

Soleil narrows her eyes but answers playfully, "not to my knowledge."

My mind wanders and Evalie scoots out her chair, the legs grinding on the terrace floor. Evalie and Soleil kiss each other's cheeks, and Soleil and I bow our heads before Evalie walks her out, church bells ringing across the estate. I sit again and stare out where I last saw Daphne and wonder why I'm feeling so frustrated.

～

I decide I'm going to go look for Arden and talk to him. I'm tired of the tension between us and I want him to be my friend again. I thought we *were* friends. I lean over the terrace and look in every direction, but I don't see him, so I wander the palace. The corridors are mainly empty except for servants carrying laundry, or pushing carts with steaming pots of tea. It's quiet.

Large double doors in the center of the hall open and Arden walks out, stuffing something small into his cloak pocket. I recognize the door as Calix's chambers. What did he just take? I follow him around until he goes outside and to the stables. Through the slats in the barn walls, I watch Arden kick dirt and straw and mumble under his breath. He pulls the item out of his pocket and walks back towards the castle and then stops, stuffs it back in his pocket and sighs deeply before flopping down on a bale of hay.

I walk around the side of the building and step in the stables. Arden has his head in his hands but looks up just as I enter.

"What are you doing here?," he asks.

I don't want him to know I was following him, and I realize I've made a dumb mistake by appearing just as he's stolen something. "I wanted to go for a ride. Are you alright? You seem flustered."

"I'm fine." He stands up and pulls a saddle from the wall. "Let's go."

"As in, *we*?"

"You can't go alone."

"I can manage." I say and grab another saddle, but it's so heavy I drop it on the ground.

Arden snorts. "Are you sure?"

I glare at him and it only makes him laugh. I roll my eyes, but step back and let him pull out both horses and saddle them, and I even let him help me mount the female. Arden leads us from the stables and down to a small orchard full of citrus. He tugs at a branch and tosses me the fruit while already biting into his own. I take a bite and the taste is sour, but juicy.

"The first time I ever saw this castle I was just a kid." Arden says to no one in particular. I take another bite and wait for him to continue. "I took my father's bow after my parents died. Then I went looking for my sister," his eyes dart to me. "She lived here at the castle."

"I'm so sorry about your family. I know what it's like, to a degree. When Lieve and I lost our parents, we had to take care of ourselves at a young age, too." I toss the pit of the fruit on the ground and Arden does the same. "Lieve ended up taking on the role of a sort of father," I say with a sigh. "Whether I wanted it or not."

Sometimes I just wanted Lieve as a bother. Once our parents died, I lost a piece of Lieve. I was allowed to grow up a little slower than him. I resented him for it, but also needed his protection, and none of it was fair to Lieve. I should have taken care of him more than I did, but I didn't. I let him be the leader, and Lieve kept my adolescence intact as best he could. No wonder he fled to Prinav, he needed an escape as much as I did. I shouldn't judge him for coming here without me, but it makes me wonder how many other secrets he has.

"What was your sister's name? You've never said."

Arden's eyes darken and I realize my mistake, the answer to all his tension with Calix suddenly clear. "Oh Arden, I'm so sorry. Your sister was Narah, wasn't she?"

Arden tilts his head down and he doesn't say anything back. He snaps the reins and trots ahead, ignoring my question. We ride along in silence, the somber aura now filling all the space around us. I want to ask more questions, but I don't want him to be faced with whatever memories he's trying so hard not to revisit.

"You saw me in Calix's chambers, didn't you."

He looks me in the eyes and I nod slowly. I don't know where this is going, and my palms sweat. He pulls out the item I caught him taking from Calix's chambers, and holds it up in the air. "This was Narah's ring —my mother's ring, and I wanted it back."

I give my daughter, BLANK, to this man BLANK, along
with a dowry of BLANK from BLANK. I say this and
agree to it, my word in good standing and good faith. I
betroth them, and this contract is binding and lawful.
– *Marriage contract template of Prinavian Law*

CHAPTER 26

LIEVE

T ime goes by in a blur. King Niall isn't doing well, and I've been
called to come to the King's chambers and speak to the Healers.
I'm dragged out of bed, still drunk and hungover at the same time. The
King's health has gone downhill for months, and there's never any new
updates. So, when I see Finn, I want to lay in bed and be left alone. I
know the routine. They'll give me an update, I'll look at his growing
infections, and then leave. It's pointless. The King isn't even conscious.
Finn forces me to bathe and I hate him for it. He walks with me, unable
to hide his disappointment that I still reek of wine. I stumble as we walk
through the halls, and Finn grips my arm with a strength I wasn't aware
he possessed.

When we arrive at the King's chambers, Finn side-eyes me. I
know that he knows I'm still inebriated. Guards in front of the King's
apartments open the thick wooden doors and step aside so Finn and I
can enter. The room is muggy. I shrug off my robes and hand them to
Finn while Calix, Esven, and the Healer, Valence, give me a nod.

"His Majesty has died," Valence murmurs.

Finn drops my robes to the ground. "I'm sorry," he stutters and picks them up hastily.

"When?" I ask.

Esven answers. "Moments ago."

I walk around Esven and Valence so I can get a better look at the King. He wears a patch on his eye from the arrow, and streaks of green and purple color his face with infection. His complexion has yellowed since I last visited, and even in death he looks clammy. I touch his hand and the King's moist skin makes me recoil.

Esven clears his throat. "We'll need to begin funeral arrangements immediately."

My heart hammers in my chest. "Okay."

"And you'll need to be crowned."

At those words my stomach sours. The wine and fear create a storm of nausea, causing me to curse these chambers for not having windows that can open to fresh air.

"Hail King Lieve," Finn whispers and bows deeply.

Valence and Esven follow his lead, then bows Calix. Calix and I lock eyes and I shake my head, the vigorous motion making my temples pound. *This can't be happening.* I run from the room and down the hall, throwing up in a tall and presumably expensive vase.

———

I sit on a small throne in the center of the dias overlooking the crowd in attendance for the funeral. Everyone is dressed in mourning clothes, dark colors, black silks and velvets, even in the heat of summer. Calix is in the front row of the audience, seated next to Lord Esven. Next to Esven is Daphne's father and sisters, with Daphne and Arden filling out the rest of the pew.

Daphne began coming to my chambers nearly every night after Narah's death. First it was only to speculate about her murderer, or to drink with me, but it quickly turned into using each other as a means to ignore our pain. Our bodies mask our wounds, and I'm happy to cover myself in her, instead of dealing with the reality I'm living in.

Daphne locks eyes with mine and I nearly whimper. Her copper hair reminds me of lying with her on the fur rug in my chamber, flames blazing in the fireplace. I could watch her hair flow across her shoulders and down her back, dancing across her skin like flames dance in the darkness forever. She looks away, face flushed pink, and tucks a lock of hair behind her ear.

I imagine what a crown will look like on her gorgeous head.

The only benefit of becoming the next King is that Daphne might actually be a real prospect for me now. I haven't allowed myself to fall in love with her again since her father denied my proposal, but now that I have the means to change his mind–

Daphne's corset is pulled tight, drawing my eyes to her curves. I swallow. She makes it hard to focus on the ceremony when all I can remember is what her creamy skin feels like underneath my satin sheets. Her lips look soft and plump, and she's painted them a deep burgundy today to match her gown. My eyes drift down her body and I feel my heart flutter when my thoughts wander to what she tastes like.

Benito Matisse and his brother, Baptiste, the Sagart Priest, stand on each side of me. The Sagart steps up close to me and holds out his arms to those in attendance, his deep purple robes catching the light of the sun and soaking up the rays like a sponge.

"On this day we mourn the passing of His Majesty, King Niall Brone–," his arms now high above his head–, "May Sybill welcome His Majesty with open arms."

He begins to hum, and so does the congregation. The sound fills Gwen Abbey from ground to ceiling. I close my eyes, humming with the others while a young boy and girl beat on drums and wail a prayer in ancient Prinavian.

When I open my eyes, I catch Esven eyeing Daphne. My fingernails dig into the wood of the throne as Esven whispers into Lord

Cortwright's ear. Daphne's father glances at Daphne before producing a toothy grin and patting Esven's thigh. Lord Cortwright sits up straighter in his seat, his chest puffed out like an oversized pigeon, while Esven slicks back his dark hair and crosses one leg over the other. I don't know what I've just witnessed, but it can't be good.

Once the funeral and burial are complete, I head back to my chambers. The room is stifling hot so I shed my heavy mourning robes and toss them in the hamper before lying shirtless on the bed. It's so hot. About an hour later, Finn enters with a knock.

"Would you like me to draw you a cool bath?" Finn asks.

"No," I answer. "I want a bottle of Tussian liquor and the power to turn back time."

The thought of time reminds me of the pocket watch I lost in the trenches. I feel an aching in my chest over losing it, losing my token of the last moments with Vera. None of my Hunters have found it.

Finn's face is disappointed yet again with my request for alcohol. "We are out of Tussian liquor, Your Majesty, but I can send word to Lord Bramford's men to bring some on their return."

I sit up. "Their return?"

Finn pours a glass of water from the jug on the table. "Lord Bramford and his men left moments after King Niall's farewell's. I assumed he informed you."

"Clearly not."

"Your council thought it best to secure the borders to alleviate any incoming threats to your crown. I overheard them speaking and thought it was your own orders."

I stand up and pace the room. "This was not discussed."

Finn takes a deep breath. "Your Majesty, not to meddle in your affairs, but with the amount of drink you consume–"

"Get out," I growl.

Finn sighs and sets the jug back on the table, bows, and leaves. When the door closes behind him, I race over and toss the jug and glass across the room, shards of glass exploding over the floor. Anger festers on my skin like boils. How dare Finn bring up my drinking? He knows next to nothing about what I'm going through, what I've lost. I continue to pace around the room and fume until I realize Finn, everyone, *they're right*. I need to apologize to Finn and thank Calix and my advisors. I'll need to remind them to keep me informed, but that I appreciate their swift action.

Calix wasn't wrong to send the militia to the borders. Now that Niall is dead, his last wishes are all that keep Prinav with a secure ruler. Without me sitting on the throne, war will erupt. Not only will the other Kingdoms, Madoria, Tussia, and Teyrnas, attempt to secure the Prinavian crown for themselves, but so would hundreds of noble Prinavian families.

Without patrols, Prinav would succumb to another war, just as it happened four hundred years ago when the Brone family itself gained control. We do not need a repeat of Queen Rosalind Brone. My temper gentles. I might not have been immediately informed of the plans, but they are good plans.

A gentle rapping on my door grabs my attention, and because I dismissed Finn, I answer the door myself.

Daphne stands in the doorway with a smirk on her face. "May I come in, *Your Majesty?*"

She exaggerates the words and my skin grows warm. I open the door wide so she can enter. The lip of the guard stationed at my door twitches as Daphne enters my room, and I throw him a look that screams "*discretion.*"

Daphne's eyes flutter as she scans my half naked body. She must be feeling reckless, so again we are to smother our feelings with our mouths, our hands, our bodies. I yearn to tell her that I want to marry her and bed her and give her a crown that weighs more than she does, but I can't think straight when she's in front of me like this.

I want to say that I'm not a peasant anymore, even though I still feel like one. I can raise her station. I can be someone that her father would allow her to marry. I get distracted with her breathing and I could listen to her voice plead my name in my dying moments and kiss every inch of her until I take my last breath.

Daphne parts her lips. "How are you feeling?"

I step forward so I can push my body into hers, relishing the gasp she lets out as I ease her up against the wall, crowding into her space. Her head knocks against it with a sigh, and I finger a stray wisp of her hair, kissing it before gently tucking it behind her ear. "Better now that I have you in my chambers."

"I don't want to talk anymore–," she breathes harder–, "I don't want to think. Just take me, here, and now."

Daphne makes any sort of civilized thought impossible. The thought of her being as aroused at our close proximity as I am is slowly turning me feral. She glides her hands down my chest, a faint golden glow erupts from her fingertips, sending pleasure through my veins and stars burst behind my eyes.

I bring my lips right near hers, so that they brush against each other with every word, "You are my undoing."

Daphne bites my bottom lip and I become what I say–*undone*. My hands glide up her numerous skirts, sliding up her thighs until I feel what my hungry hands are searching for. Daphne tilts her head back and I slide my finger–

A knock on the door is an unwelcome sound. We separate immediately, covered in sweat and practically panting.

I clear my throat. "Yes!"

"Your Majesty," Finn calls, his voice muffled by the heavy door, "Lord Esven requests your presence"

Daphne brushes her skirts and smooths her copper hair as I open the door. "On my way, Finn," I say while trying to cover the evidence of my encounter with Daphne.

He takes one look at us and our flushed skin and turns a deep red. "So sorry to interupt."

"No interruption." Daphne pushes her chin up in the air and straightens her back, walking past both of us hastily.

I try to feign a royal sounding voice even though I feel guilty as Finn places a bottle of liquor by the bed and bends to clean the broken glass. "Show me the way."

He does a deep bow, his face still red as a beet, and scurries to the wardrobe to fetch me lighter weight mourning attire. I place the thin silken fabric over my back and follow him toward the door.

When we arrive at Esven's apartments, he's seated on a large tufted chair near the window. There is an identical mate across from it and Esven waves his hand for me to take a seat. The dark green cushion groans with my weight, and Esven's servant, a teenaged boy with ginger hair and a face full of freckles, pours each of us a cup of tea.

"You're dismissed, Tenile," Esven says, waving the boy from the room.

I nod at the boy before I pick up my cup of tea and blow the steam off the top of the liquid. "You called for me."

"Ahh, yes. We need to get you coronated as quickly as possible."

"We do," I sneer, "so then maybe I can make my own choices about my army."

Esven blanches. "We only thought it wise–"

I smile to myself, happy that I've scared him a little. "I will speak with Lord Bramford, but see that it doesn't happen again without my consent."

"Of course, Your Majesty."

I stand to leave his chambers. "Is that all?"

"No," Esven picks up his own cup of tea. "Lord Cortwright has given me Lady Daphne's hand in marriage."

"What?" I snap.

An evil smirk appears and Esven oozes. "I shall have her from this day forth."

My vision blurs and I want to rip his throat out. "Why would Cortwright choose you–"

"Over a potential King?" Esven finishes my question, "I'm a nobleman of the realm, my family goes back for generations. I'm not going anywhere."

I grit my teeth. "Is that a threat?"

Esven pours more tea into his cup. "No, but you *are* the Foreigner King, and not everyone is pleased by that." He takes a sip of the piping hot tea. "Now, I see that this is a difficult day for you, so we can begin the coronation arrangements tomorrow."

I march to the door.

"Oh, and Lieve–" Esven taunts, "Please do me the honor of keeping your distance from my fiance."

～

I send for Daphne as soon as I return to my chambers, Esven be damned. Waiting is an agony. I try to busy myself, but it's no use. Thoughts of Daphne's fate are all that occupy me. *What is taking her so long?* I can hear the click of ladies' boot heels on the marble floors ad I perk up. *Daphne.* My leg bounces so fast it vibrates the dishes on the table. *What if she wants to stay engaged to Esven?*

Daphne walks in and glares at me, taking a seat at the other end of the table.

"Good evening," I say.

She eyes me up and down and pops a berry into her mouth. "No it isn't."

"So you know about your–," my voice shakes along with my knee. "Do you want me to end your engagement with Esven?"

She takes a deep breath. "It doesn't matter what I want."

"I'll talk to your father," I say. "I had asked for your hand before, and he denied me because I was only Regent."

She looks at me with wide eyes. "He never told me."

I feel like my heart is going to burst. "I'll ask for your hand again, if you'll have me."

"Lieve, I–"

"My coronation would surely change your father's mind."

Daphne drops her head. "That's not how it works here, Lieve. They've signed contracts. It's done. I'm betrothed to Esven."

"I'm King, that has to have weight behind it," I retort. "How can I be unable to change the laws?"

"Wiser men and women have tried, and the throne punishes such actions. The only way to end my betrothal would be my death, Esven's death, or a Sol ball."

"Sol ball?"

"It's a ritual they used to perform during Solurnalia. A man acts as Sol and steals the Dia from Oriel. Essentially, you'd be the god Sol and you'd have to take me, the Dia, from Esven, the Oriel."

My heart leaps. "Then it's settled, we'll have a Sol Ball."

"It's not that simple," Daphne grumbles. "Esven has standing in Prinav and you don't. The soldiers may love you, but the citizens don't know you. You've been drinking a lot–" I open my mouth to argue but she waves her hand– "you've been drinking a lot, Lieve, and Esven could produce a myriad of problems for you."

"I don't care about what problems Esven may or may not produce." I walk over to her and take her hand in mine. "If I am who you want, I can make this ball happen."

"You'd have to have the entire week's worth of festivities, the Feast of Bram, the Festival of Light and Dark, as well as the Sol Ball."

"Done."

She laughs. "You can't just say 'done'. It's expensive, it's–"

"Worth it to end up with you."

"Esven said your coronation is approaching quickly and he wants to marry me before then. No doubt for something he can brag about to his political colleagues who will no doubt be in attendance." She scowls. "Like I'm some kind of prize he won at a carnival."

"Well, I can't blame him for that, can I?"

She rolls her eyes. "Having a huge celebration before your coronation is dangerous. You already have a target on your back, and Father said a vast majority of the army is on patrol and wouldn't be here to keep you safe in the event of an attack. Solurnalia is huge, there would be thousands of people in attendance."

I smile. "Thousands of people to watch me take you from him."

Daphne shakes her head. "People would hate you. Plus, he'll know what you're up to if you plan this festival, he'll know it's all leading up to the ball."

I hold her hands and tell her, "I can send Esven away on some mission to another Kingdom so he won't even hear of the festivities until it's too late. I'll tell the help to keep plans quiet and give Esven a date to come back the day after the ball. Your engagement to him will be moot by the time he returns."

"You're asking for trouble."

"Then tell me not to do it. Tell me you'd be happy married to him, and I'll drop it all."

A tear falls from her cheek and she smiles weakly. "The Kingdom will hate us."

I grab her face and kiss her, my heart bursting with happiness. I don't care if people hate me, as long as Daphne loves me.

Daphne, my mother has passed and has left me terrible
news in her wake. I need to speak to you, and I wanted
to ask about your gifts because…I think I might be gifted
too. I don't know if it's grief or stress, but I've been able
to do things I couldn't before. I can't say what, in case
this letter is intercepted, but I'm coming to Brone Castle
to see you.

– Letter from Lady Soleil Toun to Lady Daphne Cortwright.

CHAPTER 27

VERA

The portrait gallery is an enormous one room chamber nearly two
hundred feet tall. There are stained glass windows with etchings
of past monarchs, and the sun drenches the dark, wide plank floors, in
a flood of color. Calix pulls me behind him gently as he points out the
paintings. We stop in front of a portrait of Rosalind Brone, with her
dark hair and nearly silver eyes. She's beautiful, and she's smiling, but
the smile has a vicious hint to it. At the bottom of the painting there's a
scratch, as if by a nail or a claw. I step on my tiptoes to read the plague
underneath it and it says '*all hail King Roz.*'

"Ah, Rosalind. She was interesting." Calix says from behind me. "But
troubled."

"Indeed," I answer, not taking my eyes off hers. "Her story is a violent
one."

He nods. "I understand her though."

I turn from Rosalind to look at Calix. "How so?"

"I understand revenge."

My heels click on the floor and echo in the large gallery as I get near enough to reach out to Calix. "I can't imagine." I slide my hand up his arm and rest my palm on his cheek.

He kisses my palm. "What happened to my wife is similar to what happened to Rosalind. Betrayed by people she should have been able to trust. Her death haunts me."

"It seems Narah was very loved."

"She was." Calix gives me a weak smile and then leaves my side to stand under Rosalind's painting. "Narah had a diary and she wrote of so many things. About me, and our baby. About Lieve entering Prinav through the tree. And she was so invested in the war. Since her parents were killed by Dops, and Lieve and I fought in the war, she felt it was her mission to learn about them. She wanted to learn all she could to defeat them."

"Did she learn anything of value?"

"Yes. She learned that Queen Rosalind interacted with her own Mimic without any harm done to herself. In the diary Rosalind kept, it talks about having the blood of gods in her veins, and that her Dop was nice to her because she needed her help or something."

I ponder what that means, that Rosalind with all her rage could have had devine ancestry. *I bet she's a descendant of Hode.* Then I think about Doppelgangers. What could a Dop need help with, and why did that keep Rosalind safe from them?

We look around the room at the other paintings, and I notice that none of Rosalind's children look like her, except for one. A man with long, black hair. I continue to scan the portraits until I get to Niall and his wife, Venus. I notice every Brone monarch from the dark haired line looks just like Rosalind, all the way to Niall. I search for Niall's son, but the painting is missing.

"Where's the portraits for Niall's son? I know he had a son, but I don't see a painting, and I don't even know his name to search on another wall."

"His name was Monroe," Calix answers. "He went missing years ago. Hunters and nobles took all his portraits across Atatacia looking for him. They never found him, and the paintings were never returned." He looks up at Rosalind and the others, scanning all the faces.

His brow arches. "Vera, can you stand under there for just a moment?"

I give him a coy smile and do as he asks. He looks from my lips and eyes, to the paintings and back again, his brow furrowing. His golden-honey eyes twinkle and then he points from me to Rosalind.

"What?" I ask with a laugh.

"You look so much like her, like all of them really. It's uncanny."

I turn and look up. We *are* similar. Dark hair, light eyes, full lips. Even our complexions are a match. Calix pulls me right under Rosalind's painting and wraps his arms around me. My knees grow weak as he lends in and purrs in my ear, "I see why Corde was content with being just Rosalind's lover. Who could ask for more than love, when a woman captivates you as she did him? As you captivate me?"

His warm lips brush against the shell of my ear and my breathing quickens. His hand cups my breast and I freeze. I want to continue, but I don't know if I should. We aren't married. Calix's hand then travels down my sides and his fingers sneak under my skirts. I don't know how to react to my body, although I like the feeling. I *like* his hands raking over me. I turn to face him, threading my fingers through his messy hair and tug him closer, slowly pressing my lips against his.

"I'm growing rather fond of you, Vera dear."

"I'm growing rather fond of you, too," I whisper into his mouth.

Calix kisses my neck, my collar bone, sending a ripple down my spine. *Fuck it. I want this.* My hands find Calix's belt, and I tease him, dragging my finger across the waistband of his leathers. He moans in my ear and I clench my legs together. The door to the gallery opens and I see Soleil entering with Lieve and a few of the palace staff talking in the hallway. Soliel's eyes widen in shock and he clears her throat, allowing Calix and I time to seperate.

"Oh look!" Soleil exclaims to Lieve and the servants. "The Princess!"

I appreciate Soleil trying to cover for us, but Lieve walks in and I can see he's trying desperately not to laugh. I'm glad he isn't angry, but I really wish he wasn't privy to what we were just doing.

I feel my cheeks heat and Calix graciously answers for us, "Hello to you Lady Toun! What's going on then? Renovating the gallery are you?"

"Not yet," she laughs. "Just preparing for the Princess's welcome dinner. His Majesty heard I was visiting and asked me to make sure the dinner goes without a hitch, as the Queen has been too busy to coordinate the event." Soleil says. "The King was just giving me a short tour before heading to the dining space."

"Soleil, do we really need to make an ordeal about my arrival?" I ask.

All three of them look at me like I have two heads.

Soleil reaches for my hand. "Yes, my dear, we do. You're the talk of the Kingdom!"

Both Lieve and Calix's brows are furrowed and Lieve asks, "have you met?"

"We have," I say. "We met before she–"

"Yes," she says nervously. "Before I spoke with Evalie, her chambermaid. I wanted to ask if she was willing to make me a gown. Evalie's an incredibly talented seamstress and no other lives up to the outrageous designs of my imagination."

Lieve nods. "I've seen some of her work. I even own a piece from her myself."

Calix and I say our goodbyes to Lieve and Soleil, leaving them to finish dinner planning so Calix can take me to the library for research. I can't help but to latch on to Soleil's nervous behavior in my mind, when mentioning what she was really here for. I was only going to say that she was here to see Daphne, and it feels like she didn't want me to mention that in front of them.

"Do you know of a woman named Daphne?" I ask Calix.

His jaw twitches. "I do."

"Who is she?"

"Someone you should stay far away from, for Lieve's sake, and yours."

~

The following morning Lieve asks me to meet him at the pond. He wants to go boating for a bit and spend time with me before the Queen arrives from her summer holiday. We aren't supposed to meet for several hours, so I make my way to the stables to see if Arden would like to go on a ride with me. I'm hoping to learn more about Daphne, and learn why Calix doesn't want me around her.

On my way there I see Arden and Daphne walking together again. People stare at them as they pass by, and then they round the corner of the palace and out of sight. The sundial in the garden tells me I still have plenty of time before I need to meet Lieve, and I wring my hands trying to decide if I should continue on to the stables, or follow Arden and Daphne. *I'm just going to wait.* I can ask questions another time, I shouldn't spy. But, I'm too curious for my own good and quickly race around the corner to catch up to them.

I spot Arden's hood, and Daphne's gorgeous red hair, darting to the back side of the castle. I follow their steps behind large walls separating the stone walkway from the grassy area of the estate where several nobles are playing lawn games.

"Oh hello!" One of the nobles shouts to me.

No, no, no. I don't want to talk to you. Two women leave their game of rolling fist sized balls into small iron hoops on the ground. They approach me, sweaty and out of breath.

The woman who shouted does a deep curtsey, "Your Highness."

"Hello," I say and curtsey back, "nice to meet you."

She looks absolutely delighted. "I heard the King's sister arrived and I've just been dying to meet you."

The second woman frowns, but she nonetheless agrees. "Yes, we both have."

"I apologize for not being able to chat, but I–" Arden and Daphne are gone, –"need to go."

Hastily gripping a large bunch of my cumbersome gown, I run down the stone walkway and end up at a fork. To the left is an empty walkway that leads to a dark set of stairs. To the right are more courtiers. *They must have gone down the dark stairs.* My heart pummels inside my chest. I hate being in the dark.

I stand at the top of the dark stairwell and look down. I can't see the bottom. Shoving my skirts all into one hand, I use the railing to guide me down. With each step the light fades until I am deep enough that I can't see in front of me. It's pitch black at the bottom of the steps and my heart beats so hard I imagine it pushing through my skin and falling in front of me on the ground. I use the walls, gently sliding my hand against the rock. It's cool and damp beneath my fingers. I continue to run my hand along the uneven surface, begging to find a latch or a door that Arden could have gone through.

As I step carefully on the ground beneath my feet, metal touches my fingertips and I wrap them around a door knob. I pause. I should turn around, but I don't. The door isn't locked, so I push it open just enough for me to fit through sideways. A creaking fills the silence, making me wince. It's dim in this hallway, but there are oil lamps on hooks at even intervals as far as I can see. I shiver, but at least I can see now. *This must be the dungeon.*

The hallway only goes in one direction, so I follow it. At the end, it splits left and right, and I choose the right side on a whim. Up ahead I see a faint red glow coming from underneath a door. My heart pounds. I sneak up as close to the door as I'm comfortable with as bottles clang together. A woman's voice hums and then a crackling sound snaps loudly. I take a step forward. *Is Daphne a witch?* She says something to Arden, but it's so low I can barely hear her.

I dare to stand directly in front of the door so I can hear her muffled voice, "I *have* to Arden."

"No you don't. I've told you I would marry you if it came down to that," Arden replies.

Something in Arden's words makes my stomach churn. Why would he have to marry this woman? The red glow brightens and light floods the bottom of the door frame, spilling onto my shoes and the ground around me. Then a scent leaks into the hallway, smelling faintly of vanilla. The aroma is intoxicating and makes me a little light-headed.

"I'm not marrying you." Her voice burns through the haze. "Stop offering."

Arden scoffs. "It's better than this."

I quietly lay on my stomach so I can see under the door frame at what they're doing. The room they're in is small and dark. The only light is from the red glow in the center of the room. There's a small wooden table, and the red glow is coming from something sitting on the top of it. Arden and Daphne stand on opposite ends of the room. His boots dig into the soot on the floor, but his steps are silent. For his size, he is incredibly graceful. Daphne wears shoes of a noble, laughably high heeled and covered in gems. She seems to float around the room effortlessly in them, as if by magic.

"Maybe Gelhert will take me back?"

Arden huffs, "doubtful."

"He's widowed. Single."

"Pick someone else, he won't forgive you."

The woman slams her hand on the table, startling me. I suck in a hard breath and hold it, praying they didn't hear me.

"Then I'll put this in his drink at the feast!" She exclaims wildly. "*Or maybe Lieve-*"

"I would never let you, so get it out of your mind," Arden says hotly.

"He loved me once."

Arden strides over to her, boots not making a sound. "He's had years to be with you, and he made a mockery of your–"

I can hear the venom in her words when she interrupts, "Lucette had a lot to do with that, along with *your* failures all those years ago."

"You can't believe that it's *my* fault that your actions came to haunt you."

"No, but you certainly didn't help. You were late, weren't you?" I hear a small amount of liquid being dropped into a larger bowl of liquid. "I guess I'll just have to use this on Calix if I don't secure an engagement by the time the ball commences."

"You wouldn't dare." Arden growls.

"You'll have to put all that angst for him aside," she snaps. "The little Princess is a small hiccup, I agree, but everything will be fine. We were friends once, it won't look suspicious, hell, he might even agree to it. And if not, men like him are easy to control."

My blood is boiling. I will *never* allow her to sink her claws into Calix.

"I only have until the Ball to secure a notable suitor or my father is moving me to Madoria, or gods forbid, Teyrnas. You know that getting rid of me is his deepest desire–," a burst of red light explodes, washing the room in a blinding flash–, "and I *refuse* to let that happen."

Calix was right, she's trouble. I have to tell him, I have to tell Lieve. I push my hands against the ground to get me to my knees. But when I stand, my shoe gets caught in my skirts and I slide on the ground, grabbing the door knob to steady myself. The knob shakes, and an uneasy silence follows.

Fuck.

I lift my skirts and run. My head still feels light, making my steps slower. I kick off my shoes and push myself faster. The door opens and that's when I hear Arden's boots. I turn the corner, hoping I can get into the dark stairwell before he can catch up to me. My stockings slide around on the stone floor and I lose grip of my skirts. I don't even make it half way down the tunnel before I'm shoved into the wall.

"How much did you hear?" Arden's voice is low. Deadly.

I've never been afraid of him, but as he stares into my eyes I feel how dangerous he could be. He leans in, his body only inches from mine. His chest puffs out, muscles straining against his leathers. *What have I done?* Each beat of my heart crashes. My breath is ragged and I can't swallow. Arden narrows his eyes at me and I freeze under his gaze.

"Vera." Arden squeezes his eyes shut like he doesn't want to do this. "Don't make me ask again."

"I heard nothing," I breathe.

He wraps his strong fingers around my wrist and repeats, "*How much did you hear?*"

I tug my arm, but he puts pressure on my wrist causing it to pinch. "You're hurting me."

The pressure immediately dissipates and he takes a step back. *"Vera."*

"No."

He grabs my wrist again and yanks me a few steps back towards the door hiding Daphne and her magic. I can't fight him. I can't run from him. So I lift my head and walk ahead of him, back to the red glow. If I'm going to die, I'll die as a Lady. A Princess. And they'll have to explain my murder to a King.

I pick my shoes up from the ground when we pass them and Arden snorts. Tucking them under my arm, I stop walking when we reach the door. Arden swings it open and we both step inside. Vanilla wafts in the air and the beautiful red-headed woman leans against the stone wall with her arms folded and her eyes burning like fire.

Sir Finnigan Challit, betrothed to Lady Ana Stark. Lord Thomas Cartier, engaged to Lady Wendilin Port. Lord Gelhert Esven, betrothed to Lady Daphne Cortwright. Captain Jurian Ira, betrothed to Lady Bridget Durant of Madoria.

– Engagement and Betrothal Announcements, Mercat Cross Podium, Kelby Drake, Barault, Prinav

CHAPTER 28

LIEVE

Daphne and I have had several secret meetings in my chambers, her chambers, the dungeons, the stables…basically anywhere we can. I feel like I'm doing something wrong though, like I'm taking something that belongs to someone else. I suppose I am, in a way. It feels good to do something bad, something I'm not supposed to do. Loving Daphne is dangerous, but I need her as much as I need air.

"I think a Doppelganger killed Narah," Daphne blurts out one day as we're lying on the floor of her chambers, our naked bodies covered in sweat from our most recent encounter.

Before I can ask what she means, someone knocks on her chamber doors. I scramble to slip on my shirt and trousers and hide under her bed. Daphne wraps a robe around herself and cracks open the door. Marguerite barrels in, her small feet scurrying past the bed and over to the bathing room, tossing soiled garments into a hamper.

"Marguerite, what's going on?"

"Lord Esven is on his way to bid you goodbye before his trip to the border," she scolds. "And by the looks of this room I can tell you've been entertaining a gentleman again. You're lucky I'm here to clean up your messes."

"I have not been entertain–"

Marguerite shoves the garments down and turns on her heel to face Daphne. "Please don't insult my intelligence by lying to me."

"Fine, but you don't understand," Daphne pleads.

"I don't need to understand, you're *engaged*."

"*Betrothed*."

"It's the same thing," Marguerite argues.

Daphne's voice turns cold. "No, it isn't."

"Does it matter? If Esven finds out about your–*activities*, you'll be ruined. And so will I with your sins."

Daphne and Marguerite continue to fuss over one another, but I'm not listening anymore because I see something tucked in the stitching of Daphne's mattress. It's a teardrop shaped vial, and it's half full. *Lopter's blood*. Using my knees, I scoot myself forward so I can reach the vial without making any noise. The women have entered the bathing room, and I should really take this opportunity to escape from under the bed, but I *need* that blood.

I hear water running and use this golden moment to rip the vial from the threads and stuff it in my pocket. Daphne and Marguerite are still in the bathing room, so I slide out from under the bed and tiptoe towards the door. I reach my hand to turn the nob and standing on the other side is Esven.

He makes a face like he's smelled something foul. "Hello, Your Majesty."

"What brings you here?"

He cocks an eyebrow, "I could ask you the same."

"I was congratulating Lady Daphne on your betrothal." I smirk and wipe my bottom lip.

I see a muscle in Esven's jaw twitch and I bump his shoulder on my way out the door before I call back to the ladies, "Daphne, your door is open and you have a gentleman caller."

Marguerite's head pops out from the bathing room, white as a ghost. "Just a moment!"

I saunter down the hall, fingering the vial in my pocket. Egging Esven on isn't a good idea, but *damn* it feels good to be able to do it, just this once. I arrive at my chambers, but I see Finn milling around. I don't want to interrupt his work or see the shame in his eyes again, so I turn down a different passage.

As I walk, I think about the news that Daphne delivered to me. Her supposition. Could a Dop have killed Narah? Was one in the castle? I suppose it could happen, especially when her killer still hasn't been apprehended, no matter how aggressive the investigation. I'll have to speak with Esven about this and ask if there's a possibility that Brone Castle could be infiltrated. I lean my forehead against the cool stone wall. Just another problem to my endless list, another worry. Another failure.

My fingers wrap around the vial and my heart skips a beat—*can the blood show me if the Dop will strike again?* There must be a way to see it's next move, and maybe I can stop it before it happens.

I find a powder room where I can be alone, and with shaking hands I pull the bottle of death from my pocket and unscrew the lid. The aroma of salt water and mud fill the small room and I inhale deeply. My heart flutters in my chest, the anticipation making me dizzy. The blue liquid swirls around and fizzes in the bottle and I hold it up in the air so I can get a taste. Daphne's warning chimes in my mind '*just one drop*', and I do as she says. *One drop.* The moment that one little drop hits my tongue, the world is gone.

The thick goo coats my mouth and the back of my throat. I know what's about to happen and I'm not going to let myself panic this time. I'm not going to scrape the thick sap from my tongue. I'm going to let it sit there so I can absorb it all, so I can get the full effect from Lopter's magnificent high.

Breathing through my nose steadies my breath, and I'm glad I was prepared for the side effects this time because if I weren't sitting, I would have cracked my head on the sink and passed out. My eyes flutter as I fight the urge to black out. I want to feel this as long as I can when suddenly, I'm not in the powder room anymore.

I'm Narah again, standing in the window watching the snowfall. I hear a shuffling of boots behind me. No, that's a *limp*. Light flashes and now I'm me, in a dead Shadow Grove, covered in ice. I hear clicking and chattering but I'm too weak to look for the sound. Another flash. I'm Vera, standing in a creek watching minnows swim around my toes. Another flash. I'm watching Vera and myself jump into the Lopter Tree and my legs propel this powerful body forward, and I dive headfirst into the endless void of the tree.

I blink and I'm back in the powder room, drenched in sweat. My head is throbbing. I stand on shaky legs and wash my face in the sink. A small stool I hadn't noticed before sits in the corner, and I slide it over so I can sit on the stool and dump cool water over my head as I suck the leftover syrupy blood from my lips. *I need more.* I can feel an energy under my skin, flowing in my veins and I crave it. I crave what it can show me, teach me. I know the answers are near.

I look at the bottle, and there's plenty of blood left. What would the harm be if I had just one more drop? I lick my lips and hold up the bottle one more time, waiting for that delicious sap to fill me once more.

~

I tried two more times with Lopter's blood, and I vomited so violently that blood began to mix with the bile and I forgo any more attempts for knowledge. I find Esven and tell him that I believe a Doppelganger might have killed Narah. He orders guards to interrogate everyone on the property, coordinating it so that no one panics, or even knows why questions are being asked.

I head back to Daphne's chambers to ask her about Narah's killer. I need to learn more to determine if it's a real possibility. I knock on her door and Marguerite answers, that same sour look smeared on her freckled face.

"I need your Lady," I say.

Without taking her eyes off me, Marguerite shouts, "Lady Cortwright, the King is here."

"I've been announced," I say and push past her. "You're dismissed."

Marguerite scoffs but she can't argue with me, so she grips her skirts in her hands and stomps down the hall. I should care that she didn't bow, but I don't. Daphne emerges from her sitting room and when she sees me, she blanches.

"Lieve, what have you done?"

"Nothing."

Her eyes flick to her mattress and then back at me as she shakes her head. "You found the vial and you've been draining it, haven't you?"

"Do you really believe there's a Dop in the castle?"

"I do," she says and folds her arms across her chest. "There's no other explanation for what happened to Narah. Whoever did it couldn't have left the room, there was too much blood." She gives me a stern look. "And don't ask me who it was because I don't know who it was. But it damn well wasn't Arden."

I nod. "I agree. Neither Arden's or Calix's stories suggest they harmed her."

"There was no time for anyone to run out of the room without being caught or leaving footprints. They had to have escaped through the mirror in the room. So that would mean Dops can go back into the mirrors, as well as come out of them." She says.

I shiver with the notion that Dops can travel that freely.

"I–," I see Daphne's eyes dart to my lips and she narrows her eyes angrily before continuing–,"I know Calix didn't do it, I know that. But, what if his *Dop* did?"

"There's no way Calix's Mimic is in this castle without me knowing. The Cal walking around is the real Cal, I would know." I scoff. "Daphne, you know that's impossible."

"Lieve, listen to me. By your own account, Cal's reaction with Arden was completely out of character."

"He wasn't thinking straight," I argue. "His wife and child had just been murdered."

"Lieve, please–" she steps towards me. "Calix is my friend too, but I just can't reconcile his behavior. Not just that day, but for weeks, even months now."

But I can't bear to hear this attack. It's not true. Calix is my brother, my truest friend. He's not a Doppelganger. I storm back through the double doors of her rooms and keep going until I find myself wandering to Calix's chambers.

When I arrive at his room, the door is locked. I ask his servant to let me in, and he does begrudgingly. I pace around his chambers for hours, going over my memories surrounding Narah's death. I can still see Narah's blood pooling around Cal's knees while he cradles her body. I can still hear the pain in Arden's voice when he screams that he loves her. I pace faster as Narah's face materializes before my eyes, drained of all her warmth.

My neck grows hot. I rip open my collar, buttons scattering the ground. My heart is pounding and I'm starting to drip with sweat. I pull at my hair and pace faster and faster, wiping my moist hands on my pants with every step.

The sound of Narah's head smacking the floor crashes around me, then the screams of my men in the massacre of Madoria, then the drums of the battlefield. I run to the bathing room and douse myself with water to try and cool down. It's so hot, so, so, hot. *There's no way Cal is a Dop.*

I rip open the wardrobe, the drawers, desperate to find proof that Calix is real. Desperate to find my friend is my friend, and that I haven't lost another person I love.

The vial of Lopter's blood bounces against my leg.

I rip it from my pocket, unscrewing the stopper frantically. If I ingest more, will it help me? Are answers worth my sanity? I take a deep breath and think of my men, of Hal, of Vera, of Narah, and Calix. *It's worth it.* I leave the bathing room to sit on Cal's mattress so I don't hit my head on the floor if I fall.

Pressing the lip of the vial to my mouth, the thick liquid touches my skin, but I'm distracted. The sun glints on something metallic in the corner of the room. I lick my lips, letting the tasteless syrup soak into me while I roll from the bed to the floor. My eyelids are already beginning to flutter, but something is pulling me to the reflective surface in the corner.

I crawl over to it and stretch my hand out to touch the tip of a black dagger. As if in slow motion, I pull it from the bundle of swords that it's barely hidden in. The urge to black out is strong, my heart pounds as I turn the dagger over in my hands. I see words etched in the blade and it takes me a moment to read it, but before my eyes roll I see: *Calix Bramford.*

Blinding white light flashes in my eyes again before I see Vera running in the dark, screaming for me. Then I'm back on the battlefield, severed heads rolling at my feet. Another flash. I'm running through a labyrinth smearing blood on massive stone walls. Flash. I'm in the trenches of Shadow Grove with Calix. Doppelgangers step out from behind the trees and Calix launches his black dagger into his own Doppelganger's leg.

I blink a thousand times and I'm lying on the wooden floor of Calix's chambers again, a puddle of vomit next to my head. The room is hazy and my forehead throbs. My eyes water from the strain of the flashing light, so I cover them with my hands.

A hand on my back pulls me to sit up, I instinctively grab and twist.

"Ahhh!" Calix's servant stands over me, eyes wide, "I'm sorry!"

I let go immediately, "I'm so sorry, I–"

He rubs his wrist, but waves off my concern. "Are you alright, Your Majesty?"

I nod my head, and catch sight of the onyx blade again. I'm still holding the black dagger in my hands. *Calix Bramford.*

Calix threw this dagger into his Doppelganger's leg. I remember it. Lopter just *showed* me. Calix never got that dagger back. So how is it that I'm holding it now?

Daphne was right.

I think about the last visions Lopter showed me. *The limp approaching Narah.*

Daphne was right about everything. Calix's Dop killed Narah. So where is the real Calix? How long has he been replaced by a fake? Pin pricks dance across my skin. My body shakes and my muscles cramp. I vomit until there's nothing else to spew and begin dry heaving. The servant fetches me water and I sip slowly, and once my legs stop shaking, I stand. My mind races, anger simmering under the surface of my skin.

"Aaaggghhh!" I roar and tear through the chambers and look at myself in the mirror.

Mirrors. They must be shattered. I grab it off the wall and smash it to the ground. Guards enter through the door, startled, and see me standing with shards of glass all over the room. The servant darts past them and runs.

"Find Calix Bramford and bring him to me unharmed." I push past the guards and run from room to room, smashing every mirror I see.

People watch me tearing through the palace, smashing things. They run from me.

"Smash your mirrors, now!" I yell. "If you see Lord Bramford, tell a guard!"

They scurry all over the castle, smashing mirrors in their own chambers, or running away in fear. Fear can be a good motivator. There will not be another Dop in my castle. I cannot lose another person I care for. I can't, and I *won't*.

Magic shall be banned from this day forth, unless by use of the Holy Order. All others shall perish, for that is the Deal with the Fae. To keep the peace, sometimes violence is necessary.

– Decree of the Ancient Monarch, King Rafi Durant of Madoria, during the Mador-Seelie War of the Drols, two centuries into the Durant Dynasty.

CHAPTER 29

VERA

I can hear my heartbeat pounding in my ears. *You're a Princess. They aren't going to kill you.* I repeat it in my head while Daphne glares at me. I stare right back at her, my jaw set, even though I'm shaking on the inside.

"I don't like eavesdroppers," she says.

"I don't know what you're talking about."

She rolls her eyes at Arden. "Well?"

Arden leans against the door. "I have no idea what to do."

"Think of something," she hisses.

The rapid beating of my heart and the intoxicating aroma of the room make me light headed. I feel my pulse quicken, and notice it's uneven. I keep my eyes trained on the woman, the witch, and she drums her claw-like nails while she contemplates how best to kill me. *I shouldn't have come down here. What was I thinking?*

"I know who you are, *Princess,* and you're lucky that I do," the woman says with a voice like silk. "If you weren't who you are, I would curse you this very instant."

"Lucky me."

"*Very.*" She narrows her emerald eyes.

Since my title seems to have some sway, I seek refuge in it. I straighten my shoulders and turn my nose up, as haughty as any Lady's I've ever seen. "I don't know why I even came down here. I was only exploring *my* castle. Now," I say with a step to the door and my heart slamming against my ribs, "I'll be leaving."

She smiles. "Not so fast. I know you caught me doing magic, and I can't let you tell anyone. I don't need the Queen's Court to *finally* have a reason to hang me."

I stop and furrow my brow at her. Is the court that ruthless? "Hang you?"

"Magic is illegal," Arden answers.

I cross my arms. The more I learn about the real Prinav, the more confusing it is. "Prinav is full of magic."

"The people understand that the land is soaked with power, but those of us with particular gifts aren't afforded the same compassion." Daphne's eyes darken. "For the few of us who dare to learn the secrets in the soil, our lives are often the consequence of testing our extraordinary abilities." Daphne walks on the other side of the table and stands next to me so that our noses almost touch. "You'll want to keep my secret, *Princess,* for your brother studied magic under my instruction for a very long time...it would be a shame for a King to be hanged for such a crime."

"You wouldn't," I snarl.

"If you say anything to him, or to anyone, about this, I'll have a mob at the front gates by nightfall. He's the Foreigner King, and many Prinavians would love to see him crumble; and if he goes down, so do you." She then snatches my chin with her sharp nails. "So don't toy with me, I've been in the game for much longer than you."

I jerk my chin out from her claws and try to get past Arden. "Move."

Arden looks from me to Daphne, and then opens the door to let me out. Once I step into the hallway, I run. I don't look back to see if they're following me, I only want to get out. Returning to the dark stairwell, I hold my breath before going into the black void. Slowly, I ascend back into the light of the spring sun and have to hold my hand at my forehead to keep the sunrays from blinding me. It takes a moment for my eyes to adjust to the light, and I step back into my shoes while I try to calm my breathing.

Finally returning to the main entrance of the castle, I brush the dirt from my skirts with shaking hands before I dart as quickly as possible back to my chambers to think. I'll have to keep my encounter with Daphne a secret until I can figure out how I can expose her while keeping Lieve and Calix safe, and myself. The thought makes me shudder.

Would Daphne really put him in danger like that? What history is there between them for such a viscous response? *Does Lieve really know magic?* Frustration and fear build in my chest. All these lies, all these secrets. I'm so sick of being in the dark. It's yet another reminder that I don't know Lieve anymore, and his secrets could ruin him, ruin us, even ruin an entire Kingdom.

I stay in my room all night alone, pacing back and forth and coming to the conclusion that I need to fix the pocket watch. If I can't get Lieve and Calix out of this mess, then I have to save Lieve another way. Arden's warnings about Dops make me pause, but then I think of Calix. He said Rosalind's Dop didn't hurt her. I'm terrified of seeing my Dop again, but I tell myself that if I only look at myself in the watch, she shouldn't be able to get to me. I'm also terrified of seeing the madman with the cane again. But if I fix the watch, maybe I can use it to bargain with him. Maybe he'll help us if I give it to him. Maybe neither will even show up.

Envy isn't green.
— *Roe Oleander*

CHAPTER 30

LIEVE

C alix is nowhere to be found. The Doppelganger who took his form is gone, and all of my guards and soldiers stay on high alert. I've barely slept for weeks, and often use Lopter's blood to try and discern where either Vera or Calix could be, but nothing has worked. Daphne attempted to use her skills to find him, but all she could see was darkness. We didn't know what that meant, Daphne had never seen nothingness before.

Daphne eventually found the vial of blood and took it back; hiding it behind countless wards in the dungeons. We argued over it. Viciously. She said I was turning into a shell of a man, but she's wrong. The visions seem to be coming true, and I need to see what will happen, so I know where I should search. In the moments Lopter's blood touches my lips, I feel like a god myself. The knowledge the blood gives is divine. Although it comes with the consequence of illness, doesn't she understand the blood's worth? Doesn't she care?

Without access to that euphoria, I turned back to wine and liquor. I drank myself stupid for several days, unable to do any of my royal duties. I spoke with Arden and my band of hunters looking for Calix and Vera, and for another source of blood daily, and everyday was a failure.

My guards and servants try to coax me into a better disposition, and I appreciate their efforts, however useless they are. Nothing will save me anymore. Narah is dead, Calix is gone, Vera is missing, and now Daphne refuses to speak to me. I don't blame her. Daphne tried to console me, to talk to me in the days after all of the mirrors were destroyed. I could see the pain in her eyes when she would look at me. I could see the concern for my well being, and I know she cares about me. But I need to care about more than her. I need her to see that the torment is worth it. This is bigger than both of us.

While cut off from the god's blood, Daphne secretly took over the duties of the court for me while Esven has been away speaking with Ambassadors. I vomited continuously for days at a time, and I was nasty with her. Every time she walked in the room I started to pick fights with her. I accused her affection as just trying to raise her station. I became a monster to protect her from me and my wrath. I made her hate me. I flaunted myself in front of other women at court even though it made me sick to do so. I dismissed her when she would attempt to speak to me. She wrote me letters, and I ignored them entirely.

After every encounter I could see tears well in her eyes and I wanted to say I'm sorry. I wanted to hold her, kiss her. I wanted to drop to my knees and vow my life to her, my heart, my soul to her. I wanted to worship her in every way. The amount of love I have for her is the amount of disdain I unfairly threw her way. I don't know why I behaved that way. I think she was right about the blood. Having too much of the blood does force you to go mad, but again, mental anguish is a small price to pay for finding Vera and Calix.

I sent word to her that I think it would be best if she married Esven. Her reply was the stain of a kiss on parchment. I could see where her tears fell on the paper, and I knew it was her goodbye. I knew she had finally had enough pain. Even though I was in agony every second of the day without her, this is how it must be.

Tomorrow night is the Feast of Bram, and I have extra guards at the castle for the event. Multiple teams of soldiers are still on their missions of finding Calix, his Dop, and searching for Vera. I pray to Bram that the manhunt will be over soon, for the Festival starts tomorrow. Esven is still out of town, but I'm sure he's heard about it by now. It doesn't matter if he knows, because I've lost Daphne. Just like I've lost anyone I've ever cared for. I don't want to go to this Festival. I don't want to go to the Feast. But, I have to.

This damned feast. I don't want to attend, but my coronation is right after the week-long festivities and I must return to being King. My advisors have done a wonderful job of taking care of my affairs and keeping the people calm, along with Daphne, while Esven has been away. But I accepted the responsibility. It's time I take the position King Niall left for me.

⁓

The next day starts early for Brone Castle. I imagine everyone is working diligently to make the Feast incredible. Servants ask my opinion on a multitude of things and relay my answers to a new event planner, Soleil. I chose colors, lighting, food choice…I make my decisions and watch the beauty unfold before me like magic.

She's turned the castle into a mythical wonderland. Vera would be in awe at the sight, it's exactly as the books described. If I didn't know better, I would have thought the Fae enchanted the space. Wisteria hangs from the ceiling, twinkling lights are strewn across every inch of the estate, and *barrels* of wine line the back wall.

Wine. This week will be a battle.

Every member of the court is in attendance for the Feast, except Daphne. My eyes scan the room for her, my heart racing every time a woman enters my field of vision. The banquet hall in all its fantastical glory, changes moods when the lights dim. Nearly naked women dance in gilded bird cages while men drool over their exposed bodies. I lean back, slumped down in my massive tufted chair and watch the belly dancers swing their hips and pout their lips. The charms dangling from their curves create music that perfectly matches the seductive melody of the musicians.

In the corner are poufs, with courtesans flung across them, smoking from long, silver tubes. Billowing tendrils create a thick layer of berry-scented fog, intoxicating those who stand too close. Near the back of the room are naked women sitting in gigantic crystalline glassware. They float in champagne and pour their drunken liquid into the mouths of those underneath who are straining for a peek.

My attention goes to a dark haired man talking closely with one of the jesters, clearly making some type of wager. The man twists around his hand and wins against the jester. The jester, with his ridiculous pointed hat, shoves the winnings into his opponent's hand and the man pockets the coins while snatching a tiny glass of smoking liquor and downing the contents in one gulp. He smiles, the rune tattoo on his cheek glistening like ink under the dim lights.

There are other dealings going on. Middle aged men stand huddled together, talking in hushed tones and passing things from one to another. I squint, but I can't tell what they're doing. Each time a scantily clad young lady walks by, they stare and smile, and when she passes, they go back to business.

I scan other tables and catch a glimpse of a woman with red hair. My heart stops. She turns and smiles at the man next to her but it isn't the beautiful face I want it to be. My eyes brush past her, wishing it was Daphne, and I notice who else is sitting at the head of the table near me. A few courtiers, and the Healer, Valence. I watch Valence laugh and flirt with an attractive young woman with almond eyes and sleek, black hair. They seem to know one another, and by the looks of it, they might be a couple.

The musicians perform and I get lost in the melodies, each one darker than the last. The rhythm mirrors my soul, tragic and desperate. They strike up another tune, this one sending a toe curling ripple through me. Several dancers shimmy their bodies to the tempo, and one of them climbs on top of the banquet table. She wiggles her thighs and her bronze garment flicks with her, back and forth. With bare feet, she steps over the mounds of pomegranates, cakes, and meats, waving her body like waves in the ocean.

The song is coming to an end, and the woman locks eyes with me and smirks. In her version of a bow, she leans forward and picks up a ripe berry with her teeth, the juice dripping down her chest–

"Your Majesty," Finn interrupts my focus, "it is time to address the Court."

I scoot my chair back and stand, the court rising with me. I look around for Daphne, desperate to gaze upon her just once more. I need to quit fooling myself, this is all my doing. I intentionally ruined things with her, and because of that, she isn't coming. Why would she?

"Thank you all for attending Brone Castle's Solurnalia," I say. "This will be the first of many celebrations this week!"

"Huzzah!" the crowd cheers.

A servant pours a glass of dark red wine and places it directly in front of me. Finn looks at me with a pained expression, pleading with me not to pick it up. Without Daphne or Calix here, I don't think I can fight the urge. I drum my fingers on the table, every eye in the audience boring holes in my skin, and lift the glass.

"To the parent gods, to Sol, to our insatiable entertainment brought to us by Lady Toun, and to what I hope to be a week of salacious debauchery!"

The crowd claps and whistles for Soleil Toun, the Lady of Entertainment, as I down the glass of wine.

Everyone cheers and takes a sip of their own drink, returning to their conversations. I wave to a servant to bring me more wine, and the young man delivers an entire bottle to my side. Finn scowls and I scowl back and pull the cork out with my teeth. I fill my glass to the rim and lift it to him and wink. Finn purses his lips and disappears behind a group of illusionists.

Then the large dining room doors open, and flaming copper hair dances in the entryway. The chalice was already on my lips, and I know wine met my tongue, but I don't taste what I'm drinking. I only see Daphne, and she's wearing the most revealing article of clothing I've ever seen.

Her gown is black and the twinkling lights and candle flames make every inch of fabric shimmer. Nearly translucent, there's only enough to make out the shape of a gown. The neckline is open at her collar and the v trails down, ending at her navel. Her collar bones are bare and the cut accentuates the roundness of her breasts that seem to barely be held in place by delicate lace. It teases and taunts me, causing me to fantasize about tracing the neckline of her gown with my mouth.

Daphne purposely sits at the furthest chair from me and I can't take my eyes off her. I drink in her existence like wine, savoring the sweetness of her presence. A shirtless man wearing silver horns and skin tight silver bottoms pours her a glass while Daphne nods at him and throws me side long glances. Her skin is flushing and the pink that appears in her cheeks becomes my new favorite color.

People mingle in the dining hall, chatting and flirting, even though every eye in the room longs for Daphne. For several minutes I just stare at her, even when people vie for my attention. I haven't moved or spoken to anyone since Daphne arrived. She talks to several men, but she doesn't give them any real attention. I know the expression on her face. This performance, that gown, it's all for *me*. She wants to make me jealous, and it's working. *This is what I've given up.*

"Envy isn't green." That's what my father used to say to Vera and I when we were children, and I never understood what he meant until now. Tonight, right here, I've discovered truth in the statement. Envy is black and *maliciously* beautiful. Envy is dark and cold, shameful and arrogant. Envy is lust and disgust that your hungry teeth wrap around, desperate for more to chew on. Daphne's black dress and painted black lips curl around my heart like dying fingers clinging to breath, to life. No; envy isn't green. Envy is a shimmering black gown.

The Feast of Bram has strange traditions. Everyone who's married sits near the back of the dining hall, merely spectators at this event, as the Feast is the catalyst for the week. Unmarried courtiers mingle together, flirting shamelessly to find a partner. The feast is where young women are introduced to the court as potential wives, and it's a great time to wear your heart on your sleeve. Men who pine for a particular woman can freely proclaim their intentions, women can verbalize their desires without shame. This was the week for me, and for Daphne, to make our relationship known.

I wanted to enjoy this week, but watching Daphne even *pretend* to entertain another man's affections has me considering putting an end to this frivolity. She floats from table to table, smiling at them. Talking to them. Tempting them. If I had a sword in my hands I would gut every man in this room and revel in their pain as I watch their entrails spill onto the freshly polished floor.

"Your Majesty," I hear a soft voice to my left.

It pains me, but I tear my eyes from Daphne and focus them on the owner of the soft voice. It's a young blonde woman with round eyes. She curtsies and smiles, her dimples giving her a youthful look of innocence. She's the personification of Siva; pale skinned, light haired, and covered in diamonds.

"Good evening," I stand up with unsteady legs that I'm sure are due to that second bottle of wine. "Forgive me, I don't recall your name."

A flicker of rage flashes across her face but she replies sweetly. "Lucette Matisse."

"Ah, Matisse," I bow. "The Viscount's daughter, and the bane of Sir Arden."

"Correct, Your Majesty," she replies and quirks a brow.

Out of the corner of my eye I see Daphne dancing with the man who gambled with the jester earlier this evening. His hand wraps around her waist and they sway together, whispering. Heat prickles my skin.

"Care to dance?" I say gruffly at Lucette and shoot out my hand.

She takes my hand in hers and we twirl to the beat of the musicians. The crowd watches us, wondering if this is the one I'm going to choose as my partner for the week. It won't be long before they wonder if this girl is the next Queen. Maybe she will be. She's pretty. The longer we dance, I can see that Lucette is smart, calculated. Every twirl is a game of chess. I grab her waist with one hand and firmly hold her against me. She doesn't waver, she only tightens her grip on my other hand. There is no sweat on her palms. *No nerves.*

When the song ends, we part ways and Lucette gracefully returns to her table surrounded by all her noble friends. Some of them look happy for her, and some look utterly offended. *Bravo Lucette.* I can only hope I've made the same impression on Daphne.

Strangely, no other women attempt to dance with me, not even Soleil Toun, my event planner, so I claim another bottle. Each glass I consume seems to create another couple. They leave the dining hall in pairs, some to talk of dowries and inherited fortunes, and some just to bed for the night. I drink so much that at one point, I'm startled to realize that Daphne is no longer present. One of the entertainers tells me she left with the man she was dancing with. *Who is this man?*

It's the end of the feast and I'm alone in the dining hall with only Lucette, some nobles, and a handful of entertainers and servants. Couples are progressing to intimacy in the dark corners of the room, while others sleep on the poufs they were smoking at. *Why did Daphne even come tonight?* I slam my fist on the table and push my chair back. Everyone stops moving. *If Daphne wants to bed someone else, then so will I.*

I grab Lucette's arm. "Let's go."

She doesn't say a word, only looks back at her friends as her feet tap the floor in a hurry to keep up with me. I half drag her through the corridors until we reach the Royal Wing. I push her into the wall and kiss her. She kisses back, hesitantly at first, but then her guard falls. Her fingers drag along my scalp and she grabs a handful of my hair and tugs. The pain feels good. I bite her lip and she whimpers. Our mouths continue to roam and I lead her drunkenly to the door of my chambers.

The guards turn from us as we stumble through the doors, our arms tangled around each other. Lucette tears away from me and coyly pulls the pins from her hair so that it drops past her shoulders, brushing her waist. I watch her loosen the fastenings of her gown, the outer layer falling to the ground around her feet. Then she pulls one shoulder strap down, then the other, exposing her pert breasts. I know what she expects next, and the thought sours my stomach.

"I can't do this," I say and lean my head in my hands.

"Did I do something wrong?"

Her voice pains me. I can't look at her or I'll retch. "Get out."

"Your Majesty," she says softly.

"Get out!"

Lucette gathers the pieces of her gown from the floor and dashes out of the room as the guards come in, swords drawn.

"I'm fine." I wave my hand to shoo them away.

I need to talk to Daphne. Right. *Now.* I rush out of my chambers and towards Daphne's. *Who is the man she flirts with?* All I know is that he doesn't reside in my estate, which means he has no bed to sleep in. In that case, she must have taken him to *her* bed. I march through the halls, stopping right in front of her door and bang on the wood with my fist.

"Daphne!" I roar, "Daphne!

Bedsheets rustle before the door opens. She wears a nightdress, tousled hair, and a clean face. It looks like I just woke her up out of sleep. Before she can say anything I step inside and search the room for the man, any man, so I can wring the life out of them.

"What's the meaning of this?" She snaps at me.

"You–" I pant–, "*you* are the meaning of this. You're the meaning of it all!"

She shakes her head angrily. "You aren't making any sense."

"You instilled a jealousy in me that I did not know could exist in a person. You–that gown–" I growl loudly as I circle the room again.

Daphne opens her mouth to argue but I hold my hand up. "That gown is witchcraft, and it has ensnared me. You have ensnared me. I can't stop thinking of you, and I can't be without you. I'm sorry for pushing you away, but I thought it best with how we left things."

"It *wasn't* best." She snaps again and turns her head from me.

"Every fiber in my being longs for you. You are the only thing that occupies my mind and I realized today that I was wrong. I was wrong about it all. I need you. Seeing you speak to someone else, entertain someone else," I pause to breathe. "It made me sick. I can't watch you with another man. It can only be me, if you'll have me. I'm sorry for everything. Daphne, I– I worship you, I am mesmerized by you. Your mind, your voice. I don't think you grasp the power you have over me. You are my life. You are the sun and the stars. You are–*everything*."

A tear runs down her cheek, but she doesn't look at me.

"Daphne," I place her delicate hand in mine, "I love you."

Her lip twitches, and she wipes the tear from her cheek. "I love you, too."

You are cordially invited to the Welcome Dinner for the
long awaited sister of our dear King Lieve. Please join us
in greeting Princess Vera at Brone Castle on the...
— *Invitation to Prinavian Nobility, sent by Lady Soleil Toun*
and His Majesty, King Lieve Oleander

CHAPTER 31

VERA

How am I going to stop Daphne from using some kind of spell to trick Calix, or any man at court for that matter? I can't talk to anyone about it, Daphne said she would ruin Lieve if I did, and I believe her. I can see how Lieve would have tried anything to stay alive, and to find me. I don't know how powerful she is, and I can't risk putting him in danger just to find out.

Everything seems wrong. All I've ever wanted was to live in Lieve's stories, but now that I'm in one, I'm not sure I'm happy. Maybe I'm feeling out of sorts because I'm in Prinav, but my experiences now are all my own. I didn't get to share them with Lieve, and I have to admit, I'm still angry with him for keeping this place from me when he knows how much I craved an adventure like this. If he would have taken me with him earlier, maybe none of this would have happened. I'm angry that he got himself into a mess with a witch, and I'm angry that I can't even ask him for help.

I sit at the desk in my chambers and pull the *Watch Makers* book from the drawer and open the pocket watch with shaky hands. The gears are stuck, so I use makeshift tools I found and get to work. Once the gears turn with the help of my finger, I flip the faces of the watch so I can look in the mirror. I see my eye, and I stare at it for several minutes as my heart pounds in my chest. I blink and my eye turns black. I want to scream and throw the watch across the room, but I don't. I tilt the mirror to look at her better, and her gaze drifts to the other faces of the watch. I can see her eyes widen, not with shock, but with excitement that I'm fixing it.

Then loud church bells ring and I realize I've been working on the watch for hours. The sun is beginning to set, so I must change my dress for my welcome dinner. It's a pain to have to change my outfit several times a day. Do the rich really have nothing more to do than show off their clothes to one another? This isn't how I pictured life as a Princess would be.

Evalie knocks on the door and enters, carrying a letter and a gorgeous dress draped over her arm. The color is a deep green, and it's made of satin. There aren't any sparkles or ornate embroidery, it's simple and soft. In the candle light it looks like a dream, a fantasy. It's perfect.

She hands me the letter with my name scrawled across in Calix's handwriting. I tear it open and read aloud:

Vera Dear,

Your presence is the spark that will light the flame of change in the King's life, and my wish is for it to ignite a spark in my own life as well. I feel all the waiting and grief might have been worth it. This is just my way of saying, I'm thrilled you're here, and so is Lieve. I want to ask if you'd be my partner for Solurnalia, and I hope you'll wear this gift at your welcome dinner tonight.

Most Devotedly Yours,

Cal

Evalie's whole face lights up. "Isn't this lovely!"

I could burst with happiness. Maybe I really am inside my own fairytale. Could I get my own happy ending? After all these years reading of girls becoming royalty, and of meeting their White Knight,

I might just be writing my own tale in these very moments. I just have to tie up some loose ends with the red-haired witch, and I'll be living in my own perfect little story. I laugh at Evalie as she jumps around the room.

I bounce around the room with her. "Oh Evalie, now I feel like I'm in a dream."

"I imagine so! Becoming royalty *and* having the attention of Lord Bramford? That would make anyone feel like they're dreaming."

"You know, I've always been a lover of stories. Lieve would often recite poems to me about Prinav and tell me wild tales about the gods. I've been feeling like coming here was a mistake, but now with this dress... I feel like Dia meeting Oriel for the first time and falling madly in love, so in love that they defied everything they knew to be together."

"A love like that is rare." Evalie nods.

I wonder if she's thinking of her husband. I don't want her to be sad, so I tease. "So is a face like Calix's."

"Lord Bramford is such a wonderful man, and very handsome." She pats my arm and winks at me. "You're quite lucky to have caught his eye. Many have tried and failed."

"Why *hasn't* he chosen someone since his wife passed?" I ask.

Evalie pulls the dress from her arms, careful not to snag the fabric. "He was so in love with Lady Narah that no one could compare to her." She turns me around to help get me out of my current dress. "At least, until now."

My face grows hot. "I'm nothing special."

"Why of course you are! You're a Princess!" Evalie exclaims.

"I suppose," I say, "but I wasn't always Princess. I've had to resort to thievery so we wouldn't starve to death, and that wasn't so long ago."

"Not every Princess starts out as a Princess. You should know that with all the tales you consume."

"It's a miracle I'm here. It's a miracle I'm even alive," I say to her. "I need to be more grateful."

"King Lieve has searched for you day and night for years. I've heard so many rumors of people who claimed to have found you, and it was a lie. The King was distraught each time a girl was brought to the castle, only to discover an imposter. People are cruel, and I'm betting this all must be terribly overwhelming for both of you."

"It's a surprise, there's no argument there," I reply. " I don't know who to trust in the court, and I'd love to have a real friend."

Evalie pins my hair away from my face. "Well look no further."

I'm so glad I've made a friend in Evalie, and to have a friend in Soleil as well. Maybe there's a way I can confide in them to help me with Daphne. Evalie completes the finishing touches on my look for the night and rummages in the wardrobe for a hairpiece. I return to the desk and slip the pocket watch in my dress as Evalie's back is turned. I don't know why I want it with me now, but it's beginning to give me comfort. I cling to it and vow to keep it close for Lieve; in case I'll need it later. "Thank you, Evalie."

"No need for thanks between friends," she says with a smile and places a gold hairpin dripping with emeralds in my hair.

I make my way to the dining room to meet with Lieve and his wife. I hope I make a good impression on her, not only as my new Queen, but as a sister. I'm nervous as I wander through the halls. To calm myself, I admire the art. It's beautiful here. Grand paintings of the gods fill large spaces of the walls, and many of the windows have stained glass etchings of past monarchs.

A noble man passes by me and I do a difficult little curtsey and my heel slides on the stone, making me wobble like a baby deer. He snickers, bows back, and leaves me in the hallway alone. I hope Calix is already at this dinner to be a buffer to my inevitable awkwardness. I straighten my back and catch myself in the window's dark reflection and frown. I look like I'm trying too hard to fit in.

When I round the corner, I'm right in front of Arden's room. I hear him talking to someone, and I lean close to the door to listen. Arden says my name in a strained voice. *Shit.* He's talking about me. My breath hitches and just as Arden's door opens, the witch pops out.

Her eyes narrow. "Let's walk to dinner together, little eavesdropper."

I swallow the lump in my throat. As we walk, we pass by a window and my reflection smiles at me and then disappears. Is she following me now? My palms sweat as I recall Arden's warnings about the Dops. Then I realize that Arden isn't following us.

"Isn't Arden coming?"

"No." Daphne replies in a flat tone.

We arrive at the dining room doors together, and the ever-present Finn announces our entry. "Lady Daphne Cortwright, and her Highness, Princess Vera Oleander."

When we walk in, Daphne shoves her arm under mine and holds my elbow. I try to shake her off, but her nails bite into me.

"What are you doing?" I hiss.

She smiles broadly and we walk arm-in-arm around the table full of courtiers. Once she lands on a seat that she finds worthy of her noble ass, she gently lets me go. *Now I understand.* Daphne wants the entire court to think we are bosom buddies. If I tell anyone of her gifts, then her retaliation will look genuine, like she might have even turned *me* into a witch. This is a dangerous lie for me.

There's a seat near the head of the table that one of the servants directs me to. Across from that seat is Calix. His eyes scan my body wearing his satin gift and licks his lips. I bite my lip and Calix's eyes darken, causing my knees to weaken. A servant pulls out my chair, but before I can sit, Calix jumps up from the other side of the table and pushes the chair in for me. My heart leaps. Calix basically informed the entire Court that he's interested in me, including Daphne, with that gesture. I smirk. *That just makes her plan that much harder, and that much harder for the court to believe.*

Calix returns to his own seat across from me. The room is buzzing with chatter, but he and I don't make a peep. We just look at each other and smile, both our thoughts lingering on where this evening might end.

"Great dress," Cal says to the man next to him as he not so subtly nods in my direction.

My face grows hot and I know I'm blushing. I fidget in my seat, not knowing what I should do or say.

"Hmm, why yes it is," the man says back without even looking, his eyes stuck on a point at the other end of the table.

The man wears a wig of tightly wound curls covering his head and has deep wrinkles in his face. His hands are clasped together on the table top, mindlessly rubbing his thumb across the other. I follow his eyes to where they focus and see what he's so enamored with. *Daphne.* Looking around the table, most of the men, and some of the women, are also staring at her. I roll my eyes and Calix shrugs, making me laugh.

"Hello, Your Highness."

"Oh, hello again–" I realize it's the noble woman who greeted me on the lawn earlier today.

She leans in and speaks softly, "I am so happy to be seated by you tonight!"

"I am too, and I'm sorry I wasn't able to talk to you earlier."

"Nonsense," she pats my arm gently. "Of course a Princess is busy! I must admit I bribed the staff to sit near you, I hope that's alright and not too forward of me. I'm desperate to be friends, I don't have many friends at Court–"

She makes a face like someone pinched her, and I lean forward a bit and see who the pincher is. I'm not surprised to see the woman with the pursed lips who I met on the lawn with this sweet girl.

"Oh, you know what I mean, Brenna," the girl says. "This is my cousin Lady Brenna Silks, and my name is Lady Poppy Silks."

Poppy visibly trembles as Brenna scoots her chair closer to her. Brenna tilts her head and she's so close to Poppy now that her hair brushes Poppy's arm. Poppy smiles and shimmies her shoulder so that

Brenna's hair falls away. Poppy herself has mousy brown hair, thin lips, and oversized teeth. I had a pet mouse for a short while when I was a child, and it trembled exactly like Poppy is doing right now.

"Well, Lady Poppy," I lean in and feign a whisper, "one can never have too many friends."

Poppy smiles with all her teeth and smooths out her dress while her cousin, the pincher, snaps at a servant to fetch her a glass of wine.

Seated near Daphne is Soleil. They start chatting and laughing like old friends. I catch Soleil's eye and we wave to one another. Daphne's jaw ticks and I think through how I can ask for Soleil's help. I'll have to be careful, for Daphne's warning was clear that I can't tell anyone what's happening, and it's even clearer that she and Soleil are close. But, Soleil didn't want to talk of Daphne in front of Lieve, so maybe they aren't as close as it seems.

"Entering, His Majesty, King Lieve Oleander!" Finn announces.

Everyone at the table slides their chairs back to stand as my brother enters. I don't scoot my chair right away, the sight of everyone standing for my brother puts me in a momentary daze. Lieve walks in a few steps and stops while holding his hand in the air. I can see dark rings under his eyes and wonder if it's from being King, or being drunk again. I plan to tell him I'm willing to help with this Kingdom should he need it, and I hope he accepts.

Finn clears his throat and scowls at the floor. "Entering, Her Majesty, Queen Lucette Matisse Oleander!"

Matisse? Evalie claimed they were horrible people. How could no one have told me this Lucette was a Matisse? I lean forward to try and catch a glimpse of her, but I can't see her. I see only a long white glove, wrapping fingers tightly around my brother's outstretched hand. Her gown matches Lieve's outfit, down to the threads. They both wear ice blue fabric of heavy crepe, with silver buttons along the left sides. My eyes quickly fix on her outrageous hair. Her white-blonde locks are piled two feet high atop her head and there are blue and silver flowers stuck all over it with pins. She looks like a cupcake.

This is the woman Lieve married? I know she's a Queen, but *seriously?* She's the kind of woman we used to make fun of, the kind of Lady that we'd never cross because they're so vindictive. It's peculiar that he would choose someone like her, she's the opposite of his tastes. My eyes flick to Daphne. She's actually more of what Lieve would have been interested in. I dart my gaze back and forth between the two women and think, *Lieve has poor taste all around.*

Lieve and Lucette stare into each other's eyes and they are both glowing. Looking at Calix, I can see that he seems happy about them being together too. Maybe she's different than the Matisse's Evalie spoke of, because Lieve would never marry a woman if she were anything like what Evalie described. Lieve and my new sister walk around the dining room, hand in hand, and stop right in front of me. I make my back rigid, regal, and try to look happy.

Lucette performs a deep curtsey as Lieve takes my hand and places it on top of theirs in an awkward hand shake, hand hold situation. I give a tight lipped-smile and just stand there while everyone watches us. This display is so ludicrous that I have to drop my head for a moment and giggle. I dip my knees an inch or so to curtsey, but it just makes the whole thing more uncomfortable.

"Vera, this is my wife, Queen Lucette," Lieve says to me.

He looks at me with such joy that I feel bad for judging her. Maybe she really is the love of his life. Maybe she's great. Gossip isn't always true and clothing doesn't make a person. Hell, I should know that. I'm going to try and be friends with her, it's only right that I give her a chance.

"Nice to meet you," I say and do a second awkward curtsey with my hand still trapped in our hand pile.

"Yes, well..." she looks me up and down and scrunches her nose. "Lieve has talked of his sister for so long that I had begun to believe you were a figment of his imagination."

"Now now," Lieve says before I can reply and pulls Lucette's arm a little, "let's take our seats."

He winks at me before letting me go and parades Lucette around the dining room again, finally placing her in a high backed chair opposite of his at the two heads of the table. Everyone claps before returning to their seats. *I think Evalie was right about her.*

Jousters for Solurnalia, Day one of the Festival of Light and Dark: Captain Dalis Dugg, Sir Helman Tames, Royal Knight Sir Yul Bowden, Blackband Alexi Briggs, Blackband Julius Montague, Blackband Oliver Blackwell, Blackband Remi Vail, Thomas O'Malley, Rudy Valentini, Gregor Karofski...
– List of Joust Participants

CHAPTER 32
LIEVE

Waking up with Daphne next to me makes me feel like I'm alive again. Her eyes flutter in her sleep and her hair is wild and messy. This is the most beautiful version of her I've ever seen. I wrap my arms around her and pull her close to me, and in her sleep she snuggles against me. She smells like vanilla and I breathe her in. *She loves me. She loves me.*

"Mmm, good morning," Daphne murmurs.

She rolls over and stares into my eyes. I brush her fiery locks back and she holds my palm to her cheek. Our lips press together, slowly, gently. This is paradise. We lay together in silence, just holding each other and soaking in this moment. I'm reminded of our first night together, alone in the dark abbey. I loved her even then. I loved her at the tavern. She's more than I deserve.

Outside the window, muffled swear words drift into Daphne's rooms from servants and workers finishing last minute setups for today's games.

Daphne covers her mouth and we laugh together at the sounds of the men arguing on the grounds below.

"I haven't been to a festival in so many years. This is going to be fabulous," she says.

Energy rises in me and I wink at Daphne. "I admit I'm excited to watch the games and stroll around with you all week long."

"As am I."

"The Game Master told me he was able to entice Skillsmen from all over the continent to join the festivities, so it should be a solid affair."

Daphne's breath catches. "Esven is sure to know about the Festival then."

"There's nothing he can do about it now."

Daphne sighs. "I suppose not."

"All is well," I say and tangle my fingers in her hair and grin. "I can assure you, that if you exchange a kiss with me right now, we shall be forever linked, and no man or god can undo our connected heartstrings."

"A kiss for my heart? That's a hefty wager."

I lean in close to her so that our foreheads touch. "Is it a deal?"

She hesitates. Her eyes burn and before kissing me she whispers, *"Deal."*

Every inch of my body tingles, from the point where her lips press into mine, to the tips of my fingers, and down to my toes. My heart aches with happiness and when we part, silent tears stream down both our faces. Daphne wipes her eyes and I let go of her hair, the electricity between us slowly simmering.

"I hate to tell you this–,"she kisses me again–, "but you need to get back to your own chambers."

Daphne's right. I need to sneak out of her chambers, undetected, and get ready for the day. Daphne and I must keep our escapades secret until the night of the Ball to retain her reputation, and to make sure Esven doesn't try anything against us. Although most of the week's activities largely surround frivolity and lust, there still remains a standard of decorum for a prospective Queen. Daphne must remain pious, and I must keep the nobles on my side. Including Esven, *eventually*.

I kiss her hand and leave the comforting warmth of her bed, "always one step ahead."

"I'm a clever little fox," she teases.

Daphne watches me dress and when I get to the door she smiles the brightest smile, making my heart melt. "I'll see you at the Festival," I say and open the door just a tiny crack and whisper, "*my future Majesty*."

She squeals and kicks her feet, and I just laugh and leave her in her excitement. Esven is intelligent and wealthy, he'll easily find another bride. All will be well, and Daphne's father will come around. He'll accept our marriage once Daphne is Queen of Prinav. How could he disapprove then? I'll keep her safe and become the man she thinks I am. I'll be the man Daphne deserves, the man Prinav deserves.

I act as naturally as possible as I roam the corridors back to my own chambers. The servants all bow and offer me food from the breakfast trays they wheel down the halls. I scoop up a handful of berries, wink at the servants, and almost skip the rest of the way back to my room.

When I enter my chambers, Finn had already drawn me a bath and had a tray full of food and tea waiting on me. I clean up quickly, but with care. I want to look good for Daphne and I can't wait to spend the day with her. I'll stage bumping into her at a tent or a show and we'll lazily wander the shops together.

～

The sun shines over the entire estate as I walk onto the lawn where most of the Festival will be taking place. Dew on the grass dampens my boots, and I slightly sink into the wet earth. Honeyed spices, perfumes, and damp soil fill the air. Now that the sun has risen, it illuminates the estate, and the white of the castle seems to sparkle in the early morning. Today I feel as I did the first day I ever arrived in Prinav. Full of hope and magic. I'm light on my feet as I make my way to the enormous field the workers have turned into a vibrant carnival.

The Festival of Light and Dark begins at dawn and ends well into the night for four days. Mornings consist of breakfast foods, shopping in the merchants tents, playing lawn games, and watching Skillsmen perform great feats. The afternoons have acrobatic shows, grand lunches, and duels, while the evenings are full of theater, lavish drinking, and gambling. It's a safe way to be with Daphne all day without people spreading rumors.

Crowds of people are already gathered, dressed in traditional Festival attire. The women are wearing pastels, creams, and white day gowns, while the men don dark jewel tones, maroons, navy, greens, and blacks. The contrast alludes to the River of Light and Dark, as well as Dia and Sol. Everyone mills around, excitement buzzing like bees.

I scan the faces around me for Calix's Dop, but the guards assure me that he's not here, but that they're watching for him. Daphne has tried having a funeral for the real Cal, but I can't. I can't come to terms with his probable death and I won't give up hope that somehow he's still alive. I've had men searching as far as Prinav's borders, and we have reward posters scattered all across the Kingdom for him, as well as for Vera.

"We won't stop looking for either of them, Sire," one of the guards says to me with a bow and hurries away.

There's nothing more I can do but wait and hope, so I walk along the grass in between the tents and let my mind drift to more pleasant thoughts. The tents are laid out in rows on either side of me and I try to count them, but they pepper the fields as far as the eye can see. Merchants run the tents, selling everything from necklaces, books, and cloaks, to arrows, daggers, and leather armor.

It's just like the stories I would recite to Vera to calm her down before another night of sleeping on an empty stomach. I brush my memories aside and peek into the booths as I pass them by. One has a young man with ginger hair and a pointed nose getting a tattoo of Sybill, the death god, inked into his forearm. He scrunches his face up as the tattoo artist hammers the needle into his flesh. I wince before moving onto the next tent.

Another booth is full of books. *Books.* My heart breaks as I walk in the tent when I read one of the titles: *An Ode To Prinavian Lovers,* Poems by T C Marra. Vera would love this. I pick up the book and the cover falls, hanging on to the rest of the binding by mere threads. The merchant, a young woman with sunkissed skin and golden hair, looks at me and flushes.

"Oh dear, that book is a disgrace."

I hold it up, the cover swinging and I chuckle. "My sister would love it."

She flushes, "I can't let you buy that, it's horrendous."

"Then I'll just have to take it as a donation." I smirk and place a handful of coins in her hand and walk out of the booth.

I ruffle the pages, catching glimpses of words like adore, admire, and desire. I can see Vera's hands in my mind, turning the pages and devouring text after text until the candle's all burned out. She couldn't get enough of the written word. I place the book in my pocket and keep trudging along the tents, my eyes peeled for Daphne, when I hear a voice call to me. I turn and see that it's another merchant, calling from an artisans booth.

"G'day, Your Majesty," the merchant says.

I nod at her in reply, and freeze when I realize what it is. *A Lopter Tree.* Not a real tree, but enamel brooches depicting it. Am I going to be reminded of Vera in everything I see today?

"How much for a pin?" I ask the girl.

She scoops the pin from the table and walks around to stand in front of me. "I've had these for years and they never sell. They say it's bad luck if you wear them, so you can take this one for free. Maybe if the others see you wearing it they'll flock like birds to my booth and buy the rest of them without superstition clouding their judgment."

My voice falters a little. "I will leave you more money than it's worth. This is special to me, it reminds me of someone."

Her lips curl into a smile and she pokes the pin through my vest and adjusts it for me. The merchant's hands remind me of Vera too, small and long-fingered. She doesn't look a thing like Vera. Her hair is short and curly, and adorned with colorful charms and beads, but she reminds me so much of my sister anyway. Even the way she tilts her head while adjusting my vest is exactly how Vera used to do.

I see another set of pins, two foxes, male and female. The female is a copper color and has a sly look on its face, and the male is a dark, a silver fox, almost black in color. They're placed on the table next to each other, almost in a scene of the male chasing after the female. Daphne's words from this morning echo in my mind, *'I'm a clever little fox.'*

I pull out a handful of coins and point to the fox pins, "I'll take those, too."

Once I pay, I go in search of my real-life vixen. My heart leaps from my chest when I find her with Arden at the jousting arena.

"There's been no sign of Calix," Arden says.

Arden wears his usual black leathers, cloak and mask, to hide the scar on his lip from the day Narah died. Guilt ripples through me when I remember the blood flying from his mouth as my blade accidentally cut him.

"I heard," I reply.

Arden nods at the Skillsmen. "Are these the best you could find on such short notice?"

I smirk at him. "Have *you* entered any of the contests?"

"And ruin the festivities?" He waves his hand out to the participants lined up inside the arena. "I wouldn't want to win every tournament and bring shame to your soldiers."

"To be fair, that's probably exactly what would happen," I say as my eyes meet Daphne's.

She winks at me. "It *is* true," she says and pats Arden's shoulder, not unlike a mother would when validating her teenage son. "You're quite talented."

It's amazing watching her with him. Months ago, Daphne was sure that Arden couldn't handle himself, but she stepped up after Narah's death to fill the role his sister had. She coaxed him out of his shell a bit, and helped him channel some of his rage into more productive avenues.

He's even been helping the stable boys with the horses recently. Daphne's patience is something to marvel at. She's been patient about my drinking, and about Lopter's blood. Every time I behave erratically she just leans against the stool in the corner of her potion room, or a chair in one of our chambers, folds her arms, and closes her eyes. She listens. She waits.

What a gift love can be for a person when it's freely given. Daphne's unwavering care for me is a beacon of hope that I now cling to. My parents loved Vera and I, but they were always busy, always working. Mom would listen while folding laundry, and then interrupt me to have me help her with another task, never allowing me to finish a full thought with her. Dad, well, I don't remember having an actual conversation with him that didn't surround survival.

No one cared about what I had to say, except for Vera. She clung to every word. She would fight me, but I always knew I was heard. Daphne's version of love is similar to Vera's, and maybe that's another reason why I'm in love with her.

Daphne is similar to Vera in that way, of always listening. Daphne will hear you out, whether she likes what you're saying or not. She might argue with you, but I've never wondered if Daphne heard me or saw me; and I've never felt misunderstood by her. Arden is lucky to be partially raised by a woman like that. He will always know there's at least one person who will always be there for him, and hear him, see him, even when he isn't talking. Daphne is a gifted seer, in every way that matters.

Daphne leans in close, her lips brushing my ear and whispers, "father agreed."

"Agreed to what?"

"To your proposal. He's going to talk with Lord Esven about it tonight."

Bewildered, I turn and face her, trying desperately not to grab her and kiss her in front of everyone. "You're joking?"

Daphne grins as she shakes her head. "I talked him into it this morning."

He agreed. I'm speechless as the three of us watch the joust together in the front row of the stands as the participants mount their horses and secure their helmets. I feel like I could fly over the crowd and sing. Arden notices that there's a shift between us and his eyes crinkle with a hidden smile as the jousters begin to warm up.

The clank of metal-on-metal stings my ears. I haven't heard that sound in a while. I train, and I've trained Arden, but this is different. The noise of the crowd, the thunder of the horses' hooves. My throat tightens as the horses snort and paw at the dirt while people clap, rooting for their favorite Knight. I swear I can taste the tinge of blood in my mouth.

A loud voice booms over the crowd. "Are we ready!"

I'm not ready. I see King Niall on his pearl horse in the valley, an arrow stuck in the socket of his eye.

"Three!"

Heads rolling on the ground at my feet, their lifeless eyes staring into mine. I'm sweating. My hands ball up into fists and my fingernails slice into my palms.

"Two!"

The world around me is drowning in red. *Blood.* My heart hammers in my ears, pulsating just as loud as the cheering crowd around me.

"One!"

I stand up too fast and my head spins. Daphne reaches out and holds my hand, and a fizzing sensation pulsates in my fingers. The bubbles travel up my arm and pour into my chest, filling my lungs. I've never felt anything like it before, it's a tickle, not unlike having a tickle in your throat. The fizzing begins to calm me down until I see the tiniest glow in between our interlaced hands. Daphne performed magic. *In the open.*

She doesn't look me in the eye, only looks forward at the joust. I cough and she releases my hand, still focused on the show in front of her. Carefully, I glance around the audience. Thankfully no one seems to have noticed her glowing bubbles of tranquility. Everyone around us rises from their seats to jeer and shout at the jousters, and when the victor claims the win, he rides over to our section and does a small bow.

I wave at him and turn to wave at the crowd around the arena too, and the people wave back cheerfully. My stomach churns when I think of this beautiful day full of lovely people, and how they would turn on us without so much as a moment's notice had they seen what Daphne did for me. That familiar acidic taste of bile begins to rise from my stomach and into my throat.

"Lieve," Daphne whispers through a tight smile, "are you okay?"

I glare at her while mentally pushing the tang of vomit back down. "No."

Daphne stands up and loops her arm in mine to pull me away. Arden begins to stand but she places her hand on his shoulder, telling him without words to stay seated. Sweat beads across my hairline and trails down my face as every eye in attendance follows us. Daphne smiles and waves as we walk by. Many narrow their eyes at us, but with a confident look from Daphne, their faces soften.

"His Majesty must have had one too many glasses of wine last night," she giggles to a group of nobles whose expressions could cut glass.

We reach the bottom of the arena and Daphne continues to pull me along. Now that we're out of the crowd, I don't feel like retching. I lean on a fence post and breathe, but then my stomach flops again. Not more than twenty feet away stands Esven, and if looks could kill I would have fallen over dead. I don't know what to do as he strides over to us, a venomous scowl painted on his face.

"Good day," he hisses at the two of us.

Daphne curtseys. "Good to see you Gelhert. His Majesty wasn't feeling well so I brought him from the crowds."

"Hmm." He eyes the sweat on my brow. "It does look like you are unwell, shall we get you a Healer? It seems like you need one."

"Wonderful idea, my Lord," Daphne says graciously, and yanks my hand to follow her away from him. "I'll take him to Valence and meet you at the arena later on."

"Do that." Esven snarls.

More thunderous cheering erupts from the stands. The next joust must have begun. We scurry around to the back of the arena, out of Esven's poisonous stare, and step behind the backside of a large merchant tent.

"When did he get here?" Daphne panics. "The contracts are signed. What if he won't agree to the new negotiations now that he's seen us together? He could force me not to go to the ball and all hope might be lost for us."

I rub my temples. This is bad. This is *really* bad. Esven is bound to ruin everything. Anger and fear bubble up within me and I spew, "Are you insane!".

"Am *I* insane?" She throws her arms out. "Am *I* insane!" Daphne points at me. "You were losing it! I had to get you away from the crowds."

I swipe my hand across my brow to wick the sweat away. "We can't be seen together again now that Esven has returned, not until your Father has annulled the contracts. And you can't do magic in the open like that. Never again."

"It helped, didn't it?"

"That isn't the point," I say and take her hands in mine. "What if someone noticed? You'd be killed. You can't just perform magic out in public, I was sick thinking that the entire arena could have turned into a mob and taken you from me."

A rustle from the side of the tent startles us and we drop each other's hands. I swallow the lump in my throat as a foot appears from the shadows. The foot is attached to a leg, a leg with expensive stockings, and they are attached to a noble woman, and that noble woman is *Lucette Matisse.*

Lucette raises her icy blonde eyebrow and licks the top row of her perfectly pearl white teeth and says, "Yes Lady Daphne, what if someone noticed?"

I beg of you to help us.
– Correspondence of King Rafi Durant of Madoria to Queen
Ursula Brone of Prinav during the Mador-Seelie War of the
Drols.

CHAPTER 33

VERA

Servants place our dishes in front of us. The smell of buttery duck wafts around the room, making my mouth water. With everything that's been on my mind recently, I'd forgotten to eat. I pick up my fork and Poppy politely taps my knee and nods in Lucette's direction. Lucette scrapes her fork and knife together and slices into her duck, peeks at the meat, and smiles. Everyone at the table, including Lieve, seems relieved and then picks up their own silverware to dig into their meals. It seems as if the Queen is in charge of the court, and not my brother. *Is Lieve really okay with this?*

"Thank you," I whisper to Poppy.

She cuts into her own duck. "What are friends for?"

Calix is tearing into his food while Lieve is talking to the noble with the ridiculous wig, the noble whose eyes are glued to Daphne figure.

"Your wife must be distraught without you," Lieve says to him.

I poorly hide a snort of laughter under a quick sip of wine. Lieve noticed the man panting over Daphne as well.

"Yes, but I'm sure her multitude of lovers are ready to quench her loneliness." He huffs.

"You and your wife don't get along?" I ask him.

His eyes dart to Lieve before he finally looks at me. "Arranged marriage."

"Oh Cavel," Lieve says with a wide grin, "Lady Janelle is lovely, don't pretend like you weren't overjoyed at the union."

"She's Madorian," Cavel mutters and shovels a large bite of meat into his mouth.

"What's so wrong with Madorians?"

"Nothing," Soleil interjects, "it's a beautiful country–"

"They're greedy." Cavel growls.

"Greedy?" I ask.

"Greedy. The lot of them. They needed money to fund their war over the Drols, we paid. They needed workers to rebuild their palaces, we sent them. They needed men to marry their women to keep them out of poverty, we married them."

Cavel then glares at Lieve while taking a long draught of ale. *I wonder what that's about.* I swirl around my glass of wine before taking another sip of the tart juice.

"Lady Janelle wasn't poverty-stricken." Calix rolls his eyes.

"Janelle wasn't titled either, she may as well have been homeless for all I'm concerned." Cavel grunts.

I bite my tongue so as to not cause a scene during my first interactions with Lieve's court, but Cavel is making it very difficult. Everything about this man grates on my nerves. He's why Lieve and I never liked aristocrats, they're all the same. They all judge the poor and carry resentment for them, when without them, the rich wouldn't exist.

"Trash." He shovels another mouthful in his face. "Madorian trash."

My hands clench my silverware and my arms tremble as I strain not to stab him with cutlery. I watch Cavel's face as sweat beads across his forehead with every bite. *Let him choke.*

With his food bouncing around his open mouth, Cavel points his fork at me. "They need us. Not just the trash in Madoria, but the peasants here in Prinav. We give them jobs, we let them attend Solurnalia, we tax very little compared to our neighboring Kingdoms–"

The servants around the table stiffen. Cavel goes on and on about the difference between those with and without titles, and what he would change if Lieve gave him the grace to create new laws. *What a complete and utter ass.* At least Lieve hasn't bought into this way of thinking. I would eviscerate him if he ever agreed with these outlandish opinions.

"You say the people in Madoria are without a lot of wealth–," I swirl my wine–, "so what do you think should happen with them? Abandon them?"

Soleil scoffs. "Surely not. Mardoria has been a faithful ally for two hundred years."

"They've been a nuisance for two hundred years," Cavel argues.

"Nuisance? No. Peasants aren't a nuisance, they are strong. Imagine what you would do if everything you knew–everything you had–was taken away from you." I say.

The room turns silent, and everyone stops what they're doing to listen to me. Silverware clicks against plates, someone at the end of the table coughs. My hand, still slightly trembling with rage, brings my drink to my lips again and I take another sip of wine to steady my nerves.

"Place yourself in the boots of another for just a moment," I say while boring a hole into Cavels skull with my stare. "Your ally, *wealthy* ally, decides they don't want to help anymore. No more gold. No more workmen. You don't know how to grow your own crops and the 'peasants' you once dismissed in your own kingdom won't sell their produce to you. Your noble friends don't want anything to do with you anymore, because now *you're* considered a peasant, a *commoner*. You become a servant for wealthy families, but it's degrading work and doesn't pay nearly enough. You bounce from manor to manor with bread as your only sustenance for the majority of your meals. Eventually hunger possesses every thought you have and you must steal to survive.

But, you've never done this before and you get caught. You might go to prison, you might be whipped, you might even be hung."

"Where is this leading?" Cavel scoffs.

I place my glass on the table and notice I'm not shaking anymore. "When you insult peasants you insult me, and you insult your King. For that is the Oleander story, sire. Be grateful for what you have and stop judging those without. Anyone could fall on hard times, even those sitting at this very table. I imagine many of the Madorians who asked for help were once in positions of wealth, and I'm sure the Madorians don't like the situation any more than you do."

"My wife may not like her situation, but she doesn't complain about it, especially when she's spending my money so frivolously."

"Well, for her sake, I hope she's getting your money's worth." I say.

Poppy sputters and spits dark red wine across the table, showering Cavel in tiny droplets. He wipes his face with a cloth napkin, shaking with fury.

"Huzzah!" Calix exclaims and holds up his glass.

The rest of our party bursts into laughter and clinks their glasses together. "Huzzah!"

Cavel dismisses himself and I take another sip of my wine, meeting Cal's gaze. He grins at me, that devilish grin, and I fail to hide my smile. My heart is beating wildly. I've never talked to a nobleman like that before. I've never talked to anyone like that before. I sit up straighter in my chair and eat the rest of my meal with confidence.

The staff all serve me with more care than even Lieve and Lucette after that display and many of them outwardly smile at me, making sure my drink is constantly full. I notice them walk with a little more ease, and a few of their faces seem to beam with pride. It feels good to stick up for my kind, especially in front of *these* people. But the fascination with me quickly ends, for when I study the other faces in the room, the courtiers at the table have already forgotten what happened and returned to their conversations of mind-numbing gossip. All but

Daphne. Daphne has a tiny smirk and coyly glances at me while she eats.

When the meal is over, the court all bow to me or raise a glass as they leave the room. I wonder if taking Cavel down a notch earned me a bit of real respect from them. I nod back or raise a glass to each one in return, and soon I'm left with only Lieve, Calix, and Lucette.

"I'm tired darling," Lucette says to my brother.

Lieve strides over to her, loops his arms in hers and winks. "Goodnight, you two."

"Goodnight," I reply and turn to Lucette with a curtsey. "It was a pleasure meeting you, Your Majesty."

"Hmm," she purrs, tapping a finger to her lip. "It was quite–*enlightening*."

Lieve doesn't say anything, he just has an anxious expression and pulls Lucette from the dining room before I open my mouth again. I thought Prinav was going to be perfect. I thought the royals and nobles would be just as Lieve described, but now I'm disappointed. Prinav isn't much different than Adamston, only my feelings about it have changed.

"Lucette is–" Cal puts a finger to his lip, mocking her–, "difficult."

I chuckle and lean my bottom against the dinner table. "Is she always like that?"

Calix leans forward, his forearms resting over the back of the chair beside me, our faces now at eye level. "For the most part, yes."

"If she's–" I struggle with the right words to describe her and gesture at the door she walked out of–, "*difficult*, then why did Lieve choose her?"

"He was set on Daphne Cortwright, but that ended poorly. Lucette is attractive, intelligent, loyal to her country–" He stops his defense when I fold my arms and huff. "Her family, the Matisse's, are prominent. Lieve made a wise political choice with her."

"Does he love her?"

"Only commoners marry for love," Calix says while running a hand through his dark hair.

My heart drops.

"*Usually*," he grins again and that familiar twinkle returns to his golden eyes.

Calix is a whirlwind. An adventure. I watch the muscles in his arm flex with only subtle movements and my mouth waters. An adventure that I desperately want to embark on.

"That dress really does look nice on you." The tone in his voice lowers, sending a ripple of excitement coursing through me.

I look down at myself in mock disgust. "Oh, this old thing? I found it in my wardrobe."

"It's a miracle it fits," he says, creeping closer like a cat ready to pounce.

Calix comes close enough to share a breath. He runs his hands down the bare skin of my arms and goosebumps follow in his wake. He holds my hand in his, lacing our fingers together, while the other travels up to push a strand of hair behind my ear. My breath hitches as my body anticipates our lips touching again.

This kiss isn't as hurried as the last. It's no longer a stolen moment in the hall, or behind the stables, it's the culmination of days of tension. His lips meet mine with confidence, the confidence Calix always has, as though he always knew we'd end up here. Like he was sure he'd be kissing me again. His lips are sweet with wine against mine as he gently nibbles at my bottom lip, then sucks at it to soothe the sting. I gasp into his mouth and he swallows my breathy moans greedily.

"Don't be too loud, Vera dear. After all," he says with a smirk, "we can't let the servants hear us."

I nod and he tastes me again, tilting my head to deepen the kiss. His free hand starts in my hair and wanders, and I can feel my core tighten. His tongue explores my mouth, and I let a moan escape when he cups my breast. My own hand travels first to his waist, and then finds the firmness between Calix's legs. I push myself against him and rock my hips. He then digs his fingers into my flesh and hoists me up so I'm sitting on the table and I wrap my legs around his waist. Calix's mouth leaves my own and trails to my neck, leaving me reeling for more.

Church bells fill the air, and it distracts me. I open my eyes and Calix lets go of me. He uses his thumb to wipe his lip and grins, so I grab the collar of his shirt and pull him closer once more, his firmness hard against me. The bells ring again and I hear a servant on the other side of the doors say our names and then begin to pray to Bram, and Siva, and even Hode.

Calix laughs softly. "I think we've been discovered."

The bell chimes once more and Calix places me on my feet. He grabs my face and kisses me again, causing every nerve in my body to catch on fire. The praying gets louder and we both know this won't be the time or place for us to get intimate, so I smooth my dress and stand next to the door.

Before Calix opens it, he kisses the back of my hand. "Another night, perhaps."

"Perhaps," I breathe.

Once in the hallway, we part ways. When I arrive in my chambers I place the pocket watch under my pillow before taking off my dress and slinking under the covers. Everything about Calix is so perfect. He is the answer to all my dreams, and I can't believe I've found a man like that. I guess anything could happen now that I'm here. Look at me now, I *am* a Princess after all.

My fingers wrap around the cool metal of the watch. I have so many questions about this watch, and Lieve, and about Lucette and Daphne. Why is Lieve being so submissive to her? What happened between him and Daphne? There's a lot for me to learn about Prinav, and not all of it is pleasant. I tuck the watch close to my chest and sigh. Prinav might not be exactly as I imagined, or how I wanted it to be—but that doesn't mean I can't change things.

Monroe Brone, Crown Prince of Prinav, only son of
King Niall Brone and the Queen: Missing.
– *Announcement at Mercat Cross, Barault, Prinav.*

CHAPTER 34

LIEVE

"What do you want?" Daphne snarls.

Lucette twirls a strand of her icy blonde locks around her finger and pouts her lip, "I just want what I deserve."

Daphne rolls her eyes. "I'll ask once more; *what do you want?*"

Lucette stomps her foot like a toddler and her face turns red. "I want to be Queen."

My eyes dart back and forth between them as they circle around each other like sharks circle their prey. I need to step in, but I don't know what to say. How much does Lucette know?

Daphne then snorts at Lucette's wish. "What makes you think the King would choose you?"

Lucette prowls towards me and her face is slowly turning back to its shade of milky peach. "I was the only courtier he chose to dance with last night, and I'm sure I'm the only courtier who was in his bed chambers after the Feast."

Daphne's eyes snap to mine and her face hardens. *Shit.*

"I undressed in his room–" Lucette begins but I cut her off.

"That's enough."

Daphne marches past me and I grab her wrist, but she wrangles it free and leaves me alone with Lucette.

"You're playing a dangerous game," Lucette says to me.

"Drop this."

"Unless you want all of Prinav burning Brone Castle to the ground with your precious witch inside it, I suggest you listen to me." Lucette twirls her hair again. "You will announce our engagement by the end of the week."

"I will do no such thing." I sneer.

Her face turns red again. "I guess I'll go to the Priests and tell them what I saw then."

"They won't believe you," I say. But I'm not sure if that's true.

"I am the daughter of a Viscount and the niece of Prinav's most notable Sagart, and you are the Foreigner King. You may be feared by the people for your battle skills, but I'm not so sure you're loved just yet. Are you sure you've got unwavering loyalty already?"

I grit my teeth. "Your point?"

"My point, *Your Majesty*, is that you should think long and hard about who the people will believe more." Lucette then takes her fingernail and traces my jaw. "You're the one who brought me to your chambers for the entire court to see. You made such a display with me last night, it's no secret we spent time alone together. I'm not entirely cruel though, you have my permission to keep the witch as a mistress, just as long as *I'm* the one wearing the crown."

Lucette then hikes up her skirts and walks away like nothing happened. "Oh, and I've told my father about last night, and he witnessed Lady Daphne's secret little magic show too...He was seated in the stands only a few rows back from you. So don't even think about trying anything, you'll only get the two of you killed. You've ruined my reputation, so take the day to accept my merciful offer, and I'll let you keep your life."

I rush from behind the tent and back to the stands of the arena. Daphne isn't there, and neither is Arden. My heart drums against my ribs, and the only breaths I can manage are sharp and painful. I was right in what I saw in Lucette last night. She's cunning. I don't know how to get out of this mess. How many people saw Daphne's spellwork? How many people know I took the Viscount's daughter to my room?

I leave the festival and go back to the castle to see if Daphne went to her rooms. I'll explain that nothing happened with Lucette, and that I only brought her there out of jealousy. She'll understand. She always understands. Everything will be fine, we just need to figure out our next step.

Arden opens Daphne's door when I arrive. He won't move out of the way so I can pass, or even look me in the face. He just stares at the floor. Daphne sits on a bench at the end of her bed with her back to me.

"Daph–" I start.

She holds her hand in the air, and that small gesture seems to grip my throat. All the words I want to say to her are choked and gone.

"You brought another woman to your chambers," she whispers without turning around.

"Nothing happened," I say as delicately as I can. "I stopped it before it even started."

She turns to me, face as hard as stone. "You have every right to bed anyone you wish."

"I don't wish to *bed* anyone," I say, my face growing hot when I remember that Arden is still in the room.

"And I don't wish to be hung, so I suggest we finally let go of whatever this is between us." She stands, gesturing from me to her.

"Let's figure out how to remedy this," I cry. "I want *you!*"

"I'm going to marry Lord Esven. *That* is the remedy."

I shake my head. "No, please. Talk to me, help me."

"I have no more words to say."

I reach my hand out to touch her shoulder and she recoils like I'm diseased. My heart beats hard enough that I can feel it bruise me from the inside out. This can't be the end of us.

"I will fix this." I say and storm from the room.

～

There is no remedy. I stay up all night trying to find a way out of this, but find no solution. Lucette and her family have orchestrated her ascension to the throne with such precision that I question the rest of the court's loyalties now. I feel like I'm being watched. Everywhere I turn there's a new Priest to meet, a new hand to shake. I imagine every person scrutinizing me, like they know all my secrets.

Lucette was right, Prinav fears me...but do they trust me? Do they love me? I am to be King by the wish of Niall, chosen for reasons I'll never learn. They accept me as their King for now, though, but what good have I done since that horrific battle? I've drank anything I could get my hands on and I've barely been present in recent meetings. It wouldn't be hard to turn the court, and then the whole Kingdom, against me.

Daphne and I could run away together, but everyone knows who I am. I couldn't take care of her like I took care of Vera, I would be picked out of a crowd in an instant. We could go to a neighboring country and live as commoners if I can convince Daphne to leave behind this life. I could hang Lucette, her Viscount father, and her Sagart uncle for treason. But how many courtiers know my secret? How many will come forward for the Matisse's? If the paranoia never stops, I'd have to hang half the nobles in Prinav. *Maybe I should.*

～

The following morning I scour the festival for Daphne. I'm going to ask her if she wants to run away with me, or if she wants me to hang

Lucette. I'm happy to do either and pay the consequences when they come. I spot Arden near the sword fighting arena, but he's alone.

"Do you know where Daphne is?"

Arden leans in. "Esven requested to have breakfast with her."

"And?"

"She went." He leans in even closer and lowers his voice."Leave her alone. She just wants out of this cycle with you. Everything is very hot and cold."

I bite the inside of my cheek so onlookers can't see my rage. "Is she still with him?"

"Yes."

"Well, where are they?" Arden is trying to defend Daphne, but he must know I love her. "Arden please, I love her."

"She loves you too, but it just isn't going to work." He pats my shoulder. "I *know* you know that."

I bury my face in my hands. "I can't let her go."

"If you cannot do this for her, you'll start a civil war with the Matisse family." Arden looks around, making sure people aren't listening in. He pulls back his hood and scratches the top of his head. "The Dops don't even compare to how vicious the Matisse's are. They would kill every noble in Prinav just to prove a point, and they've done it before. The court you have is only half a century in the making, and they're made up of nobles handpicked by the Matisse's."

My fingers grip the fence dividing the audience from the Skillsmen. "You don't think I can defeat them?"

"You don't have the numbers. The Viscount has a hand in every pocket in the Kingdom, and most of Prinav owes their good fortune to him. Over time, the people will give you their loyalty, but there's nothing that can be done at this moment."

"So now they're using Lucette to gain access to the crown. Why didn't they try this with King Niall?"

"The Brone bloodline were the monarchs of Prinav for centuries, the True Rulers picked by the Crystal Throne. They were handpicked by the gods to rule over everyone else. The Matisse family is deeply faithful to the old lore of the gods and would never go against their wishes, but Niall only had one child. He went missing many years ago and his wife was hanged as a witch. He had no siblings–"

"No heirs," I finish his sentence for him.

"Exactly." He pulls his hood back up. "So when a foreigner was handed the throne–"

I interrupt him again–,"They decided now was the perfect time to snatch it up, and the drunken foreigner King who hasn't chosen a wife yet was the perfect pawn."

Arden looks me in the eyes. "Even if all of this weren't true, Daphne has been distraught over you for a very long time. Please let her go."

Arden's wrong. Daphne and I are meant to be together. I'll play Lucette's game for now, but I'll find a way out of this. Prinav deserves more than a phony Foreigner King, they deserve the Conductor of Death. They deserve a defender of the crown, and that's *exactly* what they're going to get.

Parasite: *an organism that lives on or in another organism and benefits doing so by deriving its needs at the other's expense.*

CHAPTER 35
VERA

In the morning, I return to the dining room for breakfast and I find Lieve, Lucette, and her father. Servants bring in the food, and again we wait to see if Lucette is going to approve the meal before we can take a bite. This ritual is so ridiculous. I try to catch Lieve's eye, but he seems enamored with her. She cuts into her quiche and the servants hold their breath. Lucette scrunches her nose and places the food in her mouth. Her expression softens, the mood in the room softening with it.

"Where is Calix this morning?" I ask.

"He'll be gone for a little while," Lieve answers. "He's doing some errands for me."

"How long will he be gone?"

Lucette scrapes her dish with her knife. "I would like to spend some time with you today, Princess."

Great.

"Of course, it's just that–"

"Then it's settled." She pats Lieve's hand while keeping her eyes on me. "You and I will have tea this afternoon."

"That's a wonderful idea!" Lieve exclaims.

"Agreed, our royal ladies should get to know each other." Lucette's father says and winks at her. "We're family, afterall."

Although I have no desire to spend a moment alone with Lucette, maybe this tea will bring us closer. I can ask her about their relationship. Maybe spending time with her alone will help me get to know her and see if she's as bad as her family. Just because Evalie says the Matisse family is horrid, doesn't mean Lucette is. I doubt Evalie was lying, but I owe it to Lieve to try and make friends with her.

Evalie helps me get ready for tea with Lucette. She dresses me in a gown covered in floral embroidery and sweeps my hair out of my face. I don't know if I'll ever get used to the idea that Lieve and I are rich now. Not just rich, but *exceedingly* rich. Every inch of fabric reminds me of our old lives, of how much has changed. Even Lieve has changed. He's been to war, he's married, he's a King. I just hope it's for the better.

I guess now, to fit in with him again, I have to fit into this new life. I have to be friendly with Lucette, even if it kills me. If she and I cannot get along, that will be a tear in the fabric that binds Lieve and I together. I *must* try.

"Just be nice," Evalie says while she secures the last of the buttons on the back of my tea gown.

"She needs to be nice too," I pout.

Evalie laughs. "No she doesn't." Her hands fluff the flowing lace of my skirts. "She's the Queen."

I pull the skirts playfully from Evalie. "And I'm the Princess."

"Just be nice," she says again and gently shoves me out of my chambers, praying to Siva as I stumble from the door.

I pull up my skirts and stride down the corridors to the tearoom. Evalie says that's where Lucette has tea with her maids, ambassadors, and guests. I imagine the room to be a doily lined, frilly curtained, pink nightmare. My floral gown is going to blend into the sofa and the tea will be so sweet I'll be sick to my stomach. I could kill Lieve for this. Why would he say it's a great idea? *Why!*

Standing in front of the door to the tearoom, I take a deep breath, preparing myself for the heavily perfumed air that will undoubtedly hit me in the face when the door opens. Servants open the double doors, which surprisingly aren't made of heavy wood. They're made of stained glass, with brass frames, and crystal knobs.

I'm led inside by one of Lucette's maids, a short woman with a face full of freckles and a sour expression. She takes quick steps and when we pass through the entrance and into the main room, my jaw drops at how beautiful it is. It's *nothing* like I imagined. The ceiling is tinted blue glass, letting the sunlight spill in and cast cool toned beams across the room. There are massive crystal chandeliers, more stained glass windows, and plenty of brass inlays around the window trim. The air is warm, but not stuffy, and the scent of jasmine floats in the air.

"Watch the water on the ground, Your Highness," says the maid.

As she warns me about the water, my feet step into a tiny puddle on the stone floor, soaking my satin slippers. I don't care about wet feet though, because it's hard to stop myself from spinning in circles to look at everything. I'm astonished to find that the water comes from an indoor waterfall. Droplets mists my face as we walk by, and the coolness is refreshing in this warm solarium.

If Lucette created this, then there has to be something we can relate to each other with. There must be something good in her, to design something so beautiful. Evalie might be wrong about her. I stand there and let the water dampen my gown, but then my thoughts are interrupted by the maid.

"Please keep up, Your Highness." Lucette's maid's voice is sharp and her steps are quick. "The Queen doesn't enjoy being troubled with waiting on others."

With a sigh, I pick up my heavy skirts and follow the maid to the tea space. We round the waterfall and on the other side is another surprising scene. Lucette, in a small pond, *naked*.

"Oh–" I gasp.

Lucette points her nose in the air. "I do all my best thinking in water."

"I thought we were having tea," I say and avert my eyes.

"We are."

I keep my gaze focused on the glass ceiling. Lucette splashes around the water before stepping out of the pond. The maid, who's name I still don't know, rushes to bring her a robe.

Lucette giggles. "You can look at me now, princess prude."

I scowl. "I'm no prude, I was just surprised."

"See! This was a great way to break the ice, was it not?" Lucette's robe flows behind her as she chooses a seat.

I laugh, I guess she's right. It *was* a unique way to bridge the gap, and if she has a sense of humor, then there's hope of being friends. Then I notice the furnishings in the solarium are different from the rest of the castle. They're oversized, plush, and embroidered with a multitude of designs and colors. I've only seen furnishings like this in my dreams. Around the solarium are plants, trees, and colorful flowers. Some of the petals are as small as buds, and others as large as dinner plates. I'm amazed to see butterflies floating around, their wings glistening with condensation and reflecting the colors around the room. I'll never tell Evalie, but I love it here.

"Now–," Lucette says while she's devoured by the pouf she flops in–, "we need you surrounding yourself with the right people."

"What do you mean?"

The freckle-faced maid carries over a crystal tea tray laden with fruit tarts, smoked fish, sugared berries, yeast rolls, and cheeses. She then hurries away, behind the waterfall, to fetch the teapot and cups. Lucette picks up one of the tarts and takes a bite. Her face recoils in disgust and she launches the tart into the pond. My eyes widen as they follow the tart and I see a bright red fish as large as a cat gobble up the tart in a matter of seconds.

"Marguerite!" Lucette screams.

The maid rushes back, her face drained of color. "Yes, Your Majesty?"

Lucette stands up and throws the entire crystal tray into the pond, her face flushing to shades of deep red like I've never seen before. She shakes her fist and points to the pond. "Get those vile tarts out of my sight!"

My heart races. *Is this why everyone lets her eat the first bite?* She and I could never be friends. Evalie was right, the Matisse family is awful and Lucette is a tyrant. I want to scream as poor Marguerite lays the steaming pot of tea on the glass coffee table and wades into the pond, fully dressed. To reach all the food, she has to enter the deep end, and the water reaches all the way to her waist. I watch her, not knowing what I should do, as she retrieves the tea tray, picks up the tarts one by one, and places the tray at the edge of the pond.

A brass framed mirror left undraped stands behind Lucette, and my reflection catches my eye. Instead of me locking eyes with myself, my reflection imitates Lucette. Her face turns red and she pretends to throw tarts in the pond and stomps her feet like a toddler. I cover my mouth to stifle a laugh, and that makes Lucette *smile.*

"Ah, yes–," she flicks her hand in Marguerite's direction–, "It is quite funny to watch them do things for you."

Did Lucette really just say that? I clench my fists around my skirts and bite down on my tongue so I don't say something I shouldn't. Lucette chuckles again when Marguerite slips in the pond and all I want to do is strangle her as Marguerite's face flushes with embarrassment. I try to tell her with my eyes that I don't think her situation is funny. I try to tell her that I'm nothing like Lucette and that I hate her too. I should say something, do something. But I don't. I just sit there as she climbs out of the pond and disappears again.

My reflection, no, my *Doppelganger,* is frolicking around in her own version of the solarium, tossing tarts and playing with her floral skirt.

Damnnit. I hate that she made me laugh. Her eyes find me and I give her a stern look. Then the Dop throws an obscene gesture towards Lucette. I furrow my brow at her and she flashes her eyes black and holds my gaze. My pulse quickens. She's showing up more and more, and this feels like a challenge now.

"Vera," I hear from Lucette, but I ignore her, distracted by the mirror. "*Vera*," she says louder.

I shake my head and my reflection turns back to normal. Strands of loose, wet, hair stick to my face and neck, so I brush them from my cheek, terrified that Lucette saw what I did in the mirror. "What?"

"As I was saying," Lucette hisses. "You need to surround yourself with the right people."

I clench my jaw. "I think I can find who the right people are for myself."

"I don't think you can. You came to dinner yesterday with the harlot of Prinav, Daphne Cortwright."

I grip my skirts tighter. "I did *not* come to dinner with her."

"Don't play with me, girl." This time there's venom in her words. "Daphne isn't a friend of the Court. She is a parasite. A blood sucker, desperate to attach herself to a suitable host. Lieve and I have no intention of befriending her. She's only allowed to remain a Lady because her father is an important man."

"I am not her friend."

Lucette's eyes narrow. "Good. You may go now."

I'm relieved to find Evalie in my apartments when I return. She gasps when I tell her what happened in the Solarium, and my stomach churns again at the memory. I forgo telling her about how I laughed and made whole thing worse. Admitting that I'm seeing my Doppelganger everywhere I turn isn't something I'm ready for, and I don't think it wise to ask anyone about them. I wish I had books so I can learn about their nature. There has to be information about them somewhere.

Evalie sets a plate of food down on the table beside me, throws salt over her shoulder and says a small prayer before leaning against the wall. "I can't believe she did that to Marguerite."

"It was horrible," I say, and take a bite of a cucumber sandwich.

"I'll check on Marguerite later this evening." Evalie pours me some tea. "She's probably furious."

I hand Evalie a sandwich. "She looked mortified, as was I."

She takes a bite just as a loud knock startles us. Evalie then sets her sandwich down and brushes any crumbs from her hands before opening the door. In steps a young girl with frizzy auburn hair, olive skin, and servant's attire. She looks to be no older than twelve and has a letter in her hand.

"Hello dear, can I help you?" Evalie asks.

The girl's cheeks flush when she sees me and she stuffs the letter in Evalie's hand without a word. Evalie looks at the letter, her eyes growing wide. "The Royal seal."

My heart thumps in my chest and I call out to the girl, "Did the Queen give this to you?"

The girl nods her head vigorously, curtseys, and then takes off running down the corridor. What could possibly be in this letter? A summons? A punishment? Whatever it is can't be good. I take it from Evalie and snap the seal with shaking hands. Evalie sits on the edge of my bed as I open the parchment to read whatever horrible punishment Lucette has in store for me.

Princess Vera,

The shocking display and lack of decorum you've shown in the miniscule time you've been a part of my court disturbs me. The King has clearly overestimated your ability to fall in line, and I'm disappointed. I don't like Sir Cavel, so I allowed your horrific attitude at your welcome dinner, but I will not tolerate that same attitude towards me, your sister and Queen.

I understand that you were not of nobility before my dearest husband was crowned King, and you are ignorant of the customs of the court. So, I am appointing you an etiquette tutor. This person will teach you how things are run in my court, and I expect immediate changes. Do not disappoint me again.

Her Royal Majesty,

Lucette Antionetta Malesha Valoria Matisse Oleander, Queen of Prinav

"I have to take etiquette classes."

Evalie's shoulders loosen as she strides over to her abandoned cucumber sandwich and stuffs the whole thing in her mouth with a laugh. "Maybe she'll let me be your tutor."

⁓

Evalie was, in fact, not allowed to be my tutor.

I received a note the next morning that I should meet my tutor in the library. Along with etiquette, I'll be learning Prinavian histories, astronomy, and the languages of Madoria and the other Kingdoms of the continent. Lucette is a dunce. For me, this isn't a punishment. I want to learn as much as I can, and a private tutor is something I've never dreamed I could have.

I barely eat any breakfast, and I only let Evalie quickly braid my hair into a crown so I can be in the library as long as possible. If I get there early enough, maybe I can find a book about Doppelgangers, or even a better text for fixing Lieve's pocket watch.

The doors to the library are at least twenty feet high and made of solid wood. Similar runes like the ones in the Crystal Throne Room are carved into the wood, but they don't dance off the door like the ones that danced off those walls. The guards open the doors for me, and my breath catches.

There are more books in this room than I ever knew existed. Rows and rows of shelves line the walls, and there are ladders on wheels all around the space. Sturdy wood tables and chairs have stacks of quills and ink ready for students, and a fire is already roaring in the enormous marble fireplace. It's dim, but not too dark, and there are plenty of lamps around the room. The deep colors of the drapes and rugs, and rich wood tones make the enormous space feel cozy.

As I walk inside, my feet echo on the stone floor. This library is enormous. I have to crane my neck to see the top of the bookshelves, and there are tiny stained glass windows near the ceiling. I blink, realizing they probably aren't tiny, they're probably taller than me. Some of the books are cloth bound, their once-vibrant colors faded with age. Some are plated with gold lettering, and some have bindings with unknown material. The rest are leather bound and titled in languages I've never seen before.

I grab a stack of books that are so heavy they're hard to carry and plop them on the nearest table. I open the first one and flip through the pages. It's a textbook on the constellations and contains mythos of the gods they're named after. The second is in a language I can't read, and the third was nothing more than a list of servant's duties.

I push them aside and open the last one in my stack. It has tons of illustrations of the Fae, depicting the anatomy of their translucent wings and pointed ears. I shiver remembering nearly entering the fairy ring in Shadow Grove. If Arden hadn't stopped me from going with that Fae girl, who knows what would have happened to me.

Someone else enters the library. "Good morning, Your Highness, I'm so delighted to be your tutor!"

I spin around and see Poppy, bouncing on the balls of her feet with a basket in her hands.

"I didn't know who I would be studying with." I sigh with relief. "I'm glad it's you."

Poppy carries her basket to where I'm standing with the books and looks at the drawings of the Fae on the pages. "They're a terrifying people, aren't they?"

I look back at the drawing and shiver again. "Yes, they are."

Calix remains absent over the next few days, so I spend all my time in the library, either learning with Poppy, or trying to fix Lieve's pocket watch. After finding me asleep on the library floor, Evalie forces me outside for some fresh air. It's warm out by the time I reach the stables. I haven't had to saddle a horse myself before, and when I lift the saddle off the hook, the unexpected weight of it sends me tumbling.

A horse whinnies like he's laughing at me, so I point at him when I sit up. "Just for that, I won't give you any of the sugar cubes in my pocket."

The dappled horse snorts and turns from me. From the back of the stables where Siva and Malsu sleep, I hear more whinnies, and a familiar voice. I poke my head up from the haystack to see what was going on.

In Siva and Malsu's stall, I see Arden. He is brushing Siva with a gentleness, and it's hard not to stare. His strong arms glide over the horse's back, calming and protective. I watch him coo at them, pet them, and nuzzle them. There must be more to Arden, more to Daphne, and much more to their friendship.

I walk to the stall with the heavy saddle in my arms as Arden spins around and scowls. "Why are you here?"

His tone makes me bristle. I have a right to be here, same as anyone. If he didn't want me here, he shouldn't have rescued me. "I can be anywhere I want, this is *my* castle."

He continues brushing Siva, refusing to glance my way. "No, it belongs to Lieve."

"I'm the princess, in case you've forgotten."

"Indeed. Then let me help you, Princess." Arden takes the saddle in my arms and moves to Siva. I chafe at the thought that I need his help, but at least I get to ride this beautiful horse again. I take her reins and walk her out of her stall. But before I can begin my ride, Arden has mounted Malsu and is following me to the fields.

I raise my nose in the air, pulling from my etiquette lessons to add an air of courtly irritation. "I can ride a horse just fine, I don't need a chaperone."

"You can't go alone. Your brother would have my head, he's appointed me as your riding instructor."

"Fine," I say and climb onto Siva. "But we aren't chatting or anything."

"Fine."

"*Fine.*" I snap and kick Siva's side, forcing her to gallop towards the treeline near the edge of the estate.

The estate is beautiful and I'm glad I took Evalie's advice to get out of the library for once. I've now read up on the history and ecology of Prinav, and I'm able to spot a few plants I recognize. I think of mentioning it to Arden, just as he showed me the plants and berries in Shadow Grove, but then I remember how cross I am that he's followed me out here in the first place. I'll have to speak with Lieve. I hardly need a bodyguard now that I'm within the safety of the castle grounds.

And is Arden even a reliable guard? He's friends with Daphne, and I still haven't figured out how I'm going to stop her from giving Calix that love potion. Daphne needs to go. Maybe Arden will go with her? That would be great. I don't need him here, taunting me and distracting me. I have to make sure Calix is safe from her, and that she never has a chance to threaten Lieve again.

Arden's voice startles me when he breaks the silence. "Are you going to tell anyone about what you saw the other night?"

"I don't know."

"Vera, please listen to me. You know nothing about Daphne."

Oh, is this his game? To lecture me when we're away from the castle? Did Lieve even order him to ride with me? Irritation flares within me and I nudge Siva to trot faster but she doesn't speed up. "I know enough."

"No you don't, she—"

"I know she's a witch, and that magic is illegal. She told me herself. And I know she threatened me, and my brother, and that she plans on poisoning Calix." I nudge Siva again, but she stays at Malsu's side.

"She just needs her secret to stay secret. She's not a bad person and would *never* poison anyone." Arden replies.

I furrow my brow. "She threatened her King."

"She only–"

"Vera!" A voice calls from the distance.

I turn my head and see Calix. My stomach leaps. *Calix is back!*

I kick Siva's side again, and she snorts at me angrily.

"Snap the reins if you want her to gallop." Arden says softly.

So I do. I snap the reins and she finally runs. I hold my breath as I steer her towards Calix, and once she gets close, Calix grabs her to slow her down. I climb down from Siva's back and jump into Calix's arms. I slam my body into his, crashing our lips together. The world spins around me and all I care about is right in front of me. He picks me up and twirls me around, kissing me over and over again until we have to pause to catch our breath. *Calix is back.*

Blackbands were introduced to the arena in the year
of Queen Rosalind, but not as a merciful example of
generosity, but as a show of her power.

– Excerpt from: A History of Prinav

CHAPTER 36

LIEVE

I 'm going to bring the Matisse family down. They think they can
win against a King? I'll play along with Lucette and make everyone
in the Kingdom think she's going to be the next Queen. It will flip
the Matisse family right on its head when they're kneeling in front of
Daphne at the end of the week.

Disposing of the Matisse family helps everyone in Prinav. No one will
be bound to them anymore, not financially, not politically. It's brilliant.
By taking away their power, I'll actually be doing some good. I was
chosen by Niall, a ruler the people loved, and this could be the thing
that makes the people love me too. I would have unconditional loyalty.
I just have to figure out how to do it.

Lucette and her father enter the stands and make their way towards
Arden and I. Arden's hands ball into fists and his eyes narrow.

"Just play along, I have an idea," I say to him in a low voice.

He doesn't respond, but his hands loosen. I try to loosen up too. This
must look natural, not just to onlookers, but to Lucette as well. I have to
make her believe that not only have I given in to her scheme, but that
I *agree* with it.

"Your Majesty," Lucette greets me, her dimples hiding the vicious snake beneath the surface.

"M'lady," I coo and kiss her hand.

She looks puzzled for a split second, but quickly blinks away her confusion. "It's wonderful to see you so cheerful, you were in such a state yesterday."

"I've recovered." I say as I bow my head.

Lucette smiles brightly and turns to her father. "I believe you know my father, *the Viscount*, Benito Matisse."

Benito does an exaggerated bow. "Always a pleasure, Your Majesty." He raises his voice so everyone in the vicinity can hear him. "I am elated that you've taken such an interest in my greatest treasure. You won't be disappointed with your choice."

I grip his hand firmly and apply just enough pressure to assert my dominance, but not enough for him to suspect that I'm resisting their plans. "I genuinely believe that."

Lucette's face is glowing, and she giggles and waves at those who pass by. Every face in the stands watches us, gaping, pointing, whispering in each other's ears. I hold out my arm to lead Lucette and she takes it, smiling broadly at onlookers. The Viscount follows with Arden trailing behind. I place Lucette on my left, where a Queen would normally sit. People are openly gawking now. *Lucette Matisse is sitting in the Queen's seat!* She makes a production of sitting down, waving at strangers and winking at her friend a few rows ahead of us.

"I'm glad you saw things my way," she whispers to me.

"You left me no other choice, but when I mulled it over–," I lean in to make it look like the two of us are flirting–, "you were right."

She grins and places her hand on mine. "You'll find I often am."

A few people gather nearer to us in the stands, I'm sure to watch the show of courtship and not of the Skillsmen, so I pull her hand onto my lap so the onlookers get a better view. The Viscount turns to a brooding man with thick black hair tied back with twine and a long braided beard sitting next to him. They tilt their heads at our interlaced fingers, and the brooding man passes Benito a small coin pouch.

"What about the witch?" Lucette whispers through a smile.

Everyone around us continues gossiping, whispering, and staring at us. Arden was right, the Matisse family *are* well known. Much of people's stares have nothing to do with me, but the fact that the Matisse's look as if they are coming into even more power. My plan is going to work. I just need everyone to believe that I'm madly in love with Lucette and come up with how I'm actually going to overthrow them. Looking like I am infatuated with her won't be hard. Lucette is very pretty, and her family are nobles. I won't have to do much to add to the illusion. At least that part of my undeveloped scheme is easy.

"Daphne is to stay engaged to Esven," I reply.

"Not a mistress?"

Arden coughs, I know he heard the question.

"No. She didn't want to compete with you."

"Her family is prominent. Why not?" Lucette demands.

"Because–" I stare into her eyes–, "you're *Lucette Matisse*."

Lucette dons a venomous smile and turns her attention to the sword fighters. I pray to the gods that she believes me. Then, Skillsmen of all shapes and sizes enter the arena. Many of them are from other Kingdoms, and they wear their country's colors as a band around their arms. White for Teyrnas, Purple for Madoria, Green for Tussia, and Gold for Prinav.

A smaller group of Skillsmen enter together after the Royal Skillsmen, wearing black bands wound tightly around their biceps. They look completely exhausted. Each with tattered clothes, disheveled hair, and several don't even have shoes. I furrow my brow and watch them as pairs are drawn. The pairs of Skillsmen are randomly selected to compete as ushers place them in wooden circles for their fights. These earlier battles determine who moves on for the chance at larger and larger prizes like weapons, women, and wealth.

I must look like I'm enjoying myself too, so I watch the matches and cheer with the crowd. I can't help but pay special attention to a fighter with a black band. He's skilled, precise. This fighter allows his opponent to get dangerously close, even wound him slightly, but just as you think he's lost, he's won. He lures his opponent into a false sense of victory and then sweeps them off their feet. This is a swordsman who knows what he's doing.

"Looks like I'm going to get a payment this evening," Benito says with a chuckle to his friend. "He's lucky, I was growing impatient."

"A payment?" I ask Benito with curiosity.

Benito nods at me, his curls bouncing on his shoulders. "Blackbands, those without a countryman's colors, they're indebted to someone. That one, over there–" I look and see that it's the Skillsman who just won–, "he owes me more than a years' dues."

Each time a Blackband wins, they wave around their swords like Kings. All but the Skillsmen for whom I'm so impressed by. Instead, he bows to his opponents and takes his winnings gracefully.

My great swordsman wins his last match. When the announcer declares him triumphant, he removes his mask and my stomach flips. I recognize that dark hair, those gold rings, and that mysterious rune tattoo on his cheek. It's the man who was dancing with Daphne at the Feast.

"Let's cheer for the Blackband!" The announcer bellows, "Remi Vail!"

"Do you know him?" I whisper to Arden.

Arden studies Remi's face but shakes his head. "I've never seen him before."

A stranger, a skilled fighter, a man indebted to Benito, and a man who's on my list of people I don't care for. He's perfect. Remi Vail is the answer I've been looking for.

When the afternoon festivities have ended, Arden and I leave Lucette and the Viscount to gossip with their friends while we go on the hunt for Remi Vail. I buy a commoner's outfit and masquerade mask to hide my identity so people think I'm just a regular man celebrating at the Festival. No one must be aware that it's me when I talk to Vail.

Arden discovers that Remi is staying in the large makeshift shed on the estate that's temporarily erected for out of town commoners to have accommodations. The best athletes and Skillmen room here along with commoners who have extra gold weighing their pockets down. They all journey to Brone Castle to display their talents for the aristocracy and make some money, while the rest are on the prowl for someone to bed.

Arden opens the door to the building and we walk inside. Laughter, shouting, and the clanging of metal on wood fills the room. Men young and old stand on tables and sing drinking songs, engage in sparring games, and some play cards. Women with tight corsets and loose morals dance on tables, pass around drinks, and kiss the lucky men closest to them.

This place is bigger inside than it looks from the outside. There are bunk beds sectioned by Kingdom with linens in each countryman colors, wash basins, and barrels of wine lining the walls. Many contestants seem to know each other and laugh like old friends. It reminds me of the Hode, and of my time with Calix, sleeping in bunks next to each other and talking into the late hours of the night, laughing, drinking, dreaming. If I wasn't King, I would want to be a Skillman. Calix would have loved this.

Arden takes in the people around him, and it's so interesting to watch him read the room. Narah wouldn't be happy that Arden was here, she would have said he's too young to be around this kind of revelry. Maybe he is in age, but in experience, he's been a man for quite some time. He pulls his hood down and scratches the top of his head, trying to determine who's sober enough to ask about Remi Vail's whereabouts.

Arden settles on a man playing cards. He seems to be in his fifties, with the rough face of a sailor who's been at sea for decades, a man who's shrewder than he lets on. Under the lamp light, I can tell that the sun has browned his skin and bleached his hair. When we get up close I swear I smell salt from the ocean. I've only ever seen an ocean twice, the Mauroc Sea, on the borderlands of Prinav many years ago as an adolescent and again as I wrote Daphne letters of the waves. This man reminds me of that sea and sand. Gritty and rough.

"Evenin'," Arden says with a slight bow.

The man doesn't look up, he just grunts and plays his hand.

"Sorry to bother you but–"

"I'm in the middle of a difficult game, boy." He picks up a card from the table and grunts again. "What do you want?"

"My friend and I are looking for a fighter–"

"Which one?" He loses a hand and slams the table. *"Damnit!"*

"Today's victor, Remi Vail."

The man chuckles and so do the rest of his table mates. "Vail's a nobody. What do you want with the likes of him?"

Arden doesn't answer, he just looks at me and shrugs, so I step up. "The Royal Guard is interested in talking to him about a position in His Majesty's army."

"He's around the back of the building. But the King should know he runs from any fight he cannot win. He's a coward."

I want to tell him that Remi sounds like a survivalist. He sounds a lot like me, and even though I hate him for dancing with Daphne, I can't help but like him.

Arden and I nod our thanks and dash away before anyone recognizes us. We take a breath outside before walking around the back of the building.

"What are you up to, Lieve?" Arden asks.

"I'm going to take the Matisse family down, and I'll explain it as soon as I get Vail on board."

I take a long stride around to the back of the building when Arden jumps in front of me, stopping me in my tracks.

"You're playing with fire." His eyes darken. "This is a bad idea."

"It's only a bad idea if it doesn't work."

It's empty behind the building except for Remi. He's leaning on the wall and staring out into the distance towards Mount Oriel. The drumming and shouting from within are muffled by some quieter parties outside and the buzzing of evening insects. As we step closer, Remi spots us coming and pulls out a dagger. *Good.* A man always on guard is exactly who I need.

"I have little money," he says in a cracked voice. "They haven't paid me all of it yet, and I won the sword fight, so you'd best back off."

"Settle down," Arden replies. "We aren't here to rob you, and I'd slice you to ribbons if we were."

Remi's hands wrap tighter around the handle of his blade, eyes darting side to side, desperately searching for an escape.

"Ignore him," I say and take my mask off.

Remi's eyes widen and he drops to his knees. "Your Majesty!"

"Please stand, I'd like to speak to you."

Remi stands up and narrows his eyes. I want to talk to him, but who knows who else is listening, so Arden and I get closer so we can speak to him quietly. Remi grips his dagger again and I hold up my hands to show him I'm not armed.

"What brought you to Prinav?" I ask. "Your accent sounds Madorian."

"The match, Sire, they offer quite a bit of prize money."

"They don't offer that in Madoria?" Arden asks.

"They do, but it's not nearly enough to pay my debts. My father's debts, really."

I furrow my brow. "How much are you indebted that you would need to travel such a substantial distance for prize money?"

"A thousand pounds, Sire, and I owe Viscount Matisse even more for my own debts."

That's all I needed to hear.

If I can convince Remi to get others like him to stop paying the Viscount, then the Matisse's will eventually be poverty stricken. Not right away, but it will be enough of a blow to either make them back off, or get a big reaction from them. The people will band together, feeling safer the larger their numbers become. They'll lose debtors, servants, and power.

I can turn Prinav against them and at the very least, postpone the scheme they've concocted for Lucette until I'm coronated. It won't matter if they try to out Daphne for her sorcery, because the whole Kingdom, the whole realm, will be loyal to me for saving them from their greed and wickedness. They'll be outcasts. I could even hang them as traitors if they attempt a coup. *This is perfect.*

There has only been one case of a Doppelganger not taking the life of its reflective host. It was recorded in the year of the gods, 1458, by Queen Rosalind Brone. Scholars haven't proven the existence of a docile Mimic, and Queen Rosalind was known as a liar and a brute herself. Her stories of being handed godlike powers from Hode are quite dramatic, and her surviving children never claimed to have witnessed her Doppelganger. In chapter 3, the Forgotten Heir's own words are transcribed from ancient Prinavian

– Legends of Atatacia Texts

CHAPTER 37

VERA

"I'm so glad you're back," I breathe in Calix's ear.

He kisses me deeply, running his hands all over me, tangling his fingers in my dark hair. Peeking through my lashes, I see Cal's beautiful face. He has stubble growing on his firm jaw, and I notice a grin forming on his lips.

"I'm glad to be back," he murmurs and lifts my chin again, giving me another kiss, this time softer than our crashing reunion.

Siva whinnies and Calix scurries to her. He picks up her rein and guides her to me, and the three of us make our way back to the stables to unsaddle her. I don't even look back to see Arden, I just walk with Calix and bask in the knowledge that he's returned.

Hand-in-hand Calix and I stroll the castle grounds after returning Siva to the stables. I smile at people as we walk, but not everyone smiles back. *I'm still new here,* I tell myself. A group of women a little older than me walk by and roll their eyes as a group of teenage girls laugh in my direction.

My hands start to sweat as Calix and I continue strolling the grounds, and now the attention is making me uneasy. I enjoyed it at first, but now I feel their furious jealousy pressing in on me, drowning me. My stomach flips when I see a woman with red hair pass by, but it's not Daphne.

"It's only gossip," Cal says without a care in the world.

He's right. The gossip isn't even gossip really, because anything they're saying about us is probably true. Lord Calix Bramford, Knight of the Oleander Dynasty, The Witan, the right hand of King Lieve, is romantically interested in the once missing Princess Vera. *Wow.* It honestly sounds like something out of one of my fairytales. I would devour this story if I were reading it now. It's no wonder people are talking, this is big news in Prinav. *I'm big news.* I need to follow Evalie's advice and 'just be nice.'

~

A ray of light spills in through high windows near the ceiling of the library, landing on a book with a faded gray cover. It's small, barely bigger than my hand, and only about one hundred pages.

The title is called *Legends of Atatacia.* This might be the kind of thing I've been looking for. I flip through the book, taking in the beautifully illustrated pages of creatures. But then I stop short when I catch an image of a woman standing near a mirror, and on the other side of the mirror is a woman with black eyes. My heart beats wildly and I read the paragraphs under the drawing.

Doppelangers, also called Mimics, are copies of humans. These humanoid creatures are cruel in personality, and dangerous. Although they do not possess light or dark magic, it is widely accepted that they were made using such mysteries.

To come in contact with your own Mimic is grave. Doppelgangers slowly take your essence. What we as humans call the soul, they call the mask. They don it and pull it from their human host so that they retain power. Eventually, the Doppelganger depletes you of all energy, leaving you a husk of your former self, insane and hollow—

"We're dancing today, Vera!" Poppy announces brightly, interrupting my reading.

"Are we to dance together then? I see that you haven't procured me a partner."

The giant library doors swing open with a loud creek and Arden strides in. "Don't worry, *Princess*, I'm here to dance with you."

"You've got to be kidding."

Poppy's eyes widen and her body starts trembling. "Oh no, I'm so sorry, I thought you were friends." She starts to shoo Arden away. "Go now, Sir Arden."

Arden's eyes blaze and he doesn't move even with Poppy nudging him. "I'll leave if Vera wants me to." He steps forward and whispers so Poppy can't hear him. "But then you'll have to tell Poppy *why* you want me to leave."

My blood is boiling. I very well can't tell Poppy why I want him gone. Not the real reason anyway, and if I make up something, I'll just look petty. Why would Arden even want to be here? Why would he want to be a part of teaching me to dance? This is just another way to get under my skin, to watch me. He's only here to get back at Calix, and to keep Daphne's secret hidden. I know that, and he knows that, but there's no explanation that will make sense to Poppy.

"It's fine," I snap, "let's just start."

Poppy pulls a small music box from her basket and places it on the nearest desk. "The tune in the box is a traditional Prinavian Waltz, also known as the Sparkstep. It will most definitely be played at the Ball and nearly everyone there will know the dance."

I move to the open space between the desks as Poppy winds up the music box. I watch Arden remove his gloves, cloak, and hood, tossing them arrogantly over the back of the nearest chair. He joins me between the desks just as Poppy finishes winding up the box.

"Do you know the dance?" She asks Arden.

He nods.

"Alright, first thing," Poppy says, her voice timid. "The gentleman takes the hand of the lady."

Arden bows deeply, his eyes never leaving mine, and then steps forward to take my hand. His skin is rough and calloused. Strong. He then puts his other hand on my waist and I feel his thumb drag across my rib before resting on my hip. I pretend not to notice and place my free hand on his shoulder.

Poppy walks over to us and adjusts our hands slightly before returning to the music box. "Now, Arden will lead. He steps forward, then to the right, then back, and lastly to the left before twirling you and going back to first position."

The music begins and Arden steps forward, his broad chest touching mine. I inhale the scent of pine and moss, the scent of Prinav, and almost stumble when Arden leads us to the right. I regain my footing and continue to follow Arden's lead.

"Great recovery," Poppy calls. "Keep going."

Arden leads me through the steps, even through the twirls. The longer the music plays, the easier it is to forget why I'm angry at him. I focus on breathing, his and mine, and hold tightly to his shoulder as we go faster and faster around the library.

Poppy claps at the end of the song. "Now that you have the general moves, let's try putting a little spark into the Sparkstep. This next song uses similar moves, but you need to sway your hips, get your bodies closer, and the last twirl ends in a dramatic dip."

We get into first position again and Arden squeezes my waist before pulling me against his body. I slide my hand behind his neck to keep myself close just as the next song starts. With each step I let my hips sway and wiggle, moving with the beat. Arden's eyes rake my body with a predatory gaze, his grip tightening with every step.

The climax of the song erupts from the music box, and Arden dips me so far back my hair brushes the floor. I can feel his breath on my neck, even through his mask. Then, as the music dies, Arden pulls me upright–*slowly*. Both his arms wrap around me and before I know it, we're so close I can feel our heartbeats dumming wildly together.

We hold one another's gaze even as the music ends. I don't let go, and neither does Arden. Then Poppy claps and we break apart quickly. I'm nearly panting and before anyone says anything, Arden grabs his things and storms out the door.

Poppy calls after him, but he doesn't come back. I watch his shadow disappear, and something inside me wants to go after him, but I don't know if I should. *What's come over me?*

I tell Poppy I need to go, and pick up the book I was reading before darting out of the library myself. I need to leave before Poppy can ask me any questions, because I don't know the answers. What just happened? What am I feeling? I shake my head. Nothing happened. Nothing. It was just the music.

CHAPTER 38

LIEVE

A rden leans on the wall of the shed and picks at his fingernails with a blade while Remi slides his dagger back into its sheath.

"I have a proposition for you, and I can pay you more money than you've ever imagined." I pull a small coin purse from my cloak and toss it to Remi.

Remi catches it with one hand. "What's this?"

"An advance."

Remi opens the bag and his eyes light up. He sits on a pile of wood and rubs his chin with his shoulder. "What would a King need with a Blackband of no importance?"

"You and I have a similar goal. To get out from under the thumb of Benito Matisse."

Remi's body turns rigid and he starts shaking his head. "No, no, no."

"Don't you want the money?" I ask him.

Still shaking his head Remi replies, "Of course I do, but–"

"But you're a coward." Arden chimes in without even the slightest glance in Remi's direction.

Remi's eyes dart to Arden. "I'm not a coward, I'm just not willing to die because I don't feel like owing Benito Matisse any more money."

"It's more than that," I say. "Benito is forcing my hand in marriage to his daughter. If they even have a whisper of royal power, the whole continent would be their playground. People's lives are at stake, Remi, people just like you. If I can't stop this, there's no telling how far Benito will go."

"Your right, and they shouldn't be in power," Remi says and places the bag of coins back on the stack of wood. "But I have someone in Madoria more important than your entire kingdom. She's more important than the whole continent."

Arden steps forward. "Bastard."

"I go by many names."

"Dead will be the next," Arden says coolly.

"Drop it, Arden."

Arden pulls his mask down, uncovering the scar on his face and looks Remi in the eye. "That wasn't a threat." He takes a few steps closer.

Remi's hand brushes the hilt of his dagger. "I can take care of myself."

"Do you really think that once you've paid your father's debt to Benito that he'll just let you live your life?" Arden asks. "Your own debts will only grow, and you'll owe him forever. Don't you see that?"

"Of course I do," Remi answers. "But once I've won the prize money, I'll have enough gold to buy passage on the next ship out of here. I'll be gone before he knows what happened and he'll never take another coin from me again."

Arden shakes his head. "Who do you think owns most of the ships in Prinav?"

Remi pulls out a note from his pocket and shoves it in Arden's face. "How dumb do you think I am?"

Arden snatches the parchment and hands it to me. "Dumb enough to swing around whatever this is."

I have to hand it to Arden, he knows how to push people's buttons. While Arden and Remi argue, I read the note. It's a passport that calls Remi a Ship Captain by the name Cedric Matisse. It looks authentic, but I feel the tingle of magic covering the paper. This passport has been *enhanced*. What a dangerous lie.

"Cedric Matisse?" I wave around the passport.

"He and I look like brothers, I met him on the ship to Barault." Remi answers.

I grin at him. This is an interesting spell, and I might be able to use it against Benito. Maybe I could even use it to change the marriage contract between Daphne and Esven. "How did you do it?"

"Do what?" he asks.

"How did you change the letters to Cedric Matisse?"

"I didn't." Remi swallows hard. "I stole it. It's real, I swear."

I rub my thumb over the name Cedric and I can see R-E-M-I appear. "This passport has been altered with magic, so just tell me how you changed the letters."

Remi's eyes widen with fear and he takes off around the building. Arden chases him and a few moments later Arden has forced Remi back by holding Remi's own dagger to his throat.

"Witch or Drol?" Arden sneers.

"Neither." Remi spits blood onto the ground. "But a Drol helped me at your Feast. She had long red hair, and she said her name was Delphi or something."

"Daphne?" My heart beats so hard my temples throb.

"Yes!" Remi shouts. "Yes, her name was Daphne!"

Arden drops the dagger to the ground and we both look at each other with our mouths hanging open. It can't be. Daphne? *A Drol?* My body freezes. Daphne can't be part Fae, she would have told me. She just knows some spells, nothing more.

"That's impossible," Arden whispers.

Remi lowers his hands and looks back and forth between us. "You know her?"

Arden's head snaps to Remi. "Yes, we know her."

"You must be mistaken," I say to Remi. "We've known Daphne for many years."

My thumb glides over the name on the passport and I can feel the tingle of magic again, just laying on the surface of the paper. The magic feels *so* familiar. It's the same tingling I feel with Daphne's touch, the same I felt when she tried to calm me at the joust. *It's true.*

Her magic has always seemed to flow out of her, as if the magic runs in her veins. Drols pull magic from the soil, they don't learn it. Their magic lives inside them. It's in their blood, their skin. The tingle of magic in the paper lingers on my thumb, barely tangible, but still present.

Memories of Daphne's lessons rush around, coming to the forefront at the same time. Daphne always taught me by doing the spells myself after watching her. If we ever had a text surrounding the magic, it was mainly lore, not instructional. It makes sense. Remi is telling the truth.

"I'm not mistaken." Remi snatches his passport from my hands and stuffs the parchment in his pocket as he turns the corner.

Arden takes a step as if he is going to chase him, but I wave my hand, letting Remi walk away. There is more going on in my Kingdom than I am privy to, and that ends *now*. I need to learn if Daphne's hiding anything else, and I need to think of a way to get Remi Vail on my side. If he can convince the other Blackbands under Benito's thumb to stop paying, that could trickle out to others to stop paying. I need Remi to want to help me, and continuing to chase him won't accomplish that.

I walk over to the pile of wood and lean my head on it. Daphne is Fae. Is that how she got Lopter's blood? Did she really have nothing to do with cutting the Lopter tree, or was that another omission? Another lie? My fists curl as the rumble of anger rises slowly to the surface. I can hear Arden talking to me, but it sounds far away, muffled. His chatter is like insects dancing near my ear. I slam my fist to get him to stop talking, and the force rattles the coins in the purse I offered to Vail. The sound gives me an idea. *The prize money.* That's how I can get Remi to help.

~

"This plan is—"

" —genius." I answer Arden.

"Manipulative."

It is manipulative, yes, but it's also genius. Remi Vail will have no other choice but to do as I say. Tomorrow is the last day of the festival, so I need to decide if I'm going to go through with it—and I need to decide right *now*.

Arden and I meet inside my chambers. We were up all night, Arden questioning everything as I worked out the details of the plan. I open the heavy wooden door of the room and turn my head to see Finn waiting in the hall.

"Get me the Treasurer and the Festival Announcer."

With a small bow, he dashes through the halls to collect the people I asked for. Arden sits in a chair on the opposite wall, leaning back with his feet crossed on the desk in front of him.

"This is a bad idea," he sighs.

"Come on," I close the door and lean on the desk next to Arden's feet. "How else am I going to get him to help me?"

"Just *make* him. You're the King."

I push Arden's feet from the desk and he wobbles around, almost falling out of his chair. Arden doesn't understand. I would love to just 'make him', but Remi won't be loyal that way.

I shake my head. "No. I need him to *want* this." I have to make him yearn to help me. He must think he has no other choice.

I pace around the room as we wait for Finn to bring back the treasurer and the festival announcer. This has to work. I cannot allow Benito and Lucette to have control, and although I have many questions for Daphne, her safety comes first.

It's as if Arden can see the thoughts bouncing around in my mind because he says in a soft voice, "Have you spoken to Daphne?"

I shake my head no. "Have you?"

"No."

Arden taps his fingers on the table as I pace the room. I know he's wondering if I really think Daphne is a Drol. It doesn't matter, not really. Even if she is a Drol, my feelings for her haven't changed. Daphne is Daphne, whether I'm angry with her or not.

"It doesn't matter," I mutter.

Arden looks at me confused. "Huh?"

"It doesn't matter if she's a Drol or not." I smile at Arden weakly. "I still love her."

Arden's face turns hard and he looks away from me. "It matters."

Finn returns with the treasurer and the festival announcer. Each of the men look like they were rushed out of bed and forced to run here by my servant. The treasurer, Quinn Grey, seems happy enough to be here. He's young. I've only met him a handful of times before he took over the position after his father, Reginald Grey, passed away a month ago.

"What can we do for you, Your Majesty?" Quinn asks.

"Well," I look from Quinn to the announcer, Kelby Drake. "I need you both to do something for me."

Kelby almost throws himself to the ground with his obsequiousness. Kelby is a brown noser who's dying to gain more power. Kelby serves Kelby, and I can use that.

"Anything, sire," Kelby practically wails.

Arden rolls his eyes. I walk around the room, sliding my fingers across the desk while saying a silent prayer to Bram that I can trust these men.

"Can I trust you?" I ask Quinn and Kelby.

"With anything," Quinn bows.

"Of course, sire," Kelby bows even lower.

I smile at them and adopt a Kingly voice. "No matter what, I need Remi Vail to win every competition he enters."

Quinn's eyes narrow slightly. "What does this have to do with me?"

I nod at him, "I need the prize money given to him to look stolen."

Everyone in the room freezes, barely breathing. They look at me in confusion, and a little bit of fear.

"Stolen?" Quinn asks.

I nod at Quinn and Kelby. "Yes."

Arden leans back in his chair, absentmindedly sharpening a dagger. Quinn and Kelby glance at him and look nervous. I glare at Arden and he stops sharpening the dagger so I can continue.

"Quinn, I need you to put the correct amount of prize money in the coin purse. But I also need you to take a *noticeable* amount of money from Benito Matisse's accounts and add that to the prize money as well." My voice quickens as the plan rolls from my tongue. "I need the transfer to be signed by Cedric Matisse." I turn to Kelby. "I need *you* to announce exactly how much money is in that coin purse, including the stolen gold. Say it's from an anonymous donor, and make sure that no matter what, that money goes to the Blackband, Remi Vail."

Quinn's voice shakes a little. "Anything else, Your Majesty?"

My lip curls into a broad smile. "Yes. Make sure Benito discovers that Cedric Matisse, his nephew, stole money from the Matisse accounts. He must believe it to be true. But wait just until the moment the tournament is over to show him the ledger."

"Whatever you desire," Kelby says with a bow and prepares to leave the room.

I pull out two small coin purses. "For your silence," I say and hand one to Quinn and one to Kelby.

Each of them bow, Kelby looking pleased, and Quinn looking a shade of puce and barely containing his fear.

"If you betray his Majesty, I'll slit your throats." Arden says, now twirling his dagger on the wood of the table.

They bow again and leave in a hurry. I let out a long breath of relief. Half the battle is over now.

Once the coast is clear, Arden sighs deeply. "It's not too late to change your mind, I can go right down the hall and tell them it was all a ruse."

"I'm not changing my mind," I snap.

"You're going to get Vail killed, or the real Cedric, maybe even Kelby and Quinn."

But Arden is wrong. I've not been bested yet. I am King and not even a son of Prinav. Niall blessed me, the gods of this world have blessed me, and I must trust they'll bless my hand here. "It's going to work. It has to."

Golden Clover Honey, 6 drops, Wyrmwood Root, 2
stalks, Violet Flame Orchid, 2 Petals, Hair of the Creator,
3 strands, Seagrass, to your discretion, Iron Shavings, 1
ounce, Willow bark, 2 ounces. Boil for 7 hours. Simmer
for 2 weeks. The longer you simmer after 2 weeks, the
greater the effect and the concoction will turn gelatinous.
Only the creator can pour the drink, for the pourer gains
the affections.

— *Recipe for Love Potions*

CHAPTER 39

VERA

Over the next few weeks, Arden seems to be everywhere I am.
The only moment I'm ever out of his reach is inside my room,
where I stay to avoid him, my thoughts about him, and to complete my
study of *Legends of Atatacia*. I read the entire book, and learned nothing
more about Doppelgangers than what I already knew.

The recording of Queen Rosalind Brone's account of her friendly
Doppelganger was ripped from the book, and I haven't found reference
to it elsewhere. When I'm not looking for information on Mimics, I
search for antidotes to love potions. But the only thing I came up with
was a list of herbs that increase libido. Magic is illegal in Prinav afterall,
and there aren't many books on it, even in the royal library.

I finally leave my chambers after three days holed up inside with
Evalie, to find Calix. Because even if I'm sick of Arden following me

around, I would like to see the man I'm actually courting. As I'm searching for him and praying that I don't run into Arden, I stumble across Lieve and Lucette in the parlor. Lucette called Daphne a parasite, but it seems to be Lucette who's attached herself to a suitable host. She clings to Lieve, and I've not had a moment alone with him since the day he gave me a tour of Brone Castle.

I hear Lieve say that Calix began his watch late in the night, and that he was unhappy that he keeps taking the calls, and that he needs more time with me. My heart flutters and I clutch my chest. *Calix is fighting for me! How romantic.*

I stopped listening to the conversation though, because Lucette's eyes hover where I'm hiding behind a marble statue of Lopter, and I'm sure eavesdropping on the Queen comes with a more severe consequence than etiquette classes. My palms sweat as I peer around the statue, barely breathing. *Please don't see me.* When she finally returns her attention to Lieve, I dash away as quickly as I can.

I wander all over, even to Calix's apartments, but I don't find him. He loves to ride as much as I do, so even if Arden is there, it won't matter. No one could argue that Calix couldn't be my riding instructor for the day. Unfortunately, Calix isn't there, but Arden is.

Arden looks me up and down. "I'm surprised to see you here."

"I didn't come for you."

"Loverboy is off doing whatever Lieve needs from him. So if you want to ride, you'll have to suffer and ride with me." He pulls a saddle from the hook on the barn wall and gets Siva ready.

"I'm a decent rider now, I don't need your assistance." I say.

"I know you don't."

"Then why can't I just ride alone?" I demand.

Arden tightens the saddle. "Because you're the King's sister."

I climb up Siva's back and Arden tries to help me. I glare at him and he backs off, his hands raised. I secure myself and then snap the reins.

Siva gallops away, throwing dust in Arden's face. I kick her sides and we run faster and faster through the fields.

"Vera!" Arden shouts. "Not again!"

I throw him an obscene gesture and will Siva to go even faster. I've memorized most of the riding trails by now, and I've taken to hiding in the castle wood to get away from Arden when I'm forced to ride with him. I steer Siva through the trails until the dead end and hop off her back. I know it's childish, but I want Arden to just leave me alone. That day in the library haunts me, and every time he's around I feel guilty about it. I feel guilty that I'm confused about how I'm feeling about him, and that's not fair to Cal.

I know the horse will go straight back to the stables, so I slap her rear and she darts off. I watch her pearlescent coat be dappled by the sunlight peeking in between the tree branches and smile to myself. Arden will find me eventually, but this game of hide and seek will annoy him again. I'm praying that he'll finally get so frustrated that he won't want to be around me anymore and leave me alone for good.

What Arden doesn't know is that everytime I run away from him, I sneak to the forest edge and watch for Daphne to show up. I listen to Arden complain about me, and to Daphne tell him how close the love potion is to being ready. I also watch to see if Soleil shows up, and to see if I can learn anything more about their friendship and how I can use it to my advantage. She's been busy lately and even a summons from the Princess isn't important enough for her to give me enough time to befriend her enough to divulge secrets.

I've learned a lot about Arden and Daphne. Their relationship is peculiar, but not romantic. It seems that she raised him somewhat, from what I can glean from their conversations. Daphne isn't all bad, but I just can't shake her plan of wanting to drug Calix. I've been desperate to tell Calix and Lieve about all of this, but Calix is always busy and Lieve is never alone. I don't know what to do.

Evalie and Poppy are nice companions, but Evalie would panic if she knew what I was doing, and I'm not sure Poppy would be of any help. I don't know what their advice would be, and I shouldn't burden them with this, especially when they couldn't help solve the problem.

Arden finally finds me hours later and drags me from the forest, grumbling the whole way. Once he knows I'm safe, he dashes off behind the stone wall, and I know he must be going to the dungeons to meet up with Daphne again. Looking around to ensure no one is watching me, I follow him on the off chance they make a mistake and leave the room unguarded so I can get in to destroy the potion.

I wait at the top of the dark staircase until I hear the door at the bottom creak open and then close before I make my way down. Then I wait at the bottom, in the pitch black for as long as I can, before silently, slowly, stalking inside. Soon I'm finding myself in front of Daphne's potion room.

"She keeps running off," Arden grumbles.

I watch their feet go back and forth around the room from under the door as I lay on my stomach. Daphne is wearing red satin shoes today with a heel as thin as a finger. I can't see her face, but I can hear laughter over the sound of her shoes clicking against the stone floor.

Daphne throws ingredients into a bowl and teases, "Well, good thing you're an excellent bounty hunter."

"It's not funny. Those woods can be dangerous."

"It's not Shadow Grove, there aren't any Darkthings in there."

"There are wild beasts, and—"

"No, there aren't." She adds something else and I get a strong whiff of vanilla.

The pair are silent for a few minutes, so I decide to leave the dungeons for my history lesson. I've almost been caught twice, and I don't know what would happen if they find out I've been spying on them for days at a time now. *Time to go, then.*

My breath catches as I re-enter the pitch black stairwell that leads to the outside from the dungeons. The darkness makes my skin crawl and I get terrible memories of the Darkthings in Shadow Grove. *I need to remember to bring a light next time.* My hands brush against the stone, desperate to feel the cool metal of the handrail. My toes hit the bottom stair, so I know the handrail is directly at my side. My fingers clutch the metal and just as I take a step up, I bump into someone.

"Aaah!"

My shout and the shout of whoever I bumped into mix together and echo loudly in the narrow stairwell. *Shit.* Arden and Daphne might have heard that. Frantic scraping of shoes and shuffling of skirts replace our voices. Me and whoever the other person is, panic for a moment and then when we discover there is no threat, both of us begin to settle.

"I'm so sorry," the voice says.

"*Poppy?*"

"Ye–yes–" She sniffles–, "Vera?"

"Yes."

I hear Poppy sigh and turn herself slowly on the stairs and step up to the light. I follow her up, and when we reach the top I see that she looks disheveled. Her hair has been blown by the wind, a twig is stuck in her updo, and the hems of her skirts are caked with mud. She looks like she's been drug through the forest.

I pull the twig from her hair. "What happened to you?"

She pats her hair with shaky hands. "Nothing, Your High– *Vera.*"

Something doesn't seem right. Why is she acting scared of me all of a sudden? I put my hands on my hips and repeat, "What happened to you?"

"I overheard the stable boys saying Arden lost you in the castle wood, and I thought I'd try looking for you myself." Poppy's cheeks turn pink. "But then I saw you go down the back stairs, and I–," she picks at her fingernails–, "I followed you."

"You *followed* me?" My voice hardens.

Her eyes well with tears. "I'm sorry." She wipes her face with the back of her hand. "I didn't go all the way down, I've just been waiting for you to come back up."

I can taste the tang of metal as I bite my tongue. I want to scold Poppy, but I don't know how much she knows. Does she know Daphne's secret? She might have the wrong idea about everything. What if she thinks I'm helping Daphne with that potion? A knot in my stomach tightens.

"Do you follow me a lot?" I ask her through gritted teeth.

Poppy's lip trembles. "No, of course not."

"Then let's go have some tea now and talk, shall we?"

Poppy gives me a scared smile and pats her hair again. I take a step, and out of the corner of my eye I see Lucette walking with a Priest. It must be a family member, their fair complexion and icy blonde hair are one in the same. Before I can think, I snatch Poppy's arm and pull her back into the dark stairwell. I don't want Lucette to see me, and Poppy doesn't need Lucette to see her looking like a peasant who lives in the forest. As soon as Poppy notices Lucette, she purses her lips and ducks her head into the darkness behind me.

I keep my head peeking out just enough that I can determine which way they went as church bells ring in the air. I can't hear what they're saying over the bells, but their faces look grim. They seem to be discussing something, and Lucette makes a gesture that seems to reference the bells. *What is that about?*

Lucette and the Priest switch directions and move towards Poppy and I. As quietly and quickly as we can, we fly down the stairs. Poppy opens the door and I let my feet guide us through the dungeons. Mindlessly, my body leads me back to Arden, and I'm so scared I want to throw up. I can see the glow of Daphne's spells peeking out from under the door.

I had never noticed it before, but there is another door directly across from the potion room. Soft footsteps patter down the hall and they seem to be getting closer. I turn the handle on the door, but it's locked. A soft crash inside the potion room startles Poppy and I and we crouch behind a wine barrel.

I can see under their door. Shards of glass litter the ground, and a small handheld mirror leans on its side, broken from the fall. My eyes are met by my reflection in the small mirror, and she holds her finger to her lips as if to say "shhh." Something metallic near the edge of the barrel glints from the light under Daphne's door and I grab it instinctively. It's a key. Now the footsteps are just a few yards away and I hear Lucette's voice. She's close.

I look back at my reflection and she motions for me to use the key. I pull Poppy to her feet and step towards the door, praying to the gods that Poppy and I don't get caught. While squeezing my eyes shut, I jam the key into the lock of the mystery door. *It clicks.* I shove Poppy inside before she can say a word and hold her mouth shut with more force than I mean to. My hands are shaking as not a second later, Lucette and the Priest are here. They're so close I can hear Lucette's skirt brush the floor.

The light from Daphne and Arden's room had already been extinguished and I hold my breath. What if they get caught? If I made noise, would that save Calix? No. I can't make any noise or Poppy and I will be found. I wish Arden wasn't with Daphne. This would have been a great opportunity to expose her, but I couldn't live with myself if Arden goes down with her. He did save me in Shadow Grove, and more than once. I owe him.

Poppy hunches over a stool in the corner, trying to catch her breath as I get on my hands and knees and peer under the door. Lucette and the Priest stand side by side, facing the brick wall that separates my door from Arden's. I can only see feet, and Lucette turns on her heel, looking behind her before positioning herself slightly behind the man with her.

Cracking stone, scratches, and an ear splitting snap fill the dungeon as white sparks drop from the wall. My eyes strain to make out what's happening and I have to squeeze them shut when a few particles of the white sparks bounce under the door frame making me wince. When I'm able to open my eyes again, I'm surprised to find that the hallway is empty.

CHAPTER 40

LIEVE

T he Skillsman Tournament is everyone's favorite part of the Festival. Today the victors of the matches compete against each other until there is one lone champion who gets a heap of gold and other prizes. It's supposed to be incredible, and all the victors will show off for the audience. Sometimes they even set up surprises, according to my staff. Every Skillsman from Prinav to Madoria, and even some of the surrounding Kingdoms attend. There are dozens of participants, each with a multitude of talents.

The merchants keep their booths open, hoping that passersby will purchase an item or two before finding themselves engrossed in the tournament for the rest of the day. I flip a few coins into the tents as I walk by, and the merchants gratefully wave at me and continue talking to the smattering of customers walking in and out.

"I'm betting on Vail," I hear a young boy say as he rolls a set of ivory dice on the ground. He then cheers and scoops up the handful of trinkets lying in the dirt and carefully puts them in his pocket. "What about you, Iz?"

Iz, a broad-shouldered preteen with sage green skin and white hair, replies, "I'm not allowed to bet."

"Why not?"

"The treasury forbids the bookies to allow Fae to gamble. They think we'll cheat."

The boy laughs and claps Iz's back. "Well, they aren't wrong."

Iz laughs too and picks up the dice. "No, they aren't."

I watch them roll dice a little longer, their interactions reminding me of Calix and I, before I walk away.

But I'm stopped dead in my tracks when I hear Iz say, "Especially now that they know we found a way to see the future."

Daphne said she got Lopter's blood from a Fae connection, could this kid be it? I hold my breath as I walk over to them to say hello. I greet the boys and when they look up, their jaws drop. The blonde scoots his foot to cover up their game, and Iz drops his head so that he's looking at the ground.

"You aren't in trouble," I say, "but, Iz, can I talk to you for a moment?"

The two boys gawk at one another and then the blonde boy gives Iz a tiny shove in my direction. I walk behind one of the merchants' tents, Iz trailing behind me.

"I know I'm Fae, but I promise I'm allowed to be here." Iz pulls out a piece of parchment from his cloak. "I'm Delmont's guard. His parents couldn't travel to the festival, but they didn't want him to miss it, so they paid me to accompany him. I'm not gambling, just rolling some dice. I swear it."

I smile. "It's alright, I believe you. But I want to ask you something. Do you know where I can find the blood of a god?"

"A god?" He stammers, but I notice his fingers brush his pocket. "No, Your Majesty."

"What's in your pocket then?"

Iz's face pales.

"Give it," I say and pass him a bag of coins, "and no harm will come to you."

Iz quickly shoves the coins, and his parchment into his cloak, and then rummages in his other pocket until he pulls out a tiny vial of blue liquid. "That's all I have."

"Can you get more?"

Iz's emerald eyes twinkle. "Possibly. But I don't want any more of your money. I want something else from you in exchange."

I furrow my brow. "Like what?"

"Protection."

That was not the answer I expected. Protection from what? From who? Is Lopter's blood worth getting mixed up in whatever is going on here?

I narrow my eyes at Iz. "Protection from what?"

"Queen Meritt of Teyrnas."

Shit. This is bad. I don't need blood that costs that much. I turn from the Fae boy, but I hear the liquid swirl around and my mind hyper-fixates on the contents in the vial. I close my eyes and breathe before I ask, "Why do you need protection from her?"

"Delmont was an altar boy in the Hode Basilica back in Teyrnas, and he accidentally witnessed something he shouldn't have in the Sagart Priests' chambers." Iz picks at his pointed ear and continues, "The parchment is a farce. Del hasn't any parents. We just ran. The Queen is sure to be looking for him, and we thought, *what better hiding spot than at a festival?*"

I do *not* need to get mixed up with a problem in another Kingdom, another monarch. I should tell the boys to scram and never come back. But then, Iz shakes the vile and I snatch it from his spindly fingers. "Deal."

"Deal." He says and skips away, back to Delmont and their dice game.

My lips tingle as soon as Iz says the word deal, and the tingling muffles my thoughts for just a moment. I curl my fingers around the vial and stare at the contents. There's no telling what Delmont witnessed in Teyrnas, and it must have been bad if they think a Queen is looking for them. *Shit. Shit. Shit. What have I done?*

I jam the blood in my cloak and peek around the corner, making sure no one noticed that I was behind the tent with a member of the Fae. It doesn't seem like anyone was paying attention, their minds are set on the upcoming matches, and of the underdog, the Madorian hero, Remi Vail. I haven't seen any of Remi's other performances, but I've heard comments from the spectators around me. He's been winning. A lot. Whether he's winning because of skill, or because Kelby is rigging the matches, is neither here nor there. All that matters is that he's winning.

I hear Kelby bellow the names of the next Skillsmen in the ring. "Umal Crowley versus Remi Vail!"

I venture to the stands to watch, perched like a hawk with Lucette and Benito on my left, and Arden on my right. Finally, Remi is set to have a match in the Royal Grand Stands. Umal appears from the left side of the ring, shirtless, and wearing chainmail from head to toe. The crowd roars as he pushes through them, creating his own path with his extreme mass. He has tan skin and dark, wavy, hair that he's tied in knots away from his face. His eyes are painted with kohl and his muscular arms are covered in unreadable tattoos.

Umal's legs threaten to tear through the wooden step that leads inside the arena, and the colors moving around over his face from the sunbeams coming through the tent top only create a menacing appearance. If I hadn't paid off Quinn and Kelby, I'm not sure Remi would win this fight. Umal looks like he was built for war. My knee shakes a little, but I stifle my nerves by drinking a full dram of ale passed to me by one of the entertainers cruising through the stands. Arden gives me a withering stare, but I ignore him. I need something to calm me whether Arden likes it or not.

Remi's entrance is the complete opposite of Umal. It's quiet. I hope Remi is up for the challenge because Umal looks like he could snap bones as easily as a child snaps twigs in the forest. Several people in the crowd cheer for Remi, but not nearly as many as those who cheer for Umal. He doesn't seem to mind. On the contrary, Remi sports a devilish grin and winks at a pretty pair of young women sitting in the front row.

Another mug of ale is passed to me, and I guzzle it as Umal and Remi bow to one another. Remi's bow is deep, and his hand flicks against his blade. Umal's bow is miniscule and stiff. He clearly believes he's going to win, and he smirks before tightly gripping his weapon. The gong rings, and the match begins.

For the first round, Remi is falling short. His sword is much shorter and assumedly lighter than Umal's, so it would be no surprise if Kelby hands match one to Umal. Remi looks tired. If it looks like he's going to lose the second match, I'll have to send Arden to remind Kelby of his promise.

A juggler walks in front of us, blocking the end of the round and Lucette snaps at him to get out of the way just as they finish and another gong rings out, barely audible over the cheering crowd.

"Round two!" Kelby announces.

"Will go to Umal," a pale man with short-cropped hair shouts in front of me along with their group of friends.

They better be wrong. I look past the group and instead, focus my attention on the Skillsmen. Remi looks increasingly tired, but he continues to dodge Umal's impressive strikes. He backs up, holding his sword high above his head, obviously attempting to gain traction, when his boot slides in the soot. Remi's knee is suddenly jerked inward and a painful screech escapes him as he crumples forward. Umal rushes at Remi, pressing his advantage.

Like a flash of lightning, Remi leans back and slices from side to side with all his might and his blade somehow penetrates the space between Umal's chainmail. Umal doubles over, his abdomen and hands covered in blood. Remi didn't cut him deeply, but he cut him. Blood spilled means— he won. *Remi won.*

Every onlooker in the audience leaps to their feet and cheers. The stomping of the crowd shakes the stands, and I imagine the cracking of wood underneath my feet. Remi stands, limping, and waves at the audience. Remi won. He won. *My plan is going to work.*

Umal Crowley is escorted from the arena and taken to the Healer's tents. Another Healer is brought to the ring to wrap up Remi's knee while Kelby and a group of other organizers prepare for the winning announcements. Two young teens, a girl and a boy around the age of fourteen, walk inside the ring carrying a red velvet coin purse, a gold-plated dagger, and a bundle of wildflowers. They stand on each side of Kelby and wait for their instructions.

Kelby raises his arms in the air. "Please give another round of applause to the Skillsmen who've entertained us through this Solurnalia!"

The crowd cheers again, clicking pewter mugs full of ale together, while the four of us in the Royal Box clap politely. Lucette turns to me and smiles, and I smile back with genuine happiness. *I can't wait to crush you*, I think to myself as she pats my forearm.

"This was delightful." She smiles wider. "I haven't seen a match where blood was drawn before."

"Give another round of applause for Umal Crowley!" Kelby bellows.

Again, another wave of applause fills the arena. Remi bows to Kelby and the crowd, pretending to show sportsmanship. He's a good actor. I know what he's really thinking. I know that his heart is pounding and his hands are sweating. He wants the gold and to split as fast as he can. He's waiting with bated breath to hear Kelby say his name so he can grab the gold, run, and never come back.

"And now...," Kelby keeps his hands in the air while he turns his body from side to side, making eye contact with everyone in the audience. He lets the anticipation build, and the spectators use their hands and feet to mimic a drum roll. "The winner, Remi Vail! This year's champion of the Festival of Light and Dark!"

The applause for Remi is thunderous. I can't help but grin. I feel like I've just witnessed a friend receive something they've been striving for their entire life. The girl with the flowers hands them to Remi and pecks him on the cheek.

Then Kelby lowers his arms and the volume in the stands dissipates. He nods to the boy holding the dagger and coin purse, and the kid takes a knee and presents Remi with the blade. Remi takes it from his hands, twirls it across his fingers, and winks again at the young ladies in the front row.

"Arrogant bastard," Arden scoffs.

I slap his back. "Like you wouldn't act exactly the same."

Kelby takes the coin purse from the boy and stands directly in front of Remi. "And of course the winner receives gold! Notoriety isn't the only prize we give our entertainers!"

He hands Remi the money and looks around the stands. *He's forgotten.* I drop my mug on the ground and don't bother to pick it up. Everything is over. Done. I'll hang Kelby for this. I'll hang him as a sacrifice to Hode or something. How could he do this? That idiot forgot to say the amount of gold in the purse and that the remainder was from an anonymous donor.

"Oh!" Kelby shouts, "and of course there is the traditional six meckles of gold from our gracious Monarch!"

The crowd claps politely and Remi raises the coin purse to me without a smile. I wave at the crowd while I nod at Remi, and at Kelby. I then stare down Kelby and let our eyes meet, applying pressure on Kelby to keep talking.

"Uh, and, this year is special because an anonymous donor also wanted to give a few meckles to the winner!" Kelby is visibly sweating and I can't believe my whole plan hinges on him. "Another six meckles to Remi Vail!"

The crowd chatters to each other excitedly, but there's at least one person in the arena who knows something is wrong. Remi. His face is completely drained of color. He tucks the gold inside his pant leg, gives a hasty wave to the audience and limps his way out of the arena as swiftly as he can on an injured knee.

$$\sim$$

My knee clatters the underside of the desk I sit at in my study. It's dead silent and I'm all alone. I knew Remi was going to run, but I thought he would be caught almost immediately. He's smarter than I've given him credit for. As soon as Remi left the arena, I made an excuse to Lucette that I needed to attend to some kind of kingly business. When Arden and I were out of Matisse earshot, I ordered him to find Remi.

"Don't let him pay Benito." I scan the people around us to make sure no one is listening. "You can let him buy his way onto a ship though, just don't let him board."

Arden nods, then pulls his hood up over his head and storms through the people around him, making a beeline towards Remi.

The next several hours are unexpected. This morning I thought I would remain with Lucette after the tournament and parade her around, but instead, I'm in my study down a hidden corridor of the castle, alone. I pull out the tiny bottle of blood I took from Iz. The liquid fizzes and swirls and my mouth nearly waters with anticipation over taking a drop. Maybe I'll be able to see what will come of my plan. Even if it shows me nothing, I may as well take it as I've probably set off a chain of murders.

If Arden doesn't get to him in time, I've just killed Remi, Quinn, Kelby, and Cedric, a man I've never even met. What was I thinking? *Arden was right.* This was a terrible idea. Right now will be the time Quinn is pretending to warn Benito that his nephew, Cedric, stole a small fortune from his accounts. It will then come to light that, no, Cedric didn't steal that money. A man who shares similar features, and who owns a copy of Cedric's passport, and who now has twelve meckles in his pocket, stole that small fortune. And that man is now escaping his debtor by ship.

What have I done?

Boots race down the hallway, heading towards my study. Benito. He's figured it out, or someone gave me up. I pop open the vial and let a drop land on my tongue. I wait to feel the euphoria, to see Lopter's next vision, but nothing happens. I shake the bottle, but I don't smell salt or mud. This isn't Lopter's blood. *I've been hoodwinked.* That Fae kid dealt me fizzy wine, dyed blue. I'm an idiot who made a Fae deal over a vial of *colored fruit wine.*

Now I'm going to have to fight, and I don't know how many people Benito would bring with him to take me down. I pull two hatchets from my desk drawer and balance them in my hands. I don't want to fight, but I will for Prinav. I'll fight for Daphne.

Fists pound on my door and I spin the hatchets around in my hand, preparing to fight to the death. Then, the door is kicked in and the sight is nothing I anticipated. Arden stands before me with his arms around Remi, barely holding him up. Thankfully Remi seems to be alive, but just barely. He's covered in blood and his limbs look contorted. I drop my weapons and rush over to them as Remi slips from Arden's grasp and drops to the ground with a thud.

It's not always blood that binds, sometimes deals are
thicker.
– *Sparrow Fledgling*

CHAPTER 41
VERA

I put my finger to my lips to hush Poppy as I remain on the floor,
my eyes scanning the empty hall. Arden and Daphne's door is still
dark. I take my time standing up and crack the door open. I need Calix.
I don't care if he's busy, I need to talk to him. It looks like Arden and
Daphne are going to stay hidden, so this is my chance to get out of the
dungeon without getting caught by them. They may not even know
I'm down here, for if they did, I'm sure they would have opened their
door by now.

We step into the hall and still nothing happens. If Poppy and I are
going to leave without getting caught, now's our chance. I reach for
Poppy's hand and we scurry out of the dungeons, up the dark stairwell,
and back to the sunlight outside.

"Was that the Queen?" Poppy asked.

I rub my temples. Poppy isn't someone who can handle this
information. Poppy isn't someone who I can talk candidly with, she's...
fragile. However, what else am I supposed to say to her?

"Yes."

"Wow." She wrings her hands. "I've never–I just–," her hair falls from
its updo and her breathing quickens.

I pat Poppy's shoulder. "Just take a breath, that was a little scary."

We have to get out of sight. There are nobles everywhere and they are going to talk if they see the two of us looking like we just did something wrong, especially when Poppy's appearance is such a mess. I don't need any other rumors flying around, and I definitely don't need Lucette hearing about this. Losing Poppy quickly and finding Calix or Lieve is top priority.

"We need to get cleaned up," I tell her.

She nods and follows me inside the castle. Neither of us speak. The only sounds around us are the clicking of our shoes and the clatter of servants working. Poppy steps to my side and guides me to her chambers. She opens the door and we step inside as fast as we can. I can't help but smile at the surroundings. Poppy's chambers remind me of the inn. There's a small fireplace, a beautiful wooden vanity, a full length mirror draped with a quilt embroidered with bunnies and ducks, and mounds of linens and pillows.

"Are you okay?" I ask her.

She sits at her vanity, rigid, and quivering slightly. Poppy's eyes bulge with embarrassment when she starts patting down her hair, but fussing with it makes it even worse. Her wide eyes meet mine and I just start laughing. At first she looks even more nervous, and then a beetle flies out of her nest of hair and flutters around the room, desperate for an escape.

The nasty insect starts to fly at me and I swat at it. This only seems to make it angry because it chases me around. I race in circles, flinging my arms in the air and cursing at it. Then an orange ball of fur jumps up from beneath the bed. It darts around the room, under Poppy's chair and between my legs. In a flash it's on the other side of the room, a thump thuds on the ground, a screech erupts, and then silence. The orange ball of fur is a cat, and it caught the beetle. The cat walks over to Poppy, beetle hanging out of its little mouth, and drops the flying terror at her feet.

Poppy looks nervously at me and picks up the cat, its legs dangling in the air as she holds it close to her and says, "This is Nigel."

We both burst into laughter.

~

I tried to find Lieve and Calix after I spent some time with Poppy so I could talk to them about what happened, but yet again, they were busy. Lieve's servant, Finn, assured me that he would send Lieve to my chambers when he and Calix finished their meeting with the Prince of Madoria.

"This can't wait," I say, and storm through the doors to the state rooms.

Every head turns to me, and I realize I've made a huge mistake when Lieve's eyes lock on mine. He doesn't blink. He doesn't smile. *No one does.* Everyone in the room is still, and the silence is deafening.

Lieve's fists clench for a moment before saying, "Apologies Durant, this is my sister."

I curtsey and swallow the lump in my throat. I can feel the heat of Lieve's anger radiating off his skin, filling the room with flames. I've never felt rage like that from him, and I'm scared of what I've walked in on. I can't pull Lieve away now, this meeting is clearly important and I've created a problem for him. Can't I ever do anything right?

A young man stands up and bows to me. The gold chains on his turquoise uniform jingle with his every movement. The color suits him. It's a contrast to his warm brown skin, and the color illuminates his handsome face. He has kind, dark eyes and a wide smile with brilliantly white teeth. I give him a small smile back, but then return my attention to Lieve.

"I apologize for my interruption," I say and turn from the table.

"Nonsense," the man says. "Join us."

"The more the merrier," a man with slicked back hair sitting next to Lieve echoes.

I turn back around to see the kind eyed man beaming at me, but I freeze. Should I stay, or should I just leave? Lieve's hand clenches again and I know he's going to yell at me the second this meeting is over. I don't know what to do, so I look at Lieve for an answer. He gestures sharply to the seat between him and Calix. So, I pull out the heavy wooden chair and sit without a word.

"Wonderful," the kind man cheers. "Nice to meet you Princess, my name is Florian Durant–," he bows deeply–, "Crown Prince of Madoria." Someone clears their throat and Florian smiles again. "And this is my beautiful sister, Princess Saima."

Florian wasn't exaggerating, Saima *is* beautiful. Her hair is as dark as mine, but thicker, and shiny, and hangs down to her waist. She doesn't wear a tiara, but a crown of delicate gold chains that hangs in her hair and across her forehead, connecting to a hooped nose ring. Her skin is smooth, and she has the same dark eyes as Florian, but they are sharper, cat-like, and have a ring of emerald green around the iris.

"It is a pleasure to meet you," Saima says with an encouraging smile.

"And I'm Lord Esven, your brother's Grand Visor. Apologies for missing your welcome dinner, I was in Madoria with our guests."

"Pleasure to meet you all as well," I reply sheepishly, as I'm aware that prolonging introductions will only make Lieve angrier.

"Shall we proceed?" Lieve huffs.

Esven stands and signs a stack of documents, Florian signing after him. They pass them next to Lieve, and when Lieve scrawls his signature, Esven rolls the parchment, tucking it deep into his robes and smiles at me before turning his attention to the Durant's. "Prinav is always here to help." He holds out his hand and Florian shakes it. "We're all friends here, aren't we?"

"Of course we are," Florian replies, a muscle ticking his jaw.

"Calix, please show them where Saima will be living from now on, and ask one of the servants to furnish Florian his own chambers for his stay." Lieve says.

"I hope it's not a bother that I'm staying too," Florian says. "I want to make sure Saima will be comfortable here without me, and my journey back to Madoria is a long one."

Lieve opens the state room doors, ushering the Durant's out. "Not at all, I hate that you've had to travel in secret. This whole situation is wretched."

"Truer words have never been spoken, Your Majesty." Florian replies to Lieve with a smile as he wraps his arm around his sister and steps into the hall.

Esven bows and says his goodbye's as Calix quickly grabs my hand and squeezes before passing by me to lead Florian and Saima through the corridor. I close my eyes, steadying myself for Lieve's reaction. Once everyone is out of the room, he closes the doors with his back turned to me.

"Lieve, I—"

"You have no idea what you walked in on," Lieve growls.

"I know, but—"

Lieve cuts me off again, "No excuses. You have to learn your place."

"My place?" I snap.

"Yes!" Lieve spins on his heel. "You know nothing about my Court. You shouldn't have barged in on that meeting."

Tears well in my eyes, "Maybe I would know more if you would have brought me here years ago!"

"What are you talking about?"

"I'm talking about the fact that you'd been to Prinav before the jump through the Lopter tree. You kept this place from me! You told me all those stories, knowing how much I yearned to get out of Adamston, and yet you still kept it from me. We were barely living, barely eating, and you still chose to keep Prinav to yourself," I spit. "My ignorance around your Court is your own doing."

Lieve slams his hand on the table. "Anyone, even a *beggar*, would have known not to barge in like that."

"I'm sorry I *barged in*, but I needed to tell you something important and I didn't think it could wait."

Lieve knocks over one of the chairs at the table and it rattles on the stone floor. "What Vera? What could possibly be *so* important that you had to interrupt a meeting with monarchs from another Kingdom?"

"Lucette. I saw her–"

Lieve shakes his head vigorously, "No."

"Lieve, she was in the dungeons and–"

"I don't care what she was doing." Lieve waves his arm. "She's the Queen of Prinav, she's my wife, and you're–"

"I'm what?"

"A child." Lieve pinches the bridge of his nose. "Although you're taking classes with Lady Poppy, I can see now that you still need time to adjust."

I start breathing hard through my nose.

"You aren't ready for life in court yet, and I understand that," his face softens. "But you need to start learning now. Absorb Poppy's lessons. There are rules here. It's not like when we were stealing from the markets. I have standards, secrets–"

"I understand." I say and stand up.

Lieve reaches for me when I pass him but I rip my arm away from him.

"Where are you going?"

"To learn my place," I curtsey to him, "*Your Majesty*."

As soon as I leave the state room, I run in the direction that Calix was taking Florian and Saima. After several minutes of tracking down Calix, I can hear his voice from around the corner.

"Florian, I can promise you that your sister will be safe here."

"I know. It's just going to be difficult leaving her behind when I have to go home."

"Of course, and no one knows better than King Lieve about missing a sister."

I can hear curiosity in Florian's voice when he says, "Yes, the news of Princess Vera being found has traveled far and fast. Has she talked about what happened to her? I thought the King's sister was his age, but she looks very young."

"We aren't sure what happened, but speculation only creates rumors. And you two know how dangerous rumors can be." Calix answers sternly.

Florian replies, "Indeed."

I hear Calix's boots walk in my direction and when he rounds the corner I hug him. His strong arms wrap around me and I take in his scent, that clean fresh mint fills my lungs and tears stream down my face. All the stress that I've been bottling up comes flooding out and I cry into his neck. "I hate it here."

Calix rests his chin on the top of my head and I feel the weight of whatever he's carrying ease a little too. He squeezes me and I squeeze him back. This is what I need. I need someone to just listen, to care about what I say. He releases me and takes hold of my hand, leading me away from the Durant's living quarters.

"I know I haven't been around." He drags his thumb across mine as we walk through the halls. "I'm sorry I've been so busy."

"I should be the one apologizing. I shouldn't have barged in on that meeting like that. Lieve was right, I need to adjust to the protocol here."

Calix rolls his eyes as we continue walking. "You don't need to do anything different. But why *did* you barge in?"

"Lucette."

Calix stops dead in his tracks. "What about her?"

"I was in the dungeons and–"

Calix rounds on me. "You were in the dungeons?"

Here we go. Now Calix is angry with me too. More tears well in my eyes and I start shaking. When will I ever learn to just keep my mouth shut?

Pressing my eyes closed, I prepare for an argument. "Yes, and Lucette was down there too."

"What was she doing?"

I open my eyes and when I look at Calix, I don't see anger. I see concern. Maybe even fear. I place my hand on his cheek. "I think Lucette knows magic. At least a little. She was with an older man, a Priest, and they performed a spell."

Calix's eyes scan the corridor to make sure we aren't being listened to. "What makes you think that?"

"Because I saw it."

His eyes narrow. "What did you see her do?"

"She went into the walls."

"Show me."

Have you ever felt out of breath? Or felt your rib catch?
That's the Fae taking a little bit of air from you to help
another.
— *Ancient Atatacian Nursery Story turned Religious
Superstition.*

CHAPTER 42

LIEVE

"What happened?" I ask Arden.

"What do you think happened?"

"I get it, you're angry." I kneel down near Remi, pressing my hands on a large open wound. "I'm not arguing with you right now. Go get Daphne."

"Do you really want me walking around the castle like this?" Arden waves a hand at his blood-stained clothes.

He's right. I can't have him wandering around the castle covered in blood.

"Hold pressure here," I say, and stand up.

Arden drops down next to Remi and firmly bears down on his abdomen, the flow of Remi's blood barely slowing. I swallow a lump in my throat and my eyes sting. *He can't die. Please don't die.*

Arden looks up at me and I nod. "I'll be right back."

The door shuts behind me and I make a bee line to Daphne's room only to discover that she isn't there. *Damnit Daphne, where are you?* The back of my tunic is sticking to my skin as I sweat more and more with every step. *If I don't find her, Remi's dead.* I scour the castle, desperately searching for a glimpse of her red hair.

What am I going to do if Remi dies? Arden was right, this was a stupid plan. Everything I've ever done is stupid. Losing Vera in the tree–every battle where my friends died–Lucette... Hell, I'll have another young man's blood on my hands by the end of the night. If Calix were here he would know what to do. Calix would help me. He always helps me. As I'm dashing through the halls, tears pour down my face thinking of Calix. *Where is he?*

Calix was always there to calm me, to bring me back from my demons. Without him, I'm not sure I can be King, I'm not sure I can even live. I lost him and I don't know if I'll ever find him again. I don't know if he's even alive. The ground beneath my feet begins to sway and I lean on the wall to balance myself. Stabbing pins and needles cover my skin, my arms, my chest. I try to breathe, but each attempt is more shallow than the next. The earth is swaying harder, my vision blurring. Black nothingness forms in the corners of my eyes, but then I hear something.

Laughter.

I hear laughter from a few rooms away, and the voice sounds familiar. *Daphne.*

My legs are unsteady as I follow her voice. The solarium. I forgot this room was her favorite place. I can make out her shape even from behind the stained glass, her head being thrown back in laughter. I walk inside without looking up. I don't want to see any pain on her face, I don't want her to ask questions. I just need her to listen, and to come with me without arguing.

"Daphne, I need you."

Don't look.

"I am incredibly sorry, but I cannot come with you right now, Your Majesty."

I look.

Daphne isn't alone, she is sitting on a pouf less than a foot away from Esven. My eyes blink rapidly as I process what I'm looking at. A date. Daphne has been in her favorite place, and laughing. Laughing with *him*.

My heart begins to beat so fast I hear it in my ears. Every inch of skin burns and my muscles tighten and clench. I feel heat boiling, rising higher and higher as a tightness in my throat threatens to cut off my air supply. But instead of blackness, I see red. I don't want to make her come with me. I don't want to throw my position in her face, but I need her to come without question. Fuck Esven. Slimy, slick, Esven with his greasy hair and greasier palms. I can't think straight. Every thought swirling around spins and spins like a top, making me dizzy.

"Lady Daphne," *don't say it, don't say it*, "it's an order."

My heart pounds in my chest as the words pour from my mouth. *Damnit, Daphne.* Daphne and Esven stand. She takes her time, showing me that she will respect me as her King, but that she isn't someone that I can push around on a whim. I don't want to make things worse, or reveal the situation, but I need her to hurry.

"I'm sorry you must go," Esven says. "I shall wait with bated breath for your return."

"This was a lovely tea," Daphne replies.

Is she serious? I want to scream. I don't have time for any of this. Remi's life is on the line and we need to run.

"It was, m'lady," he coos, "and I would love to speak with you soon, Your Majesty. There are bills that need tended to."

I wave my hand in the air. "In due time." With a stiff nod I snatch Daphne's hand and pull her away. "Good day!"

Esven didn't even have time to bow by the time I had Daphne out of the solarium and into the hall. My fingernails dig into her skin and I'm dragging her more forcefully than I should. Everything about this is, well, *wrong*.

Her expression is as hard as stone when we're finally alone, and she wretches her hand from my grasp. "*Let go.*"

"I'm sorry but I can't," I pull her again. "You have to come with me."

"No." She yanks her arm away. "Not until I know what's going on."

I look up at the ceiling and take a deep breath to try and calm my nerves. "You and I made terrible mistakes the night of the feast, and you're the only one who can help me fix them."

"What's on your hands?" Daphne's voice quivers.

I look at my hands and they are stained with blood, some of it already crusting under my nails. "Daphne, *please.*"

〜

I lock the door behind us. The metallic tang of blood fills the room, threatening my sanity. Without a word Daphne dives head-first into the storm. She pushes Arden away and raises her hands, palms down. She bends her elbows in and pinches her fingers together in a claw like movement as if she's pinching magic directly from the air around her. Sky blue light forms into marble sized balls and floats in the air, following her hands as she waves them over Remi's body, steering them into his airway.

It's not working.

"Take his shirt off, I need to see the damage," she orders.

Arden slides his dagger from its sheath and tears through the fabric. Not only is Remi's face crushed and his stomach bleeding from a large gash, his ribs are badly bruised too. There's no doubt they're broken.

"He's not breathing," Arden says quietly.

"I know that."

Remi's lips have turned a purplish blue, and I don't know how long he hasn't been breathing. He may already be dead. He looks dead. I pace around the room while Daphne works, pulling more blue light and guiding more and more of it into Remi's open mouth.

"Where are the Healers?" She snaps at me while she works.

I shake my head at her. "No one can know he's here."

She continues trying to push the blue spheres into Remi's mouth, but it isn't working. "Who is this man?"

Arden growls, "Your passport friend."

Daphne's face blanches and she covers her mouth, Remi's blood sticking to her pale skin. "I couldn't tell." Her voice shakes, "His–his face." She stares at Remi in stunned silence for a second or two, brushing her blood soaked hand across his arm before turning to me. "I need your help, Lieve."

I look at my own hands and see Remi's blood. "I can't."

"You can and you will. This is your mess too, so get over here and help me!"

I drop to the ground beside her. I don't even feel my knees smack the hard stone floor, I just lock eyes with Daphne and listen.

"Good. Now just do what I do." She makes the pinching motion with her hands again and another ball of blue light appears.

I put my hands up as she says, and she nods her head. "Good, now, in your head you must visualize breath."

"Breath?"

Daphne closes her eyes and pinches the air again, patiently teaching like she always has. "Pinch the air, grab the breath."

I close my eyes and pinch the air, imagining the blue light that magically appeared for Daphne. I can't feel anything. No breath, no tingle of magic. *Please don't die, please don't die.* Daphne cups her hand around mine and slowly she uses my fingers to pinch the air. I strain myself, trying to visualize the blue light, again and again. A small wisp of blue flicks in my hand, but it's so small it wouldn't be of any help.

With a worried tone Arden announces, "His whole face is turning blue."

"I know, Arden," Daphne snaps. She takes a deep breath and addresses me next. "Do you trust me?"

"Yes."

"Then lie down."

I lay on my back next to Remi, his blood becoming darker by the second. A shiver runs down my spine as my body sinks in the dark red puddle next to his body.

Daphne breathes out slowly. "Open your mouth."

I open wide and Daphne hovers her hands over my face. "This is going to hurt, and you are going to feel like shit for a few days, but I promise you'll be fine."

Then, I'm electrified. My body feels like it's on fire and I can't move. I can't scream. I can only lay there. Burning. Daphne pinches the air right above my mouth and pulls. I can feel a white hot string being drawn from my lungs, and every tug scorches me. She pulls harder and my throat burns and sizzles, the pain nearly blacking me out. Then the white hot string leaves my body and floats out to her fingertips like a fluid bolt of lightning. The string pulls something much larger from my lungs. Something heavy.

Stop.

I'm going to die if she keeps pulling. I can't take it anymore. *Stop, Daphne.* Please stop.

"You're killing him!" Arden screams.

"Shut up!" Daphne screams back.

"Witch! Drol!"

"Shut up!"

Then Daphne yanks hard and I feel like she's ripping out my heart. If I could speak, I would scream. My lips fry as a large ball of blue light rises from my mouth and Daphne quickly waves it over to Remi and shoves it into Remi's mouth. I don't feel like my body is on fire anymore, but I can't feel my limbs. Every sensation is gone, like I'm deflated. I'm too weak to keep watching as Remi's chest shudders with the strength of what can only be *life* being plunged into his chest.

He coughs and opens his eyes, while everything before me goes dark.

~

I feel a warm hand on my forehead. It's soft. I only ever got a hand on my forehead from my mother when I was sick. *So, I'm sick?* I must be. My body feels weak. I try to move my arms but they feel as heavy as lead, but also weightless. I don't even know what I'm thinking. My skin is moist and so are the linens around me. I must be feverish.

The warm hand on my forehead brushes my hair away and slides down my cheek. I can't open my eyes, even though I try. Through my eyelashes I see a woman, but I can't keep them open long. *Mom.* She's here. She's here because I'm sick. She found me. She traveled so far to be by my side. *Gods, I hope she has Vera.*

I whisper, "Mom." My scorched throat feels raw.

Mom doesn't answer me, she just presses her lips to my forehead and walks away. I can hear her fuss around the room and I feel safe knowing she's here. My heart feels light. I'm glad she's here, I've missed her. I doze in and out while she washes my face with cool water.

~

After a while, I'm not sure how long, I can finally open my eyes. I'm in my Royal Chambers.

"Mom." My throat feels like sandpaper. "*Mama.*"

A woman's skirts shuffle next to me and I turn my head to the bathing room. Daphne wrings a rag in a basin of water and brings it over to me. She has tears streaming down her face as she dabs my forehead with the rag.

"Not Mama," she coos, "just Daphne."

~

Daphne's silhouette protects me from the harsh rays of the sun beaming through my bedroom window. She turns to wet another rag, and I notice her fatigue. Her hands and movements are unsteady. *How long have I been asleep?*

"Daphne," I croak.

She wrings out the rag and walks over to me, dabbing my forehead softly and smiling at me with sad eyes. "How are you feeling?"

"Better." Everything that happened in my study suddenly rushes back to me. Blood. Blue breath. Searing hot pain. Remi's beaten body. "How's Remi?"

"He's fine." She returns the rag to the wash basin. "Let me fetch a Healer."

"Please don't go."

She pulls out the small blue vial that I bought from Iz and sets it by the wash basin. "I thought you were done with this."

"That's not what you think it is."

"It looks like Lopter's blood."

"It's just fizzy wine that I got from a kid at the Festival."

Daphne throws me a sharp look. "I can't listen to this anymore. I'll fetch a Healer, and Finn of course. But then I think I need to salvage my relationship with Gelhert."

"You're going back to Esven? Can't you see I did all this for you? I—"

"I know you did, and it became a huge mess." Daphne sighs. "I need peace, and you have continually given me grief." She scoots the vial around on the little table and looks out the window. "I'm tired."

"We were doing so well until Lucette ruined it all," I groan as I try to sit up.

"Lucette is a horrible person, and what she's doing is awful," Daphne says as she glides to the door, "but taking her to your room undermined her chances of finding a husband. You know how it is here! People saw you, Lieve. People talk. They thought you slept with her, so to every man in Prinav, she's off limits. You ruined her reputation. You, *only you*, created this mess by entertaining her in the first place."

Shame washes over me and all my bottled up rage spews from my lips. "This is your fault! I only spoke with her because you looked like a whore in that dress!"

Daphne freezes. *Too far.* Everyone dresses that way for the Feast, it's part of the tradition. I don't know what to say, and I just let my mouth hang open. I've crossed a line and we both know it.

"And you looked like a drunk. At least *one* of our accusations is factual," she snaps, and slams the door behind her.

Daphne, I think my father is a Priest.

— *Letter from Lady Soleil Toun to Lady Daphne Cortwright.*

CHAPTER 43

VERA

Calix glides his hand across the stone wall of the dungeons. "I don't see anything, but that doesn't mean that something isn't here."

I'm keeping watch for Calix as he investigates the walls and it feels so familiar. I was always the lookout for Lieve my entire life. I would make sure no one was watching when Lieve would swipe food at the market, or pickpocket a nobleman in the street. It was fun to help him. Being the lookout made me feel important. I haven't felt that way with Lieve since entering Prinav, and Calix makes me feel that way again. Keeping watch for him feels right. Calix feels right.

"Thank you."

He brushes past me, his hands continuing to search the wall. "For what?"

"For seeing me."

He stops scanning the walls and kneels on the ground, feeling for something, anything, that can show us what Lucette is up to. When he doesn't find anything, he turns to me and looks in my eyes. "No matter how dark it is, I will always see you."

My heart flutters. He has so much patience and understanding. I should tell him everything, right now. I should tell him about seeing my Doppelganger everywhere, about the pocket watch, and about Daphne's potion.

The all too familiar church bells resonate loudly in the dungeons, and I don't understand how we can hear them when we're this far underground. We both freeze while tiny white sparks start falling from the cracks in the wall and land at our feet. One of them touches my exposed leg and burns me slightly.

"What the—"

Calix freezes and then looks at me, his eyes wide with fear. "If that's Lucette, we need to run."

I nod, and before I even know what's happening, we're sprinting out of the dungeons.

~

I meet Calix in the stables to talk privately the following day and take a ride in the woods that line the estate the following morning. Yesterday, he told me to go to my room and that he would talk to Lieve immediately. He says Lieve will handle it and that I should keep it quiet. Magic, as we all know, is illegal, and we don't want to start something with the Matisses' we can't finish.

"I don't think we should let her get away with it. Lucette shouldn't get to be above the law, I don't care if she's the Queen." I want to know if Daphne was telling the truth about Lieve, so I continue, "Unless she *does* do a little magic, and it's just some big secret that I'm not supposed to know."

"It is a big secret—officially," admits Calix, biting his lip.

I frown. "Meaning what?"

"Meaning Lucette does a few spells here and there with her uncle Baptiste, the Sagart."

"What is she doing down there?"

"I don't know, but it can't be good if Priests are involved."

I sigh. "Can't we just expose her? Out her somehow?"

Calix folds his arms and leans against the door of the stable. "The Matisse's are too powerful. They'd turn it around on you somehow, or on Lieve. It would be a nightmare."

That twinge of guilt about not sharing what I know about Daphne and her threats against Lieve, and of Daphne's love potion knot my stomach up again. I want to tell Calix and release this secret, but what if Daphne wasn't bluffing? I don't know her at all, she could tell everyone that Lieve knows magic and the mob would come for him. Maybe I should see if Arden can convince her to just leave.

"Does Lieve really know magic?" I ask.

I need to know the truth. I need to know if Daphne is bluffing, or if her threats have validity behind them. The only thing I know for sure is that Daphne has powers, and Lucette does too. In a Kingdom where magic is forbidden, who knows what lengths those women would go to, to hide their secrets from prying eyes.

"He does–"

I let out a little gasp. *Daphne wasn't bluffing.*

"He hasn't performed a spell in years, but don't fret Vera dear, no one knows about his past."

That you know of.

I force a smile and swallow my secret. I can't tell him. If I tell him, he'll confront Daphne, and then Lieve will be in danger. *Shit. Shit. Shit.* Daphne wasn't bluffing.

⁓

Poppy and I have been getting together almost daily for lessons. She's a bundle of nerves and terrified of Lucette discovering that we caught her doing magic. I don't blame her, I'm terrified too.

"Has Calix told you anything more about the queen?" Poppy asks.

I took a leaf out of Lucette's book and arranged a tea for Poppy and I in the solarium. This place has become my favorite room in the castle, apart from the library, and I wanted to have some control over the space for myself. I told Evalie that I wanted only her and that poor maid, Marguerite, to serve us and to dismiss anyone that comes by except for Soleil. I want to tell Marguerite that I'm sorry, and I'm going to talk to the ladies about all these problems I'm having. It's time. I need help.

"No." I sip my tea. "I think it might be a dead end. Lieve is handling it, and Calix says the Matisse's are too powerful to try and confront right now."

"He's not wrong," Poppy replies. "They weaseled their way into Court years ago."

Evalie places a dish of tarts in between Poppy and I and says, "they have their hands in everything, not just the court."

Evalie was right about her and her whole family the whole time. The Matisse family is a toxin that poisons everyone and everything they touch.

"Is Soleil coming?" Evalie asks me.

I nod. "She'll be here."

Near the waterfall I notice Marguerite trying to hide from me. I haven't had the courage to apologize to her, but I know I need to do it before I let it go any longer.

"Marguerite!" I call to her. "Please come here!"

I see her steady herself and then make her way to me. Her shoulders hunch forward as she attempts to make herself even smaller than she already is. I hate that I caused her any embarrassment, even if my laughter was never directed at her. Marguerite's shame stems from how I conducted myself the last time we were in a room together, and it's high time I rectify that.

"Please sit." I gesture to the pouf next to me. "You too, Evalie."

Poppy looks at me, clearly puzzled, but doesn't seem to disapprove. Evalie flops down on a pouf across from me, making me laugh. I love her confidence and her ability to be herself. Marguerite looks ill.

I soothe my voice. "There's nothing to fear, Marguerite. I asked Evalie to have you join this tea because I wanted you to be comfortable, and I wanted to apologize to you."

Her eyes leave my gaze and trail over to the pond. *I really hurt her.*

"There's nothing to be sorry for, Your Highness," she mutters.

I touch her knee and she recoils slightly, so I take my hand back. "The pond."

Her cheeks flush.

"Marguerite, please look at me."

She closes her eyes and slowly turns her head to face me. A tear runs down her cheek, and when I spot it, a tear runs down mine too.

"I want you to know that I'm sorry." I wipe my face and she wipes her own. "And I want you to know that although it looked like it, I was *not* laughing at you."

She opens her eyes which brim with tears.

"I also wanted to apologize for taking so long to apologize." I clear my throat. "I was embarrassed and ashamed of my behavior, and I hope you forgive me."

Marguerite smiles a shy smile and nods her head just as Soleil enters the solarium.

"Perfect," Evalie interjects and pours all of us a cup of tea. "Now it's time to gossip."

I nod at Soleil before turning to Evalie. "Evalie, please lock the door."

She stands up and gives me an exaggerated curtsey. "As you wish."

"As for gossip," I say, "tell me how Lucette found her way onto the throne."

Poppy trembles and then looks at Marguerite. "I don't know about the story in the world of the servants, but it wasn't a secret to the nobles that the King fancied someone else."

"Oh yes," Marguerite says, "he and Lady Daphne were quite an item."

"What happened?" I ask.

Marguerite's cheeks flush and she looks to Soleil to answer.

"Lieve took Lucette to his chambers the night of the Feast, just before his coronation. We all assumed it was drunken foolishness, but as that would have ruined her reputation, he pushed his love for Daphne aside and married Lucette instead."

"He *loved* Daphne?"

Marguerite sips her tea. "Oh yes, very much so."

With this knowledge, I decide it's time to tell them what I know. These ladies know everything that's going on here, and I need to learn. It's high time I act like I belong.

~

Brone Castle turns into pure chaos over the next couple of weeks. The Feast of Bram is tomorrow, and all the servants are putting last minute touches on the dining hall and guest chambers. Poppy tells me that every noble in Court will attend, and there may even be people from all over Prinav, Madoria, and the other Kingdoms that surround our borders. Most of them will be here all week long to celebrate Solurnalia.

Excitement buzzes in the air like I've never experienced before. Everyone seems giddy. The nobles are ordering special gowns for the ball, and specific fabrics for their attire during the festival to match the theme of light and dark. I've read about parties like this in books, and I'm anxious to be a part of it. Poppy and I have done two lessons a day so I can learn all about the rituals of the week and learn the Sol Ball dances. I've been so busy I haven't even been able to work on the watch.

"Now, we must find you something divine to wear," Evalie announces to me while she's fixing my hair.

"I hear the Feast is quite scandalous."

She looks like she's lost in a dream. "Oh yes, *quite* scandalous."

"Do you and the other servants get to enjoy the Feast?"

"Not like the nobles." She sticks another pin in my hair. "But yes, we have our own little feast in the kitchens, and we have *a lot* of wine. I like to sing hymns and I always give a pence to Sybill at my altar–for my husband."

I hate that they celebrate separately and that we can't be friends publicly. It's not right, especially when not so long ago I was much less fortunate than any servant at court. I'm no better than any of them, I'm new to Prinav, and yet I get to indulge in something that they've never gotten to be a part of, even while living here their whole lives. It isn't fair.

I stand up so that Evalie can tighten my corset.

"I'm glad for you. You'll love it." She then finishes making me look like royalty and forces me to walk around the room as if I'm on display. "Lovely!" She exclaims.

"Thank you." I look in the mirror, half expecting to see my reflections eyes flash black, but they don't. She must not be following me today.

I just see myself, happy, pretty, and royal. I'm wearing a silver ball gown and a delicate diamond tiara. I'm not going to a ball today, I'm just going on a date. *I look like I'm trying too hard.*

"I know what you're thinking, and no, it's not too much," Evalie says.

I turn my head to face her and wave at my tiara. "Really?"

"Lord Bramford is taking you on a carriage ride through the *glimmer trail*." Evalie's face pops up next to mine in the mirror. "You'll need to sparkle brighter than the stars."

"Alright." I sigh and spin around so my gown flows around me. "Don't stay up. I'm hoping to be back late."

Evalie turns serious. "And first thing tomorrow, the Solarium Sisters are destroying that potion. Calix is *yours*."

"Exactly. Everyone will be so distracted with the Feast that we can slip down and grab it before Daphne has a chance to use it. I'm so glad Marguerite and Soleil know how to get in that potion room."

"We just need them to get in the room before she puts up the wards."

I cover the mirror with the drape. "Let's just hope they can manage it."

In the heart of the royal palace, where silks and jewels shimmer, alliances are forged and broken on the ballroom floor. Each twirl of a gown a calculated move in the game of thrones, and every dance step could shift the balance of power in Atatacia.

— *Corde Dashar, Healer and Consort for Queen Rosalind Brone in the year of our gods.*

CHAPTER 44

LIEVE

A few hours later I feel strong enough to stand. The Sol Ball is tonight and I can't miss it. I have to host with Lucette by my side and make a show of it, and I pray Daphne forgives me and gives me one more chance to earn her love. Arden was successful in keeping Lucette away from me while I was unconscious, but now that I'm alert, she wants to talk. She and her father must've figured out my entire plan. I hear a knock on the door, followed by Finn attempting to dismiss her, but Lucette tramples all over him and comes inside anyway.

Finn dashes in after her, "Madam, I'm afraid I'm going to have to ask you to leave."

Lucette makes a clicking noise with her tongue and glares at Finn coldly. "Go. Away."

Finn looks at me and I wave him out, "I'm fine, Finn."

He backs out of the room and closes the door. I know he's listening in from the other side, untrusting of anyone with the name Matisse.

"The help have been whispering about some sort of malady you have." She purses her lips and looks me up and down in disgust. "So what is it?"

"Nothing, just lost my breath," I answer.

"Uh huh." She walks over to the window, waves at people walking along the grounds below, and smiles that innocent lie of a smile. "You cannot die on me, I want half the crown, remember?"

It takes every ounce of strength that I have left not to fling her out of that window. I imagine her on the ground below, crumpled from the fall, a crowd gathered around her mangled body. I smile at the thought, praying she thinks I'm just happy she's here to see me. I must keep her oblivious if I still want to attempt my plan. Remi is okay, everyone is okay, there's still a chance. I just need to talk to Daphne. I need to make her see that I want her, and that I'm fixing everything.

I go back in time to when I was a master thief in Adamston and put on my best honest face. That face got me free berries sometimes, or fish. I'm hoping that while I'm still not feeling my best, it will be even more believable. My *malady*, as Lucette called it, might be beneficial at the moment, and I pray to Bram that I'm right.

"Oh Lucette, don't you worry about that, you'll be queen soon enough." I open my eyes slightly wider than normal and soften my voice for that added sincerity.

It must have worked because she smiles wide enough that her dimples peek out from her cheeks. "Alright then, I'll see you at the Ball."

She doesn't let me say anything else, she just turns to leave my chambers. Finn stumbles a little when the doors open. I was right, he was listening. I smile to myself. She believed me. *This is going to work out just fine.*

Not a moment later, a red-faced Esven barges in my room. Finn again tries to stop him, but I let him come in. I know he's probably upset about me taking Daphne from their date.

"How are you, *Your Majesty*?" He sneers.

"Better."

"Good. This will be easier to say if I know you're well." He snaps the door shut behind him and says, "I know you and Daphne have a history, but those feelings must remain in the past."

"Who are you to tell a King what to do?"

"I don't see a crown. So I'll say it again, *leave those feelings in the past.* She is to be my wife, as her father declared."

I want to rip his throat out, but I can't really argue with him. I'm supposed to be with Lucette, and he's still legally bound to Daphne. Even though I want to kill him, for now, he's right.

"I'll take your words into consideration, *Advisor.*"

Esven exits the room, his ashen cloak flowing behind him like shadows.

~

The ballroom is filled with people. Lucette grips my arm, digging her nails into my skin like talons. My legs are still weak. Finn offered to fetch me a cane, but Lucette refused to let me appear weak. So I begrudgingly let Lucette guide me as I walk, and every step I take with her pains me.

Our outfits match perfectly, down to the color of the stitching. Deep red with gold thread and buttons. Lucette is a master of illusion and she's got the entire court in the palm of her hand. Our matching attire makes it obvious we're courting, at least to onlookers. It's brilliant really. Lucette and Benito have created a perfect ruse, and knowing I'm their pawn turns my stomach. Their scheme is genius. While we walk around the room, seemingly arm-in-arm and smiling happily, she has convinced all of Prinav that we're in love. Everyone believes she'll be the next Queen, I just hope they're all wrong.

Two thrones sit on a stage in the front of the ballroom. Although our engagement hasn't even been announced yet, Benito Matisse has convinced my staff to give his daughter a throne. It seems like he's already started having them treat her like the queen she is "destined to become". Each throne is made of red velvet and they have solid gold legs. I look around the room and the decor is all matching red and gold. *Lucette thought of everything.* How long have they been planning this? This isn't the work of just a week.

Nobles greet me, bow, and introduce themselves if they hadn't yet had the chance to throughout the week. Lucette interrupts at every encounter, and I have to bite my tongue. I can't blow up at her or dismiss her in front of everyone, even though any other King would chide her for her actions.

I have to wait until I'm officially the King to ruin her. If I don't, she and her family have a small claim to the throne, and with all of their supporters, they might wage a civil war to get it. According to Arden, they have so many supporters that they might even *win* a civil war if it came down to it. I have to stifle the fire that rages inside me, at least until the Royal Jewels are atop my head. Only then can I drown her in her own poisonous actions.

Across the room, Esven appears with Daphne at his side. Seeing them together makes my skin crawl. His hands touch her bare skin. My eyes trail up her arms and to her smiling face, and my heart aches. She is radiant. I've messed up so many things in my life. Vera. Calix. Maybe even what happened to Narah. I can't mess this up too. The light in the chandeliers dim, and the musicians begin playing. I hear a woman's voice singing with the instruments, and it makes my ears tingle. It's that same tingle that I've felt a million times before, Daphne's tingle.

The whole room quiets so they can hear the music, and like a spell, we all search for the woman with magic in her voice. Each note sits deep inside me, brimming against my soul. My eyes well with tears and everyone goes silent. It's like a siren's song, holding the listener captive with its beauty. I see her, the singer, as she belts out a high note just as dancers find their partners and spin around the room to her melody, and she's gorgeous. She has dark eyes, angular features, warm brown skin, and dark, thick hair. She looks like royalty, but wears not a crown, but delicate gold chains in her hair.

"My sister has an incredible voice, doesn't she?"

I blink several times, pulling myself out of the beautiful woman's audible spell. "She does."

The sibling of the singer bows to be and reaches his hand out for me to shake it. "Nice to meet you, Your Majesty." He winks at Lucette. "My name is Florian Durant, Crown Prince of Madoria."

He's charming and polite, and makes a great impression. I shake his hand and he takes a seat on the edge of the stage, one leg hanging off the ledge. I admire his confidence and casualty. He seems real. Authentic. Maybe I can make friends with him. Maybe he can help me with Lucette and her family.

"Eldest of the Durant sons, correct?" I ask.

He puffs his chest, proud. "That's right!"

Lucette joins in and I can see it in her face that she's charmed by Florian too. "So nice of you to come."

"We wouldn't miss it! Saima and I." He nods in his sister's direction. "We used to come to the Sol Ball as children. We were thrilled to hear that it was reinstated."

"All thanks to my darling," Lucette purrs and drags those talons of hers across my forearm.

I produce the most genuine smile I can muster. Lucette pulls Florian into a chat about the ball, the costumes, the food, and the decor, and I can tell he's not impressed with her. It makes me want to laugh, but I let Lucette have her moment while I watch the dancers. Through the sea of guests, it's hard to keep track of Daphne, and everytime I see her red hair my breath catches.

I hear a cry from across the room and Lucette snaps her head to inspect where it came from. She then clenches her jaw and hastily curtseys to Florian and I before excusing herself to tend to her friend who's escort ran off with another woman. I can feel my muscles relax and my shoulders loosen as Lucette disappears behind a pillar.

Arden appears out of nowhere and climbs up the stage with graceful ease. Like a predator, he strides over to me and whispers in my ear, "Vail is in. We're leaving immediately, he's ready to destroy them." He pulls his mask up higher. "We'll see you at your coronation tomorrow."

My heart leaps. *Vail is in.* I could jump for joy.

"Thank you," I say and squeeze Arden's shoulder. "Be safe."

Arden nods at me and climbs back down, ignoring everyone and everything around him. The sea of people part for him, giving him a wide berth to pass them by. I don't think anyone has given up on the idea that he may have killed Narah. Arden has a ruthless reputation, and he uses it to his advantage. I hope it helps him tonight.

I shake my head and think. Now that Lucette is distracted with her heartbroken friend, I can try to run off with another woman myself. I scan the room frantically to find those fiery locks. I see her, I see Daphne, finally. She looks like she's having a good time, her smile is wide and her hair is coming loose. Clearly she and Esven have been dancing, I can almost see the droplets of sweat on her collarbone from where I'm sitting. Florian is talking to me, but I'm not paying him any attention. I nod at Florian, but then I notice Daphne curtsey to Esven and walk towards the powder rooms. *Now's my chance to talk to her alone.*

"I'm afraid I'll need to postpone this conversation," I pat Florian's shoulder and drop from the stage to the floor in one jump.

That jump was steeper than I anticipated. A stinging sensation climbs up my feet and into my shins. It's painful, but I shake it off and head towards the powder room after Daphne on my wobbly, stinging legs.

Florian's eyes travel to Daphne, and he gives me a two finger wave and laughs. "Not a problem."

The music and the chatter in the ballroom quiets when I enter the hallway nearest to the powder rooms. Soleil pops out of the servants passage, a handsome man in a cooks' uniform wrapped around her. They break apart quickly and the servant dashes to the kitchens.

Soleil laughs, "that's Reggie."

I bow to her and say, "Not my business, Lady Toun. This is a lovely ball you've created, a lovely week's worth of artistry to be honest. Your work is impeccable, I'll be sure to continue to hire you."

"I would love that," she replies and curtsies. "Do you mind if I escape the crowd and take Reggie with me?"

I laugh. "Not at all. Have fun."

Then I hear water running a little ways down the hall and hear Daphne mumbling to herself behind the door of the powder room. Soleil winks at me, "same to you."

Once the hall is empty, I hurry towards Daphne's voice, stopping at her door. I don't knock, I just turn the knob on the powder room door, but it's locked. I turn it again, and fists pound on the other side.

"Give me a moment, damnit."

I chuckle and wait patiently for her. The door clicks, and when it opens, her eyes widen and she looks down both sides of the hall. She takes a step back into the powder room and puts her hand on the door to close it in my face.

"Please," I murmur and reach my hand out to stop her from closing the door on me.

"No."

"Daphne–"

She shakes her head, a loose curl falling from its pin. "Gelhert cannot see this."

"Just listen to me," I beg, "only for a moment."

Daphne taps her foot and huffs. "Be quick."

I step inside and instantly regret my decision. This powder room in miniscule. There really isn't room for one person, let alone two. Daphne's dress takes up the majority of the space, and our bodies are pressed closely together, close enough that I can feel her breath on my skin.

"What now?" She sneers. "Were you not finished degrading me?"

"I deserve that."

"Damn right you do." She turns her body away from me, at least, as far as it will go.

I lean my head on her shoulder. "*I'm sorry.*"

"What do you want, Lieve?" She sighs.

"I wanted to let you know that everything I've done, everything I've messed up–," I gently use my finger to turn her chin towards me–, "it's getting fixed as we speak."

Her brow furrows and her eyes narrow. "What do you mean?"

"The man you saved, Remi, he's helping me take down the Matisses'."

"You're not serious?" She shakes her head vigorously. "You've actually gone insane, Lieve. This–this is mad. Are you drunk?"

"No! That's the beauty of it, Remi and Arden–"

"Arden!" She shouts and the shrill pitch of her voice rattles my ear drums.

I wiggle my finger in my ear, trying to ease the pain. "They're already gone, and it's going to work."

"What *is* this plan?"

"Arden and Remi are going to talk to people, recruit people." I answer.

"Recruit them for *what*?"

"For a sort of coup," I can hear how my own words sound now. Ludacris.

"Against *Benito Matisse*?"

"Yes."

Daphne lets out a slow whistle. "You *must* be drunk, or *high*, if you think there will be enough people to stop Benito."

I run my hand across the bare skin of her shoulder. "Remi's going to talk to other Blackbands. They're skilled fighters and they don't want to be indebted to Benito or anyone else. They're going to talk to everyone they can so we have enough people to go up against him, to stop payments to their tyrant. And if it doesn't work, I'm announcing every single grievance about them in front of the entire Kingdom immediately following my coronation. They will either be turned into peasants or hung for treason."

"Or *you* will be," she says coolly.

"It's going to work."

Daphne's voice shudders. "What if the people Arden talks to give him up, or hurt him–"

"Arden is sixteen. There are men his age in my militia."

"I know but–"

"He isn't your child, Daphne," I say sternly. "He isn't a child at all anymore."

Then the door is flung open, and standing before us is Lord Esven. I'm sure the scene is not what he imagined he would find. His lip curls into a terrifying sneer as he realizes his fiance is in a small powder room, chest to chest, with the Foreigner King of Prinav, a man he despises. His eyes darken and his fists clench hard enough to turn white before he storms back to the ballroom. *Shit.* Daphne calls out to him over and over, but Esven doesn't look back.

Love cannot be destroyed. It can only be taken, or given.

– Ode of Guenivere, The Holy Book of Bram

CHAPTER 45

VERA

When I step outside the castle, a warm breeze meets my face. I close my eyes and let the air waft my skirts and hair, breathing in the floral aroma of the nearby gardens. Hooves click on the cobblestones and a carriage appears. It's pearl white and has a glossy luster. Gold filigree adorns the trimmings and it looks to me like a giant pearl from the ocean wrapped in gold ribbons. Siva and Malsu are hitched to the carriage and their coats gleam in the moonlight. I walk over to them and they whinny with excitement. I reach my hand out to pet Malsu, and Siva nudges me impatiently with her nose until I pet her too.

"Evening, Princess," says the driver. He's a young man, around seventeen, with long dark hair, pale skin, and a mischievous grin.

Calix arrives at the entrance to the castle about ten minutes later and he grins when I meet him under the chandelier. The glitter in my gown catches the light and dapples the entryway in silver sparkles. Calix holds up a finger and makes a circular motion, so I do a spin for him. The sparkles dance across the floor and walls, giving the illusion of shooting stars.

"You look great," Calix purrs, and kisses my hand.

Calix looks great too. He's dressed in black from head to toe. He wears a black silk tunic with a black velvet vest and silver buttons. His trousers are black leather with silver buckles and studs down the outside of the legs, and black riding boots. With his dark hair and tan skin, he looks like stars dipped in ink.

I stand under the twinkling lights of the chandelier while Calix speaks with our driver and let my mind drift to Lieve's fairytales. The Glimmer Trail was briefly mentioned in a rare leather book that Lieve stole for me two years ago. I know the glimmer trail we are taking tonight isn't the same one, the one I read about was in Shadow Grove, and it was full of beautiful Fae and Nymphs. But a girl can pretend.

Calix then turns to me and holds his arm out towards the carriage. I scurry down the entrance steps and Calix kisses my cheek, my skin instantly warming with his touch. The driver opens the door to the carriage and Calix holds his gloved hand out as a guide for me to climb up. I wrap my fingers around the leather and cling when I fail to play my part as a distinguished lady, hoisting my gown up above my knees and clamoring inside.

"You are never dull," Calix chuckles.

Calix climbs up, wincing a little from his leg, and settles himself next to me. We lean back on the plush, white, interior of the carriage and let the quiet of the night wash over us. Calix places his hand on my thigh and I squirm in my seat, reveling in the memory of the last time he had his hands on my thighs and smile.

"What are you smiling about?"

My cheeks flush. "Oh nothing."

"Liar," Calix whispers in my ear and bites on my ear lobe.

I grab his wrist and slowly pull his hand higher up my thigh, but then we hit a bump in the road and knock our heads together. We both laugh, and I turn from him to look out the window. We're on the side of the estate that I haven't explored much yet. The driver takes us beyond the pond that lays on the far side of the stables, and up to the edge of the wood that Arden never lets me ride. I can see twinkling lights in the distance, like insects bouncing around with tiny lanterns. This is further than I've traveled on the castle grounds, and my stomach flutters with anticipation.

"I've read about glimmer trails before," I say in a hushed tone.

I have no reason to whisper. We aren't in Shadow Grove anymore, and there's nothing to fear in the Brone Castle Wood, according to what Daphne said while I was eavesdropping. However, giving in to the silence makes it all feel more fantastical. Whispering makes me feel like there's something here that is a little bit forbidden, or a little bit magical. Whispering is how Lieve would recite his stories, so it just seems fitting that our voices should be low.

"Arden hasn't taken you here on one of his riding lessons has he?"

"No." I sit on the edge of my seat when we get closer to the soft light. "And I wouldn't want to come here with anyone but you."

The carriage stops at the edge of the woods, right in front of a narrow path that leads deep into the thick trees. The driver hops down and opens the door for us, and the minute we exit the carriage, he tips his hat and hurries back to the castle. There are wisps of light flickering around us, and it enhances the sparkles of my dress. Evalie was right about my outfit, I'm sparkling brighter than the stars.

"Ready?" Calix asks and offers his arm for me to hold.

"Yes."

A bright wisps flies by Cal's face and blinks just above his brow. The light illuminates his honey colored eyes, making my knees weak. I loop my arm in his, and together we take our first step onto the Glimmer Trail. The instant our shoes touch the path, the grass beneath our feet glows. I take another step, and another, and another, while tiny flickering lights bob around us.

"This is incredible!" I say and spin around and around, all the glimmering lights creating this beautiful glow around us.

"I'm glad you like it." Calix smiles as he watches me dance around. "There are so many stories surrounding the Glimmer Trails and I wanted you to see one while it was still here."

"It's so much better than reading about them."

I go further down the trail, watching the glow of the grass shimmering under my feet. I feel a magnetic pull to delve deeper, like a gentle hand guiding me to somewhere I desperately want to go. I continue walking almost in a daze, but Calix grabs my arm before I can go too deep.

"Be careful, you'll end up in the Fae Realms."

I swallow hard, thinking about the Fae girl near the fairy ring in Shadow Grove and nod to him that I won't venture on without him.

"What do you know about glimmer trails?" He asks.

I shake my head and run my hand along the leaves, and they twinkle around my fingers. The tiny lights fly off the leaves and into the air around me, so I spin again to watch them float higher and higher in circles. It may be dangerous out here after all, but there's no doubt it's beautiful.

"I've read a short passage about them years ago, and it said the trails are made by the Fae for temporary travel." I stop spinning. "There are speculations that it could be a trail that tricks humans and leads to the Fae Realm. Others believe they use it for code, as Fae messages to those who need to hear them, temporarily lit up, and then perfectly faded in the morning light, along with the stars in the sky." As I answer Calix the Fae lights flicker and a soft melody, like a bird song, plays in my head.

Blood of my blood is the answer alone.

A drop from the mortal divine is all you need.

Both live within and for that I am pleased.

"Did you know that there are half Fae that roam Prinav and the other Kingdoms, that the Fae aren't just in their woodland and underground realms?" Calix asks, pulling me from the song.

I shake my head and feel as if I've lost a moment of time, or an important memory. My head feels groggy. Calix touches my shoulder, and I ask him to wait so I can try to remember the lyrics, but I'm already forgetting the words.

"Vera, did you hear my question?"

What does he mean? He didn't ask me anything. "I didn't, I'm sorry. It's just so beautiful here I must have been too focused on the view. Can you repeat your question please?"

He smiles. "Of course, Vera dear. Did you know that half-human, half-Fae live in Atatacia?"

"I didn't."

"High Fae married humans, centuries ago, and had children, the Drols. The Drols are highly magical and have similar powers to their ancestors, both taking their magic from the soil itself." Calix runs his hand along the leaves, softly lighting up the vegetation with his touch. "There is a sect of Fae, the Unseelie, who despise the offspring of the Seelie and humans."

"I remember reading about the Fae courts from a book in the library."

"There are two courts in the Fae realms, Seelie and Unseelie. The Fae of the Seelie Court are for the most part, empathetic and good. They've helped humans and humans helped them for many generations. Their cousins, the Unseelie, thought that humans were beneath them, and they waged a war against both Seelie and Humans when they discovered that human offspring had Fae magic running in their veins."

"Is that what Cavel was going on about at my welcome dinner? That Pinav helped Madoria in a war over all this?" I ask.

Calix nods. "Yes, except those were the Drols that were left *after* the Unseelie slaughtered the Seelie, their human friends, and their Drol offspring."

I shake my head, trying to keep up with this story. "Why was Madoria even fighting the Drols?"

"That's the whole reason why magic is outlawed," Calix sighs. "The Madorians are the select group of humans that the Seelie had children with, and to end the catastrophic war with the Unseelie–"

I chime in, "The Madorians made a Fae deal with the Unseelie, didn't they?"

Calix nods. "Any Drol found in Madoria should die, so the Madorians can live."

"That's awful."

"The Drols had to fight to save themselves, and so did the Madorian humans so *they* could live. The Unseelie are not empathetic to the plights of humans or Drols and didn't care what was happening here as long as it didn't harm their realm. Then, Prinav was roped into that war on the grounds that we're allies to Madoria." Calix runs his hand through his dark hair, sighing again. "So Prinav was bonded to Madoria's Fae Deal."

"Wow." The twinkles dance off the leaves and grass around me and seem to be blinking brighter and brighter as the story continues, almost as if they were screaming at us, at me.

"That's why Princess Saima is here." Calix looks me in the eye. "She's Fae. Well, she's a Drol–," he cocks his head to the side–, "and she was discovered."

"Why are you telling me this?" I ask.

"You saw her, so now you have to keep the secret." Calix takes both my hands. "No one can know that she's here, her presence in Prinav, and her abilities, can never be shared publicly."

I feel the hair on my arms raise as the twinkling lights blink faster and faster. "What would happen if someone found out?"

Calix's eyes darken, "the Unseelie."

~

The rest of the date in the Glimmer Trail was overshadowed by Cal's ominous warnings about the Unseelie and the fact that now I have yet another dangerous secret to keep. I'm glad that Calix took me there, and I'm hungry to learn, but I thought last night was going to be different. I was hoping it would be an escape from my problems in the castle. I was hoping to feel Cal's hands beneath my skirts again, but all I've gained is another thing to wonder and worry about.

"I thought last night was going to be more romantic," I complain to Evalie. "Intimate even."

She sits in the corner, sewing the finishing touches to my gown for the Feast and rolls her eyes. "It *was* romantic."

I cross my arms and pout. "How?"

"The setting was gorgeous, he brought you there in a carriage, and he told you intimate secrets!" Evalie answers. "There's your intimacy if you ask me."

Although I didn't tell her about Saima, I *did* let her know that Calix revealed a secret to me and that I can't tell anyone about it, not even her. Evalie thought this was a great sign that Calix is falling for me, but I didn't tell her that Calix probably only told me because I walked in on that meeting and saw Saima with my own eyes.

Evalie then says that people don't tell each other intimate details about themselves or something they care about, unless they care about the person they are telling the secret to. I suppose she's right. It is a huge, dangerous, intriguing secret. In a way, last night was more romantic than the night I thought I was hoping for.

"Evalie, how are you always right about everything?"

She finishes attaching the last section of lace and raises her eyebrows at me. "Years of marriage."

Evalie stands and holds my Feast gown in the air, shaking out the wrinkles. *It's a work of art.* The silky fabric is a pale shade of gold, with a plunging neckline, and a dangerously high slit in the skirt. Peeking through the leg slit are delicate lace appliques, along with an open back, lace also lining the hem. Lieve was right about the Feast. It must be even more scandalous that I realized because this dress leaves me very exposed.

"Lord Bramford had this fabric shipped here from Teyrnas for you." She hangs the gown on the door of my wardrobe. "I've never touched anything this soft."

"Is Teyrnas known for their fabrics?" I ask her, touching the silky material for myself.

"Oh yes," Evalie replies. "I used to import whatever fabric I could afford from the capital, Affames, in my shop. Nearly everyone in their lands works in the industry making gowns, tapestries, bed linens...Their queen has impeccable standards."

Evalie helps me into the gown and she's right, it is the softest silk I've ever felt and hangs off me perfectly. The fabric is so thin that I feel naked, but luckily you can't actually see any skin underneath. It hugs my body in all the right places, emphasizing what little curves I have. Although, now that I'm eating regularly, I don't present as gauntly as I did when I first arrived at Brone Castle. I've gained a little weight, curves finally starting to form on my thin body. I feel like a woman for the first time in my life, and I grin anticipating Cal's reaction to this dress.

"Alright, now I have to help some of the other staff finish up some errands for the Feast, but I will meet you in the Solarium with the others in twenty minutes." Evalie kisses my cheek and then sprinkles salt around us, praying in a language I don't recognize. Then she looks me in the eye and nods. "We are going to keep King Lieve safe, and any spells and potions that Lady Daphne divvies up will be poured into Calix's glass by your hand, not hers."

We came up with the idea for me to give Calix the potion myself during one of my lessons with Poppy. As we were reading about love potion antidotes, we stumbled on a book of spells. We read that antidotes take a month to conjure, and love potions cannot be destroyed.

Any potion's magic will continue to flow until someone finally drinks it.

However, the drinker will fall in love with the person who pours the potion, regardless of who made it. So, we're going to snatch it up, and I'm going to pour it in Calix's glass myself. Marguerite and Soleil stated that they can get past Daphne's wards, so the plan just sort of fell together.

I have a little time to kill, so I root around in my desk to find my copy of *Watch Makers*. I've barely had time to work on the watch lately, but I can spare a few moments to try before I have to meet the ladies. I didn't want to do this plan this late in the day, but Soleil said Daphne would be busy until right before the Feast, and we know that means we can't get the potion until the room is empty. We're sure Daphne made enough to take with her, but as long as he drinks it from me first, whatever she gives him won't work. So we have to wait until the room is empty to steal some for ourselves.

I sit on the edge of my bed, careful not to ruin any of Evalie's hard work, and crack open the book. I've been itching to work on the watch as a backup plan, but haven't found the right tools to complete the repairs. I just hope that our plan works so I don't have to call out Daphne for her magic and be forced to flee Prinav with Lieve and a broken pocket watch.

My few spare minutes have passed and it's time to leave. A screech from outside my chambers startles me, and I drop the book on the floor. I lay my ear against the wood, but I don't hear anything in the hallway. Slowly, I grip my door knob and crack the door open. The hall is empty so I open the door wider and poke my head out. Nothing is there.

I have to leave anyway, so I step into the hall and turn to just shut the door behind me, but then Poppy's ginger cat darts between my legs. The orange ball of fur runs straight to the stack of books about watches and Doppelgangers and Brone monarchs I borrowed from the library and picks up a loose sheet of parchment sticking out. Nigel scrambles around my chambers, prize in mouth. I grab for him and miss, while he knocks over candlesticks and runs up the curtains before bolting out the half open door.

"Nigel!"

I can't afford to lose any of the pages in these books, one of them could be the key to mending the watch, and my relationship with my brother. I follow Nigel through the maze of hallways that make up Brone Castle, only catching glimpses of his orange tail before he picks up speed around each corner.

"Come back!" I shout. "I don't have time for this!"

Then, like a miracle, the cat stops. He uses his back leg to scratch behind his ear and it's the perfect time to grab the paper if I'm fast enough. I sneak up to Nigel while his back is turned from me and he's distracted with his itch. Quickly, I snatch the paper from his cute little mouth. Nigel must believe we're playing because he swats at me, and his sharp claws get caught in the intricate lace that Evalie sewed onto my gown.

"Oh no!" I bend down and release Nigel's claws from my dress. " Nigel, you rascal!"

Nigel meows, swats one more time, and then disappears around the corner of the hallway, leaving me alone with a torn dress and a piece of paper with a list of Brone Monarchs and their pictures drawn with ink. One of the portraits catches my eye. Monroe. I study his eyes, the curve of his jaw, and feel uneasy. He looks eerily like my father. I stare at it, and notice he even has the same scar. As I'm considering what this might mean, a door right in front of me opens just wide enough that I can see an eye watching me.

"I can fix that," a woman says, pointing at my dress, and I realize it's Princess Saima.

I hurry inside, knowing that she's supposed to be a secret. "Oh, thank you!"

Saima's room is small. I think this was once a servants room. There's a washroom, seating area, desk, poufs, and a manageable but not princess worthy bed. A window in the corner overlooks the stables and the forest that houses the Glimmer Trail. It's a small window, but at least the view is beautiful. The air in the room smells of some sort of fruity smoke, and a slight fog hangs in the air. Saima walks around me, her long skirt dragging the ground and the tassels on the hem jingling with her steps.

She snaps the door shut behind her and I remember. *Saima is Fae.* Well, a Drol, but magical nonetheless. Maybe I shouldn't have come in here. Her nostrils flare, pulling on her nose ring. It's connected by a delicate chain that attaches to the chains that adorn her hair and slightly pointed ears. It's intimidating, and breathtakingly beautiful.

Saima gestures towards a pouf so we can sit, but I don't budge. I need to get to the Solarium. She notices my hesitation and looks me up and down. "There's nothing to be afraid of, *Princess.*"

"I know that," I say and stand a little straighter, trying to convince myself more than her at this point.

"So you aren't afraid of the Fae?" She smiles.

I take a step toward the door and Saima waves her delicate fingers in a twisting motion and the lock clicks.

"I think you might be. Most people are."

I fold my arms across my body. "What do you want with me? I refuse to make some kind of Fae deal with you, and you aren't even fully Fae, so—"

"I saw your little date at the Glimmer Trail." She looks me up and down again. "And by your own words, you now know my secret." She looks at her fingernails absentmindedly. "Calix must have told you, and it wasn't his secret to tell. So now, I want one of yours."

A nervous burst of laughter erupts from my chest. "You've got to be joking."

Saima's eyes meet mine and she hisses, "Do you want to find out?"

I feel a tingle in the air, drawing closer, stifling my breath. "I'm not going to tell anyone your secret, nor did I ask to know it–"

"I needed to hear you say it out loud. And just so you're aware, *that's a bargain*." She shoots off the bed and grabs my dress.

I try to pull from her, but her grip is strong. "*Let me go*."

Saima runs a long nail across the tear in the lace and it sews itself back together. I rip the fabric from her hands and try to open the door, but it's locked.

Saima turns her fingers again, the lock clicking so I can get out. "You said out loud that you wouldn't tell my secret, and I fixed your gown. *See?* I can hold up my end of a bargain, and that means you have to hold up yours."

"What if I don't have any big secrets?" I ask.

She holds up the parchment that Nigel stole from my book and I'm astonished. I didn't even see when or how she got a hold of it. "When you're ready to tell me, I'll give this back to you."

With that, I'm pushed out of her room and the door slams in my face. I've made a Fae deal, and I think I'm going to have to make another. I don't know why, but I have to know what that parchment says. But first, I need to get to the potion. The others are waiting for me, and I'm already late.

Borders clear. No Dops. No sign of Lord Bramford.
Found young woman matching the description of
Vera Oleander but was soon discovered an imposter
with a Teyrn accent. Squabbles near the Black
Diamond mines resolved. Shipment of Tussian Liquor
and Teyrn Iron arrived on Damaskan Highway
yesterday and heads to Breka at daybreak.
– *Correspondence from Captain Issel Paloma, head of the
Royal Hunters, to Regent King, Sir Lieve Oleander.*

CHAPTER 46

LIEVE

We manage to escape the powder room and Daphne chases
Esven down the hall. I'm still weak and I have to push
myself just to stand. My muscles strain when I use the doorknob
to get to my feet, and then scream at me with every step. Luckily
there are chairs, statues, and other furnishings in the hall that I can
lean on to walk because I don't think I can make it without support.
I should have used the cane Finn offered. My chest heaves realizing
Daphne is long gone, running after Esven like he's the one she loves
and I'm a nobody again.

It takes me several minutes, but I catch up to them. They're arguing in
a secluded part of the servants' halls. Esven is shaking, his fists clenching
and unclenching repeatedly. Daphne is desperately pulling on her hair,
her skin damp with sweat. She reaches her hand out to caress his forearm

and he flings his arm, smacking her into the stone wall. Daphne's body sinks to the ground, her hands covering her face as tears stream down.

Daphne reaches out to him again. "Please listen to me, Gelhert–"

Esven's nostrils flare. "Siren, you will not speak to me so informally." He rears his arm back to strike her again.

White hot rage floods my veins. "If you lay another finger on her, I won't play nice." I drag my exhausted body one foot at a time so I can get nose to nose with him and push my finger into his chest. "I'll rip your head from its body and feed you to the Darkthings."

Esven takes in my heaving chest, strained from over-exertion. "Will it satisfy you? You are no true king, sire. The throne will see to that." His eyes flicker to Daphne and then back to me. "Enjoy the whore while you can, I am no longer bewitched by her."

I pull on the hilt of my dagger and before the blade is fully released from the sheath, a strong hand grabs my wrist. I don't turn to see who it is just yet, I wait a moment for Esven to notice what I was about to do. I want him to see that I am his King. I am dangerous. I am The Conductor of Death, and I can swiftly bring death upon him.

Esven merely raises an eyebrow. The hand around mine tightens, even as I try to swing.

"I suggest you go back to the ball, Lord Esven." *Florian.* The Prince stopped me from killing my advisor in a fit of rage. My grip loosens and the blade slides into its sheath as Florian slowly removes his hand from me.

Daphne flees to her rooms. I start to follow, but Florian gently puts a hand on my chest. Esven hasn't moved. Florian stares him down, Esven glaring back at him. I wager that he's not used to anyone telling him what to do.

"Esven," Florian commands, "*leave.*"

Esven draws his cloak to his chest and shoulders past me, storming in the direction of the ballroom doors. I didn't know that my free hand was clenched so tightly, and when I release my fingers, crescents of blood are left on my palms.

"Gelhert is as unrelenting as ever," Florian sighs.

I wipe my palm on my pant leg. "You know him?"

Florian shrugs. "Unfortunately."

I start shaking and a wave of nausea hits me. Heat pours from my skin and then a chill runs down my spine. It's hard to keep my eyes open and another wave of heat pulsates in my neck, flowing from my collar. Back and forth, the hot flashes repeat and now in a cold sweat, I lean against the stone wall, letting the even cooler rock rest against my forehead.

"Lieve," Florian's voice seems worried, "are you alright?"

I wave a hand at him, but my vision is fuzzy.

Florian's hand rests on my shoulder. "Something isn't right. Let me help."

"Get Daphne," I croak as the room grows hazy around me. "She'll know how to–"

"I'll be right back."

I'm on my knees now, barely awake when Florian's footsteps return, with the click of women's heels. It's not Daphne. I'm dying and I'll never see her again. I'll never get to tell her I love her. I can't smell her vanilla scent.

"He's lost his breath Flor," the woman says.

"Can you help him?"

"Of course, but it will be difficult." The woman leans down and her dark hair tickles my nose. "Sire," she whispers, "did a Fae take your breath from you?"

"Not Fae," I manage, "a Drol, we–" I take a shallow breath–, "we were saving a young man's life."

"I need you to relax." She runs her soft hands across my lips, neck, and chest.

Through the haze I can make out who she is. Princess Saima. And floating in her hands is a familiar, blue orb. How many of these nobles are truly Fae?

"Lay him flat," she instructs Florian.

Then a piercing cold pain travels from my lips to my chest. It freezes my lungs, paralyzing me from the inside. Even my eyes feel frozen shut, the sweat on my skin so cold it burns. I force my mouth to move and the skin on my lips crack. Saima wraps me in Florian's cloak. I shiver on the ground for a few moments, and when I open my eyes I see my breath frost the air.

Florian and Saima watch me breathe, looking relieved. They hold each other's hands and do a motion with their arms, a thanks to the mother goddess, Gwen, for saving me. Then they start speaking to one another rapidly in Madorian.

Will he tell anyone?

I doubt it, he's working with another Drol.

Should I bind him in a deal?

It wouldn't hurt.

Saima looks at me and tilts her chin up. "Obviously I require that you don't reveal my secret."

I assumed she would want reassurance, not only for her safety, but for Madoria's safety. Florian looks around again, keeping a close eye for passersby. They're a great pair. It makes me think of Vera and my heart breaks. We were a great pair too, and I miss her.

"What are your terms?" I ask.

"Until your dying day, you will be indebted to me and my brother. You will provide safety for us, and discretion. You must never tell anyone of my gifts."

"Those are harsh terms, Saima," I cough, as my voice returns to me. "I will accept on one condition."

Florian and Saima glance at each other before Saima says, "go on."

"That you do the same for myself, and if you ever encounter my sister, Vera Oleander, you do the same for her."

Florian shrugs. "It's a good deal."

Saima folds her arms and narrows her eyes. "Fine. We have a deal."

They bow and curtsey as tingles from her magic flood my skin. After, they turn to reenter the ballroom, and Florian looks back at me and winks. I pray to the gods that Vera meets them someday, somehow, and they are indebted to help her. At least there's something I can do for her, even if it's small.

I stand alone in the hall, trying to decide if I should go after Daphne, or return to the ball. I yearn to follow Daphne, but I steel my resolve. I must remain calm and focused for just one more day. The coronation is tomorrow. Arden and Remi will be back with citizens ready to speak against the Matisse's. I'll be crowned, and the coup against my enemies will commence. I will rid Prinav, and the entire continent of Atatacia, of the Matisse family, and then I can work on getting Daphne back.

The guards open the doors for me and I enter the ballroom with my head held high. But the mood has shifted within the room. People are no longer mingling and dancing.

Something is wrong.

Every head turns towards me. I scan the crowd, trying to figure out what's happening when I see the problem. *Esven.* He's whispering to a large group surrounding him. Our eyes meet and I can feel the wrath in my chest begin it's all too familiar bubbling to the surface. I break eye contact and look toward the stage to see Lucette sitting on her throne, her face stoic and stark white.

Ignoring everyone else, I walk to Lucette. I have to make sure that she and her father don't start their own coup tonight. I'll send Prinav, and all of Atatacia into ruin, handing over the crown to a family of monsters if I don't appease Lucette immediately.

I smile and nod at people, and their gaping mouths tell me that Esven has talked to several of my guests already. My legs drag me to Lucette before I can even think of what to do next. Then, like I'm possessed, I'm on the stage, kneeling in front of her.

I hear myself utter words that make me want to plunge my dagger into my own chest. "Lady Lucette Matisse, will you marry me?"

No one speaks. The musicians stop playing and all in attendance watch our every move. Out of the side of my eye, I can see the gossip commence. My ears ring with deafening silence and I swear Lucette can hear my wild heartbeat ramming against my chest.

Lucette stands, and as I kneel at her feet, nausea takes hold. I'm going to retch on the stage. My eyes dart from her to Benito and I watch closely as she looks at her father who stands at the edge of the stage.

Benito looks *delighted.*

My blood curdles. He nods at her and she turns to the crowd, smiling, drinking in the moment. Lucette tangles her fingers in my hair and pulls. She smiles that wicked smile as pain sears across my scalp. Benito chuckles.

"Yes," Lucette says to our audience and not to me, "I'll be your Queen."

Love is gentle and kind when true, but fickle and tried when forced.

— Seelie Proverb

CHAPTER 47

VERA

My hands shake while I walk to meet up with the others. Several members of the court gather in front of the dining hall. There's no other passage from Saima's room to the solarium or the dungeons, so I'm forced to go this way. *Damn that cat.* I pin my body against the wall and walk quickly hoping no one will notice me. The clock at the end of the hall tells me I'm already late. The potion must be stolen before the Feast so I can slip it in Calix's drink myself before Daphne does. I have to hurry or there's no point in trying.

Pushing my way through the half-naked guests, my shoulder slides on a particularly sweaty nobleman's arm. I press my eyes shut and continue walking, praying, that he doesn't speak to me. I let out a sigh of relief while the sweaty man wraps his moist arms around a young, blonde, noblewoman dressed in a tight corset, bloomers, and nothing more.

I slowly turn my body to slip around the corner and out of sight when another nobleman with black hair and a silver stripe at his part notices me.

"Why hello, gorgeous." His steel gray eyes light up as he trails his gaze over my body. "Leaving so soon? The fun hasn't even begun yet."

The blonde noblewoman rolls her eyes as she lifts her breasts up higher in her corset. "She's probably scared to join. The feast seems a little too saucy for a girl like her."

I stop and plaster a fake smile on my face and join the group. "Yes well, it's not becoming for a Princess to participate in salaciousness when she's courting someone already."

The blonde's face drains of color and she shoves the sweaty man off of her and curtseys. "Apologies, Your Highness."

I raise an eyebrow at the rest of them and they bow deeply, the steel-eyed man still grinning.

I move to leave, when I hear Lucette. "Princess Vera, join me."

What do I do? I look around, panicked, and everyone is staring at us. I can't go in, I have to meet the others. My legs feel like lead.

"Vera," Lucette's voice cracks like ice, "let's go."

I feel something moist and squishy pushed into my hand and I turn my head to see Soleil and Poppy standing in front of one of the castle guards, merely an inch from my side.

"Good evening, Princess," Poppy says with surprising confidence.

"Hello," I say as I fiddle with the slimy object hidden in my palm.

When our eyes meet I can see that she is in distress. Sweat beads on her skin and has made its way through the delicate lavender fabric of her gown. The rest of the guests turn from us and walk into the dining hall while I stay focused on Poppy.

She nods at our hands and I realize that whatever is in my hand *must* be the potion. *They succeeded!*

I smile at Poppy and take Lucette's arm, walking into the dining hall and hoping that no one notices my clenched fist. I take a turn with her and then pull away as soon as I can because the squishy ball of potion in my hand is starting to grow warm and melt.

Shit. Where's Calix? I walk over to a champagne tower. If I can just dump this into a glass and take the glass myself, then *voila!* Potion ready for Calix to drink! I look around the room for him, and it's hard to make out specific faces in the dim lighting. Women in lingerie hand out tiny bottles of smoking liquor, and shirtless men pour glasses of wine in the empty chalices dotting the tables.

I spot him. Calix wears a loosely fitted tunic and leather pants, no belt, and no shoes. His hair is tousled and when he sees me, a predatory smirk curls his lip and my core burns at the sight of him. Cal's muscles flex as he pulls out a chair at the dining table and sits, then cocks his head to the open seat next to him.

I fumble with the potion in my palm, and with my hands behind my back, I gently drop the squishy blob into a glass. I hear it plop and fizz, speeding up my already racing heart. *Here we go.* My body tenses as Cal's eyes rake my curves and I bite my lip hoping that I'm doing the right thing. *He already loves me, right?*

I flick my eyes to Poppy and nod at her. She looks relieved and takes her seat beside Soleil at the table a few chairs away from where I'll be sitting with Calix. With a deep breath I head over to him, squeezing the stems of the champagne flutes tight enough that I fear they may bust.

"Look at you," Calix purrs. "Dia herself wasn't ever as captivating."

I hand Calix his drugged drink. "And you look like Dia herself made you just so she'd have something beautiful to gaze at."

Calix's face tightens, just for a second.

"Did I say something wrong?"

"No, Vera Dear." He smiles, raises his glass in a toast to me, and drains it.

My heart sinks. Why did he tense? Does he know what I've done? Calix's eyes meet mine and his hardened expression leaves, replaced by a crooked grin. But that look doesn't melt my heart this time, it breaks it. I give him a soft kiss on the cheek.

I stare at Calix for the rest of the cocktail hour like he's an animal at a menagerie while my thoughts bounce inside my head. This was the best option, the only option. I had to have him drink it or he'd fall for

Daphne. He already loves me, or at least, is close to loving me. I didn't do anything wrong. I've saved him. *Right?*

Then the dining hall doors open again and Daphne enters. She looks livid. Without speaking, she takes a seat right beside me. Poppy's eyes dart from me, to Daphne, to Soleil, then Calix, and back. I freeze. The world around me seems so far away, it's as if I'm watching myself at this feast and I'm not inside my own body. Jugglers and courtesans walk by and say hello to Soleil, couples grope each other in dark corners, but my attention stays on Daphne. The look she's giving me is sharp enough to cut glass and I'm terrified to even breathe.

I can hear Lieve welcoming his guests near the head of the table, thanking them for their attendance and thanking the servants for their work. I hadn't even noticed he'd arrived. Lucette recites a passage from the Book of Bram, and the room applauds around us, though Daphne, Poppy, Soleil, and I remain locked in place. I'm brought back inside my own body when I hear Calix say my name.

"Vera, dear," he says. "You're pale. Are you feeling alright?"

I look down at a plate full of food a servant placed in front of me and then back up at him. "I don't know."

"You seem unwell."

"Oh my, you're right!" Daphne exclaims. "She looks like she's going to be sick." Daphne's eyes flare and I almost believe I could see *actual fire* behind her eyes.

"I can take you to your chambers, Your Highness," Poppy squeaks.

Daphne stands, her hand now on my arm. "I wouldn't want you to miss the Feast, Lady Poppy. I'll take her."

Poppy backs down in the face of Daphne's glare, and before I know it, the witch is guiding me out of the dining hall. I don't fight it, I know better than to make a scene at this point.

"Goodnight, Vera dear!" I hear Calix shout. Good. Daphne might kill me, but at least Calix is safe.

I don't reply to him. I'm not sure I even can. Daphne's nails dig into my skin as she leads me to the dungeons. I was right. She's going to kill me.

While almost everyone in the castle is celebrating, I'm coming undone inside. Daphne will end my life tonight, and I might let her. Our footsteps thump on the hard ground beneath our feet. The sound of our steps and the heaviness of our breath put me in a trance. I try to memorize everything around me. The smells. Vanilla. I look at Daphne and her hair matches the flame of the lanterns in the dimly lit dungeon halls.

I hear a man's voice up ahead and it's familiar. It has to be Arden. We round the corner and I see him standing in front of someone, a woman, with a dagger in hand. My mind catches up to me and I realize it's Evalie.

"Arden!" I cry, finding my voice to save a friend. "Please don't hurt her!"

Arden turns to me, sheathing his dagger. "I don't plan to. Is that what you think of me?"

Daphne lets go of my elbow and I rush to Evalie. She throws her arms around me and I can see fear all over her tear-stained face. I put my body between Evalie and Arden, spreading my arms out to protect her.

"I'm not going to hurt anyone," Arden insists.

"But I might," Daphne snarls, pushing Arden aside.

I force myself to meet Daphne's eyes. "The potion is gone. I gave it to Calix." My legs shake as I clench my jaw. "You can kill me if you want to, but leave Evalie out of this."

Arden's brow furrows. "The potion's gone?"

He looks from me to Daphne and no one says anything.

"What is going on?"

"My former maid betrayed me," Daphne says. "And if we don't get Marguerite out of my potion chamber, she'll be dead before morning."

"So get her out!" I shout at her. I cannot allow Marguerite to die as a result of my scheming.

Daphne rounds on me. "I made a Fae deal with her, you ignorant–" She cuts herself off and paces around the darkened hall. "She's stuck."

Dia save me. "You're Fae?"

"Yes. And Marguerite is going to die very, very soon."

"So undo the deal."

"If I undo it, then *I'll* die.".

I'm sick of this, of nobles protecting themselves while the lives of their subordinates hang in the balance. I'm sick of Daphne having the power of life, death, and love, over me. "Do you think I care if you die? Do you think I would waste even a second of my day thinking about your fate?"

"Back off, Vera," Arden says flatly.

"No." A strange rush fills my chest. "I am the Princess of Prinav and I refuse to take orders anymore."

"I want to help her." Daphne pushes her hair from her face. "Why do you think I dragged you down here? I ran here the moment I felt her cross my wards, but I was too late. The moment she handed that potion to someone outside the door, the deal broke. She betrayed me." Daphne gets in my face. "And that's on *you.*"

"Like hell it is." I bark at her.

"We can all argue until we're blue in the face, but none of that will save Marguerite." A voice says softly behind me. Soleil.

She's right.

I lean against the wall and glare at Daphne. "So what will?"

I had not expected to be at Saima's door again so soon. My entire body shakes as I lift my hand to knock. If she doesn't help, then Marguerite will die, and I will have played a large part in that. I will not let my actions cause her any more pain. Before my knuckles even touch the wood, I'm being dragged inside.

"Do you have a death wish, Princess?"

"I need you. A life hangs in the balance."

Saima raises an eyebrow as she slips on a pair of shoes. "I keep the letter."

"Fine."

~

The fast pace of my heart makes me lightheaded. I have to word everything exactly right. I have to make sure I have the upper hand. We're close. Voices echo in the dungeon and Saima stops hard and looks at me with daggers in her eyes.

"You said you needed to save someone." Saima sneers. "You lied."

"No I didn't," I whisper. "They're a part of this."

Evalie calls my name, and she, Arden, Soleil, and Daphne appear from around the corner. Daphne's jaw drops when she sees Saima, and Saima's face turns beet red, her fists clenching in rage.

"You—you—" she stumbles over her words, wrath spewing from her mouth and shouts loud enough for them to hear. "You told *everyone* I was Fae!"

I smile and a wave of relief and excitement pulsates through me. "No. *You* just did."

Saima lunges at me. "You—" she swings and misses—, "thought—" and swings again but this time her closed fist meets my jaw and the connection rattles my teeth—, "you could—" lightning shoots up my jaw and into my eye—, "trick me!"

I don't fight back. I need her to save Marguerite. I understand Saima's anger and fear. Her secret is out. I've put her life at stake, and her country in danger. I deserve this. I crumple to the ground and lay in a ball. Arden has to jump in and pull her off me, dragging her to the opposite wall. He stands over her, dagger drawn to her throat.

"So you'll have this brute stab me if I refuse to help you?" Saima sneers.

I wipe blood from my lip. "Of course not." I stand as Evalie helps me to my feet. "But you'd be a monster if you don't."

Saima glares at everyone as she dusts her skirt. "What makes you think I'm not a monster already? I'm Fae afterall."

"Please," Daphne whispers, "I made a bad deal, a really bad deal."

Saima narrows her eyes at Daphne. "Wait. You're Fae?"

Daphne nods. "Half-Seelie."

"I really need your help." I say to Saima.

Saima's eyes widen for a split second and then she clenches her fists before cursing Lieve's name. Then she strides over to me, stands toe to toe with me and huffs. "Your brother made a deal with me many years ago and it just went into effect."

"What?"

"He made a deal for your protection, and I was dumb enough to accept." She pushes me into the wall and gets into a powerful stance in front of the potion room door that Marguerite is trapped inside. "He is bound to help me, and I am *bound* to help you."

I start laughing uncontrollably. *Lieve.* I've never loved my brother more.

CHAPTER 48

LIEVE

I stare at the floor, still kneeling before Lucette. *I'm engaged.* When Daphne hears of this, she'll flee. She'll withdraw from society completely, if her father doesn't disown her. Esven has ended their engagement, so if my plan doesn't work out, I've ruined her life, as well as mine.

"Stand with me," Lucette orders through gritted teeth.

For the rest of the ball Lucette and I are bombarded with cheers, bows, and kind words. There are *so many* people. My ears pick up the sound of music, but this time Saima isn't singing. The chandeliers have been dimmed and I faintly process that Lucette has pulled me to the dance floor. I'm not here. I'm not in this ballroom with *Lucette Matisse.* I'm not engaged to the person I hate the most.

Faster and faster we spin, the room blurring to the point that the only person I can focus on is Lucette. She throws her head back in laughter, closing her eyes, trusting me not to bite her neck and rip her throat out in front of all my guests. Brave of her. When the song ends we bow to one another and then separate. I notice Cavel talking to Benito as I'm walking to my throne. He and Benito shake hands and Benito passes him something, and Cavel stuffs it in his pocket. They both look at me, and then Cavel gives me a nasty smirk.

A servant with a tray of wine walks just a few feet from me and I lunge at him to grab two more drinks. He looks at me with wide eyes and then scurries away. *Good.* I down the second glass even faster than the first, and find myself back on the dance floor as the musicians have now started the Sol Ball ceremony.

Dozens of men and women gather and find their partners. I watch as they dance in formation under dim lights, and my thoughts spiral. I want Daphne to be here with me, not Lucette. I want Vera here. I want Calix to be alive even though I fear he probably isn't.

Florian is suddenly beside me. He doesn't congratulate me, he only hands me a glass of wine. "There is more to my attendance this week than celebrations, Your Majesty," he whispers.

The room is beginning to spin. *I shouldn't drink.* Florian lifts his own glass and I ignore him.

He continues, "I wanted to thank you for your help with the Dops in Madoria."

I grunt and take a sip.

He sips his own wine. "I have another, *well*, two other favors to ask."

I finish my glass.

"Madoria is in need of funds—"

"Get me another please."

"Are you sure?"

I glare at him. "*Another.*"

Florian waves over a servant and they bring me another glass of wine.

He clears his throat. "I'm asking for funding to rebuild our demolished Kingdom."

"Fine."

Screw you. He only helped me in the hall so I'd give his Kingdom money.

"One more favor." He takes another sip. "I lost thousands of men to the Dops. My women lost their husbands, sons, brothers–" he waves for a servant to pour more wine–, "They're poverty stricken, and to be frank, I don't have enough gold to help them. I thought that your unmarried men, especially noblemen, may be interested."

Someone walks in front of me and I don't even glance to see if it's a man or a woman before snatching their glass right out of their hand. I guzzle the contents like water. Florian shudders. Out of the corner of my eye I see Cavel flirting with a beautiful young woman. He slides his giant paw of a hand up her ebony skin and she grimaces in disgust.

"Sure Florian, I can make that happen," I say.

"Really?" He breathes a heavy sigh of relief.

"Start with Cavel." I point to him. "He's very wealthy. You pick a woman for him to marry, and make sure she's safe and her needs are met. If you do that, I'll help you with the rest of your favors after my coronation."

Florian bows to me and dashes off, I'm sure to talk to Saima. I for one, dash off to find the servant who's filling the wine glasses and ask him for a bottle. I want to be drunk enough that if Cavel fights me, I won't even feel it.

Daphne, these are the only known religious members
of the Order working where my mother would have
had mass during the weeks I could have been conceived.
These are the Priests actively performing sermons
from that start of spring to start of autumn: Fissa
Barlow, Cordelia Gatelby, Rolz Dugg, Cameron Briggs,
Lord Baptiste Matisse, Lord Devlon Ashbury, Lady
Iola Mantilli, Prudence Vaughn, Russ Kingsley, Fischer
Toll...
– *Letter from Lady Soleil Toun to Lady Daphne Cortwright.*

CHAPTER 49

VERA

S aima breaks through the wards Daphne placed on the door, and
severs Daphne's Fae deal, but it took hours. Saima is sweating and
clearly in pain by the time Evalie can jump in the room and tend to
Marguerite. Marguerite is barely alive. Breaking the Fae deal does some
damage to Daphne too, I noticed her hiding her own pain just as Saima
broke through the barriers.

Saima and Daphne heal Marguerite enough that Evalie can get her
to her room. Daphne told her she would be a little weak for a few days,
but that Saima did a very clean break and she should return to full health
very soon. Relief floods my veins at her words and I hug her tightly.
Daphne stiffens, but then gently wraps her arms around me and strokes
my hair while I sob.

"I'm done now," Saima announces. "And you are all now obligated to keep my secret."

Daphne chimes in–, "As well as mine."

We all look at eachother and a thought pops into my head so I say, "We will accept your deal if you help me find out what our little Queen is up to."

"Deal–," Daphne stretches her arm out to me and I take her hand and shake.

Saima crosses her arms. "I cannot stand you."

"I know." I shrug. "Deal or no deal?"

She marches past me and bumps me with her shoulder. "Deal."

I smile as familiar tingles travel from my hand and land in my chest, confirming the bond.

～

"I've been to festivals before," I tell Poppy, "but nothing like this."

Spinning around and around I see everything all at once. Giant tents with beer and wine, tents with merchants, tattoo artists, some even with scandalous courtesans, and tents with things I've never even heard of before line the dirt pathways on the estate.

The merchant tents are black and white striped, but inside each are an array of color. We pass by a baker's booth and a young man with curly blonde hair sells me a pastry and I rip it in half to hand the other half to Poppy.

"I just love the Festival," Poppy says brightly.

We walk into one of the booths and see Arden. He's bartering with a grumpy looking merchant with a weather beaten face, and he apparently wears him down because Arden tosses him a copper coin, sliding something wrapped in linen into his cloak.

"Sir Arden," Poppy greets him hesitantly.

He turns and looks at me, eyes blazing when they meet mine. He slides past us so he can exit the tent and I gesture to Poppy that I'm going to follow him out. Before he gets too far, I grab his cloak.

"What do you want now?" He snaps.

"I haven't seen Daphne this morning and I just wanted to ask how she was feeling?"

He scoffs at me. "You might have wrangled *her* into another idiotic scheme, but not me. I'm not telling you anything."

"I'm not trying to scheme," I scold him in a low voice. "I saw that Daphne was hurting when Saima ended the Fae deal, I was just concerned for her."

Arden's eyes darken. I've said something wrong yet again.

"Don't ever talk about Daphne and her–" he scans people walking past us–, "*gifts*, ever again."

"Arden, I'm just–"

A low growl comes from his chest. "Let it go."

"You can't order me around," I spit.

He pulls his hood tighter over his head and leans forward so we're closer to the same height. "I do as I wish."

"You're insufferable."

"And you're a spoiled brat messing with people's lives." He turns on his heel and walks away.

"Come back here!" I shout at his back.

He just raises his hand and places his middle finger in the air, waving it around above the crowd. I stomp back inside the tent to see that Poppy has a basket full of books.

She blushes at me. "I don't want to pry–"

"Pry away," I reply hotly, my eyes still following Arden's back.

"Sir Arden and yourself, are you–"

"No."

"It just looked as if–"

"Drop it Poppy," I snap and she trembles. I sigh. "I'm sorry, he just gets under my skin."

She looks down at the ground, a smile quirking her lip. "I couldn't tell."

～

Calix meets me in a section of outdoor stands to watch the joust. Just the sight of him smiling at me makes my heart ache. Daphne told me, after saving Marguerite, that the person who drinks or eats the love potion will be so intoxicated with the person that gave it to them, that they would willingly end their life for them. Every second of their day will be consumed with that person. There are potions to dampen the effects, but they can take months to concoct. Daphne agreed to make it for me, but I'm not sure I trust her.

Calix puts his hand on my thigh as we watch the joust, and even this tiny action feels different. I want to cry, or tell him what happened, but he would still be infatuated, so it's no use. The crowd jeers as one of the Skillsmen falls from his horse with a sickening thud.

"Are you feeling better?"

I touch my lip, afraid that Daphne's healing spell wore off and he could see where Saima pummeled me. "Yes, I'm fine."

"Glad to hear it," he whispers in my ear. "The Feast was a bore without you. I went to bed shortly after you did."

"You could have stayed at the party," I say.

Calix's lips brush the curve of my ear. "No amount of debauchery could tear you from my thoughts, Vera dear. I went to bed, alone, because you weren't well and I couldn't warm yours."

His breath on my skin sends a shiver down my spine. I *like* that he's now obsessed. I like that he's breathing on me, touching me, and I hate myself for it. *He was already courting me, though.* I keep repeating that line over and over, making myself believe that tricking him is okay. I repeat the line so I can convince myself that we're meant to be, that

Calix already feels this way about me, that I did nothing wrong. It's not working.

After the joust, we walk around hand-in-hand. People stare and gossip, some smile and some grimace. Calix isn't paying attention to anyone around us, he's been hyper-focused on me all day long. I have to pull him from every tent because he attempts to buy out the goods for me. *He has bought you plenty of gifts already, this is nothing new.* Another line I tell myself.

Lieve and Lucette join us for the midnight show in the Grandstands. Flames illuminate the massive arena, casting a fiery glow over the crowd. Entertainers pour out and do acrobatic feats in center rings made of solid wood, most of their tricks I've never seen before. They climb up each other's bodies, flipping and bouncing several feet in the air. Some throw each other high enough to touch the top of the enormous multicolored tent covering the arena. The crowd cheers and gasps at every trick, and I do too.

Lieve and I haven't interacted very much since our spat. He keeps side eyeing me. I know he wants to talk, but he's too stubborn to speak first.

"I'm feeling much better," I assure him.

"That's good."

"I'm sure Lucette told you I wasn't feeling well last night. But I suppose it was just some silly little bug," I go on and emphasize to him, "*but I'm fine now.*"

He smiles and the lines in his eyes deepen, "I'm glad to hear it."

"What about you?" I ask.

He nods. "I'm fine too."

Good. Argument over. The show ends and the audience piles out. Calix takes my hand again and the four of us head back to the castle to rest for the next day's activities. Once inside, we say our goodnights to Lieve and Lucette.

"Can I walk you to your room?" Calix asks.

No, I won't be able to stop myself if you come on to me too strongly. It wouldn't be fair to Calix if we take things too far before he can get his antidote. It would be a lie that could break our entire relationship if he ever found out. Until Daphne makes the love potion's antidote, I have to be the voice of reason. I have to tell him no.

"Um," I hesitate.

Calix looks at me like he won't be able to breathe if I say no. *I won't take it too far.* I think I can hold back. Lieve's eyes bounce back and forth between us and I wonder if he is going to tell Calix to go to his own room so I don't have to. I stand there like an idiot, practically begging Lieve to realize that I don't want Calix to walk me to my room because I have no self control. Lieve looks at me, and then to Calix with a knowing glance.

"You have an early morning, Calix–," Lieve claps his shoulder–, "and I haven't spent much time with my newly found sister in quite a while. I'll walk her to her rooms."

If I could hug Lieve right now, I would.

～

I don't think I'm going to be able to continue to keep away from Calix. After nearly escaping ecstasy tonight, (*why did I reject him again?*), I found myself crying on Lieve's shoulder in my room.

"Calix is so fond of you." Lieve pats my knee. "But it's okay if you don't feel the same way about him."

A jolt strikes through my heart. "That's not it."

"Then what's wrong?"

I have to make up a lie. I don't want to, but I can't tell him about the love potion. Or the entire situation with Daphne. Or Saima. My actions have created a barrier between Lieve and I that I don't know how to mend. I've made a mess of things. He was right when he said I don't know anything about Prinav or how to act here. Maybe I should just leave before I ruin Lieve's entire Kingdom.

"He's so wonderful, and I'm afraid I'll never be good enough." I didn't have to lie about that at all-, "and now-"

"Your whole world got flipped upside down." Lieve looks at the floor.

My lip trembles. "In a good way."

"Becoming royalty in a matter of moments is difficult." He kicks his foot. "I would know."

I let the weight of the past few weeks slide from my shoulders with a sigh. "It's difficult to navigate."

Lieve lays back on my bed. "You can always talk to me, or Lucette, about how you're feeling"

I roll my eyes and Lieve sits up straight. "I was trying to be nice to you, but you keep pushing me, Vera. What's your problem with my wife?"

"She's rude," I say hotly.

"She demands perfection."

"She threw tarts into a pond and forced her maid to fetch them from the water."

Lieve stands up now, his face flushing. "And you *laughed*."

My heart stops.

Lucette *told him* that I laughed. Lieve must think I'm a monster. Of course, he's been so distant with me, who wouldn't be in his position? He must think I've already forgotten poverty, and how much we suffered in Marguerite's similar position. No wonder we've had such distance, he thinks I've lost all my empathy.

I can't tell him I wasn't laughing at Marguerite. I'm sure he wouldn't believe me anyway. And telling him I've been seeing my Doppelganger isn't going to help anything. In fact, telling him about the Doppelganger might actually make everything worse.

"I apologized to that maid."

"I'll be sure to tell Lucette."

Lieve exits my chambers and slams the door behind him. I wait until I can't hear his boots slap the floor before I scream into my pillow. *I hate Lucette.* I hate her, I hate her, I hate her.

I want to talk to Evalie, but she's busy with Festival duties, and when I told her I wouldn't mind helping, she sent me away. I won't get to see her until tomorrow evening, if I'm lucky. Without thinking, I leave my room and wander to Poppy.

On the way to Poppy's room, I pass by Daphne's. I stop in front of the door and just stare at it, lifting my hand to knock before putting it back down at my side. Daphne wouldn't want to talk to me. *Or would she?* I steady myself and rap my knuckles on the wood. I can hear rustling inside and then the door opens just a crack and I see Daphne's face.

"Vera," her forehead wrinkles, "can I help you?"

"You ruined everything."

Her emerald eyes narrow. "Excuse me."

"My life is a mess, I'm keeping secrets, I'm bound to Fae deals–"

"Go away."

"Lieve hates me."

Daphne sighs and opens her door wider so I can enter, and I find Soleil sitting in a chair by the window. The minute I pass over the threshold of her door, everything in me falls apart. I crumble to the ground and sob, my face and hands wet with tears. Daphne kneels on the floor in front of me and lets me cry. Her vanilla scent fills me up and comforts me and before I know it, my head is in her lap. She pets my head and just listens.

"Shhh," she coos, "I know, I know."

"I don't know why I'm crying," I say through the sobs.

She doesn't speak, she just pets my head until I've stopped weeping. My body spasms with sobs, even though there are no more tears to cry. I sit up and wipe my face while Daphne rearranges her legs so she can sit cross legged. She smiles at me weakly and I can see that her eyes and nose are red. She's been crying too.

"I'm sorry," I say and stand up. "I shouldn't have bothered you, especially when you have company."

"No, I'm glad you did."

"Really?"

"Please sit back down," she gestures to the floor.

I return to the floor and sit cross legged like her, Soleil joining us.

Daphne leans back on her hands. "I know how hard it is to love Lieve, and so does Arden. I know you hate me, but I'm not evil. I'm just—"

"Desperate."

Daphne gives me a sad smile. "Yes." She sighs. "But it's over now. I've been talking through all of this with Soleil, and she told me that you caught Lucette doing magic in the dungeons. I want to find out what the Matisses' are up to. I don't trust them."

"Neither do I."

"And we're going to have to figure it out fast," Soleil says.

"Why fast?"

Daphne wipes a tear from her cheek and reaches out for Soleil's hand. "Because I only have until the end of the week before I'm shipped off to Teyrnas. Lucette has found me a *suitor*. She had Soleil break the news to me. Just another slap in the face to have a friend be the bearer of bad news."

"I'm so sorry."

"I'm sorry about the potion."

I sigh. "It wasn't wise of you to do that."

"I know, I know. It's just—" she places her head in her hands—, "it was my only hope."

Soleil scoots close to her and rubs her arm. "It will be okay, Daphne."

"What makes you think Calix was your only hope? And only hope for what? Marriage? That can't be true."

Daphne sniffs and looks up at me. "My two younger sisters are betrothed, but they can't get married until the eldest weds." She fluffs her skirts as she talks "My middle sister is engaged, and my youngest sister got pregnant out of wedlock."

"I still don't understand," I say.

"In Prinav the eldest sister must get married first, and because the youngest got pregnant, she's being forced to marry, but–, Soleil answers. "She can't marry until Daphne does."

"But why did you think you needed a love potion? You're a beautiful noblewoman in the King's Court?"

Daphne chuckles and the laugh is a sad one. "Because the entire Kingdom thinks I'm your brother's mistress."

It all makes sense now. That's why Soleil didn't want to talk about Daphne in front of Lieve.

"It isn't true. But we *were* in love once. And the man I was betrothed to, Gelhert Esven, caught us talking––*just talking*– in a powder room together many years ago and convinced the court to shame me Your brother would have married me, and he tried, but Lucette knew about my abilities and threatened to tell the world about me unless Lieve married her."

"So he married her."

Poor Lieve. He's been so selfless all these years. He's still the Lieve I knew, the one who would do anything for the people he loves. He's probably being forced to put on a front about Lucette. Maybe his overreactions at my dismissal of his wife are to keep me far from him, to keep me safe. He could be picking fights with me on purpose. Or, Hell– he might even be cursed. Lucette *does* know magic.

"He may have saved my life, but getting caught with him in the powder room ruined my chances of another engagement, so now my father wants to strip me of my title and send me away unless I find a husband. I've barely talked to him in years because of all this, and I'm sure he and Lucette colluded in this wretched plan. Father doesn't want his other daughters to fall into the same pitiful life that I have."

"That's not fair."

Daphne shrugs. "Life isn't fair, Vera of Adamston. You should know that. And if anyone in Teyrnas finds out I'm a Drol, there will be a lot more at stake than my unhappiness."

"The Unseelie?"

Soleil shakes her head. "No. The Fae aren't the danger in Teyrnas, the nobles are. Madoria isn't the only Kingdom who made a deal with them to save themselves. To show their loyalty to the Fae, the nobles in Teyrnas hunt Drols like a sport."

"Maybe Lieve can help." I say.

"It's a Fae deal with the Unseelie, Vera," Daphne replies. "No one can help me."

Missing: Delmont Pullam, aged 11, blonde hair, light eyes. Acolyte to the Holy Order, Hode Basilica, Teyrnas
— *Announcement from Queen Merrit of Teyrnas*

CHAPTER 50

LIEVE

D rink after drink pours down my throat. Lucette hasn't spent any more time trying to speak to me at the ball, and although I'm thrilled about that, it also scares me. I keep an eye on her as she laughs with a group of noble women, waiting for something, anything, to happen. I procured a bottle of wine from a servant and when I return to the ballroom, I catch Benito and his Sagart brother whispering in a dark corner. No doubt they're already planning their next step to power. Waves of anger pulsate under my skin, so I drown them with each sip to stop myself from exploding.

I'm seated on a bench near the back of the ballroom, the plush velvet soaked with wine all the way through to the wood underneath. A woman with wavy auburn hair stands at the doorway, and she's talking to someone with sage green skin and white blonde hair. A Fae. *Iz.*

The half empty bottle in my hand drops to the floor, glass shattering before my feet. The woman snaps her head to me and stuffs something in her pocket before scrambling away. Iz shakes his head at her, smirking, until he notices me. He pales, turning to run away faster then I can blink. On wobbly legs I go after him, through the halls, out the entrance of the castle, and across the enormous lawn of Brone Castle estate. He's so far ahead of me that I'll never catch up and I watch him scurry to a Skillsmen building still erected in the field.

I search the crowd for Iz. He lurks by the wash basins and his back is turned, I stalk up behind him as he talks to a pretty girl with tan skin and a scar across her eye.

"I outsmarted the King, can you believe it?" He chuckles.

"Um, Iz–"

Iz continues. "Oh Rox, the King wouldn't deign to walk into a place like this."

I grab his shoulder firmly. "Wouldn't I?"

Rox looks from me to Iz and sprints away. I hear trays of ale falling to the ground and people shouting as she storms through the Skillsmen to get away from me. Iz stands still, frozen.

"Why did you run from me?"

He shakes his head frantically, "I didn't, Your Majesty."

"You did–," I squeeze his arm hard–, "because you bound me in a deal and knew what you gave me was garbage in return."

"Oh was it? That must have been the joke bottle, apologies–"

An almost animalistic snarl erupts from me and Iz goes rigid. He fumbles around in the pocket of his cloak and pulls out a tiny vial, hardly big enough to hold a thimble of liquid and offers it. I snatch it from him and pull Iz with me to a dark corner. While still holding Iz's arm, I use my teeth to uncork the vial and as soon as it pops, I smell mud and salt water. It's Lopter's blood this time.

"Don't lie to me again." I say to him and re-cork the vial.

He nods without a word and races away from me, out the door, and out of sight. Then I leave the Skillsmen to their games and women, slinking back to the castle under the pale moonlight alone. Craning my neck to gaze at the moon makes me dizzy and my stomach sours as the ground sways beneath my feet. The wine comes back up and I heave. Before I know it, I'm laying on the ground, my cheek pressed to the cool, dewy blades of grass. It feels good. More vomit spills from my mouth, but I don't move. I can't move, for everytime I try I throw up more. So I lay there, covered in wine and bile and drift off to sleep to the drunken sounds of merriment.

Sagart Priests are endowed with magic by the gods. On occasion, those powers can be transferred to offspring. However, this is rare, for Sagarts take an oath of celibacy.

– Ode of Barnabas

CHAPTER 51
VERA

Daphne and I decide that our little group of ladies, plus Arden, should do some sleuthing in the dungeons and see if we can figure out what Lucette was doing with the Priest down there. I explain again, in detail, what I saw to the group. The white sparks that were so bright they blinded me momentarily, and then the pair of them vanished into thin air.

"I came down here with Calix and looked around with him, but we had to run because the sparks came back and we didn't want to be caught by Lucette, especially if she's some kind of witch."

"Why isn't Calix down here with us?" Soleil asks.

"Because Calix is distracting Lucette so the rest of us can look into the wall and try and figure out what's behind the brick."

"What about Lieve?" Daphne asks.

"Lieve doesn't believe a word I say right now, and I don't want to talk about him anymore." Remembering our argument makes my stomach churn.

"You said you saw sparks, right?" Saima says. "That's not Fae magic."

"You're right," Daphne replies. "It's magic from–"

"The gods." Arden finishes.

"What makes you think that?" I ask them.

"Fae spells don't emit sparks," Daphne answers. She then looks at me and crosses her arms over her chest. "When you came to Prinav through the tree in Shadow Grove, were there sparks?"

Memories of the man with the cane and the fire mix with the mesmerizing tree we jumped through before I answer, "yes."

Daphne looks around the room and then back at me, "Lieve said the same. That tree wasn't a tree at all, that was Lopter."

My breath catches. *What is she talking about?* "Are you serious?"

"I am." She bites her lip.

And If the tree was Lopter, then, how does Lucette know spark magic, god magic? Who taught her? Is Lucette a witch? Could she be some kind of goddess I've never learned about?

"Could Lucette be a goddess?" I ask Daphne.

She shakes her head. "No. She wouldn't need blackmail to get to the throne. However, Sagart Priests are sometimes endowed with powers by the gods."

Arden gets close to the wall and digs his nails into the mortar between the brick and stone, picking and pulling at it.

I stand beside him. "What do you think is on the other side of this wall?"

He pulls a hatchet from his leather belt and takes a few steps back. "Back up everyone."

We all back up, and when we're far enough away, Arden charges at the wall. Hatchet in hand, he smashes the blade into the stone. It ricochets and bounces, causing him to shake his hand and wrist from the stinging pain.

"Great plan," I scoff.

"It seemed like a good idea–," he wrings his hand again–, "but I guess I didn't really think that through."

After about an hour of picking at the wall with no success, we're all sweating and annoyed with each other.

"This is getting us nowhere," Saima complains.

"I can't imagine you'd rather be alone in your room right now." I snap at her even though I know she's right.

"You've forced me to help you, even though I don't know anything about the magic of the gods, and I don't want to be mixed up in whatever drama you're all into. And don't you dare get Florian involved, I have enough problems of my own." She pulls her hair from her shoulders and ties it in a knot on the top of her head. "And manual labor isn't my idea of a good time."

Poppy looks up from her seat on the ground, hair a mess, and covered in sweat. "I'm still trying to see if you all are seriously suggesting that the gods are real."

"Oh," Evalie says solemnly, "they are."

"She's right. I know everything that happened the day Vera and Lieve jumped through the Lopter tree." She looks me in the eye. "Vera, Calix, my friend Narah, and your brother, they—" her voice shakes—, "they asked me to *see* you."

"You're a seer?" Saima asks in disbelief. "That's incredibly rare."

Daphne nods at her. "They thought Vera might have died jumping, but I couldn't see her, so I thought that was a good sign, and it was, obviously. But—" she turns to me again—,"after you two jumped in the tree, someone else followed you in."

Everyone stops working to listen to Daphne.

"He was dressed in all black, and Lieve said he heard thunder." Daphne states to the room.

I remember holding my ears because of how loud the thunder was. And the screaming. I remember thinking that it reminded me of Sol. "There was screaming, terrible screaming. And thunder. So loud it nearly deafened me."

Evalie gasps and covers her mouth with her hands and Soleil leans against the wall with her mouth open in awe.

Daphne clears her throat, "Sol."

I was right. It *was* Sol. The others burst into a frenzy of chatter. The gods are real. Dia and Oriel had a real love story. Not only is Prinav real, but all the stories are too.

Daphne pulls me to the side, "Lieve is an incredible thief, and Sol has searched the heavens and the earth for anything that can get him to his beloved Dia," she sighs heavily, "and I've always had this nagging feeling that Lieve found the *one* thing that Sol needed."

The pocket watch.

Daphne sighs. "I think I know what the object is."

"What?" I ask.

"Lieve talked about a pocket watch he stole that glowed blue. He told us all about the man showing up and the fire that destroyed your shop."

My heart beats wildly.

Daphne holds my hand. "Lieve lost it, and he was so obsessed with finding it and he thought it would be the key to getting you back. Arden has looked all over Shadow Grove for it, and maybe Lucette found it and is using it somehow to–"

I stop her. "She doesn't have it."

"How do you know?"

Everyone stops working and looks at me as I say, "because I do."

Poppy slinks to the floor. "If Lucette doesn't have it, then what *does* she have?"

I turn to the rest of the group and put my hands on my hips. "Next mission: we're raiding Lucette's chambers."

⁓

We devise a plan to get into Lucette's room. Soleil and Poppy are going to follow Lucette around at the festival and Poppy will warn us if she's coming back inside. Evalie went to visit Marguerite and see how she's doing, and she was given a clean bill of health. We then asked Marguerite to go inside Lucette's room and look around. It's the least suspicious because she's Lucette's maid. Marguerite reluctantly allowed Daphne to go with her to see if she can use her Fae senses to find anything magical hidden. Saima can't do anything without getting caught, so she and Evalie will be combing through books on Prinav's history in Saima's room to try and see what the object Lucette is hiding might be.

That leaves me and Arden. We're staying in the dungeon to keep looking around, and to see if Lucette or the Priest return. He's the last person I wanted to be stuck with, but there weren't any other options. Everyone breaks away, leaving Arden and I alone. He stands in the corner with his dagger, drilling the tip of his blade into the mortar and spinning it like a top.

"Do you think that's going to help?" I ask.

"Not really." He leans closer to the dagger and puts more weight on the blade. "But I'm out of ideas."

Church bells ring again. *Why do they ring at such odd hours?*

"What is the ringing for this time?"

Arden shrugs. "No idea, it's been off schedule for years."

"No mass going on or anything?"

"I don't think so." He says, still spinning the dagger. "I've tried to keep track of the bells before, but they never ring at a significant time."

"Strange."

"I suppose so." He says and glances at me. "You never mentioned the watch."

"It's broken, and I didn't say anything because I didn't want the man with the cane–Sol–to come back. It must be a very dangerous source of magic if Sol wants it."

Arden doesn't reply, so I sit on the ground and pout. There's nothing to do down here. We aren't going to find anything, Lucette is too clever. I lean back and lay flat on the ground, staring up at the ceiling.

I know it's fruitless, but I need to stop her. She has everyone under her thumb, and I hate it. I stare at the ceiling for a while and nothing happens. I don't find anything, and I'm not surprised. I turn my head and see the potion room door, slightly ajar.

It's a little off its hinges, the damage from Saima's magic barely evident to someone who wouldn't know to notice. That potion room door slightly off the hinges *is* *me*. Unbalanced. Out of place. In need of repair. If the door doesn't get fixed, the room is exposed. If I don't get fixed, I could expose everyone to *me*.

"Do you hate me?" I ask while my finger trails the mortar on the stone floor.

Arden doesn't look at me, he doesn't even stop spinning the blade of his dagger. "No."

"So it's that easy? You can forgive me just like—" I snap my fingers.

"No."

"No, what?"

"No." He stops spinning the dagger and turns to me. "I can't forgive you easily. If Daphne is forced to leave Prinav because you're a reckless fool, because you're territorial over Calix, I—" He turns back to the wall. "I don't know how I'll feel. But right now, at this moment, I don't hate you."

"Of course I'm territorial over Calix, we're meant for each other."

Arden laughs. "Okay."

"You wouldn't know what love is if it landed in your lap, you're afraid of love, of women and—"

"And you're—"

His sentence is cut short by footsteps hurrying towards us. Arden pulls me to my feet with one arm and we jump into the potion room together as quietly as we can. He shoves me behind a door past the wooden table that Daphne concocts her potions on and follows behind me, into a pitch black closet.

I can't see a thing and I bump my head on the corner of a shelf. I scoot closer to Arden and he wraps his hand behind my head so I don't knock the shelf again. His hand is warm. Solid. My heart thumps when I realize how close we are. Our chests are pressed against one another, closer than close. I can feel his heart beating against mine, his pace is slower, stronger than my own.

Boots come closer. The muscles in Arden's arm flexes, ready to attack if we're caught. My breathing quickens. Is it Lucette? Are we missing them going into the wall again? We should get out of this closet and see who it is. Maybe we can stop them.

"Let's go," I whisper.

"Shhh."

"It might be her."

Whoever was in the hall is now in the potion room. Arden covers my mouth with his hand to keep me quiet. They rummage through Daphne's herbs and books. A second pair of boots enters the hall. They stand just beyond the closet door smashing bottles over Daphne's table and leave the room in a hurry. A putrid smell fills the air and I gag.

Then that same scratching and cracking noise I heard when Lucette disappeared into the wall echoes in the hall. White sparks sizzle, and then all is quiet again. Arden uncovers my mouth gently as his other hand brushes my hip so he can reach the door handle. We both freeze. I can hear him breathe in my ear and I shiver as he presses into me so he can quietly swing the door open.

Nervously, I shake that feeling off, and we leave the closet. Arden creeps to the edge of the door near the hall to see if the coast is clear and if he can find remnants of anything. I follow him out and notice a faint glow in the mortar of the stone. Then, from a crack in the wall, one tiny spark bounces to the ground and dissolves. Arden hands me his dagger and he pulls out a hatchet, and together, we scrape the wall over and over again. Arden plunges his hatchet once more and the stone splinters. We pick at a piece of loose stone, but there's nothing behind it. Nothing.

Arden's presence now makes it hard to breathe. Watching his muscles work on the wall flutters my stomach, and I don't know what this feeling is. The way he's breathing. The way his hand felt on the back of my head, my lip, my waist. The pace of his heartbeat against my chest. I glance at him and I see him glance at me too, but nothing happens. Not with us, and not with the wall. I'm angry at myself for what I'm feeling and I chalk it up to adrenaline. We keep at it for several minutes, but with our hands already tired from the day's work, we give up.

"You should check in with the others. You need to go to the festival anyway, the Princess will be missed if she's gone for too long."

"You're joking, right?" I can't imagine thinking about attending a festival at a time like this. And I'm feeling so confused about what happened in the closet that I want to stay away from Calix right now.

"I'm not." He takes my weapon and places it back on his belt. "You, Poppy, Soleil, and Daphne are part of the Court, you all have to make an appearance."

"But what about—"

He shuffles so his back is to me and the sound of metal on stone continues once again. "What about, what?"

"About the closet—"

"Vera, just go."

"But—".

Arden rounds on me. "Leave me."

"I can't leave you alone—"

I can hear the anger in his voice when he growls. "You are the most selfish—," his eyes fix on mine—, "girl I—" then they droop a little as his speech starts to slur—, "have…" His body hits the floor with a heavy thud.

I rush to him, and my vision blurs. Each time I blink is harder for my eyes to reopen, heavier. I look at my hands and wiggle my fingers, but my limbs are moving in slow motion. I feel like I'm falling asleep, but I'm wide awake. My knees hit the stone floor and I gasp in pain. All my movements are slowed down. The air has turned to sludge, becoming thick and wet. It's hard to breathe. My lungs feel full of liquid, like a fish breathing water. I crawl to Arden, reaching out to him, and when my fingers touch his, I black out.

⌣

I wake up in my bed, covered in quilts and heavy linens. It's still bright out, the sun still hasn't reached midday, which means I was only blacked out for an hour or so. My vision is still a little blurry, but as soon as I sit up, things begin to come back into focus. Evalie and Marguerite are talking to one another, neither one looking at me. I rub my eyes, willing the haze to leave. I then rip the covers off me as memories from the dungeon come flooding back.

"How's Arden?" I ask frantically.

"He's fine," Evalie hands me a glass of water. "Lady Daphne is tending to him."

"Do we know what happened?"

Evalie sits on the bed next to me. "No. Daphne found you two laying on the ground. She ran to fetch me and Soleil and Poppy, and we dragged you both out of there as fast as we could."

"Did Arden see anything?" I ask and fling my legs over the side of the bed. "We have to go back down immediately."

Evalie catches the glass of water when I almost drop it from my hands. "Vera, he's not awake."

My knees shake. "You said he was okay."

Evalie presses her eyes shut. "Daphne believes that he will be."

My stomach churns, "So he may *not* be okay."

Evalie repeats herself. "Daphne believes that he will be."

"I need to see him."

"Vera–"

"Now."

They fall in behind me as I storm my way to Arden's chambers. I barge into Daphne's room without knocking and Marguerite flies in behind me apologizing to Daphne and Soleil as Daphne lies next to Arden on the bed, holding his hand.

"Go away," she whispers and pulls Arden's mask onto his face before I can see what his features are.

"I don't care what he looks like," I say through my tears.

She laughs a little. "He would care."

We sit on the bed and watch him. Unmoving. Barely breathing. His chest rising and falling slower each time he inhales. *I've gotten him hurt.*

"Daphne, this whole thing is too dangerous," I whisper.

"I agree. I'll be leaving as soon as the festival is over." She then sits up and wraps her hands around mine. "I'm going to ask Arden to go with me, if–," she closes her eyes– "if he wakes up."

My stomach drops. *If* he wakes up.

"He'll be alright, m'lady," Marguerite says gently.

"Yes," Daphne wipes a tear from her eye. "He'll be alright."

~

Soleil shoos us out, so the rest of the day I spend in the wood on Brone Castle's estate. I don't go to the festival, no matter what Arden said. There isn't much room in my life for celebrating right now, and I don't care about making appearances. I slip into the stables unnoticed and mount Siva, letting the warm wind whip my hair around me and dry my tears as she gallops in the treeline.

I ride the trails for hours until the sun begins to set. By the time I return Siva to the stables, the sun has disappeared behind Mount Oriel, casting massive shadows on the castle grounds. In the distance are the sounds of drunken men singing, and women laughing. The noise irritates me to the bone. How can anyone be so cheerful when the world is crumbling?

Across from the stables is a small shanty town erected for the Skillsman while they're here at the Court. The larger building houses the Skillsmen, while outside they've built fire pits to celebrate their wins and forget their losses. These people know hardship. They know pain. They're like me. It makes me miss my old life, a life where the only worry was finding food and gaining a husband.

So I invite myself to the Skillsmens' home away from home and watch them laugh together. A pair of siblings tease each other, running around the fire, and my heart aches. I miss that with Lieve. I wish this were just another story, and that I was back home with him. Goblets of wine and ale are passed around and I want some. I want to drink until I've had so much that I can't remember why I wanted to drink in the first place.

There are a few dozen people in this huddle of laughter and music, so no one cares or even notices that I've joined. Each face is flushed with drink. Everyone is sweaty and sloppy…and happy. A young girl with dark, coiled hair and a toothy grin hands me a mug full of the nastiest smelling ale I've ever had the displeasure of smelling. I sniff it and make a sour face. She laughs and holds her own mug up for me to cheers with her. I do, and then pinch my nose and guzzle the foul liquid quickly.

Sputtering, I spit some of it out and everyone around me laughs, including the girl. I pinch my nose again, and guzzle more ale, leaving half of it covering my chest while it drips down my chin. The girl grabs my hand and we dance around the fire while the group sings and cheers and drinks, long enough for the stars to come out. I don't learn their names and they don't ask me mine. It doesn't matter anyway. Tonight is a night to forget. The girl twirls me around and around, and in between songs we drink until the world spins even when we're not moving.

He who is beyond fear is eternal.

— *The Iron Tree*

CHAPTER 52

LIEVE

My chambers reek of vomit. The putrid odor makes the room stale and I want to retch again at the stink of it. The squeaking wheel of a breakfast tray outside my door pierces my ears even with my head stuffed under my pillow. *Go away.*

"Your Majesty," Finn knocks. "May I come in."

"Uggghhh," I groan.

Finn opens the door. My head is still buried, but I imagine his expression as my rancid stench hits him in the face. The squeaky wheel stops right next to me and I don't have the energy to remove the pillow. Metal dishes are moved around, clanking in Finn's hands, and then I smell breakfast. I plug my nose, the smell of the sharp cheese and meat nearly gagging me.

"Rise and shine, sire."

"Go away, Finn." I grumble.

Finn does not go away. He rips the sheets from the bed and sighs. I bring my knees to my chest as the warmth of my blankets leaves me. With my head still under my pillow, I wave my middle finger at Finn, but I don't know if he saw it or even cared, because he's already filling a plate of food for me. I grumble again and remove the pillow, the light from the sun causing me to wince. It's too early. Too bright.

Finn sets my plate of food on the bed and walks into the bathroom. Water rushes from the faucet, and I know the clawfoot tub is being filled for my bath. As soon as I've eaten enough for Finn to approve, he will force me to bathe, but all I want to do is sleep. The floor is covered in dirty clothes, and my boots lay haphazardly at the foot of my bed, covered in mud and the contents of my stomach. I look down at myself and I'm still fully dressed. I gag when I notice that my tunic is also covered in my foul mess. I'll have to burn my bedding to get rid of the stench.

Finn returns from the bathing room and rummages through my wardrobe, pulling out buckles and linen shirts, and thin undergarments as I nibble on a piece of meat. I watch him begrudgingly place the items in a neat stack and begin tidying up after me. I hate that I'm making his job harder, but he doesn't understand what I'm going through. If he did, maybe he wouldn't make that sour face.

"Stop with the disapproving looks," I bark at him. "I'm sick of it."

"I'm sure you're sick, sire," he replies.

Heat simmers in my chest. "What did you say?"

Finn doesn't shrink. He stands up straighter, taller, and glares. I'm the King, I don't cower to my own servant, but right now I want to. I've never seen Finn look like that before, and I never want to again. Neither of us speak when I get out of bed. I throw the half-eaten piece of meat on the breakfast tray and saunter into the bathing room, darting around the piles of mess on the floor.

I strip off my soiled garments, toss them to the ground, and step into the clawfoot tub. The water is scorching hot. Slowly sinking in, inch by inch, the heat melts away my attitude. I grimace with the pain of the hot water, but continue lowering myself until I'm submerged to my chest and let shame devour me.

None of this is Finn's fault. It's mine. Clanging of dishware and the ruffle of bedsheets come from the other room, furthering my shame. I don't want to hear him taking care of me. I don't want to hear anything.

I wish I were dead. I dunk my head under the water, and it scorches my face. *Why is it so hot, damnit!*

Raising my head just enough out of the water so that I can breathe, I survey the bathroom. There's vomit on the floor and broken glass everywhere. I vaguely remember breaking multiple bottles of wine on the ground after each one poured their last glass. The empty bottles remind me of how empty my life will become if Arden and Remi don't pull off the impossible. Near the sink sits the vial that Iz gave me in my drunken stupor. I know it's Lopter's blood, and I want to drink it and forget last night and my ridiculous proposal.

Finn stands in the doorway with his back to me, "I'll be back in an hour."

I don't reply, I just stare at the vial only a few feet from me, ready to be enjoyed. I hear Finn sigh again and pick up something from the floor.

"I'll clean up more once you're dressed and ready for the coronation." He smacks his lips. "I can see that this day is a difficult one for you, sire, but I assure you, it could be a wonderful one if you let it."

I dunk my head back under the water to try and boil myself alive.

～～

Finn refused to allow the tailor and the dressers to come into my chambers because of the mess and the stench, so I was carted down the hall into a formal dressing room. No less than ten men accompany Finn and I, and I'm astonished that in all this time I had no idea this room existed. There are so many options I could wear today that it makes my head spin. Every person in the room has an opinion, and I eventually just start pointing at things to get them to stop pestering me.

There are royal coronation robes in an array of colors and textures that I've never seen before. Deep purples, vibrant greens, and rich blues. In the center of the room are mounds of jewelry. I walk past the jewels to run my hand along an exceptionally Kingly looking robe made with burgundy fabric and silvery threads. A man polishing a pair of shiny, black boots smiles at me. He has shrewd eyes, small and beady, and a bald head. His forehead is wrinkled, and he has the jowls of an old man.

"Do you like that one?" His voice carries an accent that screams old money, and he's working in textiles. He must be from Teyrnas.

"I do," I say and run my thumb on the cuff of the robe.

"Tis the finest velvet in Teyrnas." He points at the trim at the bottom of the robe. "And that is the fur of a Darkthing, believe it or not."

A Darkthing? I scramble to find the end of the robe and hold the hem in my hands. It's made of thick, black fur. The texture is rough, not soft, and so heavy that it pulls my arms down with the weight of it. It would take a strong man to pull the train of the robe up the aisle of Gwen Abbey. Who, and how, could someone have killed a Darkthing? I didn't know it was possible.

"Is it really?" I ask the man.

The man smiles again. "Tis no lie. My nephew killed it and skinned it himself."

I gesture to another Dresser in the room to help me try it on. My arms slide into the sleeves of the robe and I feel changed. In my chest beats a wild drum, the heart of a man who slayed a Darkthing. This robe is the symbol of pure power. I want it.

"Who's your nephew?"

The man continues polishing the boots, "Ivar Bergman, the Iron Tree."

"Hmm, that's a strong name, the Iron Tree."

The tailors flock to me, poking, prodding, sewing and cutting while I hold my arms in the air like a puppet. The fabric is exceedingly heavy and my arms are growing tired as the tailors continue their work. I feel like this heavy robe is like my burdens, and I remember the vial in my pocket, begging to be consumed.

My palms start to sweat. No. I can't drink it. Nothing can go wrong today. Thoughts of Arden dying because of me fill me with dread and my stomach sours. There isn't much time left for him to be back. The ceremony will be starting soon, and Arden and Remi haven't announced their return to me. If I don't have a slew of witnesses to publicly raise an outcry against the Matisses', then everything I've done will have been for naught. I need them to show up.

Ivar's uncle, who has yet to tell me his own name, stands up and places the polished boots in front of me on the floor. I step into them, one at a time, and they're as soft as butter. The leather has aged perfectly, exquisitely. These are boots fit for a King.

"Tell me about this young man who slayed a Darkthing."

"His father, my brother, was a ruthless tyrant who abused his daughter and tried to slice Ivar in half as a teenager for disobedience. Ivar protected his sister and bore his blade numerous times, standing still as a tree stands in the forest. When Ivar got the chance, he then used the same blade to tear through his own father's flesh in a matter of seconds. Ivar is beyond fear, sire, he is a tree, an eternal, Iron Tree. He now works as a hunter and mercenary for that same sister, the Queen of Teyrnas."

"I would like to meet him someday," I say to Ivar's uncle, "to give thanks, in part, for my coronation robe."

His face lights up. "I shall write to him."

The team of men dressing me step back and admire their work. I tell them they should be proud, that every option was grand. They bow deeply, with wide grins on their faces. A jeweler opens a case full of gold chains and places the largest around my neck. He then slips gold bands on my fingers and clips an emerald dragon to the lapel of this glorious robe.

"Finn, please bring me the enamel pins I purchased," I say.

"Yes, Your Majesty," he replies and scurries out.

I return to my conversation with Ivar Bergman's uncle, "and what's your name, Ivar's uncle?"

The old man chuckles, "Rolf, Rolf Bergman."

"Do you also work for the Queen of Teyrnas?"

He laughs, "I do, as she's my niece."

"Oh, how lovely," I say, "to have a famous family."

"Yes, my family is special, my niece especially." He fluffs my robe, "Meritt married Sojourn, the King of Teyrnas, years ago. He died in battle, and in my country, even if you aren't blood, you are the new monarch if you were married and the blood heir perishes. Meritt became Queen of Teyrnas at only sixteen years old."

I nod. "Young."

"Too young," Rolf replies.

Just then, Finn walks in holding the pins I purchased from the merchant at the festival. I wave him over to me and he pins them to the shirt underneath my robe. My nerves calm when I see the tree and copper vixen. I then hold the black fox in my hand and run my finger across the smooth enamel.

"Shall I pin it for you as well?"

I feel my lip turn up slightly. "No, I would like to give this pin to Lady Daphne."

The room goes silent, and I don't care. I don't care that I'm engaged to Lucette. I want Daphne to know that I'm still in this, that I'm still trying. In no time at all, Arden and Remi will be back, Lucette and her father will have fallen from grace, and Daphne will see that I have loved her through all of this. She'll see that my proposal to Lucette was all a ruse and that I had her best interest at heart the whole time. She will receive this pin and know that my love doesn't waver, even if our circumstances have been more than unsteady.

"Shall we go to the abbey?" I say to Finn.

He nods. "I suppose it's time, Your Majesty."

Finn opens the door for me and I rub my thumb on the vial in my pocket. *I will not drink this unless my plan goes awry.* As the train of my robe flits across the dressing room door, I poke my head back in and direct my attention to Rolf. "It was nice to meet you."

His face beams with pride and his dressing team all smile at him, "And you, sire."

This is all going to work out.

He created a golden compass, with all the secrets of the realms inside. It is said he used it to communicate with Dia while she hid from Sol, and that he called it the...
— *Diary of Queen Rosalind Brone*

CHAPTER 53
VERA

When Evalie brings me the breakfast tray in the morning, she looks as tired as I feel. I climb out of bed and grab two pieces of bread and hand her one. She takes a large bite and flops on the chair at my vanity.

I take another bite and between each chew I ask, "have you checked with Daphne about Arden today?"

She nods at me. "He's fine. Woke up in the middle of the night and stormed back down to the dungeon."

"That's great news."

"It is," Evalie says, "but we still don't know who doused you both with that sleeping draught."

"That's easy enough, *Lucette and the Priest*."

Evalie shakes her head. "It wasn't them. Poppy said she and Soleil followed Lucette around all day and she only enjoyed the festivities. Lucette's working with someone else."

I dig my fingers into my temples. "Who else could it be?"

"There's no way of knowing, the Matisse family is well connected." Evalie blows out a long breath. "Maybe it doesn't matter who's working with the Queen. What can we really do about it? We don't even know what's on the other side of the wall."

"Don't you want to know?"

"Yes, but not at the cost of my safety, or yours. I just don't know if it's worth looking into anymore."

"I think it is," I argue.

"Then tell Calix about what happened yesterday, tell the King—"

"I tried talking to Lieve about her before and he thought I was just nagging because I didn't like her, and Calix already knows." I fold my arms. "And he's so obsessed with me right now because of the potion, I don't know how much help he'll be until the effects wear off."

"Then we wait." Evalie puts her arm around my shoulders. "Once Calix is back to normal, we tell him what happened and have him look further into this."

This all seems so dreadful. "I want to talk to Lieve about all of this. The old Lieve would fix it immediately, but I don't know how to talk to him anymore. He and I have been bickering, and I think he might actually be *in love* with Lucette. Or even cursed by her."

Evalie's eyes widen. "Or she's love potioned him herself."

That's it.

~

"It's possible," Daphne paces around her room when I tell her what Evalie and I think is going on with Lieve and Lucette. "His attitude towards her has certainly changed over the years."

I feel like I'm walking on air. All of the fights with Lieve and I make sense now. He's bewitched by her, and we can stop it. If Daphne can find a way to stay here and make the antidote for Lieve, or if Saima will do it, then he can publicly denounce Lucette and mark her as a traitor. Then we can have Lieve make her tell us what's beyond the brick wall in the dungeon and everything can go back to normal.

Excitement rushes through me and I'm bouncing on the balls of my feet. "This is it, I can feel it in my bones."

Daphne drums her fingers on the windowsill, her jaw clenched and hardened. "I said it's *possible*, but I can't continue to make the antidote, I leave tomorrow."

I cock my eyebrow. "But Saima can."

Daphne and I race to Saima's room and pound on the door. She cracks it open to reluctantly let us in, and the room is filled with a thick layer of smoke. Through the floral haze I see Prince Florian stretched out on a pouf, smiling at us with glassy eyes.

"Hello, Princess," he says, smiling coyly at me. "And hello to you too, Red."

Florian's eyes linger on Daphne and she plays into his charms. "Nice to see you again Flor," she offers her hand to him and he holds it like he's holding priceless treasure.

"What do you want?" Saima asks.

"An antidote for a love potion."

"Why can't you do it?" She asks Daphne.

Daphne sighs. "Because I'm being sent away to Teyrnas."

"Fuck." Saima breathes. She picks up a long silver tube from a silver tray and sucks on the end before removing her lips from the tube, filling the room with more smoke. "I'll do it for you."

"How fast?" I ask.

"A month."

"Thank you."

Daphne and I turn to walk out of her room but Saima stops us and says, "is it for Lord Bramford?"

"As well as another."

"Who?"

Daphne answers, "Lieve."

Florian sits up and takes a long draw from an ivory tube. "I wouldn't put it past a Matisse to do something like that. The night he got engaged he would have been an easy target. He was drinking a lot and he seemed–" he looks at Daphne and blows out a long tendril of smoke–, "emotional."

Daphne and I thank Saima and we leave her chambers. While walking down the deserted corridor Daphne says, "I can probably put a hold on my wedding for a month. I can be picky with decor, guest lists, and make a custom gown. I can stall."

"Daphne, if it was a love potion that's made Lieve continue being with Lucette–"

Tears well in her eyes. "It all happened so fast. The Matisses' are wretched people and–" she smiles–, "Lieve's behavior makes so much sense now."

"We can't tell Lieve anything. If he's under some kind of spell, he'll tell Lucette and it will all go to shit. So we wait it out." I say and hold her hands. "There's still a chance for you two, if you still want it."

The punishment for Treason is Death by Hanging.
– Prinavian Charter Law Number 213

CHAPTER 54

LIEVE

F inn and I enter Gwen Abbey after taking the dark tunnels connecting Brone Castle to the temple. It's much cooler in the tunnels than the warm air in the nave of the temple where the seats are located. I look around the room in awe. This must be how Vera felt when I told her all those tales. The cathedral is so tall I have to crane my neck to see the ceiling, covered in paintings depicting the gods and their histories. Metallic stars twinkle against the background of a midnight sky while the Goddess Guenivere throws sparks into the void. It's so realistic that it's hard to imagine that what you're looking at isn't alive.

This place is intimidating. I bring my gaze from the art and look around the room at eye-level. Lucette and her father have decorated it beautifully, yet again. Dark blue and silver adorn the space producing a solemn and mysterious aura. I meander the pews and let the soft morning light spill onto me. *Everything is going to work out beautifully.* At least that's what I'm hoping. My thumb glides across the glass of the vial in my pocket and I have to shake my head to stop myself from just going ahead and drinking it.

"Have you heard from Arden or a Madorian Skillsman?" I ask Finn.

"No, sire."

That's okay, I'm sure they're almost here.

Finn gives me a gentle nod. "Would you like me to let you know when they arrive?"

"Yes," I pat Finn's shoulder. "Thank you."

Lucette's uncle, the Priest, emerges from a door carrying a stack of white linens. He wears black robes that cling to his skin and his face has been painted as a Sagart, black tears streaming down a stark white face.

"Good day, Your Majesty," he murmurs with a bow.

"And to you," I reply and Finn bows to the Priest before nudging me along.

Finn then leads me away and up a set of stairs behind the throne at the rear of the pulpit. The stairs are narrow and steep and they seem to be never ending. At the top of the tight spiral is a single door, painted bright red and has an iron handle with runes carved on the surface. We step inside the room and it's bigger than I imagined it would be, but it certainly isn't a room fit for a King. There's a wooden desk in the center, a small brown tufted sofa, and stacks of books piled as high as I am tall.

"It may not look like much, but every king and queen of Prinav has used this room before their anointing." Finn looks around in awe. "You are standing in history."

His words open my mind to what the room holds. King Niall waited in this room before his coronation, Queen Rosalind, Fortuna. Portraits of the monarchs line the far wall in a collage, the eyes of each of them staring at me. I find Niall's, and under it, a painting of a teenage boy with a scar above his right eye. Underneath the abstract painting, a hand-carved wooden plaque reads: *My Son, from my memory, Prince Monroe Brone, Duke of Barault and Grand Knight of the Brone Dynasty*. And it's signed by *KNB, King Niall Brone*. I stare at it. This is the only portrait currently in known existence that depicts Monroe. It's hard to make out the features, Niall was clearly not an artist, but the dark hair and the scar seem familiar.

After failing to place why the painting seemed familiar, I pick up a book from the nearest stack and rifle through the pages, but the text is in ancient Prinavian and I can't read it. That's something I will decree, that at least the nobles learn the old tongue. We must preserve our history, but make progress for our future at the same time. We, I, must be better from this day forth.

"I'll leave you to ponder your thoughts, and I will retrieve you when it's time," Finn states.

He turns to leave, but I grab him and wrap him in a hug. His strong arms pat my back and for the first time in years, I feel like I have a father again. I don't want to let him go. Finn breaks apart from me and squeezes my arm before he leaves me to "ponder my thoughts" alone.

There's only one window in the room and it looks down upon the pews in the Abbey. No one below could see up this high, and I imagine the window is disguised from outside eyes. From my vantage point I can see everything, the pews, the large doors at the entrance, the throne, and all the people.

Eventually the nobles from my court, and from the surrounding cities of my Kingdom begin to arrive and mill around together, most still here from the week's festivities. My eyes strain in desperation to see Arden, Remi, or even Daphne in the crowd, but none appear. What I do see is Lucette and Benito walking across the upper pulpit, talking with the Sagart and berating a monk. Lucette points at my throne and crosses her arms. I'm sure she's demanding a throne of her own, and I hope they give her one so I can throw her off it.

Almost an hour passes and the Abby is nearly full. Finn will be back to fetch me at any moment and take me to the Sagart, who will anoint my head before presenting me to my people. Footsteps thump lightly as they go up the stairs; Finn must be on his way. *I'm not ready.*

The room is stiflingly hot. With the growing heat and my shaky nerves, sweat pours from my head and down my back, making a damp spot under my robe. Arden isn't back yet and I don't see Remi Vail either. I'm going to have to make my announcement in front of the entire Kingdom on my own and pray to the gods that they believe me, or that victims in the crowd will rally behind me. It's my only shot if Arden hasn't acquired a militia of men and women who are ready to stand up against the Matisses'.

The footsteps stop at the stop of the stairs. It's time. Before Finn can come in, I turn the handle and step out to meet him. I take a deep breath as Finn makes his way to the top of the staircase.

"I was King Niall's truest friend, you know." He says.

"I wasn't aware."

His eyes soften. "Not many were. But I wanted to tell you that you're so much like him, and even more like Monroe. You've made great changes here, with the theater and the scholarships. The people see it, even if you can't see it for yourself. I know you're suffering, but I can see why Niall chose you. I see what he saw."

I don't know what to say, so I don't say anything. Finn squeezes my shoulder and then I follow him down the tight spiral stairs that leads to either the best thing I'll ever do for Prinav, or the worst.

We stop behind large velvet curtains, hiding us from view. I hear humming from the audience harmonizing with the hum from the Sagart, Baptiste Matisse, and a few other Priests and acolytes standing on the pulpit. From the right, an organ plays and Finn bows to me before disappearing into the shadows. Then the giant curtains open. Before me are hundreds of people, and it finally sinks in. I'm going to be the Crowned Monarch of Prinav. *I wish Vera were here.*

I step into a sunbeam leaking in through the stained glass windows and turn when I see a group of teenagers pick up their instruments and play the Prinavian anthem of the gods. They each wear a music academy uniform with the new monarch's crest on the breast. An Oleander flower with a fox wrapping its tail around the stem. I did that. I smile, these students are here because of me.

The Sagart beckons me to him. He anoints my head with salt water, and then blows smoke from fragrant incense all over my face and body. I scan the faces in the crowd for Arden, Daphne, or Remi, as I recite my coronation vows, but I don't find them. I don't see *any* Blackbands in attendance for that matter. But I do see that Esven and Benito,who whisper to one another, and the look on their faces shows me that I wouldn't like their conversation.

"And now Sir Lieve, Knight of the Brone Dynasty, Regent of Brone Castle, you shall take your seat on the Prinavian Crystal Throne."

I know it's going to be painfully cold, so I disregard any want to look dignified and flop onto the seat to get it over with as quickly as possible. Frost climbs up from the thick layer of ice already trapping my arms and legs and begins to cover my neck. Every muscle is frozen except for my face. "State your name to the gods!" Baptiste shouts.

The other Priests hum loudly, and it nearly puts me in a trance.

"Your name, sire." He repeats.

"Lieve Oleander."

The ice melts at the same time something heavy sinks onto the top of my head. A crown. I hear someone cry out, "All hail King Lieve!", and others follow suit. Ice cracks and drops to the ground as I strain to stand. When I finally get to my feet, the rest of the ice breaks off and thunderous applause erupts in the Abbey, so loud it shakes the windows.

Music plays and everyone is ushered outside to celebrate. Servants have laid out long tables and covered them with food. Before long, toasts to me and my rule are made. Toasts to Benito, Esven, Lucette, and our pending marriage follow. Benito looks as if he just became King. He shakes hands with several nobles who walk by, and points to me and Lucette all throughout the coronation supper. Many of the people he interacts with look genuinely happy for him. Was Arden right? Does Benito have more followers than I realized? Where *is* Arden?

The sun hides behind Mount Oriel and still Arden hasn't shown up. I'm convinced he's not going to come. Out of the corner of my eye I see lesser nobles passing Benito coin purses, and I finally grow impatient. It's time to end his power play.

Just as I'm about to grab everyone's attention, dozens of guards storm through the supper, Kelby the announcer, and Quinn the treasurer following, their mouths gagged and their hands bound in rope. My heart hammers in my chest. What is this? What's happened?

All my guests go quiet. On shaky legs I head to the Captain of the Guard. He bows to me and so do the rest of the guards.

I point to Kelby and Quinn and ask, "What is this?"

"Apologies, Your Majesty, but these men stole from the Matisse accounts, as well as the Royal coffers. The Viscount–," he nods at Benito–, "asked for us to bring the culprits to him as soon as possible."

Benito joins me and the Captain. "What about the Blackband, Vail? I know he was working with these criminals"

"We're tracking his location."

"Capture him." Benito's voice shakes with fury.

"Was anyone working with this, *Vail?* Besides these two, of course." I say and jerk my chin to Kelby and Quinn.

Benito side eyes me and I know I've made a mistake.

"Yes," The Captain says. "Witnesses claim a man who owns the shadows and wields a mighty hatchet works with him. Our men tried to capture him, but he slaughtered all of them. All but one. The mace who killed our soldiers is a degenerate, but I say Vail's worse than him after what happened."

Sweat beads across my forehead and I fight the urge to wipe it as I ask, "and what makes you say that?"

"Because his companion was shot with an arrow and left to bleed to death, and Vail ran without looking back. One guy from the militia lived to tell the tale and ran back to Barault as fast as he could. He said he didn't attempt to arrest the hatchet wielder, even wounded he could tell he wasn't a match for him."

Shit. Shit. Shit. Is Arden still alive? Fuck Remi for leaving him. What do I do now? How do I repair this? How do I find Arden?

"Hatchets, you say?" Esven says from behind me.

"Yes, hatchets."

Esven looks me dead in the eye. "Do you know anyone with an affinity for hatchets?"

I ball my fists. "None come to mind."

Benito gestures to Esven. "What shall we do with the prisoners?"

"Well, the law states that treason requires hanging, no matter one's position at court. I would say that stealing from the royal banks warrants that conviction–," Esven smirks at me–, "and a trial always proves how high up the scandal goes."

I can feel every eye on me, anticipating how I'll react, what I'll order. I don't know what to do. I can't expose Benito now, I'll look like a criminal sympathizer, a traitor to the crown. I can stall though, or get them released secretly. I take a deep breath and don't dare look at Kelby or Quinn when I say, "Then take them to trial."

Stained Glass: Willow Tree with vibrant pink
petals...
– *Request for glass art from Lieve Oleander, to the Asteri
Polik studio, Prinav*

CHAPTER 55

VERA

*T*he Sol Ball. Even though there's so much going on, I can't help but feel excited. Lieve has been trying to sneak me into balls in Adamston for the last few years with no success. Even though he'd stolen some beautiful gowns in the past, an obstacle would always stop me from entering.

The first year was my fault. When the footmen at the Manor door asked me my name, I forgot who I was supposed to be and I stumbled when reciting the name on the ticket card. This led to being physically thrown from the property and ruining the expensive gown I was wearing. I never told Lieve that it was my fault I was denied entry, I made up a story about a Lady's maid recognizing me from the market and ratting me out.

The second year, I got as far as access to the Manor entryway inside the estate, and even flirted with a young man who was intent on finding a female companion–but he wasn't looking for a *wife*. When his wants didn't align with my needs, I was no longer someone of importance to him. I then came to discover that the young man already had a wife, and I ran from the party as fast as I could. Lieve was wrathful and had his own encounter with the young man the following week, and the next time I saw him around the village he had a black eye.

I had high hopes for the last year Lieve attempted to gain me entrance. Those hopes didn't last long because the only eligible suitor was older than our father, and I ran from the party before the music even began. And this year, when we were at the market stealing things to buy me a gown and seriously look for a suitor, I ended up here in Prinav.

"Oh Vera," Evalie breathes, "this might be the best gown yet."

I lay down my book and turn to face the bedroom door to see Evalie holding an enormous garment case. She hands me a small note before laying the case on my bed. On the front of the parchment reads, *To my Darling, my Vera Dear.*

Ripping the wax from the seal tightens the knot in my stomach. The note and the gown are clearly from Calix. I should have known he would gift me a gown for tonight, he has been so generous with me since the moment we met. Now that the relationship has been manipulated, it's hard to know how much truth there is in any words he says to me, or in any of his actions. My fingers unfold the paper and with every sentence my heart falls.

Vera Dear,

I woke up today feeling happier than I've felt in many years. Just knowing that you care for me has given me an awakening I didn't believe was possible for someone like me. Your presence is an insatiable craving that seeps into every thought and pore. According to tradition, each young woman who plays Dia shall be escorted to the Sol Ball by her Oriel. I would be ecstatic if you would allow me to accompany you tonight. I look forward to your response, and your much wanted partnership.

All my deepest affections,

Calix

As soon as I'm finished reading the letter, Evalie unfurls the gown from its case and it takes my breath away. Evalie covers her mouth with her hand as her other hand gently touches the incredible fabric. Each thread must be encased with magic. *It's stunning.* My eyes devour every inch of detail, hungry for more and more surprises.

"I'm afraid to touch it," I whisper.

Evalie hoists the dress onto a dress stand with my general shape and I help her secure it so it doesn't fall over. We just stare at it in silence, walking around it and soaking it in. The fabric is blue-green, and there are layers of white underneath. Real, preserved, exotic white flowers are sewn into the fabric, and magical appearing vines grow and slither. The bodice is tight and has boning in the corset, and the florals, leaves, and vines are beautifully applied to make the wearer of the gown look like a nymph.

"These flowers are from the Fae," Evalie gasps.

My mind reels as I continue devouring the dress. My fingers trace the neckline. It perfectly reveals the collar bones, while the shoulders and arms are covered in delicate lace and floral appliques. The sleeves are bell shaped and when you extend your arm, it reveals a wing-like illusion. On the back, there are vines of green and gold that grow up and extend above the shoulders, making it look ethereal. The train is several feet long and if I didn't know any better, I would think they picked up an enchanted forest and formed it into a gown fit for not just a princess or a queen, but a *Goddess.*

I shake my head from the trance that is this gown, and Evalie helps me put it on. Her jaw drops when she looks at me.

"Oh Vera," she says, "it's beautiful."

"Let me see!"

Evalie hurries to the mirror and rips the drape from the glass. When I finally see myself, I burst into tears. Every description of Dia that I've ever read is staring at me in the face, and I've never been happier.

"This gown is beyond what I've ever thought possible," I say to Evalie.

She fluffs the train. "You look like–"

"Dia."

Evalie smiles broadly. "You do."

Calix might be under a spell right now, but that doesn't mean we aren't meant for each other. No one but him would understand how much this gown would impact me, and only someone who genuinely loves me would know that it would make me unreasonably happy. Who cares if he's under the spell of a potion? This dress proves he really cares.

Once my hair is curled and braided, it's time for me to head to the ball. I take one last look in the mirror before I leave my room, and my reflection winks at me. Evalie would scream if she knew what I could see. I wink back at my reflection and she beams. I don't know why, but I'm strangely comforted that she's here. She saved Poppy and I once, I owe her a bit of attention. I wave at the girl in the mirror when Evalie turns her head, and she gives a little wave back. Most Doppelgangers might be evil, but not mine.

The path from my chambers to the ballroom is grand. Stained glass windows with magnificent portraits line the halls, letting the evening light spill in the corridor. As the sun sets, it creates a moving story on the ground in front of me and it looks like I'm walking through history. Gods and villains fighting, Fae spells, enchanted forests, and glimmering lights; it's the visual representation of every story Lieve has ever told me.

I take my time, slowly dancing my way through my favorite tales. I stand as Dia in the River of Light and Dark, as Siva covered in pearls, as Gwen creating life. One of the stories shows a mirror with a delicate hand protruding from the glass. I stop and stare at it, trying to remember the story, but I don't know it. I walk in the shadow of the lead on the ground for a while before noticing glass shaped like the Lopter tree in the next window. It's the only glass with a beautiful tree in it, and I'm sure no one understands what it is, *but I do*. In the bottom of the glass I see the artist's mark, and a small carving, *for V*.

That's why he chose my specific room for me. I smile to myself because even though I haven't been with him in years, Lieve still thought that deeply about me. If he ever found me, if I ever showed up, he wanted all of my experiences in Prinav and in Brone Castle to be grand. Lieve never stopped thinking of me. This Lieve that I've been fighting with isn't the brother that I know. I'll rid him of Lucette and he'll go back to being my Lieve, the Lieve who's been fighting for me our entire lives.

I carefully dab my cheeks so I don't mess up my elaborate makeup. Evalie adhered moss and glitter to my face, adding to my mystical look. She said it allowed the 'mere mortals' around me to wonder at my mysterious beauty. I don't know how I got lucky enough to have Evalie as my maid, and my friend, but I couldn't be more grateful for her.

At the end of the massive corridor is a staircase even more grand than the stairs in the entry of Brone Castle. Its size is overwhelming. The ceiling reaches to the top of a faux tower and the skylight allows for the sunset to cast a warm hue across the endless ivory marble. I can see the top of the stairs from where I stand, but I still have to walk a considerable distance before I'm even at the first step.

When I reach the stairs, I stop and look around before taking that first step down. From this angle, I can see the corridor. There are stained glass windows on the other side of the walls too, and the light sends ripples of color through the glass, the legends faintly moving around all over the massive walls and staircase. It's like moving pictures, moving stories. *It's incredible.*

In the distance music plays, and the light chatter of guests arriving leaks into my world of sun and glass and marble. I'm going to go to a ball, and I won't be kicked out this time. I'll be welcomed here. Every eye will know me as Princess Vera, sister of the King of Prinav. I get to be the people I've only dreamed to be. For once, I'll be important. I'll be noticed, and with this dress, I'll be remembered. This is my fairytale.

The marble is cool against my skin as I run my hand along the grand banister. When I get to the center of the grand staircase, a man falls into view near the bottom step. He's wearing deep green and black fabric with long coattails, and leather shoes. His back is to me, but even without his ever present hood, I immediately recognize his strong arms and sturdy shoulders as Arden. My heart hammers in my chest.

"No scary hood, no weapons attached to you," I tease. "However will you survive?"

Arden turns to face me and I catch my breath. *He's stunning.* His messy brown hair has been tamed and he's freed his face from the mask he normally wears. He looks at me with wonder in his eyes and a smile tugging at his lip. I swallow hard and feel my hands begin to shake.

His lips finally curl into a playful grin but then quickly he slides his hand up to his lip and drops it just as quickly. Arden has a scar that starts from the top of his upper lip to the bottom of his chin, running diagonally and cutting across both lips. He's wrong for covering it or being embarrassed by it. It makes him look strong. Even without the scar, he would be a work of art, but with it...he's a message from the gods.

"Wow," Arden breathes.

I can feel my cheeks flush, so I bring my eyes to the floor. "I had to dress my part as Princess tonight."

"Well, a Princess can't walk into a ball unattended, and it seems your escort is running late," he holds out his elbow for me. "Shall we?"

I hesitate. Should I wait on Calix? Arden's smile falters for a moment, but then I place my hand on his strong arm and his smile broadens. My heart races and beats so hard I swear I can hear it in my ears. Arden puts his free hand on mine and his touch sends a jolt of lightning crashing through every inch of me. My thoughts bounce around in my head as we smile at each other and stand in front of the massive doors that lead to the ballroom.

Arden beams with pride. "Ready?"

I nod and the guards bow to us and open the grand double doors. My jaw drops. I know now that my entire life has led me to this moment. There are real blooming willows, wisteria, twinkling lights, candles, crystal chandeliers, and millions of flowers. The ballroom has been transformed into an enchanted forest. I see Soleil pointing to different decorations as people ask her questions. She did a fabulous job.

A man near the door announces our entrance, "Sir Arden Madrona, and her Highness, Princess Vera Oleander."

Every eye in the ballroom turns to me. No one claps or cheers. No one speaks.

Arden leans in and whispers, "You're being seared into the memory of every man and woman in Prinav."

My breath catches as Arden's lips brush my ear. He guides me to the dance floor and wraps a strong arm around my waist, pulling me close to his chest. A new song plays, and slowly Arden spins me. The fingers of his free hand lace with mine, and I let him guide me around the ballroom to the tune of a sultry ballad I don't know the words too.

The song builds and Arden leans me back for a dramatic dip, and when he pulls me up, we're so close our lips nearly meet. The other dancers on the floor clap for us, and when I look into Arden's eyes, I see something new there. I feel something new. We stand still, breathing heavily, until the chorus begins again and we part, continuing the next steps.

"Vera, I want to talk to you," Arden says, spinning and spinning us.

"I'm listening."

His muscles tighten. "I wanted to see if you'd change your mind—"

"Change my mind about what?"

Arden opens his mouth, but before he can say a word, Calix interrupts us.

"May I cut in?"

Arden huffs and pushes past me, bumping Calix with his shoulder. I don't know how to feel now or what to think. *What did Arden mean by changing my mind?* Calix takes Arden's place on the dance floor and places a soft kiss on my cheek. I furrow my brow as I watch Arden's back, and then realize others might be watching, so I smile at Calix and take his hand; Arden's question still lingering.

I place my other hand on Cal's shoulder as he places his hand on my hip. "Thank you for the dress, it's truly divine."

Calix leans in and whispers, "*You're* divine."

He then spins me, at the same time pointing to the musicians to play another song. The rest of the guests join in again, hundreds of people re-filling the dance floor around us. Calix and I dance to a few songs together, but I can't stop thinking about what Arden meant. *Where did he go?* As the music slows, I peer over Cal's shoulder and look for him, but I spot Lieve. He looks thrilled at the two of us dancing together.

Then I see Daphne in the corner of the dance floor with Arden. Arden looks upset and Daphne slides her hand on his cheek before looping her arm in his and leading him to the dance floor. I watch them dance together, muttering to one another. They both look defeated. I lean my head on Calix's shoulder, pushing Arden from my thoughts.

On my next spin, I see Lucette. She wears a gown that makes her look like a giant silver bird. It demands attention, but not in the way Lucette intended, I'm sure. It clearly cost a pretty sum, but it's unflattering to the point of unsightly and her face is nearly purple with rage. I'm taking the attention from her, and I know I'll feel the wrath of her jealousy soon. Then I notice her father join her. They stare at me and whisper, her father's lips curling into a cruel and intimidating smile, sending a shiver down my spine.

The song ends and Calix bows to me as the audience claps. I curtsey before leaving him to join Poppy. Poppy looks absolutely delighted. She's wearing a dress full of pink taffeta that matches the color of her lips and cheeks.

"Vera," she exclaims, "that dress is so pretty."

"Thank you," I say as I fluff up her skirts. "I love this color on you."

Soleil slides up next to me and she takes a sip of champagne, her eyes darting to Arden. "What's going on there?"

I glance at Arden and he's staring at me from a dark corner. "Nothing."

Poppy just shakes her head and takes another sip of her drink.

"It's really nothing, we're just–"

"Princess," I hear Lucette call.

I steady myself and slap a fake smile on my face. "Yes, Your Majesty."

"Where did you get your delightful garment?"

Lucette is so jealous she can't stand it, so I decide to milk it. "Oh this? It's from Lord Bramford." I scrunch my nose, ever so slightly. "Where did you get your dress? It's rather unique."

Poppy spits champagne across the room.

"You are dismissed Lady Poppy," Lucette sneers.

Poppy curtsies and dashes away toward the champagne tower as fast as she can.

Lucette bares her teeth. "Did you purposely try to outshine me tonight?"

Lieve moves in between us. "No one can outshine you my darling, do not fret–," he brings her hand to his lips to kiss–, "you are the Queen."

"Get the people dancing again at once," Lucette snaps while she yanks her hand from Lieve and rushes off to a gaggle of women with pursed lips and upturned noses.

Lieve turns to the musicians and bellows. "The Sol Ball ceremony must now begin! So, Oriels, find your Dias!"

The crowd separates, men and women, until most have found a dance partner. I'm amazed as I watch them begin the ceremony. This wasn't something Poppy taught me, and I'm mesmerized. The dancers' arms make symbols in the air, and when they cross when their partner, it's as if they tell the story of the gods with their movements. This dance is ancient. Each move is precise, poetic, every movement telling a story.

Tears well in my eyes as the dance goes on. The crescendo erupts as dancers split down the middle, and then Prince Florian struts down the open aisle they created. He dons a wicked grin, winking at the women as he passes them. Most of their faces turn red, or they giggle, and I understand why. Florian is a handsome man, his brown skin almost glows in the light of the candles around the room.

"He's our god Sol this year," Lieve answers me before I can even ask. "He'll pick a woman from the dance floor and finish the night dancing with her."

"What about who she came to the ball with?" I ask.

Lieve shrugs, "that's the Sol Ball. But it's just a game." He holds out his hand to me and we join the dancers on the floor. "No one is obligated to anything, it's just tradition."

The music plays faster and Lieve and I dance for a while. I notice that Prince Florian has chosen Daphne as his Dia for the evening, and I'm unsurprised. Daphne is beautiful, and to his knowledge, unattached. She seems to be enjoying his company as far as I can tell, and they might have been a good match in another life. It's sad to watch because even if they'd be a good match, it wouldn't work. Saima, Madoria's own Princess, wasn't safe there, so Daphne wouldn't be safe there either.

Calix cuts into my dance with Lieve and kisses me. I accidentally lock eyes with Arden and he looks down at his feet. I shake the urge to run to him, because I'm with Calix, a man who's always shown me his feelings. So *why am I feeling this way?* Is it because of our moment in the closet, or on the dance floor? Or because he was my first friend in Prinav?

I shake my head. Why do I care about my feelings for Arden, or Arden's feelings about me? There's no way he's interested in me. That's not what his question on the dance floor was about. And even if he does have feelings, it wouldn't be the same as Calix's feelings for me. Even without a love potion, Calix would still be here with me tonight. He would still be dancing with me, courting me, and he would have still given me this incredible dress. Calix continues to show me how he's feeling.

The rest of the night flies by in a dream of music and drink, of sweat and stolen kisses. Calix knows what to say and how to say it. He knows how to treat someone, and how to love them. Arden knows nothing of that. Arden only berates me. Taunts me. Arden is unpredictable. Not Calix. I know exactly what I'm getting with Cal. Unconditional love and acceptance. Patience. Kindness. There is no comparison, so I need to stop comparing.

Near the end of the ball, Calix and I end up in the center of the floor. The musicians are playing a song, but Calix raises a hand for them to stop. I look around the room to try and see what's wrong, but the faces around me seem just as confused. Calix takes my hand and when I look back at him, he'd dropped to one knee.

My stomach flips. *No.*

"Vera dear." His voice echoes in the now silent ballroom.

My palms begin to sweat. *No. No. This can't be happening.*

"I've loved you from the second I met you."

I can't breathe.

"I've never known anyone like you, and I don't ever want to try." He lets go of my hand to pull out a small velvet box from the pocket of his jacket and my heart stops. "Will you marry me?"

This is the potion talking. My eyes flick to Arden standing in the back of the room next to Daphne. He clenches his jaw, waiting on my answer. I open my mouth, but I can't speak. Every eye in the Kingdom lingers, waiting with bated breath for my reply. Arden swallows.

I can't say no to Calix, I just can't. I gave him a love potion, and this proposal is entirely my fault. There's no way I can reject him in front of everyone, so I have to give him the courtesy of not looking like a fool. I furrow my brow and see Arden's fist clench as Daphne places a soft hand on his shoulder. My stomach flips again as I tear my gaze from Arden.

"Yes, Calix. I'll marry you."

Calix places the ring on my finger, and a tear rolls down my cheek. Not a moment later I hear the double doors slam. When Calix jumps up to hug me, I glance towards Arden, but he's no longer in the ballroom.

No sign of Lord Bramford. No sign of Princess Vera. Skirmishes beginning to arise in the villages. There seems to be unrest in the Teyrn. Black Diamond delivery on the way from the mines, will be delivered in a fortnight.

– *Unidentified correspondence to His Majesty, King Lieve Oleander*

CHAPTER 56
LIEVE

For the rest of the supper I'm so sick I can't eat. Esven and Benito continue to side eye me and I have a feeling they know my secret. Once the supper ends, I'm finally able to leave and find solitude and think. As I leave, I spot a member of my Hunters who was present at the supper and walk with him on the way to my chambers. I discreetly send him to find Arden. I don't let on that he's Remi's accomplice, but I make sure he sees that it's imperative that he's found.

Once in my chambers, I pace around the room, trying to devise a plan to rescue Arden, as well as Quinn and Kelby. I've made grave mistakes with my scheme, and it's up to me to remedy the situation. I pray over and over to Bram and to the death god Sybill, to keep Arden safe and alive.

Footsteps reach just outside the door as knuckles rap on the wood, the handle creaking as it's turned. Then I hear a voice that I haven't heard in such a long time that it takes me by surprise.

"Happy coronation."

Calix.

In my relief and excitement I spin on my heel and see him. Calix stands there, smiling broadly with his arms open, ready for my embrace. I take a step towards him and then stop. He doesn't look battle worn, or as if he's been riding for days to return to me. He looks like he doesn't have a care in the world. *Is it really him?* He takes a step forward –and *limps.*

Doppelganger.

"It's really me." He takes another step and puts his hand over his heart, "I'm not a Dop, Daphne checked me."

I glance out into the hall. I don't see her red hair anywhere.

"You're lying."

Calix takes another step closer and closes the door behind him, "Lieve, *brother–*"

My eyes narrow. "Prove it."

"Can't you tell who I really am?"

It's not him. It can't be.

"Yes. You're limping, and I know now that's where Calix injured you. You're not Calix."

Calix's body relaxes, his shoulders dropping slightly as he closes his eyes and rolls his neck from side to side. It looks as if he's shedding my friend off him.

"Where is he?" I demand.

He shrugs and looks around like he's bored. "The walls."

A shiver runs down my spine. *What does that mean? Is he dead?*

"What did you do?"

The Doppelganger looks at me and his eyes turn black. "I'm so sick of you humans." He steps forward, prowling like a jungle cat after its prey. "The whining never stops."

I lunge at him. Our bodies collide and we roll around on the ground. My hand curls into a fist, slamming into the bones of his jaw over and over again. The Doppelganger slides his knee up and uses his legs to throw me off him. Luckily I land on the sofa and not slammed into the desk. We both stand, circling each other like vultures. The Dop slides his hand inside his robe and pulls out a blade–the onyx dagger Cal threw at him, the one that caused his limp.

I have no weapon, so I shout for help.

He grips the handle of the blade and snickers. "Calix screams for help just like you, squealing like a pig at slaughter."

Horrified, I breathe, "Calix is alive?"

I fling myself at him. His arm holding the blade extends and I try to turn my body so I don't land on it, but as I'm in midair I panic. My thick robe has opened like wings and the Dop's blade pierces my side, in between my ribs. My full weight crashes down, the dagger driving deeper into my flesh.

For a moment I can't feel any pain, only shock. The Doppelganger rolls me off him and scrambles to stand. He looms over me as I hold pressure to my wound, begging Sybill to stop the bleeding. Each breath produces a sharp pain now, and it's hard to inhale. I glance at my wound and instantly regret it. Blood is already covering my hands, my shirt. *I'm going to die.*

Stars burst in my peripheral vision and then everything steadily grows hazy and dark. Cal's Dop strides over to the full length mirror against the wall. I can't think straight. I can't move. His blurry silhouette comes in and out of focus as he tears the sheet off the mirror.

It's nearly ten feet tall and five wide, made of solid brass. The glass almost touches the ceiling, and scrapes against the floor. I can't make out much more of it, because I then notice my reflection. My eyes meet my reflections, and the damage is even worse that I thought. Blood is spilling out across the floor. All the color has leached from my face, draining me. My vision blurs again and my eyes roll in the back of my head. A wave of nausea hits me and when I gag, blood trickles down my face.

"Get up." Cal's Dop grunts.

I think he's talking to me, so I close my eyes and attempt to crawl. Pain shoots across my body with even the slightest movement. *I can't.* I can't get up. I open my eyes again and terror replaces pain. My reflection stands up, laughing, his eyes as black as the night sky, and steps through the mirror.

It feels like hours, but it must only be minutes that my blood has been draining out of my body and spilling onto the wooden floor. The Dops have been talking to each other, peering out the window to the crowd below and *celebrating.* They murmur about putting my body in the walls with Calix so they can keep me for whatever gruesome reason I can't fathom. Faint footsteps slap down the hallway. *Finn.* I try to scream but only a gurgle emerges from my throat. Blood has now made its way to my mouth.

"Hurry," Cal's Dop hisses. "We don't have time to put him in the wall, we have to get him in the mirror, *now.*"

"It's fine. We can just kill the servant."

"Only if we have to."

The next thing I know, my crown and jewels are ripped off me. They push me on my side and I nearly vomit. Pain sears through me with the force of them rolling me over and I see double before stars burst in my eyes.

"I want the robe." My Dop says greedily.

"It's covered in blood you fool, and yours looks close enough to a match."

Then they pick me up, my Dop holding me under my shoulders, and Cal's holding up my feet. They stand directly in front of the mirror and swing me from side to side, the pain strong enough for me to get nauseous again as every inch of muscle and bone splits under their grasp. Then, they toss me. I thought the glass would shatter. I thought being thrown into a mirror would cause the glass to slice me bit by bit. *But it didn't.*

Going through the mirror was like being frozen in time. Ice covers my body while I float, numbing the pain of my wound. Everything around me is dark and cold. My body finally lands with a sickening thud on the ground, and all the pain comes back instantly. The force sends another jolt of excruciating pain ricocheting my bones and I vomit on the frozen ground. The puke mixed with my blood is warm and I lay my face in it, the air so cold I'm already shivering. I hear shattering glass and open my eyes. In the distance, the Dops crack the mirror, and as each piece of glass falls to the ground, they spark and sizzle, disappearing forever.

I think my father is Baptiste Matisse.
— *Message from Soleil Toun, to Daphne Cortrwight*

CHAPTER 57

VERA

The next couple of weeks in Brone Castle are bleak. Daphne had to leave for Teyrnas to meet her new fiance, Ivar Bergman, and Arden has refused to even be in the same room as me. He hasn't spoken to me since my acceptance of Cal's proposal. I've slipped notes under his door every morning, and I find each of them torn to shreds and slipped back under my own door the following night.

I barely leave my chambers. The good thing about that, is I've finally had time to read again. I've found interesting passages regarding spark magic. The parent gods Bram and Gwen, Dia, Sol, Lopter, Hode, Siva, and Malsu, all have spark magic. Siva and Malsu, the creators and gods of the Fae, gave them similar, but not as intense magic. They allow the Fae to take power from the soil, and so the Seelie and Unseelie live underground and in the forests all over Atatacia. Anyone with Fae lineage, or any descendants of the gods, can learn magic. It makes me wonder about Lieve, and if he really did perform magical feats. If so, what does that mean about Lieve, about me?

After Sol killed Oriel, that's when Bram and Gwen gifted humans powerful Crystal Thrones. These thrones choose the rulers and give consequences to those who shouldn't be wearing a crown. They also force True Rulers to take the throne, for they also receive consequences for not taking responsibility to rule. Many Kingdoms have suffered the consequences of the Crystal Thrones, but they also give gifts. When a True Ruler inherits the monarchy, they are to decipher a code that will lead them to a Crystal Sword that is said to wield power strong enough to kill a god.

I asked Evalie to take the book to Saima once I realized that the magic mentioned was probably the same magic Lucette was using to disappear into the dungeon walls, and I'm sure now that the Sagart has god-like powers. Lucette's family might be more powerful than we all think. Now we know that she is using some sort of ancient magic to either hide something or someone, inside the castle under everyone's noses. *But what could it be?*

Because Lucette's family has such power in Prinav, we're waiting until Saima's love potion antidote is finished and Lieve has taken it, before we bring this information to his attention. If Lucette has truly put a love spell on him, nothing we say about her will get him to make a move against her until the effects of the potion melts away. These couple of weeks have been long and tortuous, and it's become harder to stay away from Lieve now that I'm engaged to his best friend.

Lucette has forced me to attend dress fittings, wine tastings, and perform endless rituals now that I'm a bride-to-be. It's exhausting. I haven't found a way to finish fixing the pocket watch even with Daphne and Saima's help, and I'm having to stay up well into the night to continue my lessons with Poppy. I'm certain Lucette's only doing this to punish me for upstaging her at the Sol Ball, and to keep an eye on me to make sure things with Calix are going smoothly. Because I tricked Calix into loving me, I'm letting her.

I'm even letting her throw an engagement party tonight. She's wanted to throw one for about a week now, but luckily Calix has been busy enough with duties that it's been put off. We can't wait any longer for it though, the wedding is nearing. My mind is reeling at the thought.

I didn't want it to be this fast. I at least wanted Calix to have the love potion antidote first so I could fairly marry him. It all feels so wrong.

I do love him, and it truly seems like I'm getting the happy ending that Lieve and I have always dreamed of for me, but I've been close to calling the whole thing off. It's so unfair to Cal. There's no way of knowing if this is truly what he wants. I tried to put off the wedding until Saima could get the antidotes finished, but we still have out of town guests, and Lucette believes the bigger the wedding, the better.

Walking into my own engagement party is surreal. Lucette decided to have the party in the Solarium, for that I'm actually grateful. She asked what space in the castle I liked the most, and I originally said the library, but she thought it was too dark there and chose the Solarium for me. Calix chose a theme, Dia in the river, and my heart aches with his thoughtfulness.

The Solarium is beautiful as always, and everyone has dressed like druids and nymphs to blend into the surroundings. Calix and I wear white and are seated on gold wing back chairs placed near the waterfall.

All of our guests are seated around the solarium on white poufs and beds of moss, eating, drinking, and talking. Evalie and Marguerite serve drinks with the help of the other servants on staff and I'm grateful they're here, along with Poppy and Soleil. It seems like Poppy and her cousin Brenna, the pincher, have had some sort of falling out, because Brenna keeps ignoring her, and Poppy sits on her pouf alone, sipping champagne and looking anxious.

Brenna has been absorbed into Lucette's Ladies, and her ego has inflated beyond measure. Even at my own engagement party she turns her nose up at me, making sour faces all evening. I have a difficult time not confronting her and ruining this whole evening. *Maybe if I do that then the wedding would be called off.*

Evalie brings me a glass of wine. "This is a lovely party."

"It's beautiful," I say, "but I wish, I– I don't know what I wish."

Soliel lowers her voice. "Arden?"

"I don't care about Arden."

She nods and takes a sip from her own glass.

I take a long draught of my own wine. "Did he truly leave Prinav?"

"He did. He went to check on Daphne. I believe he's staying in Teyrnas with her until after her wedding."

Lucette snaps her fingers and Evalie scurries over to her and presents her with candies and a glass of liquor with a sugared rim. Her fingers wrap around the clear stem, and I imagine white sparks falling to the ground around her. *What are you hiding?* I can't stop staring at her hands. Her delicate fingers trapped my brother, wrapping around him like a snake, forcing him into a marriage. Those hands clutch a crown she doesn't deserve.

Lucette catches me staring at her, the smile on her face drops instantly. I toss her a quick nod and focus on Calix. It's our engagement party and I haven't given him nearly enough attention. That thought just adds another twinge of guilt in my stomach. I stretch out my arm and rub his shoulder. He's deep in conversation with Lieve, but he places his hand on mine absentmindedly. The knot in my stomach loosens. This man loves me. It's okay that we're getting married because the feelings are there; we're in love.

"Time for presents," Marguerite exclaims.

Gifts begin to pile in front of Calix and I, and each one we open is something remarkable. I'm handed a copper box and inside, wrapped in silk, is a necklace with an black gem hanging off a delicate gold chain.

"That's a Tussian black diamond, Your Highness," one of Lucette's courtier's calls out to me with a note of excitement. "It's very rare and said to be shaped by Drols."

Lucette purses her lips. "We don't speak of Drols in my court, Camille."

"Of course, apologies," Camille mutters.

I pick up the stone and I see flecks of gold floating under the surface. "It's beautiful."

Camille smiles at me and then I'm handed more gifts. The kingdom of Teyrnas sent gowns made of silks and satins, corsets embroidered with Seelie flowers, and a scandalous set of undergarments. My face flushes and I stuff everything back inside the wrappings and move it out of view. Tussia sent a tiara covered in pearls with matching drop earrings that must have cost a fortune; and Florian presents me with Madoria's wedding gift himself, A crystal and silver smoking pipe. I raise an eyebrow at him and he laughs.

There are so many gifts it's nearly exhausting to continue. Deeds to lands, paintings from renowned artists, weaponry for Calix, precious gemstones and jewelry, and a mound of literature for me. I want to break down and cry. This is a whole different life now, nothing like the life I had in Adamston. It's strange to own things and have somewhere to keep those things. The thought that everything in front of us is mine to keep is hard to believe. Lieve smiles at me knowingly. He understands exactly how I'm feeling.

I pick up the last gift. It's wrapped in soft leather, and I'm sure it's a book. When I open it, a note falls on my lap. The handwriting is fluid and clearly in Madorian. It has to be from Saima. I tear open the note and all it says is: *page 237.* I stuff the note inside my gown and lift the book to take a closer look. The title is *Charmed.* It looks like a romance book, but I have a nagging suspicion that it's much more than that.

The guests all giggle and jeer at the title, many of them believing it's some type of romance book as well. My skin warms. *This must be a joke.* I flip through the pages, not reading any of the words.

"Poppy, what are you teaching our dear Princess?"

Poppy flushes. "Charming others is not part of my curriculum."

Everyone laughs, and Calix leans towards me and whispers in my ear, "You, Vera dear, do not need to learn how to charm me, you have already won my affections."

I whisper back, "It never hurts to *educate* oneself further."

The party dies down shortly after the gifts have all been unwrapped and Lieve directs the servants to store the presents for us until after the wedding. Lieve says the servants will be cleaning everything up and the remaining guests retire to their own chambers. Once we're alone, Calix takes my hand and kisses my fingertips, my palm, and up my arm. He doesn't stop until his lips reach mine.

"We should go to bed," I say.

Calix raises his eyebrows. "Yes, we should." He snatches the book from my hands. "And we could read this together."

I snatch the book back playfully and he chases me around the solarium while we laugh. He catches me and we kiss for another moment. I catch a glimpse of my reflection in the small mirror Lucette uses to watch herself bathe in the indoor pond when our lips part, and I see my Doppelganger again. Her eyes are wide and her gaze is hard fixed on the book. All the playful energy evaporates. Now I know there's more to these pages than meets the eye, and I truly need to see what this is all about.

"Calix, I think I should end the night now." I press the book to my chest, "I will see you at Gwen Abbey, as your *wife*."

He grabs me, pulling me as close to him as he can. "I hate that we must be apart until the wedding. I miss you so much when I'm away from you."

I bring my hand to his cheek. "I do too."

"Our marriage will change our lives, and I can't wait for it."

"Neither can I," I say and kiss him once more.

We leave the solarium and part ways, he to his chambers, and I to mine. Once inside my room, I open the book to page 237 as instructed. My eyes devour the text until I see what the gifter wanted me to read.

It has been said that multiple realms exist and that each of the gods created their own worlds. There are portals that can take you from one realm to another, but if you aren't a god yourself, the price of your journey can be momentous. The toll a traveler must pay oftentimes requires their very lives or souls.

However, a descendant of the gods can imbue magic into certain items, gifting that item with a set of powers. In the last chapter, we learned that the crowns and thrones of Atatacia are godmade. We know that the True Ruler would be anointed and crowned and that only the True Ruler and their blood can rule without consequence.

That brings us back to our topic of charms. Throughout this book we speculate together on what objects the descendants may have bore their magic into. As we've read, there are numerous possibilities, but none more probable than the Eldertick.

My heart skips a beat, I've heard of this before. This device can tell the time of the realm you're in, and any realm you're searching for. It has celestial mapping, and magnetic forces that show you a multitude of scientific and spiritual information. I keep reading.

The Eldertick would be encrusted with gems from each existing realm, have runes of divination carved on or inside it, and store wonders a mortal could only dream of. It is speculated that Oriel himself constructed it to help him reconnect with Dia. In short, the Eldertick may very well look like a plain watch to the naked eye. Only, once you open it, it includes faces inside that seem unreal to one who doesn't know its secrets.

The pocket watch.

That's why Sol was after us. That's why he wanted it, so he could find Dia. I rip the pillows from the bed, destroying all the work Evalie put into my room. My breath becomes ragged when the watch isn't in plain sight, so I tear the linens from the mattress.

Nothing.

I hid it under these sheets earlier. Where did it go? My shoes click the ground with every hurried step, the constant tapping forcing me to throw the shoe across the room. One hits the mirror, dropping the thin drapings to the floor. The force creates a spider's web, cracking the glass almost from top to bottom. In the reflection, I see myself open a small jewelry box on a dresser against the back wall. My reflection, no, my Doppelganger, pulls out the pocket watch, and it's glowing. She then points to my desk and I see a set of watch repair tools that weren't there before.

My breath catches and the hairs on the back of my neck stand up. I should run. I try to scream but the only sound I can produce is a squeak. My Dop holds the pocket watch in the air, letting it spin around. Taking her free hand, she opens the latch on the side of the face. Her eyes, my eyes, widen in awe. *What can she see in there?*

Our eyes meet and she nods at the jewelry box, prodding me to examine the real object. *Do I dare?* This has to be a trick. Has she only been pretending to help me all along? The girl in the mirror takes her pocket watch and sits on her own mattress, a mattress torn apart exactly like mine, and flips through each face. I squint my eyes, straining to see what she's doing with her fingers. It looks like she's winding up different dials. I step closer to the mirror, my own reflections' back turned to me and the sight sends a shiver down my spine.

I can make out a little of what her hands are doing, and she's definitely winding the dials. However, there are little flicks and snaps she has incorporated and they seem to be in a repetitive pattern, tiny white sparks falling down around her. I need to open the real watch. Slowly, I walk backwards away from the mirror and stop at the dresser. I reach out and touch the little door knob on the jewelry box and stop. *What if this is a trick?*

I shake the thought away and hold my breath at the same time I open the jewelry box door. I squeeze my eyes shut, ready for something to happen. A shock, a boom, sparks, a flash of light…but nothing happens. I hastily snatch the watch off its hook and turn it over and over in my hand. The gems glisten in the lamplight. *Gems from each existing realm.* Even though it's not glowing, I have an overwhelming feeling that this is it, this is the Eldertick. I glance at my reflection, and the girl in the mirror is staring at me now.

I take the watch and go to the desk. Sitting down, I slowly open the face of the watch and flip through until I find the broken gear. My hands shake as I pick up the tools and work for a few minutes until something clicks and the gears try to spin on their own, a faint buzzing coming from the hands.

I mumble to myself, "Incredible."

My Dop waves me over to her, so I take the watch to the mirror and sit cross legged on the floor. My Doppelganger does the same. She twists the dial on the side, and I twist mine. She says something, but no words come out, so she leans in close to the mirror. I lean in too, the pocket watch still in my grasp. My reflection breathes on the mirror and fogs the glass before drawing a set of runes. I repeat her movements, slowly, but precisely. Instantly, waves appear in the glass. Slightly above my head, the waves create a small dome, no bigger than a marble and I reach up to touch it.

Bitter cold bites at my finger, climbing from my hands and up my arms. Every instinct I have is screaming at me to back away, but I can't. There's something in the mirror that I want—*no*, that I *need*. She knows it, and so do I. I push my finger on the dome and it feels gelatinous, almost fluid. My finger goes through the dome, and I have a gut feeling that I could just walk right into the mirror if I felt like it.

The freezing cold pain sends pins and needles from beyond the reflection and forces its way up my arm along with the feeling of powerful magic. I felt that magic in Shadow Grove too, but this is different. This feels raw. Flashes of the Darkthing appear in my mind, Lieve being torn apart, flesh being ripped in front of me, and I pull my hand back. I can't trust this.

The chill fades, but the magic lingers. I look in my hand at the pocket watch and it's covered in ice. So is my hand. I wiggle my fingers and the frost breaks, causing the dial to break with it. When I look back into the mirror, the girl is gone. My own real reflection is the only thing staring back at me with scared, wide eyes.

I've had the Eldertick this whole time.

A human can freeze to death in as little as fifteen minutes
if the temperature is cold enough. I've seen it.

– Saint Barnabas

CHAPTER 58

LIEVE

I 'm so cold I'm already shivering, the wetness of my blood on my clothes, already beginning to freeze. *I have to stop the bleeding.* I reach for my wound to staunch the flow, but the pain of moving my arms overtakes me and I black out.

I hereby declare that Kelby Drake and Quinn Grey are traitors to the crown. They are convicted of treason, and sentenced to death by hanging.

— Records of Court Hearing of Kelby Drake, announcer of Barault, and Quinn Grey, Treasurer to the Crown, ruling given by Justice of the Courts, His High Eminence, Nikoli Tramsil.

CHAPTER 59
VERA

I don't realize it's morning when my chamber door opens. Evalie and Poppy bounce inside carrying vases full of flowers from Calix, their happy expressions dropping the moment they look at me. I've been up all night reading about the Eldertick, about crystal swords and gods as my Doppelganger watched me from the mirror with impatient eyes.

"I'm glad you're here, I need your help with this."

Evalie and Poppy look around the room. The bed linens are still scattered on the floor, and the mirror I've been staring into for hours now has a crack in it from top to bottom. Books and notes are strewn about and I know I must look like I've gone mad.

"Vera," Evalie hesitates before asking. "Is everything okay?"

"No, it's not."

They look at each other with concern and Poppy walks over to me and places a hand on my shoulder. "What's going on?"

Evalie starts picking up the mess and Poppy sits beside me on the bed. I don't know how to say it, so I push *Charmed* into Poppy's hands and point at the pocket watch on the ground near the mirror. Poppy begins to read, her brow furrowing in concentration, and then her eyes widen. She closes the book slowly and then stares at me, unmoving. Unblinking.

Evalie picks up the watch from the floor and brings it over to us.

"Ev– that's um–" Poppy hands Evalie the book.

Evalie drops the pocket watch on the bed and wrings her hands. She does symbols over her eyes, ears, mouth, and heart, before taking a deep breath in. When she blows out, she stares at the ceiling with her hands on her hips.

"This can't be the Eldertick," Evalie states finally. "The real Eldertick? Are you sure?"

"Yes." I whisper and wind the dial. It glows blue and Poppy screams.

Evalie shakes her head frantically. "We shouldn't have this."

"I wanted to come to you both last night and talk about it, but I was afraid."

Poppy wrings her hands and stands up, pacing the room.

I snap my head to Poppy, "I'm afraid of its magic. Of Sol. Of my Doppelganger." I hesitate, "I–I've seen her."

Evalie gasps, "Bram help us."

"She's the one who showed me what this really was." Evalie looks sick and starts praying again and Poppy is visibly trembling.

"Do you think we can use it to see what Lucette's hiding in the dungeons?" I ask.

Evalie frowns. "Oh no you don't, I know that look."

"What look?" I scowl.

"That one," She answers. "We have to do more research, we need help, we–"

"I have to know what's behind that wall, what if it can help Lieve?"

Poppy holds my hand. "We'll look into it, I swear, but you have a wedding happening soon. And we should really give this to a Priest–," she lets go–, "not Baptiste, but a Priest we can trust. Or at least Daphne and Saima."

"Besides that, we need Lieve's help with Lucette, and Saima's antidote isn't finished yet, so Lieve will be of no use until it's ready."

I wring my hands. "You're right, but we have to look into this."

"We will," Evalie promises, and Poppy nods.

"Fine," I concede. "But I almost had it working. It's ticking, can't you hear it?"

Evalie picks it up and then her face loses all color. She sets it down quickly and she wipes her hands on her skirts like she's trying to rub the magic off her skin. I don't know what to do, so I stand up and walk over to the bathing room.

"Let's take the Eldertick and this book to Saima." I say and scramble to grab the items.

Poppy bites her lip. "You can't leave your chambers until the wedding. And neither can Calix."

"What?" I groan.

"It's tradition." Evalie answers.

Huffing and puffing, I stuff everything in Poppy's hands and push her out the door with a gentle shove. She and Evalie exchange worried looks and I hold Poppy's gaze. She looks as if she's going to faint and I feel awful asking her to go to Saima alone, I know she's scared of her, of this whole mess. So am I.

"Remind Saima that she's bound by Lieve's Fae Deal to help me," I say, "and tell her I'm specifically asking for her to look into this." And then I close the door before she can object.

I do believe now, that the trenches of Shadow Grove were once a great river. In the soil lives a raw material that I've tested and it gives new life. I've come to the conclusion that the trenches were indeed the location of the River of Light and Dark. My only question is, where did the water go?

— *Emmit Gadory, Second Professor's Lecture of Archeology, Lycee Hall, Ballmire Academy, Teyrnas*

CHAPTER 60

LIEVE

I've laid on the ground long enough that my face has frozen to the disgusting mixture of my bodily fluids. All of me is frozen. My hands sting with cold and the skin is painfully chapped. I try to open my eyes but my eyelashes have frozen together on the side that lays in my filth. My lips crack and the corner of my mouth tears a little when I try to take a deep breath. The only good thing about freezing is that the pain in my rib has numbed slightly, and the bleeding has slowed down.

I float in and out of consciousness, being more dazed every time I try to remember what happened. I was thrown into a mirror. So, now I'm in the land of the Dops? I have to get back, I have to stop them. I have to get Calix out of the walls. Arden isn't safe. *Daphne.* I try to sit up but I'm stuck to the ground and I'm too weak to fight the cold.

I hear the rustle of robes swishing the dirt on the ground around me. My eyes dart to the sound and there are three figures dressed all in white.

The robes they wear are severely tattered and stained, and each wears a hood. The fabric is paper thin and clings sickeningly to their skeletal bodies. I notice that the robes seem wet, like their skin is moist. Then, long, slender fingers poke out of the sleeve of their robes and the skin has a gray tint and a glossy sheen. They are so wet when they touch me that I have to fight the urge to gag.

They talk to each other, at least that's what it seems like. I can't comprehend the noises they make, it sounds like chirps and hisses, not speech. One of them reaches down and touches my frozen hair. It recoils and emits several sharp chirps to the other two. The chirping stops and then suddenly, one grabs my hair and yanks.

My skin, still frozen to the vomit stuck to the cold ground, peels off angrily. I scream in agony and the hooded creature drops my head and it thumps the earth. More chirps and hisses. Then their slimy fingers lift me from the ground and I can hear chunks of frost cracking with the force.

"Let me go," I groan.

Then they hiss together, "*let me go, let me go, let me go.*"

I wriggle, but their wet hands grasp tighter around my arms and legs as they hiss again, "*let me go, let me go, let me go.*"

I look around me as I'm being carried, and the scene is eerily familiar. It's Shadow Grove, but a grotesque version of it. The trees are bare of leaves, their gnarled branches twisting and climbing towards the sky, while a thick layer of fog hangs over the mold covered paths. Everything is cold and gray. This wood is devoid of any color, except for my bloodstained robe. I look entirely out of place, standing out as the outsider. The third creature runs his disgusting hand along the hem of my robe, carefully inspecting the hide of the Darkthing, clicking and hissing at the others. They chirp frantically in response and I'm not sure I want to know what they got excited about.

They carry me through the path, and I know where we're going because it's the same path I took a thousand times in Prinav to look for

Calix. They carry me for miles and we reach an area that should have the trench, but instead is a black river.

I try to remember the steps the creatures take, left, right, right, straight. No, *it was another left.* My head is heavy. I press my eyes shut and when I open them again, we've taken another path, this one covered in black moss and decaying leaves. My body jostles when they step over a log that had fallen, ripping open my wound. Warm blood trickles out and then almost instantly freezes, my tender skin barking at me.

Without the trench, I'm lost. Memorizing these paths is impossible. I start crying, the tears burning my cheeks from the immediate cold. My head is throbbing, and I can't focus on anything but breathing through the pain in my side.

With every step we go deeper into the forest I feel like I'm getting further and further from sanity. I swear I can hear Vera's voice, Mother's voice, Daphne's. I shake my head. *They aren't here. It's not real.* Laughter surrounds me, mocking me. Mocking my inevitable end. It's as if these woods feed on your thoughts and memories. They drain you of everything just like the Doppelgangers. They come from the mirror, and they too consume you, mind and body. If I don't die in this place, there's no doubt I'll still cease to exist.

At the edge of the lifeless forest, we arrive at a valley just like the one I named myself Conductor of Death. The name seems fitting now that I'm certain my death is coming all too soon. I thought we would cross the valley, but we don't. The creatures stay in the shadows of the tree line. We get to a part of this faux Shadow Grove that I've never been to.

After we return to the heart of the dead woods and walk deeper and deeper for longer than I care to know, we stop at another section of the river. The water is thick and black, like ink. The creatures drop me on the bank of the river and the force of the drop sends pain through every nerve in my body. Sparks burst from my fingertips and scorch the ground as they fall. I barely notice it for the pain shooting through my side like lightning, and the creatures chatter so loudly I can't think. I heave but nothing comes up. My body shakes, from fear, from cold, from pain. I feel heavy and weak. I want to cry but I don't think I have any tears left. Defeated, I tuck my knees to my chest and pray for the end to come quickly.

The three figures stand over me and continue to hiss, "*let me go, let me go, let me go.*"

A breeze picks up, chilling me even colder than I thought possible and fluttering the white robes of the hooded figures. In the center of the river, a circular current forms and an onyx crown emerges from the inky water. My heart pounds against my chest, and I find it even harder to breathe. The creatures chatter loudly and dance around, their wet robes sticking to their moist skin. Who's in the river? Am I going to be sacrificed to it?

The onyx crown sits on the head of a terrifying woman and she steps out of the river slowly, black water dripping off her gown. I press my knees tighter against my chest. There's no way I can run or fight. With each step she takes, shadows build around her, enveloping her in darkness. Everything goes black for a moment and I can't see where she went. Immense power is emitting from her very skin and up through the frozen ground under me. It sears through me like fire, scorching my already aching body.

When the shadows dissipate, I stare at the woman again. I study her movements. Quick. Agile. Her lean form moves around the bank of the river with ease, and her dress flows like water around her legs. She wears a tattered white gown that clings to her skin, not unlike the robes of the creatures who brought me here.

Her face is as white as snow, clearly beautiful at one time, and her hair is long, black, and stringy. The woman takes her time to stand in front of me, to tower over me. She crouches down and runs her long black cracked fingernail down my shredded cheek. I wince in pain, but keep my eyes on hers. Her eyes are the color of ice– gray blue and clear. She furrows her brow and tilts her head, raking her gaze over every inch of me. My heartbeat races and my breathing becomes even more shallow. This is it. This is the end of it all.

Her creatures begin hissing loudly again as the river's current flows stronger and stronger, the water crashing against the rocks and spraying me with freezing black droplets.

I love you Vera.

It comes from out and not from in. I hear her say, but the voice doesn't come from her mouth. In fact, her mouth doesn't even open. Who is she? *What is she?*

The figures chirp and screech. The woman holds her hand up to silence them. *How does it come from the out, how is it now in?* I shiver as the breeze cuts across my skin and the woman squints her eyes. *You are man?*

I nod my head, my teeth chattering. "Y-y-yes."

She cocks her head from side to side. *How get in?*

"I-wa-was, p-p-p-push-ed," I chatter.

Hmm. She scowls and her breath fogs the air. *I keep you.*

Something cherished, something bright, something
borrowed, something white.
– *Prinavian Marriage Tradition*

CHAPTER 61

VERA

I'm told that Saima is researching the watch and performing a series of spells to confirm if it's truly the Eldertick. A few days go by of me being stuck in my chambers while everyone prepares for my upcoming wedding.

The morning of the ceremony, I slip on my wedding dress. I don't feel like I'm doing the right thing. The dress feels off. The bodice is too tight, and the sleeves cling to me. The dress is understated, at the request of Lucette.

Evalie places a flower crown of baby's breath on my head. "You look wonderful, Vera. Let me show you."

I look in the mirror, she's right. The dress is beautiful, but I don't look like myself. I wonder if every bride feels this way about how they look on their wedding day. Evalie continues to talk, not daring to gaze into the mirror, but I barely register her. I just stare at myself and I wish my mother was here. I shake the thought and turn to Evalie while she fusses with my train, avoiding my reflection at all costs.

"Something cherished, something bright, something borrowed, something white." She says to herself while she ties ribbons in my hair and places earrings in my ears. "There. That's better."

Finn knocks on the door. "It's time, Your Highness."

"Check on Saima, make sure everything is still okay," I whisper in Evalie's ear and hug her as tight as my arms can squeeze.

She squeezes back. "I will." She looks me in the eye. "Leave all the problems in your mind for later. Focus on Calix, focus on your wedding."

I hug her again. "I love you Ev."

"Go on now." She touches my cheek and then drapes the mirror in heavy tapestries before opening the door so Finn can escort me to Gwen Abbey.

Finn leads me through the castle and outside to the cobblestone path that leads to the Abbey. When I see it, I freeze. I don't know if I can do this. It doesn't feel right. My stomach sours as I gaze up at the temple, contemplating running back to my chambers and hiding. Gwen Abbey stares back at me with her massive turrets, intimidating me. The dark stone blocks and stained-glass windows on every wall seem to say, *'liar, cheat, seductress.'*

Sweat rolls down my back as we arrive at the entrance. The doors to the temple are at least twenty feet tall and made of solid wood. There are runes carved into it, and heavy gold handles glint in the sunlight. I feel an ominous aura emitting from the runes. Finn turns to me and his smile fades when our eyes meet.

"Your Highness, are you feeling faint?"

"I'm just—" my head is swimming.

I can't do this. I can't marry Calix.

"It's just cold feet m'lady." He pats my forearm gently. "Totally understandable."

He's right. It's probably just cold feet. I nod at him and take a breath. *Nothing to be afraid of, and nothing to be ashamed of. Calix loves you, and you love him. It's all okay.*

A handful of guards dressed in ceremonial uniforms flank the double doors and nod to me when they see me. I give them a tight smile and take a step closer to the door. When I get closer, I notice a crest embedded in their armor. A fox with its tail wrapped around an Oleander and a small triangle underneath. No, a *V.*

Lieve incorporated me, even in the crest. Lieve never forgot about me, even in the smallest details of his life. My eyes brim with tears. All this time, he remembered me and hoped I would come back to him. I huff and lift my chin. This is my wedding day and I am loved. I am worthy of love. Everything is going to work out, and I'm going to have my own fairytale. Every story has a crazy twist in it, and starting a marriage with the groom under a love spell—well—I guess that's mine..

Not only that, but this wedding is for Lieve too, not just me. I'll finally stop being Lieve's problem, and after the wedding, I'll be the solution to his problems. I'm going through with this wedding for Lieve just as much as I am for me. He's wanted nothing but the best for me, and now I can do what's best for him. I can marry a great man, a man of status who loves me. And for once in his life Lieve can breathe without my loss, or my burdens, strangling his every breath.

The guards open the double doors and music drifts in the large entryway. The floor in the vestibule is covered with a mosaic of Guenivere. Her long red hair swirls around her like a snake while her pale white hands emit sparks onto a tranquil river. The glossy tiles shine when the sun hits them depicting Sol and Dia as babies floating on the edge of the river bank swaddled in moss.

A second set of double doors opens to a second set of royal guards. They wear the same ceremonial uniforms and my heart warms when I see the Oleander coat of arms once again. Notes from a violin spill around me. The tempo is melodic and pours into me, calming me. Finn was right, I'm just nervous. It's all going to be fine.

"They're ready for you, Princess," Finn says and knocks three times on the door. His smile travels to his eyes and the wrinkles in his kind face only make him look kinder. I smile back at him and he takes my hand and softly presses his lips to my fingers, bowing deeply. "Congratulations, m'lady."

Finn then disappears to the shadows, leaving me alone as the guards open the doors to hundreds of people turning to stare at me.

My breath catches.

Everything is going to be fine.

A sea of color illuminated by the sun shining through the stained glass takes my breath away. It's a painting. Light portraying the wedding of Bram and Gwen dances over the guests, casting them as actors in the god's stories. It's just like the hallway to the ball. Each window has sunlight showering a different legend across the room. Everyone's smiling at me as a new song starts to play. At once, the audience stands for me to walk. There are so many nobles in attendance, and I don't recognize a single face in this sea of strangers until I reach the end of the aisle.

On the left side of the pulpit, Lieve and Lucette are seated. Lieve is beaming at me and I give him a wide smile back. Lucette seems content with the number of people in attendance and she nods to someone in the audience and dons a wicked smirk. I can't wait to ruin her. I can't wait to free my brother so she can be banished. She finally locks eyes with me and I smirk back at her, watching as her face hardens like stone. *You have no idea how much I know, you wretched witch.*

I tear my eyes from her and look towards the end of the aisle to Calix. His lips curl into that familiar devilish grin and I can't help but giggle when he winks at me. Calix wears a ceremonial military uniform, stark white with silver studs on the shoulders and down the sides of the legs. His cape is white with silver trim, the beautiful contrast against his tan skin making it hard to breathe. He stands with two Priests in the center of the pulpit.

The first is a woman whose face is covered in tattoos and wears a black cape and hood with red tassles. She smiles at me and sprinkles my face with droplets of salt water from a bowl made of marble. The other is the Priest from the dungeons. Just seeing him sends a shiver down my spine. Fear floods my veins; but, then I realize that it makes sense. Lieve and Lucette would want a royal family member to conduct a royal ceremony. Lieve would never allow me to be in danger, and Lucette wouldn't pull a stunt at a royal wedding.

I step up on the pulpit to join Calix and my heel tugs on my dress. The crowd gasps and the priests wince. Before I fall, Calix steady's me and helps me walk the rest of the way up, gaining an audible *'aww'* from our guests. That simple gesture loosens the knot in my stomach and calms me down. Calix always makes me feel that way. Safe. I was wrong in thinking that this wedding felt off. Everything about him is right. His touch is right. Warm and comforting. I know this marriage is happening faster than he may have planned, but I feel his affection for me in his touch. I hope that when he gets the antidote to the love potion that he will still love me like this.

The female Priest places bowls on the ground around us and sprinkles us both with more water. Calix takes my hands in his, gently rubbing his thumb across the back of my hand. The music stops. My heart races as the Sagart begins the ceremony, speaking in an ancient language and waving his arms around us in a circular pattern.

"On this day, two will unite." He bends down to one bowl and sprinkles us with more water. "The water symbolizes the river where the goddess Dia, and the mortal Oriel, sang their vows. They declared their love, and united in that declaration, that even in death, no god or mortal can break their connection."

Calix kisses my hand as the priest continues. "The couple before us today will recite the holy vows." He looks at Calix. "Repeat after me. I take you into me, as one takes in water."

"I take you into me, as one takes in water."

"I shall remain steady as the river, gentle in good times and bad, and hold strong like the current."

Calix's thumb rubs my hand again. "I shall remain steady as the river, gentle in good times and bad, and hold strong like the current."

"We are complete. Our love as powerful as the gods who made us, and as compassionate as the humans who bore us in this life."

"We are complete. Our love as powerful as the gods who made us, and as compassionate as the humans who bore us in this life." Calix repeats, his voice low and calm.

Baptiste turns to me. "And now you repeat."

I repeat the vows, my heart hammering in my chest with every word. Each line I say makes my voice tremble. But when I look at Cal, he doesn't look nervous. He doesn't seem hesitant at all. I know he's under a potion right now, but he seems steady. Certain. Cal's smile reaches his golden eyes and they twinkle when a sunray flicks across his face. He squeezes my hand as I repeat the last line of the vows.

"Now, one final ritual before the sealment with a kiss," the Priest says.

He and the Priestess roll out something large, covered in white linens. They place it behind us, facing the audience. Everyone seated in the pews looks curiously at the object, murmuring and whispering to each other. Everyone, except for Lucette.

The Priest then pulls a dagger from his robes and I jump. What's going on? This dagger isn't like any I've seen before. It's transparent glass or maybe crystal, and has a hilt of solid gold. Calix gives the Priest his hand while the crowd whispers to each other. They all look confused. A small cut on Cal's palm opens and a few drops of blood land in the brass bowl on the floor between us. The Priest wraps Calix's hand in a white cloth and then cleans the dagger with the water from the third bowl and turns to me, palm up, waiting for my hand.

This isn't right. I hesitate, but when my eye catches Lieve's and he nods at me. Warily, I place my hand in the Priest's palm and close my eyes, waiting for the tip of the dagger to pierce my skin.

Lieve wouldn't allow me to do something that wasn't safe.

The Priest punctures my palm and I wince. My hand is squeezed until enough drops of blood land in the bowl, mixing with Cal's. The female Priest wraps my hand in another white cloth as she whispers prayers to the gods. Calix smiles at me, but the excitement doesn't reach his eyes this time. He looks different. He feels different.

This is wrong.

"Now, seal your vows with a kiss, and may your marriage be bonded by blood," the Priests bellows.

No.

Something isn't right. I back away, but Calix grabs my arm forcefully and slams his lips to mine. I push him off, and at the same time, the Priests unveil what lies underneath the white linens. A massive mirror. He then grabs the bowls with our blood and splashes the mixture across the glass. Then thunder, *tremendous thunder*, makes everyone jump, followed by a loud cracking sound that rattles the ancient windows and someone in the crowd shrieks.

The wedding guests stand up, trying to escape the temple. I panic and look into the mirror as waves form on the glass, just like the night in my chambers. The waves continue to grow larger and I know I need to get out of here. We all need to get out of here. I try to run but Calix still clutches my arm, his fingers wrapped around me, nails digging into my flesh. I tug and tug, desperate to escape, but he won't budge.

"Cal, we have to get out of here!"

I look over to Lieve for help, but he's only smiling eerily at me. Then, the waves in the mirror crash and what can only be described as a gong rings out. I watch the mirror in horror as faces with black eyes and evil smirks appear behind the fluid glass. Dozens of Doppelgangers, no *hundreds*, then flood the abbey like a tidal wave. Screams pierce my ears as I struggle to break free of Cal's grip.

"Calix, let go!"

"Vera, dear," he breathes, "everything is perfectly fine."

I snap my head around and our eyes meet. My mouth goes dry as I watch Cal's eyes flash black. I shriek, and Calix laughs as I try to free myself. I punch, kick, bite. But I can't make him let go. Calix grabs my chin and forces me to look him in the eye. I feel like I'm looking into an emotionless void. A soulless creature, a shell of a man.

"You–you *tricked* me."

"No, my darling." He plants a kiss on my lips. "You're the one who tricked *me*."

"Lieve!" I scream.

I frantically look towards where Lieve sits across the pulpit and a wave of horror freezes me. Lieve is looking at me, not in fear, but in *joy*. A fiendish grin spreads across his face and then *his* eyes flash black too.

No.

Lucette doesn't move. She looks scared but doesn't dare even flinch.

This can't be happening.

I scream again, loud enough to shred my throat. *"Lieve!"*

Then out of nowhere, something, no *someone,* knocks Calix off me. A metal chain is looped around my neck, with something glowing bright blue hanging from it, and then I'm swept off my feet. *Arden.* I press my eyes shut and curl my body tightly to his and let him carry me.

"Close your eyes."

I don't have time to ask why, or even think about what he's going to do, because Arden shoulders past the Priests, and I hear him knock them to the ground. Then he jumps with me still in his arms and I squeeze my eyes shut as hard as I can because Arden and I dive headfirst into the mirror.

Vera...Daphne...Calix...Narah...Finn...
— *Memories of Lieve Oleander*

CHAPTER 62

LIEVE

The woman from the river studies every inch of me and discovers my stab wound. Her fingers curl in a fluid motion over the wound and my skin is pulled back together. The pain of her healing is nearly unbearable and stars shoot behind my eyes as I crumple to the ground. The woman's blurry outline comes back into focus and she's studying me as I writhe before her.

She drags her broken nail across my cheek again, but I don't feel her scratch. I feel skin growing. Heat blooms across my skin and again stars explode behind my eyes. I throw up watery liquid and it freezes to my lips and chin, crusting like frost. The three hooded figures drag me to my feet. My legs wobble when they let me go, but somehow I'm able to stay upright.

Swaying back and forth and shivering in the cold, I stare at the woman. Her expression seems curious. She flicks her wrist, sparks pouring from her fingers, and I can feel a tiny trickle of warmth spread across my body. Maybe I can live. If she's healing me, maybe she'll help me get back. I need to play nice, this might work out for me. It's not impossible. Maybe this woman, these creatures, aren't evil. Maybe...maybe...

"Thank you," I whisper as my breath fills the air.

The three figures hiss, "*Thank you, thank you, thank you.*"

Name? She asks.

"L-L-Liev-v-ve," I shiver. "K-k-king of P-P-Pr-Pr-ina-v-v."

Her eyes widen and her pupils dilate. Her warm sparks dissolve into the dead grass and all hope of living dissolves with them. The woman's mouth tightens to a hard line and she points to the inky water. *Get in river.*

My heart races. I shake my head and step backwards. If I get in the water I'll surely freeze to death. I'll never get back to Daphne. I'll never find Calix or Vera or Arden. I can't get in the water.

Get in river, she commands again.

"No, p-p-please."

"*Please, please, please,*" the creatures hiss.

The woman tilts my chin up with her finger and her breath coils in the air as she uses her mouth to whisper softly, "Get in water."

I slide my robe off my shoulders, letting the heavy fabric pool around my feet. She removes her finger from my chin and pulls me to the bank of the river. The chill penetrates my skin, freezing me to the bone the minute my robe hits the ground. I plead with her to reconsider but she doesn't reply, she only flicks her eyes to the water. The creatures push me and I fall to my knees.

Shaliky, I stand back up. I scan the trees around me, trying to determine what path would be the best one to try and flee, but when I turn to run but one of the creatures grabs me by the shoulders, it's slimy fingers digging into my flesh. Its nails are sharp and they puncture my skin and graze across the muscle as they spin me back toward the river.

The creature lets go of me and pushes me forward. I take shallow breaths and lean back against it, but the creature is strong. The woman steps in the river as fog rises to the surface. Hesitantly, I put one foot in the water and watch in horror as frost climbs up to my knee. I beg her to let me go again, but she shakes her head no. I place my other foot in the river and the frost is now up to my waist. The woman smiles.

Frost continues to climb my body, now lying just under my chin. I'm frozen in place, the ice forming around my limbs and keeping me still. The woman cocks her head from side to side again, and chatters to the creatures. I open my mouth to protest the cold, to beg her to spare me, but then the woman pushes my frozen body into the inky black abyss.

~

Days, weeks, months, maybe even years go by. There's no way of knowing how long I've been here. The Twinning Witch from the river was true to her word. She kept me. I've been by her side, day and night, since the moment she emerged from the water.

The day I was submerged in the river is hard to remember. Bits and pieces of my memories eroded or were attached to memories that I know aren't connected. I get flashes of Shadow Grove in my mind, flashes of Hal lying in a pool of his own blood, of an arrow lodged in King Niall's eye socket, and of my Doppelganger. I see him walk through the mirror and steal my life.

But then, those flashes are gone, replaced by hazy segments of memories surrounding Calix. Eating fruit with him in the forest, attending his wedding, bunking together in the Hode. I try to assemble the fragments of thoughts scattered in my mind and I see Vera's face. Her looking at me, confused, in front of the Lopter Tree. Vera at ten-years-old running barefoot through a Lady's manor. Vera giggling at my tall tales and begging me to read to her. Vera just being with me.

Then Daphne floods my mind, heavy and aching and consuming me. Talking about the future, learning magic from her. Kissing her. I have to force myself from those thoughts because dwelling on them, knowing I'll never see her again, is too hard to bear. At first I would try and forget. I had the thimble of Lopter's blood still in my pocket when I entered into this backward land, and I downed the bottle at once, hoping it would just kill me. It didn't. All that bottle did was show me a war, dark and bloody. A war where magic was used as a weapon. A war where Vera fought. I was sick when I woke up from those visions, and prayed to the gods that Daphne was wrong about the blood, that Lopter was wrong.

I walk in silence daily with the woman from the river, the Twinning Witch. She allows me to learn her magic. Sparks fly from her broken nails, and she shows me how to emit sparks from my own fingertips. She teaches me to conjure objects and mold things out of thin air. I've learned to levitate, and to use religious humming to pull power into my veins. I'm powerful in this place and I wonder if I really *am* the Conductor of Death. I'm learning magic quickly. Easily. It's like the power flows through me, consumes me, *is* me. It's much easier to control than Daphne's Fae spells.

Eventually the Twinning Witch lets me wander off alone. I memorize the paths in the forest and bathe in the inky river. My skin soaks in the water and I see my complexion pale. I'm looking like the witch more and more everyday, and everyday I *want* to more and more.

It's like I hate her, and I love her. I can't separate my emotions and it's all jumbled up inside my head. I get angry that I can't organize my thoughts, and I go on long walks alone and try to tell myself stories. I recite the stories of the gods, I recount my memories with Vera, Calix, Daphne, Narah, Arden, Finn...I say their names out loud so I don't forget. Everyday it gets harder to remember who I am, and where I am. I've carved my memories on the trunks of the dead trees, into the stones on the ground, the rock walls, everywhere. I want to remember. I have to remember.

Sometimes I see Daphne's copper hair flowing behind her as she's running through the lifeless forest. I tell myself it isn't her, but over time it's harder to believe it. I run after Daphne in the forest everyday, but when I catch her, she evaporates. I've tried freezing her image so she can't leave me again, but it doesn't work.

I sleep in huts I conjure along the riverbed, and at night, *every night*, I can hear Vera's voice. She drifts through the hut and asks me for more stories, more tales. So instead of sleeping, I recount fairy tales to my invisible sister.

"Then the goddess Dia seals herself away forever."

"Forever." Vera's voice wraps around me and I smile before I can finally sleep.

The days carry on like this. Chasing Daphne during the day, and talking to Vera at night. There are days that I even believe Arden is here, throwing axes into the dead trees and attempting to hunt in this barren land. Although the Twinning Witch allows me to roam freely, I don't roam far. I fear getting lost here as my thoughts are so displaced that it's too hard to keep track of the paths and there isn't a morsel of food to be found. The Witch keeps me alive with black water and magic.

I find more creatures in this desolate wasteland. Hunched-back men with holes for eyes and needle-like teeth, black horses with red eyes, black death beetles, and butterflies with poisoned wings. Thousands of hooded figures come and go. They worship the Twinning Witch, fear her, and love her. Overtime, I think I'm becoming one of them. I, too have grown to worship her, fear her, and depend on her.

One afternoon of wandering Shallon, as the hooded figures call it, I see an archway. It's the first alteration in the bleak landscape I've seen since my arrival. I hide behind a tree as white sparks sprinkle the ground around the arch, just like the sparks from the witch. I peer around the tree trunk to see if someone is coming into this world, and why they would ever want to.

In the archway is a somewhat transparent door, and I see *Calix*. He's tied to a chair in a tiny stone walled room. *Is it really him?* It can't be. I look at him, and he seems different. He's disheveled and thin. I don't remember him looking like that, so this can't be real, can it?

Then he screams, and I know that voice.

I want to go to him, but I swear it's just a hallucination. I'm haunted by visions of my friends almost daily. This is surely just my mind coming up with another new torment.

But then a delicate hand forces a mouthful of something down Calix's throat and he coughs and sputters in protest. Lucette. Calix turns his head and his eyes widen when he—*sees me?* Is that possible? I run to the arch and reach my hand out to touch him, save him, but I'm too late. Sparks fall to the ground at my feet, sizzle, and disappear; along with Cal.

CHAPTER 63

VERA

Arden lands on top of me on the frigid ground. The wind is knocked out of me and my elbow throbs from the impact. My ribs ache. I keep my eyes squeezed shut as I try to piece together what just happened. Arden pushes his body up a little so he isn't crushing me and I finally open my eyes. We stare at each other and breathe in silence. The tendrils of our breath mix together and then rise like smoke from a fire. He unloops the chain from around our necks, and I see that it's the chain of the pocket watch. No, the *Eldertick*–and it's still glowing.

Arden stands and holds his hand out to help me up. "Are you okay?"

I grip his hand and look around us as he pulls me to my feet. We're in a dark forest in the dead of winter. Everything is dank and gray. Lifeless. Frost covers the earth and the spindly branches of dead trees that surround us. I'm not okay, but I'm alive. So I nod at him and wrap my arms around myself, holding back the hot tears burning for release.

I shiver as a gust of bitter wind cuts through the lace of my gown. My hands are already beginning to chap so I stuff my fingers under my armpits. We need to get back. We'll die in this unnatural cold. Arden removes his cloak and drapes it over my shoulders. I want to protest, but a wedding dress is no match for this frost. My fingers snatch the heavy fabric and greedily wrap the cloak tightly around my trembling body.

"Calix and Lieve are both Doppelgangers." He says.

I nod.

Arden shakes his head and his eyes scan our surroundings. "I should have realized."

Hot tears burn my skin as they slide down my cheeks, freezing in the air before they even hit the ground. I turn away from him so he can't see me cry. "Lieve is my brother, I'm the one who should have been able to see it." *I am stupid, just like you thought I was the second we met.*

Arden doesn't reply. I pull the hood of his cape over my head to hide my tears as Arden paces in circles, mumbling to himself and thinking out loud. We need to get back to the other side of the mirror. My mind races. *What's happened to Lieve? To Evalie? Poppy?* My breathing becomes ragged and it's harder and harder to inhale. What if they've died?

I watch Arden prowl around the edge of the tree line as he makes a sweep of the area. "I'll be right back, I need to check our perimeter." He states before disappearing into a foggy path.

I close my eyes and I listen to the sound of his steps, praying that he doesn't leave me here, praying that he does. I would deserve it. My heart races when he doesn't come back immediately. After a few minutes of waiting, I step onto the foggy path he wandered down, but I can't force myself to follow. Could there be worse creatures than Darkthings wandering these dead woods?

He's taking too long and there's no sight of him. I strain to listen for him over the hum building in my ears but I hear nothing. There's no sound of his boots patting the frigid ground, no swords whistling through the air, no branches snapping under Arden's step. Fog hangs between the trees so thick I can't see more than a few feet in front of me. He's left me here. He's left me here alone to freeze to death.

I walk deeper into the path, but I still can't make out anything through the cloud of gray. *Is Arden okay?* Something putrid fills my nostrils, so I back up and my foot slips into a puddle of thick, black, blood. I gag at the foul odor and turn sideways but I stumble upon a decapitated head. Its hollow eyes are sucked tightly against its skull and its lips are stretched over hundreds of needle-like teeth. *What is that?* Then a blood curdling screech pierces the air as metal crunches bone.

"Arden!"

"Vera!"

Relief floods my veins. He's okay. I run towards the sound of his voice until I see Arden. He's stepping over grotesque bodies, shouting for me between thrusting his blade into the last of the creature's skulls. I race through the blood and flesh until I reach him. Upon seeing me, he sighs deeply, wrapping his arm around me as I break down and cry into his chest.

Once we'd both settled down, Arden finds a path devoid of fog and we walk. I don't know what to say, and Arden doesn't speak to me either. He walks while holding the Eldertick up to his face and inspecting it carefully. The metal has a light layer of frost covering it, and the ice is now covering Arden's fingertips.

"How did you get that?" I whisper, just in case we're being followed. "I thought you were in Teyrnas with Daphne."

"I never left."

I stare at him and he continues. "I stayed with Saima, deciding where I wanted to go. When Poppy showed up, I was talking to Saima about my wish to talk to you–" He shakes his head. "It took a couple days, but Saima confirmed this was the Eldertick, and Soleil got it working again somehow. We went to the dungeon to see if we could look behind the wall, and Evalie was already waiting for us. Saima wound the dials on the watch and an arched passage opened in the brick. Calix–*the real Calix*–was inside, tied to a chair."

The *real* Calix. My Calix? "He was in the walls?"

"For *years.*"

Years. *In the walls.*

I put my hand on my chest. "So the eyes flashing black were real, the Calix I married–"

"The Calix you *knew,*" Arden says gently. "Calix was replaced before Lieve had even become King."

The words impale my heart. *Everyone I love is an imposter.*

Tears stream down my face and freeze to my cheeks. I don't know what's real and what's imagined. I don't know where we are or how to get back home. Arden may be with me, but I'm alone. I hug my knees and rock back and forth on the ground. Bitter cold slices my legs through the thin fabric of my wedding gown, even with Arden's heavy cloak draped over me.

I'm still wearing that wedding gown. A gown that binds me to a Doppelganger. A murderer. I start ripping the skirts with my bare hands.

"Stop," Arden shouts, trying to still my hands. "You need the layers, it's freezing."

I snap my head to him. "I don't care."

"Calm down."

"I suppose you're looking for me to kiss your boots in thanks," I say and turn my back to him. Anger burns in my chest, at Arden, and at myself. Because in all honesty, I *should* be thanking him.

But I can see it in my mind. Calix tied to a rickety chair inside the stone walls and the relief he must have felt when he was let out. Then a wave of hope turns into fear, washing over me. *What about Lieve.*

"Was Lieve in there too?"

"No, but when I realized that the Calix you were about to marry was a Dop, I ran to Gwen Abbey. I just wrapped the chain around us and jumped, I–"he sigs–, "I had to get to you."

I swallow hard as Arden's eyes meet mine. Arden came for me. Arden saved me. He always saves me. I take a deep breath and open my mouth to say something but I take too long to reply and Arden huffs and turns his head. We stay in silence and I try to think through a headache that has creeped its way to my temples. Arden rubs his thumb on the pocket watch, lost in his own thoughts.

"Can the watch bring us back to Brone Castle?" I ask.

"I think so."

"We should try."

"Calix said he hasn't seen the real Lieve in years. Lucette, Mimic Calix, and Mimic Lieve, have been coming to feed him everytime he rings a bell."

"A bell?"

Arden nods. "A bell magically connected to the church bells."

Those damned bells.

"So the erratic schedule they rang at–"

Arden's eyes darken. " I've been listening to those fucking bells for years, and it was the sound of Calix starving." Arden's fists clench around the watch. "I hate myself for hating him all these years."

"Why did you hate him at all?"

"I was sure he killed Narah, and I was right. Calix *did* kill my sister, just not the real one."

Arden shivers and I don't know if it's because of the cold, or because of guilt. I hate that he's feeling this way. I hate that the real Calix has been suffering. I hate that I don't know if my brother is safe, or even alive. I hate being in Prinav in the first place. Now I understand why Lieve never brought me here.

We sit in silence again, but then Arden says, "Saima, Soleil, Poppy, Evalie, Marguerite, and Calix are on their way to Teyrnas to ask for

Daphne's help, and the help of their Kingdom. Florian set out to Madoria to rally his troops. This was a coup years in the making and I should be there."

"We should get back, it doesn't look like Lieve is here. He would have given me signs, markings." I say.

Arden nods and then tells me what Saima says about using the watch to go from realm to realm, and I try to remember what I read about the Eldertick in my giant stack of books. We both plant our feet in the ground while Arden slings the chain around our necks and hands me the watch. I wind the dial of the Eldertick, but the dial cracks in the cold, snapping off like a piece of ice. It's broken. The dial is broken.

We're stuck in the mirror.

"Shit." Arden breathes.

My breath becomes ragged and shallow. "What do we do?"

Arden lowers his mask, his expression defeated. "I have no idea."

We scramble to find the dial on the ground and I try to put it back on the Eldertick, but nothing works. I unlock the clasp on the side and sift through the faces of the watch, willing the Eldertick to do something–anything–to get us back. I try over and over to fix it, but my hands are too shaky from the cold and the gears too delicate.

Then a twig snaps just a few yards away. Arden pulls out a hatchet from his belt and moves in front of me before spreading his arms out wide, covering my body as much as he can. His knuckles turn white as he grips the handle of his weapon. Something is coming.

Like phantoms, a group of strange figures peek out from the trees. Each one dressed in white robes that drape and cling to the wet, graying skin of the creature wearing it. The hems are stained and shredded from moving around through the forest. Their sleeves retract, revealing limbs that look nothing like living flesh. Their hands are moistened, like slime in stagnant water, and remind me of the rotting corpses Lieve and I would sometimes encounter in the canals of Adamston.

They chirp at one another, but Arden doesn't let them finish their devilish sounding conversation. He launches his hatchet, my eyes following the blade as it leaves his hand and lands sharply in the skull of the nearest hooded monster. The second it splits bone, the rest jump at Arden.

They claw and scratch at him, and Arden uses his bare hands to snap one of their necks. Some of them notice me and come my way. I turn to run and it grabs me, the slimy skin of its fingers wrapping tightly around my wrist. I hear a blade whistle through the air and land with a wet thump in my attacker's back.

The creature lets me go, just as I hear Arden wail in pain. He's defeated the rest of them except one monster. The bloodthirsty demon climbs on him and one takes off its white hood, bearing the same needle-like teeth as the decapitated head I stumbled across before. It leans down and bites Arden, and I hear flesh being torn. I scramble to turn over the creature with the weapon in it's back and see that it's a dagger.

I yank and it flies out, spraying me in thick, black blood. I roar as I launch myself onto the creature over Arden and stab the dagger through the back of its head. The creature crumples to the side with me on its back.

Arden reaches for me and pulls me close to him, breathing heavily.

I pull away from him and crouch over his body to inspect the wound and find blood pouring from a large gash on his upper arm. It's deep, but I don't see bone. *Thank the gods.* I lift the hem of my dress and rip a large section of fabric.

"This will hurt," I warn him, and wrap the torn cloth around his bicep tightly, pulling it hard so it binds his arm and staunches the flow of blood. "Is that okay?"

"It'll do." He tightens the bandage even further. "Are you alright?"

"Yes."

"You saved me."

"I had to repay the favor someday, right?"

Our eyes meet and he clears his throat. "We should get out of here in case there are more of them."

I help him to his feet, happy we agree on something for once. My ears prick to the sound of robes rustling the ground. *There are more of them.* Arden must have heard it too because we both snap our heads to the noise. From behind a dead tree comes a girl, but she's not human. It's a Doppelganger. And she looks just like *me.*

My Doppelganger smiles and waves like she always does. I walk around Arden towards her, but Arden scrambles to step in front of me.

He lifts his arm to throw his hatchet at her, but I grab his wrist before he lets go of the blade.

"Wait," I plead and walk around him slowly as the girl cocks her head from side to side, staring at me knowingly.

"Vera–," Arden grits his teeth–, "get out of the way, I don't want to hit you."

"This is going to sound crazy, but I think she's here to help me."

"She isn't, she's a–"

"I know what she is. And this isn't like the Darkthings. I've interacted with her before."

"Tell me you haven't," he growls.

"She saved me from Lucette in the dungeons, and she showed me how to use the watch." I keep walking to her. "Maybe she can help get us out of here. Maybe that's what she's trying to do right now."

"Even if she isn't dangerous, *which she is,*" Arden says, "you can't be near your own Dop for very long before they leech the life out of you."

My Doppelganger turns from us and wanders deeper into the forest. Arden and I look at each other and I raise my eyebrows at him, pleading to follow.

He lets out a sigh. "Fine. But we keep our distance."

I don't know if she knows if we're following her or not. She repeats the same chirps and hisses that the creatures did, and seems to be following a path with no predetermined destination.

"We should just go back," Arden whispers.

"Can I try to talk to her?"

Arden looks around while we walk, his shoulders hunching, and I can see every option turning over in his mind. "Try."

I clear my throat and my Dop stops walking but doesn't turn around, she just stares ahead into the mold covered paths.

"Um, Vera?" I call.

She turns around and looks at us hissing, "*Vera, Vera, Vera.*"

I take a deep breath. "Can you help us get out of here?"

"*Out of here, out of here, out of here.*"

Arden huffs. "This is pointless, let's go."

"Just a little longer, please."

"No," Arden commands. "We should go back."

Arden turns away and I open my mouth to argue with him, hoping I can talk him into continuing to follow my Dop, when she says something that stops me in my tracks. "*I need to sleep, Vera, go to bed, I need to sleep, Vera, go to bed, I need to sleep, Vera, go to bed.*"

I tug on Arden's hand. "Lieve used to say that to me when I'd beg for more fairytales." I clutch my chest and try to take a few shallow breaths. "Lieve is here."

Arden's eyes widen and he points at a carving cut deep into the nearest tree. It's an L and a V, just like the carvings Lieve has always made for me. Arden runs his fingers over the letters. "Then let's find him."

The quest for knowledge can be all consuming, driving us to seek more, even when we don't know what we're searching for. Beware.

– Fayleen, Second Scribe to the Fledglings

CHAPTER 64

LIEVE

I sit in the same spot for hours, maybe even days, waiting on the arch to come back so I can see Calix again. I throw my sparks where I remember the arch being visible, and sometimes I can see its outline, but it quickly disappears. I become fixated on finding him, but I don't even know if it's really him that I saw. I can't trust my own eyes in this place. The water that keeps me alive is slowly fogging my thoughts, and I'm starting to suspect that it isn't water that I'm drinking.

Every night when I return to the hut to sleep, or tell Vera stories rather, I think about him. Even though my thoughts are hazy, my visions of Calix seem solid. If he *is* real, I cannot tell the Twinning Witch. If he's real, I think she could free him of his captivity, but she won't. She would undoubtedly kill him for being in this place. I think I'm the first person to *'come in from the out'*, and I don't think she would think kindly of a second guest.

If what I'm seeing is real, Calix is being held as a hostage. At least he isn't dead. It might be better if he's dead if I can't think of a way to get through that arch. Maybe Calix *is* dead and I'm getting visions of him in the underworld of Ciel. Maybe I'm in Ciel. Maybe *I'm* dead.

I'm going to leave the rock wall and not come back. I can't get out. I can't save Calix. I can't save anyone. If I stay away, then Shallon might allow me to forget quicker and not be in pain any longer. I won't miss them anymore. I pull the empty vial of Lopter's blood from my pocket to leave it on the ground, and my heart races when I see there's still a drop left in the tiny bottle.

If I can't go back, then I want to forget. I want to forget them all. If I can't go back, I want to belong here, and I have to drain the bottle so I won't be shown any more visions in the future. I hope Lopter is merciful and the visions are short. With shaking hands I pull the cork from the vial and let the last drop of Lopter's blood land on my tongue and pray to the gods to remove my memories.

The gods comply.

$\sim$

My nails are bleeding when I wake up. It's happened for the last several weeks, and I can't remember what I've done. *I'll have to dip my hands in the water again.* Sighing, I drape my heavy fur lined cloak around my shoulders and step out of my hut and onto the rocky bank of the ink river.

Fog rises from the surface and the mist stings my fingertips. I take a deep breath and squeeze my eyes shut before dropping to my knees at the river's edge and thrusting my hands into the icy water. Frost nips my skin, climbing higher and higher until it reaches my elbows. I bite the inside of my cheek to prevent myself from screaming as the black water mends my fingers with blinding pain. I count down from ten. That's how long it takes for the skin and nails to be healed. Ten seconds.

Ten.

The bitter cold bites the skin of my arms, climbing higher and higher.

Nine.

Sharp rocks dig into my knees.

Eight.

I take a deep breath so that when the ice freezes my chest, I can exhale and then inhale again without suffocating.

Seven.

My neck goes rigid with cold.

Six.

It's almost over.

Five.

I clench my fists as hard as I can to break the ice that's formed around my fingers.

Four.

The ice cracks all the way up to my neck and I push my arms together and a massive chunk falls off and splashes in the water.

Three.

Slowly I start to pull my hands near the surface, wiggling my fingers as I move so they don't re-freeze.

Two.

My teeth chatter and my body shakes uncontrollably.

One.

I pull my hands out and lay on my back on the bank of the river. My fingers are tender and pink, like new skin has grown over the split and cracked layers. I pull my cloak around me and wince when my fingertips touch the heavy fabric.

A hiss whispers in the breeze. *They're back.* With stinging hands, I push myself up to greet them. Cloaked figures glide over the rubble on the ground, the trains of their stained garments swirling dust around their feet. The tallest one bows, clicking and chirping and the others follow.

"Lessons, lessons, lessons," the tallest hisses.

The Twinning Witch wants to teach me more magic. I walk over to the massive stone wall on the other side of the river, which hides an entrance to a grand labyrinth. Miles and miles of jagged stone, vegetation, bones, and glass, lead you to the Twinning Witch's palace.

For as long as I can remember, I've been memorizing the path. I spend my days following markings along the way, and for each lesson I appear in front of the Witch faster and faster.

A marking in the rock catches my eye. There's blood in the carving and it looks rather fresh. A shiver runs down my spine. *I did it again.* I've been finding new carvings stained with blood on days where I've had to heal my hands in the ink river. I think I've been scratching my fingers to the bone, carving things to tell myself something, but it's useless. I can't remember what I've done or why, only that I have a new image I can't understand.

I run my finger in the crevice of the carving and it's shaped like an archway. Dots are sprinkled around the edge of the arch and at the bottom, reminding me of the sparks that the Twinning Witch, and sometimes myself, create when dispelling magic. A pang in my chest makes me yearn to know what the arch means, why I crave the answer.

The creatures click and I'm pulled from my thoughts. I heed their warning, continuing into the labyrinth, but before I round the corner, something catches my eye. I look back to the entrance and squint. It looks like there's a new carving there. I shake my head and move on. There's always a new carving.

Nothing is Real. Go Back.
– *Unknown*

CHAPTER 65
VERA

A rden and I follow my Doppelganger through a maze of narrow pathways in the woods, each one littered with Lieve's carvings. I watch her feet fumble around in the brush as I try to memorize the path. I have no idea if this was the right decision. I have no idea if this is a trick, but I have to try. If there's a chance Lieve is stuck in this place, I have to save him.

"This seems familiar," Arden whispers, his eyes not leaving my Doppelganger.

"How so?"

I watch her too, but I make sure to scan the surrounding trees for other carvings, and threats, like Lieve always taught me. Learn. Adapt. Memorize.

Arden pushes his mask up to help keep in what little heat your breath creates and shrugs. "It's like a dead Shadow Grove."

I look around with new eyes. He's right.

The Mimic leads us to a rocky bank next to a calm river filled with jet black water. At least, I think it's water. It's so dark it reflects the sky and woods around it, absorbing the images and soaking them into its memory. This river must teem with magic. I can feel a tingle in the air, strong and electric.

Arden eyes our new companion as she uses her wobbly legs to climb onto a large tree that had fallen over the water and balances herself unsteadily until she reaches the other side. She stops for a moment and turns to look at us.

Arden crosses over the river with ease. I step on the log and my foot slips on the dewy surface, forcing me to my hands and knees. My fingers are red and chapped, and getting colder by the minute. I look up at Arden and shake my head. *I can't do this.*

"You can do this, Vera," Arden shouts from the other side, "Lieve needs us."

"Needs us, needs us, needs us," my Doppelganger echoes, eerily.

Lieve needs me. So I crawl. My fingers grip the bark and I slide my knees one at a time over the log, the tingle of magic buzzing in my ear until I reach the bank on the other side.

I'm dizzy with fear, and with the overwhelming sensation of tingles and static running through my veins. The Dop chirps just beyond the tree line, so Arden and I follow her until we end at a wall of rock. It's not smooth like the stone wall near the entrance to Shallon, this rock is ancient and jagged.

"It's a maze." Arden says.

He's right.

It's an entrance to a labyrinth with red splotches dotting the wall. My Doppelganger peeks her head out and watches me scan the rock. She steps close to me, close enough that I can notice little things about her now. She looks remarkably similar to me. The same hair and eye color. The same lips and light dusting of freckles across her nose.

But this version of me looks tired. Worn. Barely alive. She points to one of the red splotches on the wall. I wave Arden over. The red splotches are stains. Blood stains.

The nearest carving is an arch of some sort. Around the curve and at the foot of the arch are dots– like *sparks.*

"Lieve used to carve things everywhere for me," I whisper. "To track him, to map things, warn me of danger." I look Arden in the eye. "These *must* be from him."

Arden taps the carving. "That looks like the arch we found Calix in. Maybe Lieve saw him."

Our footsteps are the only sound I hear as we follow my Dop through the endless maze. Lieve's carvings continue, but they're getting further and further apart. They become cruder, and each one we find makes less and less sense.

The jagged rocks are roughly twenty feet high on each side of the maze, and limbs of dead trees hang over the top. I pull Arden's cloak tighter around me as a breeze rustles my skirts, cutting my legs with its sharp chill. My Doppelganger doesn't seem affected by the cold, she just walks on unsteady legs through the path, turning corners left and right without a thought.

The sky is turning from a drab gray, to a dark gray. Night is coming and Arden's wound is bleeding again, but there's no shelter. The maze is a dirt path riddled with divots and towering walls on either side. We're exposed to anything that may find us in the night.

Once the sky is drained of color and our surroundings become hazy silhouettes, Arden, my Doppelganger, and I, sit with our backs against the jagged rock wall. I tear another scrap of fabric from the hem of my skirt and change it out for the soiled one wrapped around Arden's arm. Even in the dark, I can make out Arden's eyes watching me mend his wound the best I can. They're darting from my hands, to my lips, to my eyes.

I tighten the shabby bandage and he grabs my hand. "We'll find him."

I nod and stifle my tears before scooting closer to him. We're close enough that I can feel the heat from his body radiate towards me, and I can't tell if it's a conscious movement or not when I scoot close enough for our arms to touch. Another breeze sweeps around us, the labyrinth walls holding in the cold air around us longer.

I shiver and pull my hood up, wrapping the cloak around me like a blanket. Arden fidgets for a moment before wrapping his arm around me and I sink into his warmth. I curl my legs to my chest and turn, letting my head melt into his shoulder. Another breeze whips my hood down and I start shivering.

Arden pulls me into his lap, squeezing my body tightly against his to conserve heat. My muscles tremble, and when the breeze dissipates, I'm still shuddering under Arden's heavy cloak. Whispers and laughter echo throughout the labyrinth, and my eyes jerk open each time I hear it. Arden moves his head back and forth, watching for anything to appear before us as my Doppelganger whistles the tune Lieve made for me.

I feel my thoughts becoming muddled, like every note she sings is stealing little pieces from me. I want to tell her to stop, my eyes are becoming heavy and I need to help Arden keep watch. But as darkness takes over the maze, I can't fight to stay awake because memories of Lieve flood my mind and I'm nearly drifting off to sleep.

"How long do you think night lasts in this place?" I whisper.

Arden looks to the sky, examining the tiny glittering stars and replies. "Too long."

~

Arden doesn't sleep. The dark is too dark, the danger too close, the cold too cold. Arden and I shiver against each other while my Doppelganger repeats phrases, clicks and chips, and scrapes her nails against the rock we lean on. The sounds are harsh and irritating in the newfound silence and driving me mad, but I think she's doing it to keep us awake and safe. When the first glimpse of dank, gray, light appears over the wall, I uncurl from Arden's arms and stand. We made it through the night, and I pray Lieve did too.

My Doppelganger seems pleased that we've begun to stir and leaves us behind to continue the maze. We're so cold and she is so far ahead, that we have to work to catch up to her. My arms and legs are stiff, and my chest aches with each inhale of glacial air. I spot more of Lieve's carvings stained with his blood. There are fingernails stuck in some of the crevices and I fight back tears when I realize he's been wounding himself to make a map. He's bleeding himself dry to stay alive.

Finally, the solid wall of rock ends and we reach a stretch of towering brambles on either side. I try to see what's on the other side of the wall, but the branches are too thick. Arden squints to try and see as well, but he shakes his head. Nothing. We must keep walking.

"*Vera, Vera, Vera,*" the Mimic hisses at me when we've stopped for too long.

She rounds a corner of brush and the path forks. On one side is smooth glass, fluid and shiny. The other is a tunnel of bleached bones that arch across a dark path. The hair on the back of my neck stands on end as my Doppelganger heads down the bone path.

"Should we continue to follow her?" I ask Arden.

He furrows his brow and looks from the glass to the bones, "I'm not sure." He takes a step and stands in front of the glass, his reflection staring back at him. His eyes grow wide and dart back and forth, like he's watching a battle before him. He pulls out his hatchet, gripping the handle tightly. Then Arden drops the hatchet and falls to his knees. He stares at the glass for a few seconds, broken words choking from his mouth and then he cradles his head in his hands and sobs.

I run into the path of glass and kneel in front of Arden. When I place a hand on his shoulder he recoils and looks at me with angry eyes.

"Leave me." He snaps. "Just let me stay with them."

I look around but the path is empty. "Arden," I say and gently place my hand on his shoulder again, "no one is here but you and me."

"No–," he says and points at the glass–, "they're here, they're here."

I look in the glass and only see the two of us. *This must be like the Darkthings, making you see things that aren't there.* My Doppelganger steps onto the glass path and looks at me with wide eyes, like she's urging me to move on.

"Arden, we have to go now," I murmur. "It's only you and I here, and we must save Lieve, remember?"

He drops his hands to his side and leans his head on my shoulder. "You really can't see them? My sister? My parents?"

My heart breaks and I sigh. "No, I can't see them."

"Am I going mad?"

"I think it's like the Darkthings, manipulating your vision." I push him from me so I can look in his eyes.

"Narah," he whispers. "My Narah."

My lip trembles. "I'm so sorry."

Arden shakes his head and takes a deep breath and I hold my hand out to him. He picks his weapon from the ground and then accepts my outstretched hand.

Before we step out of the glass path, Arden looks back at the family I can't see and mouths 'goodbye'. I tug his arm before he gets pulled back into the spell of the glass, and stumble on a shard pulling on the train of my gown. The piece of glass had been broken off near the corner and jammed into the frozen earth.

Carved in haphazard, chicken scrawl is Lieve's handwriting again embedded in a skull at the bottom of the fork in the maze, with a message reading: *NOTHING REAL, GO BACK.*

I pull my dress loose and put the shard in my pocket, thinking that it might be useful later, while Arden still holds my other hand. We look at each other, Arden's eyes red and strained, before taking a deep breath and stepping into the dark tunnel of bones together.

You'll never find it, brother. I've spit the the twins out,
the Eldertick with them.
– *Lopter, to Sol, during the Oleander jump in Adamston
Wood.*

CHAPTER 66

LIEVE

I come to a fork in the maze. On one side is a hall of mirrors, tall and
sleek, and on the other, a tunnel of bones. I know I'm supposed to
take the bone tunnel, but the hall of mirrors intrigues me. My reflection
smiles at me, a cruel, knowing smile, and I stare back at it. Behind him
stands a young woman with my facial features, long dark hair, light
eyes, and pale skin. She loops her arm through my reflection's and leans
her head against his shoulder.

Then, without warning, my reflection grabs each side of the woman's
head and snaps her neck. My fists clench as the young woman crumples.
This must be a warning of some kind, a warning to stay away from the
mystery woman.

I leave the hall of mirrors and plunge my body into the darkness of the
bone tunnel. My legs work slowly, carefully, through the tunnel as my
eyes adjust to the even dimmer lighting. Skulls and other bones line the
labyrinth walls and curve over top creating a dark, tight, tunnel. Each
step deeper into the darkness forces me to crouch through the endless
forks. This section of the maze has always been the hardest to memorize,
and I still haven't mastered it.

Left, left, right, left, straight. No light passes through once I reach this point, the only thing ahead of me is darkness. I take a deep breath and look into the abyss. This is where my master's lessons begin.

"No one helps you," she said to me on my first walk through the labyrinth.

"And if I get lost?"

Her eyes hardened. *"Then stay lost."*

I take another deep breath and rub my hands together. I have to create light, she isn't going to help me with that anymore. My hands slide together, faster, faster, and I hum a deep note in the back of my throat. My eyes roll a little and my skin warms as fingers make the symbols on their own. I hum louder. The magic within me like a sleeping monster stretching as it shakes off slumber before–

A sudden burst of light explodes from my hands, washing the tunnel in blue-white beams. The force of the blast knocks me into the wall, my head smacking against a protruding skull. I touch the back of my head to make sure I'm not bleeding before standing up and looking at what I created.

A sphere of blue flames floats in the air before me, roughly the size of my fist. The fire is warm, not hot. My lips curl into a smile as I warm my fingers over the flickering flames before gently pushing it ahead of me. It stays afloat and the glow of the fire lights up about ten feet into the path.

I notice the handiwork of my broken nails all around me. Deep cuts slashed into the bones cover the walls. I place my hands on them, following the lines to the next cut. There are carvings left haphazardly around, and my blood dots the walls and ground everywhere I look.

I see another little carving of an archway, and then one of a flowering tree. As I follow the flames, I notice more carvings. Several "L" and "V's", *whatever that means.* Some are drawings of a man kissing a woman with flowing hair. I place my palm on the woman and lose track of time, trying to figure out where I know her from. *Who is she?*

The blue fire crackles and I leave the woman behind as I wander through the bones with muddled thoughts. Tingles prick my fingertips and lips, and a warm hand touches my cheek. When I raise my hand to it, it's gone. Moonlight slips through stained glass windows, and breath heats my neck. It's like she's here with me, the woman, tugging at my heart. I almost feel invisible strings pulling me back to her. The fire cracks again and the sensation disappears. I try to focus on the memory, but it fades too quickly. I'm back in this dank tunnel full of dead smiles and lost thoughts.

At the end of the dark tunnel is a hedge maze. This section of the labyrinth is narrow, and the walls of green are at least ten feet high. Cold wind rustles the leaves of the hedge and my heart hammers in my chest. I know what's waiting for me.

The Collector.

I make my way through the hedges and I know he's there before I can see him. Metallic tang fills my lungs and mouth and I sputter as I round the corner. The Collector sits on a throne of sleek, black, stone.

"The would-be King," The Collector says. "What shall I take from you this time?"

"I have nothing more to give."

He snickers and drums his charred fingers on his throne. "You have blood and breath of life, and maybe a few more memories left."

I shrug my heavy robe from my shoulders and let it drop to the ground. Upon hearing me disrobe, The Collector smiles.

"Closer." He snickers.

I stand directly in front of him, and when the breeze blows once more, his nostrils flare. I watch him with disgust as he hungers for my mortal life and the things I can provide for him to consume. I suspect that he's the reason for the Twinning Witch's hooded creatures. A shiver runs down my spine. *How much did he take from them?*

"Do what you will."

The Collector climbs down from his throne and puts a finger to each of my temples and lets out a sigh. "*Delicious.*"

A scream erupts from my throat as pain shoots across my forehead. Then a woman's face appears before my eyes. She's the woman I saw in the hall of mirrors. Dark hair and light eyes that match my own. We're standing in front of a flowering tree and she touches the petals with a delicate hand. The sky shrieks and the trunk of the tree opens to show an endless abyss. I hold my hand out to her and watch as we plunge into the tree before everything goes black.

The twins of myth and sorrow, bound by threads unseen,
inherit the legacy of tales untold to the twins of flesh and
marrow.

*– Ophelia the Wise, Prophet of the Holy Order, Convicted
Heretic, Burned at the stake, Penjing Dynasty, Keffar,
Madoria*

CHAPTER 67
VERA

Arden's hand grips mine tightly. He's still reeling from whatever he saw in the mirrors, and I don't blame him. This place is cruel. Each step into the bone tunnel becomes darker and darker, and my free hand slides over smooth bone as I memorize the path my Doppelganger takes us through. On the other side, Arden scratches the bones with his blade.

My Dop picks up the pace, chirping and hissing up ahead. It's hard to keep up with her in the dark, and the turns feel endless. I'm glad Arden is scratching our path onto the walls. Hopefully we'll be able to use the deep cuts to find our way out, because I can no longer see any of Lieve's markings.

The darker the tunnel becomes, I start thinking of twisted scenarios. Whose bones are these? Where did they come from? We continue walking, the only sound in the maze being our steps and Arden's blade. As we walk, I think about how dark it is and wonder how many of Lieve's carvings we're missing. I wonder if we're still going the right way. I try not to panic at the fact that we're putting our lives in the hands of a Doppelganger and trusting her to take us to safety, maybe even to save Lieve.

"What do you think is happening in Prinav right now?" I whisper.

"I don't know."

"What if we don't find Lieve? Or what if we do, and he's dead?" I start to panic and lean against the wall of the tunnel. *What do I do if he's dead?*

Arden squeezes my hand. "You don't know Lieve as a warrior, but I do. He is stronger than you know. He's a survivor. We'll find him—alive."

I nod and wipe my tears. Lieve is a survivor. We'll find him. Whispers brush my cheek and I jump. I feel Arden grip me tighter and he pulls me along, the whispers growing louder and louder.

"We need to move," Arden says.

I feel something soft and wet curl around my legs just as he speaks, and my Dop clicks again to tell us to hurry. We run blindly to catch up, her clicks being far enough ahead that we can barely hear her, but we use her calls to guide as best as we can.

We walk for a few minutes and eventually the whispers dissipate. Once out of their range, we bump into the Mimic before carrying on. It feels like we've traveled for miles, and just as I'm about to ask Arden what the whispers were, and where he thinks the bones came from, we round the last corner of the bones.

Finally, light.

～

It takes a moment for my eyes to adjust, even though the sky is still overcast. In front of us are massive hedges, but even their green feels menacing in the gloom of this wretched place. Arden scans the hedges, the sky, the ground. He then narrows his eyes at the same time I hear a syrupy voice call out to us. "And who might you be?"

I nearly gasp when I see the owner of the oozing words. He wears robes of translucent fabric, so thin I can see his naked body underneath. Blood has crusted to the neckline of the garment, and as my eyes move up to his face, my breath hitches. His lips are stretched and pulled over a toothless mouth, and his nose is crushed and misshapen. A blood stained bandage covers his eyes, and I assume that under the wrapping I wouldn't find eyes, only damaged flesh.

Arden yanks my cloak and pulls me closer to him before replying. "My name is Arden, sir. I'm here to retrieve someone."

The eyeless thing cocks his head as if he's studying us. His index finger taps the arm of his chair, a massive stone throne, and then he laughs. The sound makes me want to run back to the bone tunnel and never return. I can feel it in my skin that we should leave, but where to go?

"Sorry to disappoint, Arden and friend, but retrieving is not permitted in Shallon."

"*You—*"

I grab Arden's forearm before he can finish his sentence and shout to the creature on his throne. "Do you make bargains?"

My mimic's eyes widen and she shakes her head furiously and waves her arms.

"Oh yes, I do, mortal girl," the creature says. "And you have something I want."

My mouth goes dry. *I've made a mistake.* "What could I possibly have that you want?"

Tendrils of smoke billow from the bottom of the creature's robes and swirl around on the ground, tickling my ankles. The creature's mutilated mouth curls into a wicked grin as the smoke glides up my body, lifting my chin in the air.

"I want out of here."

Arden grunts as he's fighting the smoke that's slowly climbing up his body and his mask falls from his face. "We share the sentiment."

"Then give me the Eldertick." The creature's words drip like molasses from his lips. "I know you have it and my offer won't last long."

"Never," Arden spits.

The creature's features darken, and then he's instantly in front of Arden. He takes a big sniff and his smile grows wider. "You're not the one who asked for a bargain, so I think it best you keep your mouth shut. You don't have much time to insult me, you're already becoming one of the many. I can smell it on you."

Arden and I lock eyes and I can see that his eyes have hollowed and his lips have paled. Gaunt features have begun to take over his face and he's covered in frozen sweat. The creature is right.

I try to calm myself and think straight. *Learn. Adapt. Think like Lieve.* "Why do you think we have it?"

"Only those who carry the blood of the Goddess can enter Shallon without the Eldertick."

"Which goddess?" I ask softly as my heart thumps wildly in my chest. Dia has been missing for centuries, millenia. *Could this be where she's been hiding all this time?*

"The light to the dark, born in the river and loved by a mortal man. The divine twin. The immortal witch. *Dia.*"

Arden laughs. "Liar." Smoke wraps around his neck. He speaks again, but his words don't sound as confident this time. "Dia and Oriel had no descendants."

"Ignorant fool," the creature sneers. "They had a babe. A son. He was born here, lived, and became a man in this place. He wanted more. He wanted life. So I helped him escape and he left me here to rot. I couldn't take the Eldertick from him, though I tried. He cast his magic on me, that I can only be handed the Eldertick with permission of a mortal with the divine blood of the witch goddess. Only then can my skin touch the precious metal. And when Dia discovered her blood son had gone, and that I helped him escape, she cursed me for my sins. My very being is bound to Shallon, unless I'm able to use the Eldertick. And I became,

The Collector, feasting on the delicious spirit of the mortals who get lost here." He gets in Arden's face and says softly, "and you'll be cursed to this land just like me if you don't give it to me."

"We'll never give it to you."

"Then I will not bargain with you or with the girl. And if you don't hand it to me, the mortal son and daughter of the Goddess will remain here, in Shallon–," the smoke spreads wider around the ground, slipping under the hedges–, "with *me*."

Arden scoffs. "I don't care about the son and daughter, they can rot here."

The creature snaps his head in my direction and that wicked smile stretches across his face once more. "Ignorant, ignorant mortal. Believe me when I say this: *you care*."

And Oriel made a watch of solid gold to see his beloved.
The faces a compass, a map to her, wherever she may
hide. A match he gave to her, to glow when they are
close, to radiate the love he has for her, and he called it
the Eldertick.
— *Mother's Tales, Amun*

CHAPTER 68

LIEVE

Tick, tick, tick. The sound repeats over and over. I have a splitting headache thanks to The Collector, and that will make my lesson with The Twinning Witch difficult. Blinking, everything comes back into focus and I'm not surprised to find myself at the Sea of Time. Clocks, pocket watches, and hourglasses cover the ground for miles. Each of them ticking in unison. It's another test I must pass. I sit up and see that I'm dangerously close to another one of the witch's giant melted clocks. I shudder. I must get through the Sea of Time without time itself devouring me.

In the center is her lair, and I'll hone my magic with her if I can make it through the sea. I've done my best to clear a path to her through the wreckage, but she continues to fill in the spaces with more and more pocket watches. I scoot the clocks from side to side so I can step on solid ground, but there's always a chance that you're not stepping on earth.

I've fallen into a melted clock before, and it was larger than three of me. I only escaped because my robe caught on the clock's ticking hand

and I was able to pull myself back up and climb out. From that day on, I've kept my weight planted firmly on one foot, and used the other to scoot the Twinning Witch's discarded pieces to the side before I take a second step. I do this now for miles.

Carefully, I swim through the Sea of Time until I reach the center, until I reach– *her.*

The Twinning Witch's back is to me. Sparks fly from her hands to something on the ground in front of her. There's a faint glow, and then the tang of metal fills my nose and mouth.

"I've arrived," I call out.

More sparks burst from her fingers, scorching the frozen earth around her feet. She takes a ragged breath and picks up something from the ground and tosses it into the Sea of Time. Another pocket watch for me to be wary of. Icy rage pulsates from the Witch and I'm grateful The Collector returned my robe. I pull it tightly around myself and wait for her to acknowledge my presence before speaking again.

Make time. She points into the vast sea. *I show you.*

I bow to her and take off my robe before holding my arm out for her. The Twinning Witch's hand wraps around my wrist. Warmth radiates from her skin and flows under my own skin and I absorb it. It fills my chest and I inhale deeply as she uses her other hand to etch runes onto my forearm. White hot pain sears through me as she brands me with her magic. It only lasts for a moment, but the pain is so intense I vomit.

She let's go. *Make time now.*

I wipe the sweat from my brow that's already begun to freeze and look at my arm. Two new runes glow near my elbow above a myriad of scarred ones, and I trace them with my fingertips. I can feel their power sink into my blood, the magic simmering just under the surface of my skin.

I try to do as she says, but the headache I've received from The Collector thwarts my feeble attempts. The Twinning Witch sneers at me and slaps me hard across the cheek, hard enough that I tumble backwards.

"I'm sorry," I say as I press my finger into the rune and try again. Fail again.

Even though the flesh is tender, I press harder. Sparks flow from my outstretched hand and I watch in amazement as they meld together. The sparks harden, turning into metal before my eyes. The metallic blob forms itself into a circle, hardening and melding until at last, it's a pocket watch.

Pick up, bring here. The Witch demands.

The metal of the watch is so cold it burns. I toss it back and forth between my hands, and when I give it to the Witch, my palms are red and angry. The Twinning Witch doesn't even flinch when the metal touches her, she just turns it over in her hands curiously. She conjures a slab of onyx stone out of thin air and sits down, gesturing for me to sit next to her.

The Witch takes in a breath and grabs my hand, placing it on the latch of the pocket watch and whispers, *now open.*

With bated breath I open the watch and pray that she finds what she's looking for inside, because the last time I disappointed her–well– I don't want to think about it. The latch opens with a tiny click, and opposite the clock face sits a small mirror. For a moment, I think I'm looking at myself, but when I blink, it's not me I see. When I blink, I see the eye of the girl with my features, the girl who my reflection killed in the hall of mirrors. The eye in the mirror blinks rapidly and then the Twinning Witch snaps the pocket watch closed and stares at me, fury written all over her face.

Obsessed, she makes objects containing her memories, but none can find her beloved, for her love had been taken.

— Scrawls of Amun

CHAPTER 69

VERA

"What do you mean," Arden asks, "when you say "I care"?"

The eyeless thing laughs again. "She doesn't know? How delightful."

"What don't I know?" I demand.

The creature puts his finger to my temple and white hot pain blinds me. Visions of me and Lieve enter my mind, then my father's face flashes before my eyes. Visions of him wearing a crown and sitting on a crystal throne. I see the names in the book, Monroe Brone. Roe. *My father's name was Roe.* Father then hugs a man who looks just like the portraits I've seen of King Niall. Something startles them and they look off to the right, their profiles grave and *identical.* More faces flash faster and faster in front of me, morphing from one to the next, going back further and further in time. I recognize them all. Prinavian monarchs. Descendants of Rosalind Brone and the Fae, Corde.

I expect the visions to cease, but they reach back further, on and on and on until they stop at the face of a young man with blonde hair, and a beautiful woman who sits glowing in a sparkling river. Can it really be true? Are these my ancestors? My blood? Is that what he's showing me?

Then the pain burns my lungs and I'm gasping for breath. My throat feels scorched and the cold air stings when I inhale. I can't catch my breath. I'm choking. A roar rings in my ears and I vaguely connect it to Arden. Stars burst in front of my eyes and when my vision returns, all the pain is gone, replaced by wave after wave of nausea. I heave on the dead grass in front of me until all the contents of my stomach have emptied. I lay on the ground, weak and shaking, praying for the nausea to subside.

The creature pats the top of my head. I hug my knees, pressing them into my chest and covering my face from the sight of him. His sticky breath brushes my cheek and the stench of rotten flesh makes me gag. I roll to my side and heave again, but nothing comes up. He ignores my reaction, continuing to caress my head like a prized pet and cooing softly in my ear.

"If you've hurt her," Arden growls, struggling against the smoke, "I'll kill you."

The creature stands and curls his fingers around dark coils of thick smoke. "Amusing trait that you mortals all share, that death is something to fear when there are much worse fates than Ciel."

Then he tightens the smoke around Arden's throat like a rope. Arden pulls on the bindings, but he can't break free. I push myself to my feet and dash to him, but the creature uses more smoke and pins me to the ground. I'm helpless as I watch Arden struggle, his face turning color and his limbs beginning to go slack. I scream and cry, pleading for him to let Arden go, but he only tightens the bindings.

"I'll do any deal you want!" I scream. "Anything, anything at all!"

"Give me the Eldertick."

"Let Arden go first."

"No."

A thought crosses my mind. I can use this to my advantage and get everything I want. "If you want the pocket watch, you must do as I say. Keep him safe, and let me find my brother. Only then will I give it to you."

The creature turns his head to me and drops Arden's unconscious body with a sickening thump. The smoke surrounds us, penning us in. My heart beats wildly as I gaze at his mutilated face, willing him, begging him, to let me go.

"You would trust me with your mortal guardian?"

"I have the Eldertick. So if I discover you've harmed him in any way when I return, then I'll find a way to get out of this wasteland and I'll leave the watch here. You'll stare at that watch day in and day out, never being able to touch it. Your freedom at your fingertips and yet—so far away. You'll *never* get out." I walk with faux courage, my back straight and my head held high. "I'll make sure of it."

The creature cocks his head from side to side in a fluid motion. I can't tell if it's scared, angry, curious. My chest vibrates with the force of each beat of my heart. My confidence is waning with each passing second, but I take a deep breath of icy air and continue to stare into his face. He has to agree, he has to.

"You are more interesting than the son, daughter of the divine." Blood seeps from the corner of his mouth in a thin line. "That intrigues me, child. I will make a deal with you."

Relief floods my veins and I fight the urge to fall to my knees. The solace is short lived, for then a new fear trickles from my thoughts and down my spine. *What will he ask of me?*

"I will cause no harm to your guardian, and I will let you attempt to retrieve the blood son from the witch Goddess."

I raise an eyebrow at him and wait for him to continue.

He chuckles, causing more dark blood to trickle down his pale chin. "In exchange, you will hand me the Eldertick on your return. If you should fail to return to me in due time, or if you refuse to hand me the watch, I will take every drop of lifeblood from the mortal you left in my care. I will then hunt you and the son and consume every memory you possess until you are nothing but empty flesh. You and the son will rot here with your guardian, and your corpses will adorn the entrance to the bone tunnel until the end of time."

He then opens his hand and from it emerges strands of gold and silver. They float in the air, still connected to his skin, and almost dance in anticipation.

"Do you agree to the bargain, blood daughter?"

Every muscle in my body tightens as I consider the offer and the potential of my failure. Can I do this? Lieve has taken care of me my entire life, and he needs me now. I have to do this for him. I have to try.

A lump in my throat forms and I swallow hard before I say, "I agree."

The strands of gold and silver wrap around my wrist and wriggle under my skin. It stings but I keep my arm held out in front of me while the strands connect me and the creature. They bore into the bone of my arm and settle, calcifying as one, bonding the creature and I in our bargain. A small flare of light erupts with a snap and the cords that bind us in the agreement split. The tails of the cords embed themselves in my arm, blackening the skin like a tattoo. It's a brand, a visualization of my oath. I stare at it in awe as silver and gold threads outline the black ink and shine like metal when I twist my arm.

"Blood daughter," the creature says with a grin, "good luck."

Before I part from the creature, I crouch by Arden's body, memorizing every line of his face and tracing his jaw with my finger. I bend, pretending to kiss his cheek, and sneak the watch under his shirt. "I'll come back for you," I whisper.

My Doppelganger chirps, and I follow her, not allowing myself to look back at Arden.

I can't think straight and the chirps from the Mimic are grating. The sound is like claws scraping metal and I want to bury my head in the ground. My vision goes in and out of focus and I see weird lights in the distance. *What is that?* The sky is dark, so it's clearly nightfall, but what about the lights?

Eventually my vision adjusts, allowing me to focus on whatever it is in the distance. There are thousands of glowing orbs that carry on for miles and miles. I squint to try and make out where they're coming from and then I realize what I'm looking at. It's a sea of pocket watches. My Doppelganger holds out her hand to help me up, and I reluctantly take it.

I walk until I'm standing at the edge of where the mounds and piles start. An L and a V are carved into the rocky ground. *Lieve was here.* My Dop nods at me and cuts through the ever growing mounds of metal, her feet staying on a very thin path being lit by the glow of the clock faces in front of us.

The Hidden One. That is all I'll ever be.
– *Amun*

CHAPTER 70
LIEVE

She's coming for me. I recognize the eye, it's the girl from the mirror. I was right when I thought it was a warning. She's here. Who is this girl? The Twinning Witch paces in a circle, mumbling to herself in a language I don't understand.

Mortal can't have–can't take. The Witch mumbles.

I edge closer to her. "What do you mean?"

The Witch curls her fingers in the air as sparks blend together and cool. She forms them into a sphere and it becomes another pocket watch within a matter of seconds. The face opens, but nothing is inside but melted numerals. In a fit of rage she casts the object into the Sea of Time, her body quaking with barely contained fury and snarls. She looks at me and speaks in my mind, *Amun.*

My thoughts mingle together and it's hard to pull them apart. Amun. I flip through pages in my mind until I see it scrawled in ink, written in an ancient text. The word is in a list of words–*no, names*– in a book bound in leather. Amun. A name. The Hidden One, or The One in Hiding.

The Twinning Witch opens the pocket watch I created and looks into the mirror but nothing looks back at her but her own vengeful eye. I want to ask her about Amun, but she's not in a mood to be educational.

I'm afraid if I utter another word I'll be cast into the Sea of Time and drown in her melted sorrows.

Find girl. The Witch hisses and pushes the pocket watch I created into my hands. *Kill her.*

I nod and disappear into the Sea of Time, my pocketwatch pulsating with a warm, faint, blue white glow.

Who is Amun? I scrape every surface of my mind for more information on the name, but I find nothing. Only that it means, *In Hiding*, or something of the sort. All I know is that a young woman has brought him here, and she must die for it.

I take your second eye, Barnabas, as punishment for your sins, and you shall collect sight only by the visions of others. But no others will enter my domain that can ever leave.

– *The Twinning Witch*

CHAPTER 71

VERA

The mounds and hills of glowing metal clocks climb higher and higher the further we travel along the path. My Doppelganger walks a few yards ahead of me, and each time we round a corner, I lose sight of her. I feel uneasy not knowing what could be on the other side of the next hill. Luckily the millions of clocks glow so that I'm not in the dark, because even though there's a path to follow, the surroundings seem unstable. One wrong move could send a wall of metal to crush you.

"Where are we going?" I call out.

She pops her head from around another mound of broken watches and smiles before darting off again. I sigh and quicken my pace, praying there are no forks in the path on the other side. As I round the next bend, I see that she's stopped walking. Her face looks fearful, and I open my mouth to ask her what's wrong but she hisses at me to stay quiet. I strain my ears and listen, fearful because I can't hear what she does.

The low hum of the millions of ticking clock hands gets louder, vibrating the ground beneath my feet. A familiar black beetle scuttles out from under the clock hill to my right and crawls over my foot. Then comes another beetle. Then another. And another.

I hear a crash and the Mimic climbs up the nearest mound and I watch in horror as a hoard of dirt covered black beetles chase her and climb up her legs, covering the lower half of her body in their once shiny onyx shells. I run to her and climb over the sharp pieces of broken clocks and freeze. The ticking and humming isn't from the mounds—it's the sound of countless beetles.

The beetles emerge from holes in the wood of clocks, or from underneath the metallic faces of the pocket watches. They cover the Mimic up to her neck now, some of them boring into her skin. She's helped me all this time, I must reach her. I have to help her. If not for her, but for me as well. I need her so I can find Lieve. I need her with me, guiding me through this treacherous land.

Plowing through the debris causes more beetles to pop out. They nip at my ankles, attach to my gown and cloak, some even sinking their pincers into my skin. Each bite stings, but I push the pain aside. I have to ignore it so I can get to my Dop, so I can get out of here. I ignore the pain so I can find Lieve and make it back to Arden. We'll all die in this place if I don't.

My Doppelganger has reached the top of the highest mound just as the beetles overtake her. I scramble while the beetles continue to bite and snip, dozens of them sneaking under my dress and attaching themselves to the tender flesh of my thighs. I reach the Mimic and scoop beetles from her mouth so she can breathe, and she sputters as I pull them off her face.

We smash them, pull their heads and legs off, and toss them far away from us. We could have stopped them if there weren't so many, but two lone women can't demolish an infestation of this magnitude. We stand together on the top of the mound and look out on the expansive view before us and my breath catches. There are millions.

Blood trails behind me, from the bites, as well as from the cuts I acquired from all the broken shards of glass that litter this endless sea, and the beetles are consuming it. My blood acts as a beacon and soon enough, a swarm of insects blanket the Sea of Time and they're all headed straight for me. I pick up a splintered fragment of metal from the mound and stand side by side with the Mimic. If we're going to die, we'll go down fighting. Together.

The swarm shakes the clock mound and some of the watches and clocks tumble down the hill. It doesn't stop them, in fact, more beetles appear from the ground itself, covered in dirt and ice. When they get halfway up the watch mound, the entire hill shudders. Waves of pocket watches, clocks, and broken hourglasses plummet toward the bottom taking massive chunks with it like an avalanche.

My Doppelganger grabs my hand as the unsteady pile beneath her feet quakes and she loses her balance. The dish sized clock she stands on slides out from under her and she slips, taking me with her.

I scream, but the sound of crashing metal easily overpowers my voice. My head bumps the larger clocks and slivers of metal slice my arms and legs as we roll down, down, down. The barrage of debris covers more of me with every yard I drop, and there's nothing to hold onto. I'm powerless to stop it. Helpless.

I know it was only a few moments, but it felt like hours by the time the mound finishes collapsing. I lay there under the clocks and watches, unmoving for fear that the slide would start up again. After a while, I wiggle my hands to see what would happen if I moved. Nothing happens.

I hear a familiar chirping from behind me and I call out to the Doppelganger to let her know I'm alright, and then I move. The pile under me slides, but I climb upward. I push, pull, and claw my way out with a shard of glass still in my hand. Metal and glass shift about ten yards away and my Dop's head pops up. I crawl on to her on wobbly legs and slowly drag her out.

I spot a large clock just below me on the hill, large enough for a grown man to lay across. The border melted and the sharp hands bend inward and dangle inside the clock, as if there were no bottom to it. I turn my attention back to the Mimic as her body emerges from the rubble. She clings to my arms, but because I'm still weak, my foot slips. I lose the piece of metal as both of us go tumbling once more, our bodies colliding with each other until we reach the melted clock. The Doppelganger is no longer holding onto me, and I fall over the edge of the clock head first.

Time stops.

Around me are moving images of familiar faces, the ones the creature showed me in the hedges. Dia strolls deep in an enchanted forest, pregnant and glowing. She wades in a river of sparkling water, so clear you can see the pebbles at the bottom. Her skin is clear and pale, the color of ivory. She plunges her body into the river and her dark hair swirls around her. I watch as her lover enters the water with her and hands her a golden pocket watch encrusted with gems.

Oriel then pulls another one from his cloak and brushes his shaggy hair from his eyes before showing her how to open the clasp. The watch glows a blue-white color, and then suddenly the sky, the trees, and even the river turn the color of ash and smoke. The lovers quickly leave the water and kiss each other before sparks flow from their fingertips. A mirror appears out of thin air and the woman clings to the man, sobbing, before he urges her to leave him. Still crying, she enters the mirror. The shaggy haired man smashes the mirror and it sizzles as the pieces hit the grass before dissolving into nothing.

The man opens the watch, smiles into it, and then stuffs it in his pocket before brandishing a sword made of crystal.

Soon, two new men appear on the bank of the river. One is wearing a cloak of humble gray fabrics. He lowers his hood, revealing eyes that roll around, watching, observing everything in his presence.

The other man wears all black and he looks startled to see a Crystal Sword. It's the madman with the cane, *it's Sol*. I watch him mouth, "Get him Barnabas." The man in gray hesitates, but darts forward. Oriel punctures one of Barnibus's eyes, and he screams in pain and flails his body to the ground, tendrils of smoke coiling around him.

Sol steps over him, ignoring his companion, and engulfs the area in billowing black smoke and shadows. When the fog dissipates, Oriel is clutching his chest and Sol smiles before grabbing Barnibus by his hair and dragging him out of the wood.

I scream as my palms are sliced open by the sharp hand of the melted clock I had fallen into. I'm dangling in the center of the clock, looking down into centuries of memories and my life hangs over fluid time. I close my eyes and refuse to look back down. I'll be swallowed by those memories if I fall, and I'm sure I'd never get out if I lose my grip.

My mind reels. I just witnessed Oriel's last moments with Dia and his fight with Sol, and I'm certain that Barnibus is the creator of my bargain tattoo.

Was Barnibus telling the truth? Is it really possible that Lieve and I are descendants of Dia? That we're children of gods? My arms shake. This isn't the time to think about that, I need to stop myself from falling.

Slick blood drips from my hands and lands on my face. The lacerations are deep and painful, and it's getting harder to hold on as more blood pours from the wounds. I slip a little, and grasping tighter only makes it worse. I scream for help, desperately praying that my Doppelganger didn't fall in and that somehow she can pull me out.

I scream again, and there's no reply. Not even the sound of beetles returns my plea. I'm going to die. I've failed. I've failed Lieve and Arden. I've failed all of Prinav. I'm going to die, and everyone I love will die with me. I close my eyes and pray one last time that I'll survive, when I feel two hands grab my wrists and pull.

Blood of the mortal runs in my veins, the soul of the
divine mother, binds me in chains.

— *Amun*

CHAPTER 72

LIEVE

M y steps are careful. One wrong move could send an avalanche
of metal to bury me, or I could fall into a clock and forever be
lost in time. The path tapers, and I follow the one that's more narrow.
The smaller one will take me back to the hedges and The Collector, but
I'm not in the mood to see him again. However, that's surely where she
is. I cross my arms and take the narrow path back toward the hedges,
cursing The Collector under my breath. A soft ticking echoes in the
distance and it solidifies my decision. I'm not taking the wider path even
though I want to, the beetles are out.

Eventually I come to another fork and I stop to inspect it. I've
never seen this one before, at least, I don't think I've seen it before.
Liquid shimmers faintly about sixty or seventy feet into the fork. It's a
coincidence that I even noticed it, my eye was at the perfect spot and
the gray sun just happened to reach it at the perfect time. Curiosity gets
the better of me, and I walk into the fork to see what it is. The clocks
don't shimmer. It might be a clue to find the young woman, or this
Amun, the Witch speaks of.

The shimmer looks as if it's soaked into the ground a very, very, long
time ago. There's a faint trail of the strange matter, and it looks like it

could have been blood. I follow the shimmer for quite some time until I reach a trunk made of solid gold. There are words written using the liquid across the top of the trunk, but it's been dry for so many years I can't read it. There's a heavy lock on the front and I try to open it, but it doesn't budge.

Sparks drip from my hands, but even they don't melt the lock. I circle the trunk and stop dead in my tracks when I see the word, the name I'm looking for, embedded in the back. Crystal letters spell out AMUN. Underneath the name is a plaque and a riddle of sorts engraved into it.

Blood of mortal father runs in my veins, the soul of divine mother, binds me in chains.

Shallon dear reader is not my home, and blood of my blood is the answer alone.

A drop from the mortal divine is all you need. Both live within me and for that I am pleased.

Sacrifice a drop to the creator, the blood and the soul. Twin pairings of the father and the mother, and courage foretold.

Ask the creator to save you and see, with faith and their blood, your freedom you shall receive.

I trace my fingers over the letters and the trunk shrinks small enough to fit in the palm of my hand. *What?* I pick it up so I can look at it more closely. It's exactly the same as it was, only smaller. *Why?* Before I can swipe my finger over the plaque once more to see if it will grow back to its original size, a crash in the distance booms so loud it shakes the ground.

Avalanche.

~

The tiny trunk in the pocket of my robes bumps against my leg while I run. I knew she'd come from the direction of The Collector. The ticking has stopped, which means many, if not most, of the death beetles have been buried.

Debris covers the path, and without it, there's no hope that I'll ever find the hedges again, or the hall of mirrors, the bone tunnel, or the rock walls. I try to dig it out, but there's just too much wreckage. Frustration boils my blood and sparks drip on the ground and sizzle against the metal. I'll have to climb.

I climb and climb, higher and higher, until I reach the peak of a new mound created by the avalanche. Peering over the great expanse of time, I don't see any paths at all. The avalanche destroyed all the work I had done to find my way to the Twinning Witch for lessons. All that time, wasted. My work, destroyed, just like the rubble before me.

I sneer at the vast wasteland and curse it. I throw a pocket watch from the mess and it bounces once before shattering. Breaking something makes me feel a little better so I throw another one. When the second one bounces, it's flung to the left and I see movement several mounds away from me.

I narrow my eyes, spotting a woman with long dark hair kneeling over a massive melted clock. She heaves upward and two arms emerge from the clock face. She heaves again, and a second woman, identical to the first, is pulled out. They embrace before flopping on their backs and breathing heavily, motionless. A smile lifts the corner of my mouth. *I'm coming for you.*

———

I ride one of the clocks down the slope like a sled. Sneaking around the haphazard mounds takes time, and there's no way of knowing if the women have moved or not. I can't see them from my position below. I believe I'm at the bottom of the mound that they were laying on, but I still can't find them.

Shit.

Getting on my hands and knees hurts. The broken glass and metal poke and cut as I climb to the melted clock. Familiar chirps and hisses that come from the creatures who live here in Shallon are just ahead.

So, one of the women is from here, and the other–*maybe Amun*, is from the out. Like me.

That's the one who must die.

The second woman, the one I am to kill, is crying. Through her sobs I hear her talking, but the words are jumbled. She's crying so hard that she isn't making any sense. I whisper to myself and wiggle my fingers, anticipating the crackle of sparks that will burst from my hands. Can this really be that easy, or am I being led to a trap?

Something bites my neck hard, a Deathbeetle, and I hiss in pain. The chirping woman snaps her head in my direction, but I duck just in time for her to miss me. Metal and glass clink together as she steps towards where I hide. My palms sweat, stopping me from making sparks. *What if the creature is armed?* I'm so stupid for not bringing a weapon with me. The chirping woman is now only a few feet away. She passes my hiding spot, and when she walks enough past me that I can see her back, I jump out and place my hands on each side of her head and twist.

A shriek pierces the sky from the crying woman, sending a shiver down my spine. With a snap the chirping woman's neck is broken and she crumbles to the ground, her dress pooling at my feet. It's just like the image I saw in the hall of mirrors. A cold smile spreads across my face and I turn to the other woman who's still screaming.

She looks battered and wears a soiled gown of exquisite fabric, and a heavy cloak made for a man much larger than she is. Her hair is a mess and she's covered in soot and blood. Tears stream down her cheeks and nearly freeze before dropping off her chin.

Our eyes meet and she gasps, her dirty hands clasped over her mouth. She rises to her feet, surveying me with surprise and sorrow before dropping her hands to her sides. I storm towards her, arms out and ready to snap her neck just like the other, but she retreats. I don't slow down, and she realizes now that I'm coming for her next. Her eyes widen and she runs.

She's fast. But I'm faster. I push my legs to catch up to her, both of us losing our balance over the endless piles of rubbish. Another landslide, smaller but still dangerous, stops the woman from running. She falls down and just curls her knees to her chest, rocking back and forth.

I tower over her and grab her by the hair. She wraps her fingers around my wrist, looks up and pleads, "Please, Lieve."

Lieve.

I'm pulled into myself. The girl is gone, Shallon is gone. Only the lightning speed of faces, places, and words remain. I hear stories, see bursts of color and light. Red hair swirls around me as soft lips press against my own. I'm running through a market with the young woman. Vera- *My sister.*

I remember Vera. And Daphne. Arden and Calix. Narah. *I remember.*
I remember it *all.*

Scars are just the proof that we survived. They show us who we really are, and what we can endure. Scars reveal strength.
— *Robin Fledgling*

CHAPTER 73

VERA

I've never seen that expression on Lieve's face before. I plead for him to spare me, and when I say his name, he freezes. The world freezes. Lieve's body goes rigid like a corpse found in frigid snow and his eyes glass over. He doesn't breathe or blink, and neither do I. My heart starts to pound, it pounds so hard I can hear it. *Why was he chasing me? Why did he kill my Dop?*

Cautiously, I stand up. My nerves are on edge and I expect Lieve to grab me again, but he doesn't. His face looks just like the Lieve who sits on the throne of Prinav, yet so different. He has a scar on his cheek, covered somewhat by unkempt facial hair. A beard has grown on his normally clean shaven face, and he has worry lines around his eyes. He's older. My heart breaks when I think of the Lieve I've been interacting with in Brone Castle, I saw the same lines of worry there as well.

I reach my hand to touch Lieve's face, my Lieve, the real Lieve, and he snatches my wrist.

"Vera." He says my name with command. Not a question, but with certainty.

I nod at him and place my other hand on his cheek and whisper, "Yes."

All of a sudden I'm wrapped in a tight hug. Lieve's arms hold me and he squeezes me hard enough that I lose a breath. Fingers dig into my back and I break down. My body shudders with every sob and Lieve's soft cries shatter my heart. He pulls back from me and pets my hair, moving my head side to side to inspect me. His eyes darken when he sees the cuts and bruises covering my body.

"I'm okay," I reassure him.

His mouth forms a hard line. "No you aren't. You're here."

"What is this place?"

"Shallon," he replies. "We're in the Sea of Time." His voice trails off, distant. Several minutes later he shakes his head. "All my paths are gone from the landslide–"

His words stop and he looks around as if he just realized where he is. Then he spins on his heel to where my Doppelganger lays and stares at it for a second before falling to his knees. I bend to put a hand on his back and he recoils before putting his head in his hands and rocking back and forth.

"Dead, dead, dead–"

"I'm right here," I say and grab him by both shoulders. "I'm alive."

He looks up at me, confused and in awe. It's not unlike I used to look up at him and he murmurs, "Vera?"

Lieve starts pulling on his hair and mumbling to himself. It takes about an hour to get coherent speech from him, and even then his thoughts are broken and jumbled. I need to get us back to Arden, but I have no idea what to do. The paths I took to get here are covered by the landslide, and Lieve's mental state isn't allowing for any confidence in his ability to navigate.

Once we're far enough away from my Doppelganger that Lieve can't see her body anymore, he calms down. I can't look back at her, and it's hard to leave her there. She was a friend. My friend. She brought me to Lieve, and I'll never be able to thank her or repay her. I want to ask Lieve so many questions, but something isn't right with him.

I need to ask for his help, or even console him, but every time I try he reverts back to mumbling under his breath. I take in our surroundings and memorize what I can see, but it all looks exactly the same after the slide. No paths, no markings. My eyes flick to Lieve's hands and the fingernails are chipped and broken, and the tips of his fingers are burnt. I brush a tear from my cheek and reach out to hold his hand but he shakes me off.

We're wandering aimlessly, and that has to end now. "Lieve," I say. "Can we stop for a moment?"

He continues walking, muttering and flicking his fingers around.

"Lieve!"

Sparks drip from his fingertips and land at his feet, burning tiny black dots into the ground. I gasp. That isn't magic like Daphne and Saima's. That's the magic of gods.

She created a world like her old home, but without life
in it…for it could not live. She made a mockery of
Atatacia, and of its inhabitants. And for that, we call her
the Twinning Witch.

– *The Hooded Horde*

CHAPTER 74

LIEVE

I know it's Vera, I know it is, but it's hard to separate my thoughts.
I put my hand to my forehead and burn myself. Confused, I look at
my hands and they're blazing hot from the sparks that dripped from my
fingertips. The ground sizzles and I look down to see that the frozen
dirt is peppered with scorch marks.

"Lieve," Vera says, "we need to get back to Arden. Do you have any
idea how to get back to a hedge maze?"

Arden. Arden. I remember him. *Arden?*

"Lieve–"

Vera talks to me but it seems so far away. There's no way Vera's here.
Vera. *Vera.* No, it's impossible. She can't be here. So that means, she's
a Doppelganger. A soft hand touches my shoulder and I snatch it and
twist.

"Aah!"

I squeeze her arm and pull her close to me. "You aren't my sister."

She tugs furiously and I only squeeze harder. I'm sick of
Doppelgangers, I'm sick of Shallon, I'm sick of it all. Then she bites my

hand hard, clenching down deep enough to draw blood and I swing my free arm and hit her in the jaw. She lets go of my hand and I release her.

"Lieve, it's me!" She screams. "Stop!"

She knows my name. Is it really Vera? I can't tell. I step backward with my hands raised so I can put distance between us. A large piece of metal snags my robe and I tumble into a pile of clocks and smack my head.

"Are you okay," Vera asks. "Can I come closer?"

I don't move. I don't know if I want her closer. So, I shake my head and Vera doesn't move from where she stands. Vera. Vera is here, I've found her. But where are we? My fingers slide over pins attached to my undershirt, and I remember a fox and a–

"Is that the Lopter tree?"

I drop my hand and look at Vera. It has to be her, it has to be the real Vera because the Doppelganger wouldn't know what that is. I nod, and she looks at me with love in her eyes.

Vera dashes over and sits in front of me on the pile of cool metal. Tears stream down her face and my blood has already frozen to her cracked lips. She holds out her hand and I hesitate but then put my hand in hers.

"Oh Lieve." She wipes her face on the corner of her cloak. "I love you so much." She reaches out and touches the pin. "You've always been waiting for me, haven't you?"

So that really happened? I was King? But Arden never came back. He was late. And then, and then–

"I knew something was wrong with you, I knew there had to be a reason why you'd marry Lucette."

I didn't marry Lucette. What is Vera talking about? No, no, no. This is all wrong. "I didn't marry Lucette. I've been here because– he never came back."

"Who didn't come back?"

"Arden."

Vera's brow furrows and then she stands up.

"Lieve, we need to get Arden now, okay? Do you think you could help me find him?"

Arden is here? Did he get stuck here too? That must be why he didn't show up that day.

"He's with a madman in the hedges," Vera says. "So I really need your help now."

I stand and something falls out of my pocket, clanging against all the shards of metal under our feet. Vera and I look around in the pile to see what it was that fell from my robe and we find it, a miniature trunk.

"What is that?" She asks.

"Let me show you," I say as I remember what it is and pick it up.

I lightly touch the tiny plaque on the back of the trunk and it expands back to its original size. Vera and I inspect it and she looks shocked when she reads the inscription. She runs her hand along her forearm and I see something silver, like a tattoo, peek out from under her sleeve.

"Blood of the father, soul of the mother," she mumbles and continues absentmindedly rubbing her forearm. "Blood of the father–" Her brow furrows as she mumbles the message from the trunk over and over. Then she suddenly stops and turns to look me in the eyes. "Lieve, has the man that guards the hedges ever talked to you about being a, well– *a god?*"

"What? No?"

A soft blue light flickers from my robes.

Vera starts pulling things from her cloak and orders. "Empty your pockets."

I dig around in my robes and trousers to see what's making the glow. Rocks. That's what I have in my pockets. Rocks. But it's the pocket watch I made for the Twinning Witch, the one I saw Vera in earlier, that's glowing. I pull it out and flip open the face to see that one of the multitude of faces is what is making the flickering light. The hand of that watch face is spinning and then stops directly ahead of where I stand and the hand vibrates. The flicker turns into a glow and remains steady.

"What is that?"

I hand it to her. "It's the pocket watch I made for the Twinning Witch."

Vera's eyes go wide. "You *made* it?"

"Yes."

Vera paces in circles around the trunk as the watch in her hand vibrates and the blue glow gets stronger. "Oh Lieve, oh my, I think we–"

"What's wrong?"

She locks eyes with me. "I think that witch a god, and I think–," she looks back at the trunk–, "I think we might be too."

I took the Eldertick with me, Mother.

— *Amun*

CHAPTER 75

VERA

We take a couple steps forward to see what the watch will do, and it only glows brighter. I have this nagging suspicion that it somehow connects to the Eldertick, and that we can use it to find Arden, so I suggest we follow it. There's not a lot of other options, and I'm afraid to leave Arden alone for too long.

"Can you shrink that trunk again?"

Lieve nods as he crouches down by the trunk and runs his hand over the gold inscription. The trunk shrinks down to fit in the palm of his hand and he tucks it deep into his robes. Then he hands me the glowing pocket watch. I hold it out in front of me like a compass and follow the light through the Sea of Time with Lieve at my side.

"The Twinning Witch," I say to try and break the silence. "How did you meet her?"

Lieve's hand touches his scarred cheek. "The Ink River."

The River of Light and Dark? This witch has to be Dia, it makes so much sense. Lieve kicks the pocket watches and clocks scattered around to the side and steps ahead of me, testing the ground so I don't fall into another melted clock. Even though he's watching out for me, I still can't tell if Lieve trusts that I'm real. He looks back at me through the rubble and I catch a glimpse of rage, or fear, before his face softens again.

At the end of the Sea of Time are doors that sit up on their own. Each one is made of a different material, wood, iron, and ivy. In the center of each door are runes, and when we get closer, a light shines down from the sky on the one with vines. As if he's forgotten I'm with him, Lieve darts away from the door.

"What's wrong?"

My voice startles him and he stops and looks back at me. Then vines snake across the ground towards us.

"Run."

So we run. I glance at the door to see what we're running from and my heart races as the vines grow longer and faster to catch us. They slither from the door and snatch Lieve, curling around his waist, his arms, and neck to strangle him.

I scream and race towards Lieve and pull on the vines, but they're too strong. Lieve starts gurgling and I yank and yank, but the vines don't budge. Something tickles my ankle and I'm not fast enough to move and it pulls my feet out from under me. Lieve is struggling as hard as he can, his eyes wide and fearful. The ivy door opens and behind it are hundreds of corpses tangled in dead vines. I kick and scream but that only makes the vines squeeze tighter. Lieve's face is purple now and his eyes are bulging. My heart beats faster, faster.

As I'm being dragged across the frozen tundra, something in my pocket pokes my hip and I remember I have a shard of glass from the Hall of Mirrors, so I pull it out and stab the plant. High pitched shrieks ring in my ears and the plant squeezes so hard my foot goes numb, *but I hurt it.* So I stab it again. This time the vine loosens enough that I can slip my foot out. I scramble to my feet and race to Lieve, slicing the vines as I run. When I finally reach my brother, I slice and stab over and over until the vine releases him and retreat behind the door.

Lieve's face slowly turns back to normal and when he gains consciousness he is even more unstable. He mutters to himself and won't let me touch him or check to see if he's alright. Then another light shines on the wooden door.

"That one tricks you," he murmurs. "It looks like it's nice inside but it isn't. It shows you your deepest desires and you'll beg to go in there, but don't ever do it."

I don't ask what lies beyond the wooden door. We stand firm and wait until the light goes out, our eyes pressed shut to protect ourselves from whatever could tempt us behind the door. The scent of savory food floats in the air and I'm reminded that I haven't eaten in a long time. I'm not sure how long we've even been in here, and my body shakes with want. Then comforting laughter echoes and it sounds so lovely, followed by the scent of moss and pine. I take a step towards the door, knowing I shouldn't do it, but feeling like I want to be there anyway. There's food, and friends, and love. There's safety there.

Lieve grabs my arm. "No."

I stop walking, but every fiber in my being is screaming at me to go to the door. Acceptance, respect, comfort. Those things are in there. Why can't I go? Why doesn't Lieve come with me?

All of a sudden I'm overcome with fear and exhaustion. Frigid air burns through my cloak and I swear my bones are frozen. I open my eyes and the light is gone from the door. I shudder, that door is powerful. Then the third light shines on the iron door and Lieve goes sprinting for it immediately, dragging me by the hand. He stops in front of the door and pours sparks onto the handle. It creaks open and he yanks me inside with just enough time before it slams shut again.

"This is the safe door, but if you're too slow it will kill you."

I look at my feet. There are discarded human bones and the ground is noticeably stained with blood. Lieve seems to trust me a little more and he holds my hand as we walk along a cobblestone path with wild weeds and vegetation growing on either side.

"Stay close and quiet," he whispers.

I walk so close to Lieve that our cloaks rustle together. I hear wild animals growling in the thicket and my pulse races. Lieve's grip is so tight I can't feel my fingers, but I don't say anything. My lip trembles and it's hard not to cry out.

Lieve mutters to himself, so low I can't hear him.

"I can't hear you," I whisper.

"There was supposed to be a fourth door."

I try not to think about the fourth door and what that means. Lieve doesn't talk anymore, doesn't mutter under his breath about it. He stays on high alert watching our steps and peering into the brush for danger. Water trickles somewhere to the right and we follow the fork in the path in that direction. A creek cuts through the brush and Lieve sinks to his knees and dips his hands in the water to drink.

The water is black.

He jerks his chin towards the creek. "Drink."

I squat beside him and put my hands in the water and instantly jerk them out. The water is freezing. My hands are chapped and raw already and I wring them and cry out.

"You must drink," he says. "It's cold, but this journey is long. You'll die. Drink."

I dip my hands back in the black water, pain searing my skin and cup it to my lips. It's agonizingly cold, but when I take a sip, I feel full. So I drink and drink and drink. When we've had enough and are now so cold our teeth chatter, Lieve says we can keep moving. I see his carvings on the cobblestones and run my thumb across the watch and sparks sprinkle from my fingertips and land on the ground. I nearly drop the watch and it grows warm in my hand. We watch it as it glows brighter and brighter, enough that I don't have to hold it anymore. I have spark magic too? How?

"We need to move." Lieve says.

I stuff the pocket watch in my cloak and the light shines right through my pocket. I can't think about what this means right now. I can't think about the fact that I have magic. We have to get to Arden.

I'm so thankful that Lieve made these carvings because I feel like I'm going a little crazy. It's hard to think straight, and I'm so cold and numb that nothing seems to matter but getting warm again. The sharp end of the shard of glass pokes my thigh as we walk, but I don't dare leave it behind. The intermittent stabs keep me grounded, reminding me of where I am and why.

Lieve and I continue to follow the light of the watch, and Lieve assures me that these paths will lead to the hedges. At least there's a bit of good news. We walk in silence for hours, Lieve's hand still gripping my own. I hope Arden is okay. I don't know how we're going to get out of this mess.

Fog up ahead blocks us from seeing any further into the path. A shiver runs down my spine because now the hands of the pocket watch are spinning so fast it vibrates inside my cloak. I pull it out, the glow nearly blinding, and see that the hands are spinning round and round. It's like we are exactly where it wanted us to go, and then the watch goes dark.

Lieve stops and takes a deep breath before turning to look at me. "We have to step into the fog."

My breath catches. We won't be able to see anything. I start trembling. I don't want to be here. I don't know if I can do this.

~

Arden is awake, but he's bound by tendrils of black smoke billowing from the hem of Barnabas's robes. His eyes dart to us the second we appear and he tries to say something but he's been gagged.

"You found each other," he purrs. "Unexpected outcome, but pleasing nonetheless."

"The fourth door?" Lieve asks.

A deadly smile curls Barnabas's toothless mouth. "I took it away. I thought maybe all of you would die and I could retrieve the Eldertick myself."

"But our bargain–"

Barnabas tilts his head at me. "I didn't harm him."

Then blinding pain shoots up my forearm and I fall to my knees.

"Give me the Eldertick," he demands. "*Now.*"

Lieve drags me over to Arden and with his back to Barnabas, he pulls the watch he created from his robes and places the chain around all of our wrists. Stars burst behind my eyes and I heave all the black water I drank onto the ground next to me.

"The pain shall cease when you *give me the Eldertick.*"

I rip the Eldertick from under Arden's shirt and throw it as hard as I can. It bounces on the ground near the foot of The Collector's robes, and when he bends down to pick it up, all the pain stops. My tattoo sizzles and then I smell the scent of burning flesh.

Barnabas winds up the Eldertick at the same time Lieve is winding up the dial on the watch connecting the three of us. Our watch begins to glow, a faint green light softly illuminating our faces, and I feel warmth. I hear the chirping of birds and feel the heat of a summer sun. The Collector notices that something is happening with us, and something is *not* working for him, and his face contorts with rage. Then, I feel light. Lieve, Arden, and I, are floating in the air and the tendrils of smoke around Arden disappear. We are dissolving. We'e leaving Shallon.

"Our bargain is broken, you cannot leave!"

A small chuckle erupts from my chest. "You never said the Eldertick had to work."

An ear splitting roar fills the world and Barnabas's gnarled hand snatches my ankle and pulls. My wrist slips from the chain of Lieve's pocket watch and I smack the ground, knocking the wind out of me. I look up to Arden and Lieve and they're nearly gone. Arden is screaming and Lieve's eyes are wide as he reaches for me. I reach up to him and just as they're both untangling their own hands from the chain, a crack resonates and they're gone.

No. No. No.

Lieve is gone. Arden is gone. What do I do? Before I know it, thick smoke has snaked around me like the vines, holding me in place. I can't breathe. *Please Sybill, Lord of the Dead, let me live. Don't let me die here, please, please.* Knowing that the gods are real, I don't know what else to do besides pray.

"You *tricked* me, mortal."

I won't let him know how scared I am. So I set my jaw and glare. "And I'd do it again to save my brother. I'd do it a thousand times."

He roars again and my tattoo bargain pulsates. I've fulfilled the bargain, but Barnabas must be able to manipulate it so that I'll stay branded for betraying him. He uses his power to hold me up in the air and squeezes the breath from my lungs as I try and think, but every thought bounces around, not able to find an end to my train of thought.

I try to resist and fight the bindings, but they're too strong. The smoke has reached my neck, strangling me, choking out the last bit of air as my vision blurs. More thoughts bounce around, and then I remember what the trunk in Lieve's pocket said:

Blood of mortal father runs in my veins, the soul of divine mother, binds me in chains...A drop or two from the mortal turned divine is all you need. Both live within me and for that I am pleased...Sacrifice the drops to the creator...and ask the creator to save you and see, with faith and their blood, your freedom you shall receive.

If Monroe is our father, that means Corde's magic, and Rosalind Brone's magic also runs in our veins. If what Barnabas showed me is true, it also means we're descendants of Dia and Oriel. If Lieve and I can do spark magic...If we're really the son and daughter of the divine goddess, *of Dia*–then I should be able to get out of here. But my thoughts slow and the world around me is starting to go black. Barnabas watches me dying with glee, but then the shard of glass presses against my thigh, tighter and tighter as the smoke squeezes me. My arms are still free up to my elbow and I jam my hand inside my pocket and slice my finger on the jagged edge of the glass. I feel a small drop of blood pool on the tip of my finger and quickly pull my hand from my cloak.

As the drop of my blood drips to the ground, freezing as it falls to the earth, I whisper with my dying breath, "Creator, please save me."

Crack.

I gulp down air, desperate to catch my breath. Turning to my side I feel the warmth of a fire on my skin. *I made it.* I made it out and I got Lieve out. I got Arden out. I'm out of Shallon. Tears pour down my face and my body shudders with the force of my sobs.

"What is this?"

Oh fuck, no. No. No. No. Please say it's not him. Please, oh gods, please.

"Well color me intrigued," the man says. "She made it out."

I turn to face the voice and my heart stops. I'm in the Royal Study of Brone Castle, and standing before me is my *husband*.

ACKNOWLEDGEMENTS

There are so many people to thank I can't even wrap my head around it, but I'll try.

To my husband, Jeremy…I couldn't have done this without you. You not only helped me have the time and support to finally give this crazy dream a try, but you helped in the creation of it. Your unwavering love, support, endless conversations about the lore, fantasizing about character arcs and storylines will forever be seared into my heart. I cannot thank you enough for your help with this project. You are truly the epitome of unconditional love, and I am grateful you chose me. I love you more than you'll ever know.

To my mom, Heidi…your unfailing confidence in my ability to write and your endless patience astound me. You're the best mother and friend I could ever ask for, and without your feedback, Vera and Lieve would not exist. Thank you for reading this book 700 times and going over every chapter with me in such minute detail that we would get frustrated with each other. Thank you for talking me through my panic attacks. Thank you for believing in me. I love you.

Carrie…whatever the definition of "friend" is…it describes YOU. Thank you for crying with me, laughing with me, and digging me out of my plot holes. Your creativity, critique, and support are something

I never take for granted. Thank you for bouncing my INSANE ideas off of you, and for leading me in directions I never thought possible. Thank you for reading this book as many times as my mom and being as enthusiastic about Atatacia as I am. I love you, boo.

Thank you to my writing partners, Emilee and Kim. Your friendship and critique is so important to me and I can't wait to get together for lunch or drinks or meet at the library to start book 2 in Lieve and Vera's crazy adventures.

To my discord group of writers and editors: Kourtney, Nikki, TL, and Kat…you are my personal google, and my most cherished internet friends lol…you guys deserve a medal for answering all my questions with such patience.

To my Beta reader Kirsten, your friendship and hilarious comments on the happenings in Smoke and Mirrors is what gave me the confidence to feel like a real author. I'm so glad you enjoyed the book.

To my editor, "A", there is no way in hell this book would be ANYTHING resembling a book without you. You are a GENIUS my friend. GENIUS. Thank you for answering all my questions, for giving me the most critical and inspiring feedback, for filling in plot holes and sharpening my pen. I owe you so much. Your critique taught me so much, and I'm a better writer for knowing you. Your feedback clicked something deep in my lizard brain, and I cannot thank you enough for your support and encouragement.

Thank you to the Ohio Writers Workshop for introducing me to agents and editors that wanted my book and introduced me down the line to my editor. This workshop changed my career.

To my internet critique group that introduced me to the workshop, and for introducing me to my new friends Emilee and Kim…thank you. People need to have writer friends, and joining this group changed my life.

And lastly, thank you to my readers. Without you, I wouldn't get to spend months inside the magical world of Atatacia. I hope you find yourself jumping through the Lopter Tree over and over to follow Lieve and Vera around for many years to come. I hope you all find your fairytale endings.

ABOUT THE AUTHOR

JD Laubach is an author of New Adult and Adult Fantasy. She is married and lives in the midwest where every season makes her happy (especially fall). She has 3 cats: Sabrina, Todd and Gilligan who are the lights of her life. She is a proud aunt, and proud sister.

When she's not reading or writing, you can catch JD painting, scrapbooking, watching endless streams of Gilmore Girls, and playing board games. JD and her husband are avid travelers and hikers who plan to see every US National Park and as many countries as possible.

28846253R00306